The Man with the Powe

Leslie Thomas was born in South[...] parents died he and his younger b[...] orphanage. His first book, *This Ti[...]* autobiography of a happy orphan.[...] reporter on a weekly newspaper in [...] and then did his National Service in Malaya during the Communist bandit war. *The Virgin Soldiers* tells of these days : it was an immediate bestseller and has been made into a film with Lynn Redgrave and Hywel Bennett.

Returning to civilian life, Leslie Thomas joined the staff of the *Evening News*, becoming a top feature writer and travelling a great deal. His second novel, *Orange Wednesday*, was published in 1967. For nine months during 1967 he travelled around ten islands off the coast of Britain, the result of which was a lyrical travelogue, *Some Lovely Islands*, from which the BBC did a television series. Now a director of a London publishing house, he has continued to travel a great deal and has also written several television plays. Among his hobbies are golf, antiques and Queen's Park Rangers Football Club.

**Also by Leslie Thomas
in Pan Books**

The Virgin Soldiers
Onward Virgin Soldiers
Stand up Virgin Soldiers
Orange Wednesday
His Lordship
The Love Beach
Come to the War
Arthur McCann and All His Women
Tropic of Ruislip
Dangerous Davies, The Last Detective
Bare Nell
Ormerod's Landing
That Old Gang of Mine

This Time Next Week
Some Lovely Islands

Leslie Thomas

The man with the power

Pan Books London and Sydney

First published 1973 by Eyre Methuen Ltd
This edition published 1975 by Pan Books Ltd,
Cavaye Place, London SW10 9PG
19 18 17 16 15 14 13
© Leslie Thomas 1973
ISBN 0 330 24408 6
Printed in Great Britain by
Richard Clay Ltd, Bungay, Suffolk

For my friends
David and Bob

The rain it raineth on the just
And also on the unjust fella:
But chiefly on the just, because
The unjust steals the just's umbrella.

Charles Bowen
Sichel, *Sands of Time*

One

In the first place I went to America to find my wife who had got lost in there. She was a lean and gentle girl, a dancer of twenty-two who liked to sit naked in front of our fire at home in England with our cat Levicticus luxuriously asleep in her lap. Losing her was an act of supreme carelessness. Girls like that are hard to find.

Of course I had not intended to travel from New York to Las Vegas dressed as a pseudo-Jesus and toting a large wooden Cross, but these things happen. My life has been notable for its misadventures (indeed my father has unkindly assured me that the very *reason* for my life was misadventure) and the occurrences and oddities of America were really only my existence running to form. Nevertheless it was both wearying and worrying. What with the sexual mishaps, the violence, the threats, the blood, the drink, the riots, the police, the arrests, the deceits and the downright frauds, not to mention the chronic madness involved, I felt, at the end, that I was not really cut out for a religious crusade.

And it's a big place, America. A big place to look for any-one, even someone as unique as Silvie. It goes on for such a long time. All those towns and cities and distances. All those travelling songs – 'By the time I get to Phoenix', 'You've come a long way from St Louis', 'Twenty-four hours from Tulsa'; all those different places and different people; those long, long miles; roads fingering on for ever. For me it seemed to be the richest and the poorest place I had ever known. The stranger cannot realize; it is not a country, it's an invention.

We journeyed in two motorized caravans labelled in large legend 'Jesus Loves' and 'Jesus Lives'. We set out in some triumph from Battery Park, New York, and concluded in the most hideous chaos on the Lake Mead highway in the hills overlooking Las Vegas, which was where Properjohn was arrested. Our adventures were not as gentle as those of the pilgrims going to Canterbury, but this is not a gentle age. Sometimes I felt it was more like the pioneers of the Old West, moving our waggons across the unknown horizon, reaching for the next promising sunset; ambushed and harried but still moving on. The old trails, the Cherokee Trail, the Santa Fé Trail, the Chisholm Trail, the Goodnight and Loving Trail, were joined by the Properjohn Trail. We went to Bethlehem, Pennsylvania, where they play the Easter Hymn on trombones from the church tower, to Baltimore, to the Shenandoah Valley and the Blue Mountains, through the Cumberland Gap and out into the tobacco and the pallid cotton fields to Nashville and Memphis (Oh, wicked woman of Memphis!) into the west to Amarillo and Albuquerque and through the coloured deserts in the quiet and cool of the autumn.

At each town we unshipped the Cross from the top of 'Jesus Lives' and bore it at the head of a locally staffed procession from churches subsidized by the Helen J. Jaye Foundation for Christian Love whose national headquarters, above a snake-dancing burlesque in Rush Street, Chicago, has been of recent interest to FBI fraud investigators.

On this strange and disturbing journey my companions were the Reverend John Properjohn, Minister of the Church of the Livid God, South Wales, a prince of vanities with a loud mouth, a power over people and the date of the end of the world in his pocket; his straggling wife Poor Clare; his daughter Ambrosia, a Cookeen sort of girl, plump and sweet and shrewd. There was Herbie, failed star of 'Outsize Loving' and other flesh epics; Winston, a coloured man (named, he said, after the famous Winston Churchill, police chief of Indianapolis) and the only person I ever met who gave up pot for cigarettes; and the Reverend Robert C. Hatt, a lost and lonely pastor, vicar of nowhere, a wilderness crying in a voice.

We staggered west, bickering, fighting, loving, being foul and being fair, the worst and the best of companions, taking our parade, our charade, to those who required something spectacular from the too silent God. It mattered nothing that we were a band of rogues, religious quack doctors, for some needed this much more than they needed vague promises. All

8

of us believed in something, even if it wasn't Christianity, and we all sought something more.

Naturally there were difficulties inherent in carrying a man-sized Cross (equipped with a cunning trapdoor to conceal plastic rain cape and Coca-Cola bottle) especially since I have a fair beard and long hair and was arrayed in an off-white robe. My Dolcis casual brown shoes did little to discourage those who wanted to believe and there were many anxious inquirers. Americans are, in general, folk of uncomplicated kindnesses, and numerous times I was asked by children and simple people: 'Sir, are you the real Jesus?' My English accent seemed to reinforce their belief. They would prod me as though I were invisible under my robe, they would touch the hem of the robe itself, and sniff at the wood of the Cross. At night there was another hazard. The abrupt vision of a man, bearded and robed, bearing a large wooden Cross on a dark rural road, had a petrifying effect when illuminated by the headlights of a driver going convivially home from his favourite neighbourhood bar. But these were small adventures. It was the power of people, believing what they desperately needed to believe that was so fearful; the emotional blindness of the crowd, the need that truly belched from them in their thousands as they listened to Properjohn, the man with the power, reeking with fraud. God knows what they will be like when the real thing comes along.

But even with all the ecclesiastical activity I never forgot I was looking for my wife Silvie. Our evenings naked in front of our fire ('This is the next best thing to the sun,' she would say) came to an end when she discovered that I had been lying adjacent to different flames. She left, taking our little children Kathy and James with her, and left me with the cat and the washing up.

We had long talked of going to America and making a pilgrimage to Southern California where the song says it never rains. Once we played a game, following on a map all the old pioneer trails, the Santa Fé, the Cherokee, the Chisholm, the Goodnight and Loving Trail, named after two men who set out from Texas to find a way into Colorado. 'That will be *our* trail,' she said pleased with the romantic sound.

When she had been gone for a while I began to get teasing picture postcards of places on the route from east to west, clues in her game of treasure trail. One, from Texas, simply said: 'Riding the Goodnight and Loving Trail.' Then the postcards stopped so I supposed she had found her destination. Levicticus had gone to live with the Patons, a dank, woollen-jerseyed pair next door, and had been predictably renamed Tussy. I said they could keep him and gave them also the key of our house in case there was a fire or a flood. Then I wrote some bogus love letters from Silvie to me and put them in the bureau where I knew they would see them when they were poking around. Then I locked up our house and went to the airport and America. Only the cat, sitting in the window next door, saw me go. He had never liked me. He seemed to know why Silvie had run away. I can't imagine he ever sat in Jean Paton's naked thighs. I could have sworn he lifted up two fingers to me as I went. But perhaps he was just washing.

Properjohn came through the passenger cabin door like a theatre demon accomplishing an entrance, black-garbed, his hands and legs splayed out to extremes, his eyes like bright nails, his great nose moving about independently on his face, his grey hair extended in short spikes, a condition, I later discovered, brought about by extravagant applications of Brylcreem. The moment he came in everyone, passengers and cabin crew, was aware of him. He was not one to merely enter. He was made manifest.

Topping his black suit, with flared trousers and frock coat, was a clerical collar as thick as the side of a shoe box. He blew out his fleshy lips in a sort of sustained raspberry as he stood surveying the interior of the Jumbo jet economy cabin. Those who were not already staring looked up and beheld, in the prime of his fifty-seventh year, the Reverend John Properjohn, Minister of the Church of the Livid God, South Wales.

Quickly I looked away but even before I did so I had seen him all. He was the sort of man you could see at a glance because there he *was*; hideously displayed and challenging. His wife, Poor Clare, and Ambrosia, his daughter, were mere wings fluttering behind his black back. They were settling themselves in the middle rank of seats, across the aisle. I looked resolutely out of the window at the ground men with their serpentine pipes and little trolleys. From the last edge of my instinctive glance I saw the stewardess with the panda rings around her eyes approaching with the economic anxiety of her tribe. I had watched her earlier and wondered if the pilot had been at the same party the night before. She moved quickly enough now but her arrival did nothing to subdue the spluttering grumbling confusion from the middle seats.

'Let me help you with that,' I heard her suggest. 'Will you be reading your book during the flight?'

'Book? Book?' he demanded with a Welsh howl. 'That's the Bible, that is!'

'Oh yes, I see it is,' she said, with cool, weary brightness, 'I *thought* it was a big thick book. It's a wonder they didn't charge you excess.'

'I have no excesses, young woman,' he growled. Then: 'Have you read it – have you, girl?'

'Not all of it,' she replied, keeping cool. 'We have a lot to do, you know . . .'

'Listen! Listen to this!' he interrupted, 'At random, this is, mind you. At random! Here . . . "I am like a pelican of the wilderness, I am like an owl of the desert. I watch, and am as a sparrow alone upon the housetop."'

'Lovely,' she said firmly, cutting him off. 'I love pelicans. And sparrows. Will you fasten your seat-belt. We're about to take off.'

His voice changed at that. He cackled: 'Going to get this crate off the ground, are you?' He said it like someone in an old war film.

'We're going to try,' she said. I heard Poor Clare incanting: 'John, oh John.' Ambrosia said nothing. I realized when I knew her that by then she had shrunk into her seat, into herself, trying to do anything, think anything, that would take her even momentarily away from her father.

Stiffly the aeroplane began to move, backing nervously away from the buildings as though it had done something to offend. Behind my still turned-away back I heard Properjohn call loudly, 'It's moving.' Then I heard him say: 'Ambrosia, what is that paper you are reading?'

'It's a magazine,' the girl said.

'Nothing cheap, I hope.'

There was a rustle as she turned back to the cover. 'Fifty pence,' she said.

'You know very well I did not mean that. I hope that when we are in the New World you will demonstrate the same respect for your father that you would show back home in Wales.'

'Wales, Wales,' intoned Mrs Properjohn. The first word was a little call, aching, homesick; the second a sad defeated snivel.

'Poor Clare,' said Properjohn. It was a bare unthinking response with no sympathy in it. He fell silent with the other passengers while the plane, like a fat ballerina, jogged daintily between the rows of lights and turned on its own axis at the start of the runway. It was, as ever, a brooding moment. I had never flown in anything as big as this before. It was like waiting for a cave to take off. I turned forward from the window and with sly prudence placed my feet against the bent steel legs of the seat in front of me. I did not look towards the Properjohns. I touched the buckle of my seat-belt and gave my beard a short tug, a nervous habit. Then Properjohn began.

'Let us pray!' he bawled.

'Oh, God, no,' I thought.

'Oh, God,' he insisted. 'We beseech thee, in thy infinite mercy, to help, assist and guide the pilot of this craft, knowing that he is but a *frail* man, given to all the errors and imperfections of man, that he may be given the strength and guidance to overcome his weaknesses and to take this aeroplane – itself the invention of other such imperfect men – from earth to sky and by some miracle back to earth again. We pray thy mercy on our souls which we commit to thee, and, if it be thy will, to bring us to a safe landing in the New World. But if thy will is not so, that we should quit these earthly bodies and be delivered to Eternal Life, through Jesus Christ our Lord. A . . . men.'

From the seats behind, a child, doubtless believing the prayer was all part of the service, echoed the 'Amen'. A woman began to sob and a man laughed nervously and said: 'For

Christ's sake . . .' I turned towards the middle row. Ambrosia was sitting nearest to me, her eyes tight, her face bunched with wrathful embarrassment. Her father's collared head rose above her in the centre of the three seats, serene, smiling, eyes closed like someone who has died an entirely satisfactory death. Beyond him Poor Clare was bowed forward, white hands whirling with invisible crochet work. The engine power increased and I could feel, through my seat, the aircraft straining to be off. Then astonishingly I heard several other people begin to pray loudly and spontaneously somewhere at the back. The stewardess with the panda eyes was angrily trying to get back into the cabin, lips moving vividly, struggling whey-faced to get free of her seat-belt at the front. There was a hubbub now, people praying and others protesting, and the child shouting: 'Are we going to crash, Grampy? Are we going to crash?' The plane rushed headlong down the runway and I had a sudden memory of a prayer I knew in childhood. That was the sort of effect Properjohn had.

Everyone was in terror by the time the plane eased itself demurely and safely from the ground. London was careering away beneath my eyes. Then he started again. Singing:

'Throw out the lifeline. Throw out the lifeline . . .'

This time panda-eyes was on him. She came up the gangway like some burning heretic-hunter and confronted him. He pretended not to see her at first and, in fact, he may not have done so because his eyes were closed with the fervour of the chorus. It was Ambrosia pulled his black sleeve. 'Somebody to see you,' she said bluntly.

Everyone was watching now, standing up, looking over the tops of seats and around the upholstered edges. Panda-eyes glared at him menacingly, but he smiled his great, ravaged, beneficent smile at her. He stopped whatever she intended to say and out came only the official incident-stopping sentence: 'Would you like a *complimentary* drink, sir?'

'No!' exploded Properjohn. 'Alcohol! Never.' Then the terrible smile erupted again. 'Have you got any free fags instead?'

He was quiet for half an hour. Then panda-eyes came around

with the earphones in their plastic bags. Properjohn grabbed three of the bags enthusiastically but when he found he was required to pay a pound each for the hire of the earphones he handed two back and kept one set for himself. Ambrosia, making no comment, sullenly took a pound from her purse and paid for her own earphones. Poor Clare went without, staring helplessly at the antics of the film without being able to hear a word of the dialogue. Every now and then I could see the wretched and bewildered woman trying to find out what was going on, leaning forward then across to her husband, catching his sleeve, and being shaken off, all the while asking, 'What did they say, John? What did they say?'

I had seen the film a month before. We were over the ocean now, chasing the daylight west, but it was outdistancing us. I began to doze.

Then he was standing there, in the gangway beside me, like a great black curtain. Properjohn, that damaged face, that chasm of a smile, rolled-up eyebrows, trembling nose, eyes like engines. His black arms were out, a big white paw settled on the back of the seat in front and another on the seat behind.

'Young man,' he said. 'Did you know that you bear a remarkable resemblance to Our Lord Jesus Christ?'

'There must be some mistake,' I said hurriedly.

'None at all. None at all. Your profile, your hairline and that beard. Your pensive demeanour.'

'I was wondering what the film was about.'

He dismissed the remark with a snort that left a little wet pendulum swinging from his nostril. This he dismissed with a wave of black sleeve. 'I've been watching you,' he argued. 'Observing.' With abrupt and discomforting familiarity he sat down beside me and whispered, spraying me with fine spit. 'Your profile against the oval window with the evening light coming in, shining through your whiskers, making a bright outline around your head.' His voice, thick, theatrical Welsh, dropped and the sharp rays from his fierce eyes sank to a small glow like stage lights dimming on a subdued scene.

He pulled his head back to get a complete view of me. 'Look to the front, will you,' he said with a tinge of impatience. I looked to the front, wondering why I obeyed. 'Yes, no mistake,' he sighed with almost liquid bliss. 'Jesus Christ. Spitting image. Wonder you've never noticed it yourself.'

'Look . . .' I began, turning on him.

'Look, indeed,' he breathed. His face seemed to spread as he said it. 'Look and wonder.' He jutted his large head forward truculently. 'What's your name?' he demanded.

'Willy,' I answered miserably. 'Willy . . .'

'I am the Reverend John Properjohn, Minister of the Church of the Livid God,' he announced. 'Livid, make no mistake about that. That's what God is. Livid. And who can blame Him? I'd be livid, wouldn't you?'

'I don't know,' I said helplessly.

'Livid with the world,' he said. 'This bloody world. How old are you?'

'Twenty-five,' I mumbled.

'I'm fifty-six,' he said brightly. He thrust his hand at me as though the exchange sealed something. Helplessly I shook it. He pointed across the aisle. 'She's seventeen,' he said, indicating Ambrosia. 'And she's forty-eight,' he continued, rudely pointing at Poor Clare. 'She looks older because she's had an operation on her jaw. See, how they've taken a bit of bone right out. She doesn't look like she's got a chin at all, does she? Very rare in a woman, that is.'

The young girl was regarding him with a sort of glazed hatred. She leaned across: 'I am this man's daughter,' she explained quietly, extending her hand.

I pushed my arm in front of Properjohn and took the pudgy soft hand in mine. We exchanged smiles. 'I'm Willy Turpin,' I said politely.

'Turpin?' Properjohn rasped right in my ear. 'You didn't say it was Turpin.'

'You didn't give him the chance,' returned the girl sharply. 'My name is Ambrosia,' she continued to me.

'Means "Heavenly food",' said her father sulkily.

'This is my mother, Clare,' said Ambrosia. I nodded to the lady, trying not to stare at her chin which slid backwards from her lower lip to her throat with no interruption of any kind.

Properjohn turned half-sideways in the seat, blocking the

two women from my view and me from theirs. 'We're going to New York,' he announced heavily.

'There's not much choice,' I said. 'That's where the plane's going.'

'And then . . .' he paused and his eyes revved up. 'Then – West. West on a Cru-sade, Willy. A Cru-sade that will stun America and the entire earth.' His loud tone dropped spectacularly. 'Do you know what I've got in my waistcoat pocket?'

He glared at me challengingly, as though he suspected I might have an answer. I shook my head.

'I knew you'd never guess,' he said, visibly pleased. He put a finger and thumb into a crevice in his black waistcoat, then, as though changing his mind, took it out again. 'In there,' he whispered, leaning at me again. 'In there is a piece of paper – and – listen – on that piece of paper is the date of the End of the World.'

He leaned back, obviously expecting something from me.

'Is it soon?' I asked.

'I'm not telling,' he answered, a quick annoyance in his glance. 'Not even you, Willy, and I like you. No one can know yet. I got it in a *personal message* from God. What do you think of that?'

I hesitated. Then I mumbled, 'It must be . . . very handy to know.'

'Very handy,' he agreed. 'And before long *everybody* will know. When the time comes *I* will tell!' He dropped his eye-lights and his tone to a conversational level again. 'Is New York at the seaside?' he asked with genuine innocence.

I stared at him. I could see he did not know. 'Seaside?' I answered. 'Well, it's not exactly Brighton beach, if that's what you mean. But it's on the coast . . . more or less.'

'Ah, you know about these things.' He nodded as though I was in command of great learning. 'I'm afraid I haven't done much secular reading and to tell you the truth I've never travelled. I've never been on one of these crates before.' His eyes tipped up to my face as though he had overlooked something. 'We're from Wales, you know.'

'Yes, I gathered that.'

'Oh, you knew. We have our famous little church in Wales. We're content there, although Ambrosia went to Bristol once, with Clare, didn't you, Ambrosia?'

The girl's face, a young round face, washed, but with a touch of make-up at the eyes where he wouldn't see it and with dark, full, rolling hair, emerged from around her father's shoulder.

'Yes, I'm the travelled one,' she said with sweet tartness.

To my astonishment Properjohn began to half-hum, half-sing: 'New York, New York, is a wonderful town.' He went on for several pensive bars before turning that disastrous smile on me again and explaining: 'I don't object to a little secular singing. I used to sing secular songs once. I don't mind breaking into one now and again.'

'It makes a change,' I agreed helplessly.

'It's by the sea, then, New York?'

'Well yes and no,' I said impatiently. 'Not right on. It's more or less on two rivers. You don't know a lot about it then?'

His glance was a challenge. 'Never had need before, have I?' he said. 'Not until Mrs Jaye turned up in Wales.' I did not ask about Mrs Jaye because I was hoping he would return to his seat. But he was musing about Mrs Jaye, his ragged head rocking slightly like a boulder swayed by the wind above a chasm. 'She's got all the money, you see. All the dollars. She's staging the whole caboodle, all the Cru-sade. Right to Las Vegas.'

'Las Vegas,' I said with an immediate small interest. 'What are you going to do in Las Vegas?'

'Save it,' he said in a cut-and-dried tone. 'Well, anyway, try to save it. Before Doomsday, see? Mrs Jaye's husband passed away there when he was trying to save it once before and she particularly wants it saved before she dies or the end of the world comes, whichever is the sooner.'

I was feeling helpless, hollow, needing help. There was none. 'That's understandable,' I replied haplessly.

'Very understandable,' he agreed. 'So that's what we're going to do. She came to Wales to hear my particular gift – my firebrand oratory, see? – and she has summoned me to America to command her Cru-sade. That is why I am here in this seat,

Willy, conversing with you. That uncanny likeness to Our Lord . . .'

'Look,' I said, holding up my hand. 'There's thousands who look like this these days. The beard and the long hair, and everything. Surely you've seen them.'

'I saw the light shining around you, Willy,' he intoned almost lovingly. 'Just as Mrs Jaye chose me, so I choose you. Why are you going to America?'

Carefully I said: 'I'm going to look for a wife.'

'In America?' His explosion was stifled, but his eyes were fiery. 'There's plenty of nice girls at home, surely . . .'

'I married one of them,' I nodded. 'But she got away. Now I'm going to look for her.'

His big head dropped to his chest and bobbed there sympathetically a few times. 'Ah, I see,' he said. 'I understand it now. It's a terrible thing, this. Clare and me have been happily married for twenty-five years, you know. She was a noted beauty before they did her jaw . . .' He whirled in the seat and called, 'That's right, isn't it, Clare?' I looked at her and saw that she had purloined his earphones and was nodding with incredible ugly sweetness to the music. He took the nod as an agreement and turned back to me. 'Poor Clare,' he said.

I thought he had finished then. He was quiet. But he remained huge and hunched in the seat. Then he exploded: '*You're going to do it for us, Willy! I know you're going to do it!*'

'What?'

'Carry the Cross, Willy. Carry the Cross to Las Vegas.'

I managed to stop a howl of shock. 'No I'm not,' I choked at him. 'What the hell do you think I am?'

'The right man for the job,' he said, smiling as though he had coined some rare wit. 'And well paid it is.'

'Listen,' I told him. 'I am *not* Jesus, and I don't know that I even believe there is . . . there was . . . a Jesus. I'm not even religious. I swear, I drink, I've smoked pot, I have all sorts of wicked women. So I'm not carrying any Cross for you or anybody else – and certainly not all the bloody way to Las Vegas. So there.'

'You will,' he said.

'Never.'

Two

Above the ornate plastic door on East 76th Street, supported
by a pair of synthetic Doric columns, were engraved the words
'Bonapart's Retreat', a title which caused me to lower my two
cases depressingly on the step and realize that I had the wrong
address.

The door opened upon my perplexity and increased it by the
appearance of a gigantic young woman wearing a white
starched garment, a sort of halter and a brief stiff skirt, like a
half-dressed nun. Her body was in slabs, pale lumpy arms, legs
and breasts, hanging from the garment's apertures, as though
insufficiently packed in a bulging cardboard box, and beneath
corn-on-the-cob hair a face reddened as from some steamy
exertion.

I had not rung the bell and she had obviously not expected
to see me there when she opened the door. But her surprise
was quickly transferred to my suitcases, and she said: 'Say, are
you bringing those in here?'

A much shorter girl peeped around the first's big hip. She
too had a red moist face, but her black hair was cut straight and
square, like a motor-cycle helmet, around it.

'He's bringing those in,' said the first girl.

'Let him,' said the dark girl, apparently senior. She smiled
professionally at me. 'Come in, sir. And welcome to Bonapart's.'

Picking up the cases I went blindly through the plastic door.
It was warm and carpeted inside with an imitation garden on
one side, a desk in the foreground and four men sitting around
watching television.

'Sit down, sir,' said the small, helmet-haired girl. 'Mr
Mahoney will be right with you. Maybe you'd like a glass of
wine?'

'Yes, thank you, I wouldn't mind,' I said idiotically sitting
down with the others who took no notice of me. A coloured

girl, thin as an iron bar, emerged from a curtained door and, taking the hand of one of the waiting men in hers, sat down to watch television. Neither spoke, their closeness and their attention to the television set was wholly domestic. A nice redhead, with her hair sticking to her forehead, approached me with a tray on which was a glass of red wine with ice in it. She too was wearing the white stiff affair with her ashen breasts lounging sideways from beneath the halter.

She eyed the suitcases and said: 'Mr Mahoney will be right along with you.'

'Yes, they said,' I mumbled, leaning over to take a careful look at my luggage. Nothing was hanging out.

'You're English,' she remarked with a gush of added sweetness. She went down on her haunches as a teacher might crouch to converse with a pupil. 'Have you been to Bonapart's before?'

Childishly I shook my head. She was bending engulfingly close to me; one of those women who would be more at home in a home, and in her forties, than she was now at twenty-three or whatever it was. She was concerned, confiding, comforting. She patted me.

'And you look like you've come straight away from the airport,' she smiled. There was a large sex bruise on her leg, three inches up from the bend.

'I have,' I nodded.

'Wow.' She let her eyes widen professionally but still maternally. 'You just couldn't wait?'

'Look,' I said, pulling myself out of my idiotic compliance. 'I'm looking for . . .'

'And we'll see you get it, honey. You'll get it at Bonapart's.' She patted me again on the leg before leaving. 'Mr Mahoney will be along momentarily.'

With doubt I sipped my iced red wine. I said 'momentarily' to myself several times in the American way. The man next to me, grey square-haired, was sadly hunched towards the drama coming from the television screen.

'Oh, boy,' he said quietly as though he had been waiting to speak, but without moving his face towards me. 'I sure thought you'd brought along all your own equipment.' He nodded at the suitcases. 'Shit, I ain't never seen any guy bring his own equipment to this place.'

'No,' I said. 'It's just my luggage.'

He continued to be entranced by the greying old film on the screen. '*Curse of the Mummies*,' he said, fractionally over his hunched right shoulder.

'Yes,' I agreed. 'Any good?'

'It's terrible,' he grunted wearily. 'In this joint they should be calling it the Curse of the Daddies. Jeeeeesus, look at us all, will yer? Sitting around here waiting for some kid to get her breath back from rubbing up the last guy. We oughta be home with our families.'

'I'm waiting for Mr Mahoney,' I said defensively.

'He'll fix you,' he forecast. 'He'll fix you good. They always do first time. Because you keep coming back, like I do, poor bastard that I am. Every time I get a pay check, back I come.'

Someone else came through the front entrance, a shiny short man with a strong air about him. From the back of the establishment a young man with eyes like an angora rabbit advanced and shook the new arrival's hand with summoned warmth.

'Sure, sure, Mr Trevor,' he enthused. 'How many girls will you want today?'

'Five,' ordered the bright man, briskly.

'Shit,' exclaimed the man next to me despairingly. His solid grey head went forward like a hammer into his hands. 'Shit,' he repeated. Then he stood tiredly and walked, hunched and stiff like the zombie on the television film, to the desk.

'Mr Mahoney,' he started with subdued, hopeless, patience. 'I'm a regular customer in this place. Maybe I don't spend a million bucks, but I'm regular and I don't cause no trouble. I'm a quiet sort of guy. I work hard and I kinda look forward to coming here for a little innocent fun.'

'That's right, you do,' agreed Mr Mahoney as though endorsing a certificate. The newly arrived man thinned his lips impatiently and from behind the desk Mr Mahoney eye him an apology.

The grey man continued: 'Now I've been sitting on my ass watching that crummy opera for forty-three minutes. I don't come here to watch television, Mr Mahoney. I can watch television at home with my dear wife and family. But I wait, and I don't cause no trouble. Then this guy comes in and orders five girls.' Abruptly the emotional ropes that were so obviously holding him down parted. 'Five!' he screamed. 'FIVE BROADS! ALL FOR HIM! WHAT'S HE GOING TO DO – PLAY SOFTBALL! WHILE I SIT . . .' His tone tapered and broke, disintegrating to a sob . . . 'while I sit and watch the Curse of the Fucking Mummies. Now Mr Mahoney, I'm going. I'm clearing out of here and I ain't coming back. I'm going to chase old ladies naked in the park – and it's your fault. Next time you see me I'll be grinning dead from the front page of the *New York News*.'

He stumbled out. Mr Mahoney shrugged and tripped the switch of a microphone on the desk. 'Dorothea, Pansy, Candy, Ba-Ba and . . . who else is back there?'

'Totsy?' It was a suggestion that sounded doubtful even over the inter-com. 'There's only Totsy, Mr Mahoney. Liz is taking her break.'

'Totsy's got a fracture,' Mr Mahoney shrugged to the short shiny man. 'Her right arm. Is that okay with you?'

'Sure,' he agreed after a thought. 'I guess I'll find something for her to do. Right arm, you say?'

'That's right. We'll cut the fee by ten per cent, if that's okay.'

'That's fine.'

'Credit card?'

'Sure, credit card. What else?'

A short, plump girl with the customary white garment and red face took the man away by the hand. Now, diffidently, picking up my suitcases, then leaving them, then picking them up again, I went to the desk and Mr Mahoney.

'Straight from the plane,' he smiled knowingly as though he had an arrangement with BOAC.

'Yes, I've just come from London. I'm looking for . . .'

'You'll have a wait, mister, I'm afraid. Like you saw, we just had a big order. But if . . .'

'I'm looking for a Herbie Cato,' I blurted. 'I think I've got the wrong place.'

'Herbie,' he said reasonably. 'Not at all. Herbie lives up-stairs. He's a friend of the family. Go right on through and take the elevator. But, if you don't mind, as you go through the corridor back there, will you close your eyes. It's a straight run, you won't trip.'

'All right,' I said. 'I'll shut them tight.'

'Great,' he said gratefully. 'These young girls sure get embarrassed.'

On the door nameplate it said 'Herbert G. Cato' and in a scarcely smaller flourish below: 'Actor'. The landing was dirty, deep green like the inside of a pond and stuffed behind a heating pipe was a clutch of letters and an urgent cable.

On the other side of the door I could hear him singing in his rugged, ragged baritone. I opened the cable which said: 'ARRIVING NEW YORK THURSDAY TO STAY WITH YOU. WILLY TURPIN.' I had sent it three days previously. I bent and pushed it under the door. It stopped him in mid-note. Putting my ear to the panel I heard him pick it up and open it. 'Ha!' he exclaimed. 'Ha! Ho! Ho! For Chrissake! The bastard. Ha! Ho!'

I rang the bell.

'Who is it?'

'Ho! Ha!' I bellowed. 'Ha! Ho! For Chrissake. The bastard. Fee Fi Fo Fum, I smell the bum of an Englishman.'

It was hurriedly pulled open. His big, handsome, sinful face had grown a hanging-garden of hair since I last saw him. His eyes exploded over the black moustache and beard rampant over half his face. 'Willy!' he exclaimed. 'For Chrissake, Willy! How the hell? I only just got your cable.'

'Air travel gets faster,' I said. 'Can I come in?'

'But sure, sure, come on in.' He backed away in front of me and I saw he was wearing no trousers. There was a girl in the starched white pinafore of Bonapart's shyly eating a salami sandwich while seated on a cane chair. She took a wild gnash immediately she saw me and made for the door.

'Don't go,' I protested. 'Finish your meal.'

'It's *my* sandwich,' argued Herbie. He laughed and added, 'My Hero,' as though he had just thought of a good joke. Then he said: 'She only comes up here to steal, anyway.'

The girl blurted something through the bread which I couldn't understand, and struck a sort of stage attitude before relaxing, waving airily and leaping like an urban gazelle out of the door. Her legs, bare to the backside, were lined with the impressions of the bamboo chair.

'They all want to be Julie Andrews,' sighed Herbie, staring after her through the door. 'Come in, come on in,' he said, pushing me into the room. 'That's Liz . . .'

'Yes, they said she was on her break,' I said. 'I wasn't interrupting anything was I?' I nodded at his lack of trousers.

He laughed: 'Nothing, buddy. Nothing. I was merely being comfortable. And all she was doing was eating my sandwich.' He rolled his head affectionately. 'Nice girls,' he said. 'It's a sort of nurses' . . . er . . . place.'

'They've got a nasty accident just arrived,' I observed. 'He needs five of them.'

'Five?' he said, closing the door behind me. 'Wow. That's a real emergency.' He laughed: 'Aw, what the hell. It's a therapy anyway. They're all real nice kids. Kind hearts, soft hands and hard luck stories. That one, Liz, just now, comes from Cincinnati, but she can say things in any accent from Fairbanks to Jacksonville. Fairbanks, get that. Fairbanks, Alaska. A remake of *Nanook of the North* and she's a star.'

'I couldn't understand a word,' I remarked. I put the suitcases in one corner beneath an imitation parrot in a tin cage, and took the bourbon which he poured and passed as an automatic courtesy.

'She knew you were English and she was trying to give with the English accent, but it's difficult with a maw full of salami sandwich.'

'Even an English girl would find that a drawback,' I admitted. 'Anyway I'm glad you got my cable, even if I had to push it through the door myself. I sent it three days ago.'

He laughed and the whiskers blew out in little gusts as he did so. Easy, beguiling Herbie. Silvie always said that. 'Sorry, pal. I just hate to open my mail. It worries me so much.'

'Doesn't it worry you having it stuck out there behind a pipe?'

'Sure it does, but not as much as taking it in and opening it.

That worries me more. I've proved it. Are you planning on staying here any time?'

'More or less from now,' I answered. 'Is that all right?'

'Fine by me,' he said expansively. 'I'll drop by and see you. Me, I've got to get out. The rent. The girls downstairs have a collection for me every week, but it's not enough. I shall miss them. We've had a lot of laughs. When things are slow down there I go and have me freebees.'

'Freebees? For nothing?'

'Sure, for nothing.'

'Misuse of a masseuse,' I said.

'Magic with words,' he grinned. 'You ought to write.'

'I try,' I said. 'I still try.'

'Any good now?'

'Bits and pieces,' I admitted. 'I thought I'd give it a try over here. As you so generously invited me four years ago.'

'You think you're going to find Silvie?' he said.

'I thought I might run into her.'

'It's a hell of a big place,' he said. 'You don't find people you've lost. Not that easy. Did she write?'

'Just some comic postcards. I've traced her on the map. She was going west, roughly. She always said she wanted to do that.'

'Stupid bastard,' he said. 'Letting her go.'

'There can't be that many English acrobatic dancers travelling with two kids between here and California,' I said.

He shrugged: 'It narrows it down,' he admitted. 'If she wants to be found, you may find her.' Then he sighed. 'You had to arrive when the rent gave out,' he said. 'All that time, four goddam years, I've had the rent and now you get here I ain't.' He picked up the bourbon bottle and inspected it moodily. There was about an inch left at the base. He measured it pedantically, half an inch each.

'But I thought you were *the* big star,' I said, watching him. He threw his drink down his throat with a strong jab of the arm and shook his head with large sadness. 'A household face,' I urged.

He was slow, assembling the answer with care. 'Well, I won't go along with either household or face,' he decided eventually. 'You couldn't call them the homely type of picture and my face was not the attraction. We call them budget movies. No names, no story, no clothes. And not much money.'

I watched him sagely, marvelling in his male coyness. He kept his face down, searching the empty foot of his glass, avoiding me. 'I didn't say anything before because of Silvie,' he muttered. 'I wouldn't have liked her to get the idea . . .'

'She kept looking for you in *Chitty-Chitty-Bang-Bang*, and films like that,' I prodded.

'*Chitty-Chitty-Bang-Bang*,' he sighed. 'I would have enjoyed that. Really, no shit. My titles were epics like "Big Ear," a kind of runner-up to *Deep Throat*.'

'Medical films,' I said, enjoying his embarrassment.

'Sure, sure. *Deep Throat* was about this broad who had her clitoris in her gullet. Played for months in New York before they got it banned. I was offered a supporting role in that. Some funny guy told me it was the life story of Caruso and I thought it was a chance to go legit. But they really meant *supporting* role, God damn them. Same old wet skin movie and I wouldn't do it. It made a million. So I made sure I did "Big Ear" but that got banned because some top brain at the Ear, Nose and Throat Hospital went on television and said it was dangerous. Nothing to do with morals, it was medically dangerous. *Deep Throat* was okay because broads have been doing it that way for centuries and not too many have choked to death, but the ear, that's different. Deafness, loss of balance, brain damage, even . . .' He sighed thoughtfully. 'I guess he was right,' he continued. 'You couldn't have women falling over in the street or not being able to hear the phone ring or going mad, just because of a skin flick.'

'Too bad,' I said. 'Sounds like it was educational.'

'That as well,' he said earnestly. 'The shorts that went on with the budget movies were all about the Canadian Caribou and native dances in Samoa and that sort of shit, so that these guys who went into the theatre with the horn and their brief-cases in the afternoon could go home and tell their kids all about the Caribou and Samoa. It was educational in that way, I guess. But it was lousy work for a guy. Okay, it sounds fine, screwing in front of the cameras and getting paid, but you try and get all horny on a cold Monday morning in some cowshed studio in New Jersey, leaning across some broad with craters under her eyes and weekend teeth marks on her tits.'

'I can't see Dustin Hoffman doing it,' I agreed.

'Right. Well I couldn't see Herbie Cato doing it either. Not no more. So I say to this director, Mexican guy, Manny El Elfredo, would you believe, but everybody called him El Elf because he was small, see. I say to him "I can't do this. I'm cold and I feel shitty and this broad don't turn me on one degree. How the hell can I get horny in these working conditions?" And he comes out with some trippy shit about taking the whole production to Miami Beach and getting Racquel Welch in the female lead if I'll only be a good boy and get on with the fucking because the cameraman has got to go and see his wife who is dying in the Bronx Hospital. That was it. I quit. I told him he had enough wide-angles and if he could find some guy who could get an erection on a Monday morning then he was welcome to stand in for me in the close-ups.' He stopped and beamed over his whiskers. 'Stand in,' he repeated. 'Say that's not bad, is it?'

'Write scripts,' I suggested. 'Have you got any food or do we have to go out?'

'The salami sandwich was the end,' he shrugged. 'I should have read the cable then I'd have kept it away from that thieving broad.'

'I've got thirty dollars,' I said. 'Let's go out and eat something, then we'll go and get drunk and when we're drunk we'll think of something.'

'Okay,' he said. 'I'll get my pants on.'

We got drunk in Costello's on Second Avenue, an Irish bar with wooden pews and shillelaghs out of reach on the wall. While we were getting drunk Herbie said: 'So you think Silvie's dancing?'

'Of course, dancing,' I said. 'She can't do anything else.'

'How do you know she can't?'

I ignored it. 'There's only so many towns on a line between here and the west coast,' I said. 'And they only have so many clubs where they employ dancers. I'll just take it steady.'

'You don't have no choice on thirty dollars,' he grunted low over his glass.

'It's not even thirty dollars the way you're drinking,' I said.

He didn't listen. He said: 'Maybe you'll be too late. Maybe somebody else got her.'

'I've thought of that.'

'I bet you have. What a jerk.'

'And that.'

'How you ever got her in the first place beats the assholing band, but screwing around like you did until you lost her . . . well, man . . .' He threw the remainder of his fifth pint down his throat, and looked towards me truculently. His beard was soaked and sagging and he wiped it carelessly with the back of his hand.

'Goddamn it,' he snorted. 'If I'd known she was quitting I'd have taken her off myself. Man, I was crazy about her.'

'Everybody was,' I said. The drink and the reminiscing were making me maudlin. 'I like to think I've just mislaid her,' I croaked. 'Herbie, perhaps she hasn't found anyone better than me.'

'Christ,' he said, staring up wildly. 'That's one hell of a hope.'

We left Costello's wallowy with that heavy American beer. But at Bonapart's Retreat, where it was a quiet night, they accepted us with whooping good nature and within ten minutes we were stretched naked in adjoining cubicles having free-bees.

Liz, the mistress of the accents, took me to the sauna, then the shower, and after drying me off better than anyone I can remember since my mother, she laid me out again on the massage table. Herbie had told her I was a screen and stage writer and, in this belief, she kept repeating odd lines apparently from Broadway plays, leaning close to me to deliver them as she pushed her hands around and about every protuberance and cranny of my surprised body. She had me on my face and beginning at my ankles she worked lotion into every joint, muscle and nerve. She kneaded my buttocks like a countrywoman making bread, and her fingers kept pushing down through the archway of my legs. Her face was steaming up and eventually, saying, 'Be right back' she went out of the curtained door.

'This woman's assaulting me,' I called across the half-wall to Herbie.

'I thought you'd gone real quiet,' he said. 'Enjoy it. It's free.'

'I'll be embarrassed when she turns me over.'

'It won't worry her,' he said.

'She's got long nails,' I complained.

'Pal, that's a cross you'll have to bear.'

After he had said it I did not move for two minutes. Liz returned and told me to turn over.

'I'd like to use the phone, please,' I said.

'The phone? Now? Right at this moment in time?'

'You said that beautifully,' I told her. 'Could you hand me my jacket, there's a dear.'

Sulkily she gave me the coat and I took a card from the pocket. It said: 'The Reverend John C. Properjohn – Church of the Livid God'. On the back he had written, ' *You* will carry the Cross. Good pay. Ring me at the New York Hilton.'

Obligingly Liz had brought in a plug-in telephone which she connected to a socket at the side of the massage table. She sat on a stool, the nose of one breast poking from her tunic as though overcome with curiosity.

I spoke to Properjohn for three minutes. Immediately he realized who it was he began to shout 'Glory! Glory! Glory!' to people who were apparently in the room with him. Then I said: 'I'll do it on one condition.'

'Anything, my boy. Almost,' he promised cautiously.

'I have a friend, here in New York,' I whispered. 'A great actor. Been in lots of films.'

'Yes, yes.' The eagerness was still there.

'Can he come too? He would make a terrific St Peter.'

'Glory! Glory!' he bellowed. 'Be here at eleven tomorrow. Bring St Peter with you. You will carry the Cross!'

I put the phone back. I looked up and saw the girl's eyes glistening. 'Is it for Superstar?' she trembled. 'Boy, I would make a real beautiful Mary Magellan.'

'Magellan was a sailor, love,' I said.

'Ain't there any women's parts?' she pleaded. 'Anything, sir.'

Herbie's head, like John the Baptist's on the plate, appeared over the partition wall. 'What's going on here? What was that call?' he asked.

'I've just got us a couple of prime acting parts,' I murmured, leaning back on the table. 'Good pay, travel.'

His blank look exploded into delight. 'No!' he shouted. 'How d'you do it? What is it?'

'We have to carry a Cross across America.'

'Carry a Cross? Jesus, baby, I can't do a thing like that. I'm a Jew.'

'*Now* you tell me,' I said.

Three

Properjohn was waiting for us in the lobby of the Hilton. We spotted him immediately although the concourse was full of its usual river of people, for he was standing on one of the Hilton's easy chairs and peering over everything like a tall, black lighthouse.

'Glory! Glory!' he shouted when he saw us. I felt Herbie cringe as we walked towards him.

Naturally Properjohn was attracting a good deal of attention from the people in the lobby, but it was entirely passive, for Americans are very kind, basically shy, particularly as travellers which most of these people were, and not unused to oddities. Many people had stopped whatever they were doing and had turned to look at the man in the shoebox clerical collar, the black coat and manic expression. But it was his voice, even in the saying of those words 'Glory! Glory!' which held them.

'Glory! Glory!' he exclaimed again as we approached. He loped springily from the cushioned chair and embraced us as old and loved friends. 'Glory,' he repeated, more quietly now as we were in front of him. 'Glory, Glory.'

'Hallelujah,' nodded Herbie politely.

'Hallelujah, indeed,' returned Properjohn. He embraced me again, the black arms flapping about my back like crow's wings. 'And how is my Cross carrier?' he bellowed. Without bothering to hear my muttered answer he turned on Herbie and treated him to a slightly less familiar greeting, a twin blow on the shoulders with the death-white hands. 'And this is our St Peter, is it?' he exulted.

'Herbie Cato,' I said. 'Herbie, this is the Reverend Properjohn.' For some reason I had to think of something else to say, so I added in a diffused whisper, half excuse: 'From Wales.'

There was scarcely any doubt, even for Americans, that he was from Wales. In his voice every valley of intonation was given its full sweep down and then up, with ridges and little dolloping streams in between. I have never heard anybody so dramatically Welsh. I swear he practised it in front of the mirror every night.

Now he gathered us to him like unexpectedly recovered sons, his arms cowling our shoulders, and urged us towards the elevator through the attentive crowd. As though he was afraid of losing their interest he began gesticulating to either side, to the accounting grille and the change bureau, to the information and theatre booking desk and the bookstall, and bellowed: 'What d'you think of this then? All this? BABYLON! BABYLON!'

Herbie tried to quit. He began rolling panicky eyes and violently shaking his whiskers at me behind Properjohn's back. 'I can't go through with this,' he grated at me, several tones under Properjohn's continuing howl of 'Babylon! Babylon!'

But Properjohn got us to the elevator, his arms still stretched about our shoulders, bearing our weight as he hurried forward in the manner of a man carrying two burdens on a yoke. When we got through the door he did not so much release us as set us down. Then he boomed ripely at the coloured lift-man: 'Ascend!'

'Which floor, Mac?' sighed the operator.

'Forty-two, Buster,' rejoined Properjohn. He nudged me like a huge imp and repeated 'Buster!' I remembered he had called the airliner a crate in that same accented tone; he had this peculiarity of imitating what he imagined, apparently from pre-war films, were the idioms and phrases of the Americans. Outmoded jokes, sayings, and nicknames, familiar to the tongues of W. C. Fields, James Cagney and Douglas Fairbanks, were delivered in a hideous hybrid accent, half-Welsh, half-Paramount Pictures.

At the forty-second floor he grabbed us powerfully again by the shoulders and growled: 'Right, pardners, let's go.' The lift attendant rolled his eyes quietly beneath their lids.

Properjohn slewed us into a suite almost opposite the lift. To the twenty or so people assembled there our entrance was the signal for admiring gasps and then spontaneous American applause. Poor Clare and Ambrosia were there, standing gloomily by the window as though they had considered jumping but lacked the guts. The Americans converged on Properjohn and began slapping him on the back, praising and congratulating him, until Herbie and I, standing like a couple of prize prisoners, looked at each other and then around us to see what was causing the excitement. Then we realized. It was us.

Several of the men wore clerical collars and there were half a dozen of those women there who looked as though they habitually slept with clergymen. While they were lionizing Properjohn they continued viewing us, half-slyly, but with great glee, and when he ushered them towards us they came with little, toe-point steps, heads and eyes and grins protruding, their hands half-groping as though they sought to touch us or give us a tickle or a poke.

'Ladies and Gentlemen,' bellowed Properjohn. 'These are my captures. This . . .' he pointed straight at my stomach from ten feet away '. . . is Willy Turpin who has been sent by the Lord to carry the Cross.' All the people made timid cries of approval, aaah, aaah, and one moribund hand after another was offered in my direction. I shook a few at random and then desisted as Properjohn continued '. . . and, another discovery by the Grace of God, this is . . . this is . . . ' I thought he was lost for a moment, but then he exulted: 'Our St Peter!'

The same pale hands of welcome were extended to Herbie and there were mutterings about Herbie's beard and his resemblance to St Peter as they backed away and we were allowed to walk farther into the room.

'Willy,' Properjohn boomed when the assembly had reached a raised platform at the end of the room. 'I think that we have got to avoid confusing people's minds about you, boy. They must be quite clear that you are *not* Our Lord Jesus but that you are merely carrying the Cross just as a reminder. Anything else would be blasphemy.'

Agreeing murmurs gurgled around the room. 'Blasphemy, blasphemy,' they said. He raised his finger like a candle and repeated: 'So you are *not* Jesus. Is that understood, Willy?'

'Perfectly,' I nodded. 'If anyone asks I'll say.'

There were some uncertain laughs at this but Properjohn smiled indulgently and said: 'Well, we don't want any misrepresentation, now, do we?'

While everyone around was agreeing with him I saw Winston for the first time, a slim, half-pint Negro, of miniature handsome looks. He moved to our side while Properjohn was babbling about something else, and murmured: 'I'm Winston Birtley, the public relations guy for this circus.' He glanced at Herbie. 'How about a quick miracle, man. I could use a Scotch on the rocks.' At least there was someone else like us.

Then a shyly smiling, cream-faced, young man in a maroon suit rounded off with a clerical collar arrived at our sides. His light auburn hair looked as though it might be dying by the day.

'I would certainly like to introduce myself,' he smiled, passing a diffident hand around, beginning, deliberately I thought, with Winston and ending on Herbie. 'I'm Robert C. Hatt and I'll be coming along with you on this great journey as a kind of assistant to the Reverend Properjohn. I hope we can all be good friends.'

Properjohn came back, with his carnivorous smile on each of us in turn and finally resting with a hint of puzzlement on the black face of Winston. He bent several degrees closer as though he were about to speak to a child.

'Ah, now, what did you say your Christian . . . er . . . your *first* name was?' he inquired.

'My Christian name? Winston,' said Winston with calm.

'Ahhh, yes. Your *Christian* name,' said Properjohn. He grinned with fiery indulgence. 'Winston,' he said again, bending forward informatively, 'was the name of a famous white leader we had in the war.' He stared at the Negro. 'Across the sea,' he added.

Winston said: 'I heard.'

'Perhaps your mam named you after our great leader,' Properjohn suggested.

'Ma mammy sure did, suh,' said Winston darkly.

It was lost on Properjohn. 'Ah, ambitious for you, was she?' he said.

'Sure was. Ah guess she wanted me to grow up to be a white man.'

The indulgent smile fragmented on Properjohn's face to be immediately rebuilt into an uncertain, twitching grin. Abruptly he shook us all with exaggerated hugeness by the hand, using both of his to one each of ours, and then staggered away. He had gone only a few feet into the crowd, now increased by further ecclesiasticals and their women, when he turned and beckoned savagely at me.

I was two yards from him when he reached forward and catching my wrists pulled me urgently towards him. 'That blackie,' he whispered. 'Was he taking the mickey out of me?'

'Well,' I hesitated; 'I think he was a bit hurt that you thought he was just a . . . a blackie.'

Remorse flooded his face. 'Oh, I see,' he said biting his great dirty fingernails. 'I see now.'

He seemed to be speaking to himself but abruptly he turned his secret but fierce expression on me, the eyes pleading, the nose trembling and whispered: 'I'm sorry, I'm ever so sorry, you know, Willy.' He caught my elbow now, like iron. 'Listen, son,' he urged quietly. 'You've got to help me out a little bit sometimes. I'm afraid. I've not been about very much and sometimes I may do things . . . you understand . . .' His voice dropped sadly. 'Honest, Willy,' he confessed. 'I've always been frightened of black faces. Ever since I was a little nipper in the valleys. I even used to run and hide when the miners used to come up the street from the shift – because of their faces. And if ever there was a *real* nigger in the village, you know a lascar or something from Cardiff Docks, *everybody* used to lock themselves indoors until he'd gone. They were very rare.'

'Well they're not rare here,' I whispered firmly. 'Surely you've seen that.' I glanced at him. 'Or haven't you been out of the hotel?'

Childishly crestfallen he confessed: 'No, I haven't been out yet. I thought I might get lost. But I realize they do have a lot here.'

'And they're just people, that's all,' I said inadequately. 'Just treat them like anybody else. Talk to them like anybody else.'

He seemed overwhelmed. 'Yes, Willy, I will, I will. Thank you, boy,' he said. I turned to go back to where Herbie and Winston were still standing with the Reverend Hatt. As I did so, Properjohn whispered: 'You were quite right about New York, Willy. About the seaside. Dead right. From my window this morning I could see the boats on the water.'

'What did he want?' asked Herbie.

'He more or less wants me to carry him as well as the Cross,' I shrugged. 'He's the original pre-war man. He's still living forty years ago.'

I said to Winston: 'He's sorry about saying that to you. He doesn't know anything about coloured people, that's all. He's had no experience of them. And he comes from Wales, you see, and they're very primitive in Wales.'

Winston smiled. 'Forget it,' he said and then, enigmatically, 'It's my error.'

The Reverend Hatt muttered something pacifying and Herbie looked at Winston, as though they already had some understanding, and laughed. Winston returned the laugh. Then the room's attention was taken by a clatter caused by Poor Clare toppling clumsily forward as she attempted to mount the dais at the far end of the room. She bleated two or three times with embarrassment followed by protest as Ambrosia, close at her rear, prodded her summarily with a zither-like instrument. Properjohn was behind Ambrosia, his hands urging them forward like a swineherd. Eventually they were all established on the platform and without announcement although with a certain ruggedness they launched into a lively hymn, Clare blowing into a large harmonica, Ambrosia pulling and plucking at the black instrument and Properjohn singing in a baritone as surprising as it was magnificent.

The Reverend Hatt, in a trembling tenor, and standing beside us, suddenly sang too, his face like a lily, and the other people joined in, including Winston. Herbie and I were the only mutes. Poor Clare blew out her veined cheeks while the mouth-organ flew to and fro like a shuttle. She had a deft left hand, seeming to catch the instrument by instinct as it was about to shoot off sideways from the corner of her mouth. Ambrosia's round and pretty face was intent on her harp and her fingers and Properjohn could have been centre stage at La Scala. Herbie and I felt out of it.

'Why don't you sing?' whispered Winston between verses.

'We don't know it,' said Herbie sulkily.

'La-la-la, then,' he said.

'Sure, la-la-la,' urged the Reverend Hatt.

We did.

'I'm quitting,' muttered Herbie between our shy lisps. 'Before my mind blows. Who the hell is that with the harmonica?'

'Clare,' I whispered.

'Poor Clare,' he said.

The hymn half-stopped, hobbled for a few more bars, and then was conclusively finished by the commotion of an arrival through the main door of the suite. People began shuffling aside more in fear than politeness and down the flank of the gathering was wheeled a figure in an invalid chair. A chauffeur in full livery propelled the vehicle with professional polish, a big-shouldered man blocking from our view the seated occupant.

'It's Mrs Jaye,' said the Reverend Hatt, awe nailed on his face. 'She's come to speak to us.'

'She sure ain't goin' to do no high-dive,' muttered Winston watching the ancient woman being propelled to the front.

Neither was she. The lady wheeled up a sloping run to the stage was like a lump of unbaked bread. The chauffeur's showy but dexterous three-point turn brought her face to face with the assembly who stood in collective and undignified thrall. We were confronted by a small apparition; a shrivelled creature in a puffy white fur coat and a powder-coated face, with sharp, bitter eyes that regarded us like an Arctic stoat.

Poor Clare and Ambrosia, on the stage at the side, sank a pace back clutching their musical instruments, while Properjohn made tentative dragonfly darts towards the seated figure and away again, emitting diffuse spitty noises. Mrs Jaye appeared neither to see nor hear him.

The chauffeur, having applied an elaborate handbrake, took off his cap with a military flourish and stood back at attention, the cap cradled like a grey infant in the crook of his arm. His place was taken beside Mrs Jaye by a fat man with a thin man's head. It was a strange thing to see. It was as though Laurel and Hardy had been decapitated and Laurel's head had been placed on Hardy's shoulders. And without the smile. For a segment of a second two small upward splits showed at the ends of the man's skinny mouth, but they were quickly straightened. The body was gross and morose, the large feet splayed out, the head, small and tight, like a cork surmounting a bottle.

This person now took the attention of the room. The woman remained like an antique doll. Properjohn had ceased his hesitant two-step and now stood at wondering attendance like the remainder. On the stage the tableau was as solid and silent as the watchers in the body of the room.

A digestive rumble came from inside the thin-fat man like somebody moving heavy furniture. He put his hands to his gross stomach and said: 'Good morning. To those present who have not had the pleasure of meeting her I introduce the charming Mrs Helen J. Jaye.' He made a downward curving motion, like a solemn karate chop towards the being in the wheeled chair. Then an astonishing thing occurred. A small puff of powder, like the firing of a tiny gun, issued from the area of the lady's ghostly mouth, shortly followed by another. Most of the people appeared familiar with this phenomenon and from them came a ragged and respectful 'Good morning, Mrs Jaye.'

The man beside the ancient woman stared challengingly. 'As you are aware,' he said, 'Mrs Jaye suffers a little from laryngitis and today, with this inclement New York weather, she finds speaking more of a problem than usual. So I will relay her guidance to you.' He glanced down at the figure and our heads now went as one in the same direction in time to catch an approving puff of powder, blown this time from the corner crevice of the mouth.

Straightening again, the man said: 'Most of you will know me. But for those who don't I am Oliver B. Jaye, Mrs Jaye's nephew and personal assistant. Those who are embarking on this great and momentous expedition, taking the Cross of Jesus across this heathen nation, will be seeing me from time to time'.

Again I felt Herbie make the beginning of a turn at my side as though he would have quit there and then. I caught his arm and whispered: 'Money.' He sulkily relaxed. My caution was whispered so low that even I could hardly hear it, but Oliver Jaye, from the platform, stopped in mid-sentence and looked slowly and nastily over the heads like a schoolmaster unerringly seeking out a talkative pupil.

'You have a question, sir?' he grated in the direction of our group.

Startled, I looked at Winston, Winston glanced at Herbie, Herbie stared accusingly at the Reverend Hatt, who became so frightened that he took the blame at one swallow and squeaked: 'No, no, I'm sorry. An error.'

'Sure, an error,' said Mr Jaye, considering him bleakly, marking him down. 'Now, if it is possible to have some attention through this hubbub. I want to tell you, in general terms, what the route and intention of the Crusade is, as described and dictated to me by Mrs Jaye. Those actually going along will attend a briefing after this meeting, where coffee will be available at a small charge.'

At this short bursts of puff issued from Mrs Jaye and her nephew bent down into the line of fire before straightening and announcing: 'Correction. Mrs Jaye feels that the Crusade in reality starts from today, from this moment, and to mark the occasion coffee will be free of charge.'

A rumble of appreciation acknowledged this generosity. Oliver Jaye waited for the excitement to subside. Then he said:

'At the very outset, let me leave no doubt or uncertainty about this – the primary object of this Crusade will be to SAVE LAS VEGAS!'

The three words were delivered in a trio of fearful shouts from the steely mouth. It was almost possible to feel them hit the rear wall of the room and bounce back. 'NOTHING,' he cried again. 'NOTHING LESS THAN THAT! TO SAVE LAS VEGAS!'

A primitive, almost tribal, rumble welled from the gathering and a fluttering of applause which accumulated until it was a heartfelt ovation. A long twirl of powder came from Mrs Jaye, curling out from her dead face, as though she were whistling her approval. Oliver Jaye bent smiling and solicitous to her and then straightened again. 'New York,' he muttered like a curse. 'Is beyond the Lord. Nothing here can be saved. God will destroy it with fire.'

A distinct murmur of apprehension greeted this forecast and he appeared at once to realize why. He held up a reassuring hand. 'New Jersey, New York State, Brooklyn, the Bronx, Staten Island, will be okay,' he told them. 'Your parishes will be okay and the Jaye Foundation will still finance . . . that is, support them. It will only be Manhattan Island for destruction, as I understand the prophecy at this time.'

A selfish flutter of relieved applause greeted this amendment. Reassured, the audience turned its ecclesiastical face to him once more. 'The Cross,' he said, pausing now for emphasis. 'The Cross will travel through New Jersey, Pennsylvania, to Baltimore, Washington, then through Virginia, Harrisonburg, Knoxville, Nashville, Memphis, and west – to LAS VEGAS.' Again he shouted the last two words. Then, his voice quietened, he said: 'But first, and for the most obvious reasons, from New York to Bethlehem.' There was an approving general mutter and I looked at Properjohn in time to see his puzzled black eyebrows go to the top of his head. He looked as though he was about to advance the awful question, but Oliver Jaye luckily forestalled him. 'Yes,' he growled, 'Bethlehem, Pennsylvania. We will begin there.'

His voice died and his hands, which had been rising as though he were gradually lifting an unseen load, dropped to his side. Properjohn's eyes were swivelling with dismay and ignorance. He stared across the people to catch my attention and then began shrugging his shoulders helplessly.

'The Cross,' continued Jaye. 'The Cross will be carried into each town on the route. Our instructions will have gone ahead and choirs and well-wishers from local churches, in receipt of our benefit, will be assembled for spontaneous welcomes. Hopefully our public relations advisers will have got the home-town news media, papers, radio and television, to an appreciation of the importance of this Crusade. All this on the way.' His voice paused and dropped. 'Now Las Vegas. That's something else.'

A barrage of face-powder was now shooting from the upper part of Mrs Jaye. She was patently excited and emotive because her head had commenced a doll-like rocking motion that sent minor avalanches of caked powder toppling from her forehead and her cheekbones. Her nephew bent close to hear. Eventually he came up with the message. 'Mrs Jaye wishes to remind us all,' he announced heavily, 'that her dear and well-remembered husband, Phillpot J. Jaye, led the last campaign on Las Vegas, ten years ago, and died – was taken home by Jesus – in that city while carrying out the Good Lord's works. It is with the spirit of Phillpot J. Jaye in our hearts that we go from here tomorrow on our way to finish the work that he so nobly set out to do.'

There was immediate applause which only palled as the chauffeur stepped sharply forward and with a polished manœuvre turned Mrs Jaye and propelled her from the stage, leaving behind a dusty aroma. Coffee appeared on a trolley and the clerics and their wives gathered around as though it was a relief waggon. Oliver Jaye had accompanied his aunt from the room, but he was coming back. Properjohn approached, somewhat stealthily through the people, with an uneasy smile for me.

'Well, Willy boy,' he whispered. 'It all sounds very difficult and exciting. I only hope somebody knows the way.'

An hour later everyone except for Winston, Herbie and myself, had gone, dismissed from the room, the Properjohns to their rooms, the others to their safe parishes with one laconic wave from Oliver J. Jaye. Like schoolboys kept behind we sat in an uneasy group, Jaye regarding us with unmixed sourness from the dais.

'I see you three guys,' he said with open nastiness, 'as both the strongpoints and the weaknesses of this operation. You've been around, I can see that just looking at you.' He paused and let us sit under his malevolence for thirty seconds as though daring any of us to deny that we had been around. 'From the start,' he continued grimly. 'I don't go along with having a Negro as a travelling public relations man in an outfit like this. I'm not going to hide that. It's primarily a white crusade.' He stared at Winston with eyes like northern ponds. 'You understand that?'

'Sure,' said Winston, calm as though a reasonable point had been put to him. 'Maybe your people should have looked harder along Madison Avenue. I don't want this trip any more than you want me to have it.'

I thought Jaye looked at him carefully over the word 'trip' but he only said: 'Okay.'

Winston regarded him quietly. 'I'm the only account man in the office who is currently a Christian,' he said. 'We've got three Jews, a Zen Buddhist and a Black Muslim. Maybe you'd like one of them to go along.'

Jaye's starved face seemed to be considering the challenge, but he turned aside from it. He went to Herbie now. 'You say you're an actor?'

'That's what I say,' returned Herbie cautiously. He was waiting for the Jewish question, I could tell that.

'We're paying above Equity rates,' said Jaye.

'I heard,' lied Herbie.

'Only fifty dollars now,' said Jaye cautiously. He glanced at me quickly and then went back to Herbie. 'For you, that is. But two hundred at the end. You, Turpin, get fifty and two-fifty, because yours is a bigger part. There is a bonus – provided your conduct sheets are clean.'

'My sheets always are,' said Herbie seriously.

'AND NO FUNNY BUSINESS!' the man suddenly screamed. His tone dropped to a threat. 'Get that.' He stared along the short row of us. I found myself nodding compliantly;

I saw he had reduced Herbie to head-nodding too. Winston said: 'Got it.'

'Look,' said Jaye. 'I want to make myself clear. I *know* you guys. I *know* you just by looking at you. There's not one religious impulse among you. Not a single one. Well, that's okay by me because you never fooled me on that account, never. But I want somebody who is going along on this waggon train who is businesslike, *worldly* if that's the word. Who can get the show to Las Vegas without it falling apart on the way. That crazy Welshman maybe comes strong on the Christianity, with a good reaction quotation on Oratory and Approach, O and A ...' His voice dropped reverently, 'Mrs Jaye was impressed and we've had good reports from our agents' surveillance.' Then it strengthened again, 'But he'd finish in Alaska, or the Bronx, or the Tennessee River. He don't know what the hell the time or the day is.'

He stopped abruptly, shocked it seemed at himself, and covered his tight mouth with a worried hand. 'I didn't mean that,' he apologized hurriedly, but somehow not to us. 'Not using "hell" in that context. Not as a blasphemy. I'm sorry.' He returned to our faces, having apparently corrected the error to the satisfaction of someone invisible. Certainly he cared nothing for ours for he came back with a scowl. 'So,' he said. 'If we allow that your motivation for this experience is solely commercial, that's okay with me, because you guys are going to function as the hard backbone of the business. You're the mercenaries.'

He seemed pleased with that phrase and he said it again to us carefully, as though all three had probably missed it the first time. 'You're the mercenaries.'

'But,' he said. 'Mercenaries are not always the best disciplined of troops. That's a general fact and we all know it. But, because of the nature of this crusade, and because Mrs Helen J. Jaye is financing it and this is how *she wants it to be*, anybody who steps out of line, any guy who spoils the Christian image of the experience, will be ... dealt with.'

It was a chilly sentence. Then, as though to leave us in no doubt that what the Mafia could do the Helen J. Jaye Foundation for Christian Love could do also, he continued: 'And that phrase "dealt with" does not simply mean the confiscation of all remaining fees and bonuses for the culprit, it could mean other and more serious consequences. The Helen J. Jaye Foundation for Christian Love is a very powerful organization, very rich and very powerful, and the success of this campaign is very important to the heart of that dear old lady. I aim to see that nothing happens to spoil that dream.'

His expression had softened to a strange puffiness while he recited these threats and sentiments, and his face had turned slowly and slightly upward away from us until it was in reverend profile like a saint on a stained glass window. Now when he returned to us his voice was more reasonable, comradely almost. 'Listen, you guys,' he said, as though we had been arguing against him and he wanted to compromise. 'So you know your way around the world. Great, I say, just great. Because with you on our side we'll be better able to fight the wickedness that we meet on the way. You people know all about sin and, frankly, I don't calculate the Properjohn family do. You'll know how to handle various situations which could arise.'

His voice and face tightened to slate again. 'I want you to know that I didn't want you guys. It's my estimation that too much selection was done at too much of a gallop. No character assessment, no psychological screening, no auditions, no suitability tests of any kind. And I think that constitutes a risk element. But Mrs Helen J. Jaye is anxious that the show gets on the road and Properjohn wanted to have you along. Maybe she listens to him more than she ought to. But that's how you got the jobs.' Another change and he looked appealingly at us now. His voice broke into huskiness. 'We've put our trust in you, don't betray it. The money is good for what adds up to a three-week tour across Beautiful America in the Fall. Some people pay the bus company hundreds of dollars for that privilege. And you're getting it for nothing, plus.'

We sat, our three faces turned up uneasily but attentively to him. He waved his chilly smile before us now. 'Who knows,' he mused. 'Maybe our little crusade's got its first three converts to the True Christianity right here. But maybe not. All I want to say to you men is – do a good selling job. It's just your misfortune that you are of this world and not of God's. But you can still do the merchandising – you don't *have* to believe in what you're selling. You must have an awareness of that I guess, Mr Birtley. How many of your friends on Madison Avenue really *believe* in the products they sell to the nation? Not many I guess, Mr Birtley. And you, Mr Cato, maybe you've performed in commercials?'

'Yes,' nodded Herbie. 'Sure I have. Soap, shaving systems . . .'

'But you didn't rush home and use that soap or that shaving system, did you?' said Jaye, regarding pointedly the face immersed in beard. 'You didn't truly *believe* what you were saying in that commercial?'

'No, I guess not.'

'And you, Mr Turpin. Do you honestly *believe* everything you write?'

'I've written brochures and things,' I admitted lamely.

'So even in little whitewashed England you know what it means to be commercial.'

'We're catching up.'

'Good! Great!' he exclaimed like a teacher seeing a glimmer from the eye of a long dull pupil. 'Now we have a basis, now we know what we're talking about.' He leaned at us from above like the Lincoln statue in Washington.

'Well,' he grated. 'Maybe those products were very *good* for other folks. Maybe they were just what they were looking for. Get it? That's why you're going out to do a commercial for Christ. You may not believe in your worldly hearts, but take it from me, friends, you are going to sell it real hard. Real hard.

'This means you clean up your own lives, for the next three weeks anyway. Okay? No women, or let's spell that out, because I don't know how you people operate – no s-e-x. No drinking, no foul language and no p-o-t. And especially no p-o-t, grass or whatever you might call it, nor any other drugs.' He studied our expressions. Mine must have reflected my incredulity over his performance. Suddenly he went down on his haunches as though he were going to tell a story. He was. 'I have to tell you that two years ago we became disappointed in a man who we took under the wing of the Helen J. Jaye

Foundation for Christian Love. Totally disappointed. He disgraced us in public and we cannot afford to be disgraced – and especially not in public. Somehow he let go of the Lord. Not too long after that he was able to explain his slip to the Lord – in person.'

His eyelids had dropped with melancholy, but immediately he looked up and said sharply, 'There's a thousand dollars bonus for each of you if the crusade is judged by Mrs Jaye and the Central Committee to be a success. That is to be written into your contracts.'

He stood up and looked down on our astonishment at this news. 'So keep your eyes on the Cross,' he warned. 'And your feet on the road of righteousness. Or no bonus.'

Then, as though saying that had reminded him, he said: 'Yes, the Cross. I guess you would all like to see the Cross.'

With three thousand dollars, plus fees, sitting on our shoulders, we all rose, like penitents from the communion rail, and almost shuffled after him, heads bowed, hands held with loose reverence in front of us. He led us towards a curtained alcove at the extreme end of the room, paused propitiously, then pulled the curtains apart with a tug of a gold tassel. Revealed there was a startling wooden cross, the size of a man and a half.

'It's balsa,' said Jaye practically, without taking his eyes from it. 'Real light to carry, Mr Turpin. It's not going to be too difficult. One mile outside every city it will be taken down from the roof of the trailer and carried into that town.' He stepped forward and to our astonishment opened a small trap-door almost at the foot of the Cross.

'Walkie-talkie,' he said. 'In immediate touch with the base trailers when you walk ahead into the towns.' He took a telephone receiver from the cavity and showed it to us like a military instructor demonstrating a strange weapon. Then he put it back and closed the neat cupboard door.

He turned quickly on us. 'Now, remember, we don't want any trouble with you guys. Any trouble from you and *you will get trouble from us.*'

He turned away again and spread out his wide, horrible hands. Then he recited:

'When I behold the wondrous Cross
On which the Prince of Glory died.'

Only two lines, and then he revolved again as though it were a part of a set drill ceremonial. His face was as dangerous as I had ever seen on any man. I was looking at my first religious thug.

Four

The worst part of that first of the many strange days was the putting on of the long nightshirt garments that Herbie and I were instructed to wear. These had been handed to us in anonymous parcels as we left the Hilton. Ambrosia followed us down to the lobby to give them to us. I introduced her to Herbie whom she greeted with a small smile. She immediately said: 'Are you two frightened? I am.'

'Apprehensive,' I agreed cautiously, my reply tempered by the promise of the money which Oliver Jaye had so casually thrown in our amazed faces.

'I was frightened of that Jaye man,' she said, looking carefully around her through the enclosing people in the foyer. 'That face, and that body,' she went on. 'Horrible. I couldn't help looking at him to see if he had a bolt sticking out of the sides of his neck.'

'He's certainly no Henry Kissinger,' said Herbie.

'Who's that?' asked Ambrosia.

Herbie grinned politely. 'A sort of star we have over here,' he said.

'Oh, I see. What a sexy name. We probably haven't had him at home yet.' She looked at us worriedly. 'Listen now,' she said. 'I mean it. If you two want to run away any time then I'll come with you. All right?'

'Right,' confirmed Herbie unconvincingly. 'But we ought to give it a chance. It could be a fun thing. What's that instrument you play?'

'It's a Sprott's autoharp,' she said as though there were millions of them. 'I don't think it's going to be any fun. Not with my father *and* that man. He's going to keep turning up, checking up.' She was quite shrewd even though she was young and she was looking at us carefully, working it out.

'They must be paying you well,' she guessed. 'A lot of money?'

'No,' I said. 'It's our zeal. Our religious zeal.'

'Lying buggers,' she said simply.

'There are certain conduct conditions in the contract,' I said. 'What you would expect.'

She sniffed and held out the two soft parcels, one to each of us. 'Well you can start being good little angels by wearing these when we kick off tomorrow,' she said. 'See if you think that's worth it!'

'What are they?' I asked.

'Well, sort of Jesus gear. Like a nightie.'

'God, no,' I whispered horrified. 'They didn't say we had to dress up. There was nothing about that.'

'Well, there is now,' she said tartly. 'And take it from me, with that horror comic man around they won't just have you carrying that Cross around, they'll have you nailed on it before the end. You mark my words.'

She pushed the parcels into our hands and went off chubbily through the crowd towards the lift. We watched her until she was swallowed whole by a phalanx of labelled men emerging from a sales conference.

'That ass,' murmured Herbie as though he had been asked to choose part of her. 'And those round, teenage, female tits. And that peachy mouth. Oh, Christ, Willy, that mouth. And Herbie Cato is going to be with them all the way across these United States.'

'And Herbie Cato won't be able to lay one bit of Herbie Cato on any bit of her,' I reminded him. 'Because if he does Herbie Cato might not just lose his bonus he could lose his balls as well. Herbie Cato must always remember Oliver J. Jaye.'

'Shit,' murmured Herbie. 'This is sure going to be hard.'

As it was our last night we went out and got spectacularly drunk and then returned to Bonapart's Retreat for a really disgusting session of freebees. Somehow we left our nightshirt parcels at Costello's Bar, but we regained them with some awkwardness, since when we returned there they had been opened and the two barmen were wearing the garments for the amusement of the customers.

In the dark thickness of the early next morning, in the last hour in Herbie's room over the massage parlour, we grimly explored the costumes which were to be part of our lives for the ensuing weeks. But we sat first on the edge of Herbie's wrecked bed, aching with the excesses of the night, unsweet, hanging with foul tiredness and the fungi that gather by darkness on the sleeping bodies of voluptuaries. Depravity is a very private thing and we did not ask each other questions.

The parcels, lumpily retied, sat staring at us disapprovingly from the table opposite. We sat staring back.

'What's the time?' I asked.

'Quarter past eight,' said Herbie.

'I thought Americans always said "after",' I observed. 'A quarter after eight.'

'So I'm considerate to my guest,' he grunted. 'Anyway if I'm going to be St Peter I guess I'd better speak English.'

'Why?' I argued. 'He was a Jew.'

'Listen, man,' he said, reminded of the anxiety. 'Do you think they know I'm a Jew? Or maybe they'll guess. Maybe you could teach me some quick Christian stuff, you know, like prayers. And I'll make sure I never have a piss next to that bastard Jaye. He's the sort of guy who would look over and down and draw his own conclusions. And with that nut who can tell what would happen.'

'You'd be liquidated, I expect,' I said.

'I think that could happen,' he agreed solemnly. 'A gang of Christians rubbing out a Jew. That would be kinda poetic.'

'Do you want to try them on?' I nodded towards the parcels.

'If we've got to.'

'We've got to.'

'Okay.'

We leaned forward stealthily like hunters and pounced on the parcels, grabbing them and then retreating slowly to the edge of the bed again. There was nothing in them to reduce our foreboding. We scratched the brown paper away like an old skin and each came out with an oatmeal coloured garment, a long rough nightshirt with a round neck, wide lily arms and a rope for the waist. With each was a note headed: 'The Helen J. Jaye Foundation for Christian Love'. Beneath that in strong handwriting it said: 'These garments will be worn to the Assembly of the Crusade at the Battery – 10.00 AM. Thursday 10 October. Remember and be there.' Beneath was an ominously scrawled letter 'J'.

Herbie lifted his garment first, then let it fall to full length from his hand. A childish whimper came from him. 'Oh, fuck,' he moaned. 'How can a man wear this goddam thing?'

'Put your head through the top and let it drop around you,' I said, miserably looking at mine still folded in my lap. 'You have to give a sort of wriggle.'

'Put yours on first,' he said grimly. 'Go on, you got us into this play. Stand up and put it on so, at least, I've gotten one goddam laugh out of it.'

He sounded morosely threatening, the sort of voice I had heard him take on when he had got drunk in our local pub in England. His big red eyes regarded me bleakly over the horizon of his beard like twin winter suns going down over a dark and ragged landscape.

'All right, I will,' I said. 'If it's going to bloody well cheer you up this morning, I will. Anything for that, you miserable bastard.'

'Start then.'

'I just am. Give me a minute will you, to see which end of this sodding thing is which.'

'Language!' he whistled. 'Man, you'll have to check that language. You sure will. One of your wild "fucks" when you're carrying that Cross and the credibility of the whole show will be screwed up and you and me with it.'

I had ringed the thing around my neck now, standing there in my shorts and socks, hesitating. 'Go on,' he said.

Irritably I put my arms into the voluminous tunnels of linen and then stone-faced but with a defiant wriggle I let it drop the length of my body.

'Christ!' he exploded joyously. 'Oh, God, you look lovely! You look so lovely!'

He was naked except for his ample hair and a pair of odd socks, one black and one blue, and he performed a sordid somersault over the tumbled bed, howling with excessive and exultant laughter. His mountainous, hairy arse went over in a disgusting parabola and he landed with a gigantic crash on the far side. I stood shivering with the bottled anger and shame of the moment, keeping my temper because I knew he had to put his nightshirt on yet.

'Oh, Holy cow,' he hooted. 'Do you look trippy, man! Hooooooo! I love you, man. God, that's fucking stunning. I ain't never seen nothing like that!' I stood like steel. His voice took on an idiotic pseudo-sweetness. 'And now, folks, it is my pleasure to present to you, our new model Wilhemena, showing my dazzling creation called Dead Sea. Note how the hem barely touches the unlaundered black socks . . .'

'Shut up!' I bawled. My head was thrust towards him. 'All right, so I look funny.'

'No. No,' he protested. 'Not funny – cute.' From the far side of the bed he lay his great mangled head on the end of the mattress and rocked it violently as though he were making some urgent prayer. He looked up again. I had not moved. I remained standing in my Jesus garment, sulking but defiant. He looked up and I saw the blotched eyes running water. 'God,' he repeated quietly. 'God. You sure look so cute.'

I thought I was going to snap then. I made to fly across the bed at him but he rose up, still sobbing with laughter, from his kneeling posture with his arms held up in surrender. 'No, boy, no. Keep off. You'll tear your negligée.'

He clambered across to my side again, contritely, his hilarity stifled now, holding his arms like a buffer before him.

'Sorry, Willy,' he said. 'But it looks . . .' I thought he was going to break up again, but he checked himself '. . . it looks . . . sort of different.'

'You've got to put yours on yet,' I said quietly.

He ignored the threat. He was looking at me quite seriously now, sitting back on the bedside, his head lolling sideways in consideration. 'You know, man,' he said, his voice subdued. 'You know, I think that guy knew what he was doing when he hired you. You truly *do* look like . . . er . . .'

'Jesus,' I helped.

'Sure, sure. Jesus.' He sat upright and regarded me intently. 'Apart from the socks you look great like him. Not being my religion I ain't seen too many pictures of this guy, but I've seen them here and there – I had a barber once who was a Catholic and he had one on his wall I remember. And you certainly do look the same, Willy, or very similar. Just where you're standing now, man, with that light bulb right behind your head, you do. You've got that sort of *golden* look about you.'

'Thanks,' I said sourly.

'I calculate that a lot of folks will be impressed,' he went on. 'You'll really jog their memory, man. And carrying that hunk of wood, as well. Wow. Yes, that guy sure knew what he was doing.'

'Well, I'm glad you like it,' I said. 'Because you've got to wear one too, mate. And you haven't put yours on yet.'

'I'll put it on later,' Herbie said casually. 'Maybe in the cab. We're going down to the Battery by cab, all right?'

'I'm certainly not going on the subway like this,' I said.

'You could be raped,' he agreed dolefully.

'So you're not putting on yours now?' I challenged.

'No. We don't have too much time.' He looked at the thick-strapped wrist watch and brushed away a clutch of his arm hairs that were curling from beneath it and over the dial. 'No sir, we don't have much time at all.'

'Put it on,' I said grimly.

'Aw, come on. Once you've seen one you've seen them all. I'll look great. And you won't laugh.'

'How do you know I won't laugh?'

'Because if you do I screw your mother-fucking head off your father-fucking shoulders.'

'I think you mean it.'

'Sure I mean it. And I've got thirty pounds more on me to prove I mean it.'

'All wind and piss,' I said casually. 'I won't laugh. But you ought to see if it fits. It might be tight under the arms.'

Herbie held out the linen garment in front of him with curiosity which soured to distaste. 'It just won't suit me,' he said childishly. 'I can't see myself in this thing at all.'

'It's others who have to see you in it, mate. What *you* think doesn't matter. If you were in a stage part you'd wear it.'

'Sure, on the stage. Not through the Bowery.'

'It's just acting,' I pointed out. 'Actors dress up, and that's all there is to it. Mind, it sounds like the parts you've been getting didn't need many costumes.'

'That's exactly right,' he agreed. He paused. 'You know Willy, I don't feel right about this whole thing. Straight from skin flicks to this. It don't seem correct at all.'

'It seemed right yesterday,' I said. 'When he told us about the money.'

'I'll wear it,' grunted Herbie. 'I've showed my ass to millions for half that kind of dough. I'll put it on right now.'

'Good,' I encouraged. 'Try and get into the spirit of the thing. Put on a holy face if you can. We'll have to practise that. We can't take that Cross across the country smirking like a couple of stand-up comics.'

'Okay, stop scratching, then,' he said. 'Especially there. What shoes are we going to wear with this stuff? What did they wear, sneakers?'

'Nothing, I suppose,' I guessed. 'Bare feet or sort of rope-soled sandals. But that was Palestine and around there.'

'Well this is New York City,' he grunted. 'In October.'

'Wear what we've got,' I said. 'They can't grumble at that. I'll just put on my shoes and socks, I think. They're decent enough.'

'I've only got my cowboy boots,' said Herbie. 'I guess they'll be okay.'

'Put the gear on,' I said. 'Go on.'

'All right, all right,' he said irritably. 'I'm getting it on.' He pushed near me threateningly, all hair and menace. 'And no laughing.' He pointed dramatically upwards. 'One laugh out of you, buddy, and you'll be up there where they wear these fucking things all the time.'

I did not laugh. It was not the threat so much, although as he inserted his massive and tangled body into the robe Herbie never once took his hard eyes off my face; not that, but the abrupt realization of what was happening, an awesome insight into what might happen in the following weeks. The enormity of it. To see this big bearded man, sweat and hair on his chest, his back and his arms; this rough, quarrelsome, funny, friendly, childish, and cheerfully amoral man, climbing into the garment of an early Christian martyr seemed like a perverse film or a shamefaced dream.

He let the thing drop like a shabby curtain until the hem was at his shins. As such things can be said to be a good fit, it was a good fit, except for a minor tightness under the arms and a bulge where it went over and down from his beer gut.

'You're not laughing,' he said, standing there looking oddly powerful and pathetic in the gown.

'No,' I said. 'You look all right. We've both got to wear the bloody things, so what's the use?'

'What sort of guy do you think he was?'

'Who?'

'Me. This guy. St Peter.'

'Well from what I remember from school you're not a bad fit. He was a fisherman, so he was probably a bit thick like you are. In the body that is. And he must have had a lot of fuzz on his face because they all did. And they used to say he was like a rock, so the story goes. Strong and steady. Like you, Herbie.'

He was vain enough to think I meant it. 'Was his fuzz wild like this?' he said playing his fingers along his beard like a harpist touching through the strings.

'Could have been,' I said. 'They all had different sorts. St Peter was a rough man so he probably had a rough beard. And Judas Iscariot, who was the baddie, he had a sort of thin beard, like Lenin. And then Jesus had a sort of refined beard, like mine.'

* * *

So we set out that dismal October morning, dressed in our long Christian robes and each carrying a suitcase containing the remainder of our clothes. My two suitcases, with the rest of my possessions, were left with the girls at Bonapart's, the sleepy early morning brigade, the uglier bunch brought in for the dilatory dawn shift. Beneath our robes we wore trousers, shirts and sweaters, the trousers rolled up to our knees. Herbie said it would be cold until we got to Nevada. I was shod in a pair of good Wolsey socks and a pair of Dolcis brown casuals and Herbie was wearing polished black cowboy boots with bright metal facings.

Three taxis went by without even slackening speed at our signal. The fourth stopped. The driver, a young but wizened fellow with an Armenian nose, leaned over and looked out at us with apprehension. 'You know my trouble?' he said before either of us spoke. 'I got an unquenchable curiosity. If I see something oddball I got to stop and see what it is.' He regarded us with hurt resignation. 'Where is it to? Jerusalem?'

I sensed Herbie stiffen and he leaned forward truculently towards the cab. 'Listen, Mac . . .' he began.

'Peace be with you,' I interrupted swiftly and gave Herbie an elbow. He glanced back and subsided. 'Listen, Mac,' he repeated softly. 'Peace be with you. Take us to Battery Park. Please.'

It was when we were in the back of the cab that I began to laugh. It was a delayed action, a memory of seeing Herbie struggling ridiculously into the garment in the apartment, sparked by his profile now, beside me in the taxi, beard springing out from his jaw, his face set with worry, his black and ornate silver cowboy boots protruding from beneath the worked hem of his oatmeal robe. I began to laugh and once the leak had started there was no way of stemming it. A snigger first and then a gurgle and finally a bellow. The driver looked nervously over his shoulder, at us first and then gratefully at the bullet-proofed glass screen that separated him from us. Herbie snorted and capturing my head in an angry and powerful arm lock, hooted: 'I warned you, you bastard. I warned you.'

He could use that arm lock. It felt as though an elephant had its leg across my neck. I could hear the driver gabbling an emergency call on his radio. 'Two kooks, dressed like women, brawling in the back. Yeah, wearing gowns!'

His words immediately sobered Herbie. He released me and I reminded him hoarsely about the dollars at stake. We tapped on the partition and smiled and flapped our hands in a friendly way at the driver. He regarded us fearfully over his coat collar. I waved a ten-dollar bill in the air and he cancelled his emergency call. 'Sure, they're wearing gowns,' he said, pacifying his radio contact. 'These days some guys do.'

The walls and windows of New York went by. We drove through the channel of Wall Street and out into the open again. There was an abrupt end to the skyscrapers and Manhattan flattened out and came to an end, rounded like the stern of a ship. Beyond that the grey vacancy of October sky and October rivers.

'Something going on here,' said the driver, looking to one side. 'People singing.'

'Our song,' forecast Herbie dolefully.

We looked out, curiosity overcoming foreboding but being immediately replaced by dismay and momentary panic. There were a dozen ranks of singers lined for fifty yards along one of the paths of the park beside the dull waterside. A coloured ferry wallowing in the confluence of the two New York rivers perceptibly paused fifty yards offshore while passengers and crew stood, faces like coins, watching the congregation on the bank. The singing filled the chilly Manhattan air and, by a curious juxtaposition, it looked from the point where we left the taxi, as though the Statue of Liberty, across the sound, had her arm raised like a conductor at the high note of a chorus.

I paid the cab driver who departed singing some suddenly recalled religious dirge. We walked, in our robes, stealthily to one flank of the gathering, to where we could see the maroon-clothed figure of the Reverend Hatt standing beside two sturdy motorized trailers, one bearing the news on its side in large painted letters 'Jesus Lives' and the other 'Jesus Loves'.

Even at a distance we could see that the plum-coloured clergyman was twittering nervously, doing small purple pirouettes, offering sheets of paper from a pile beneath his arm to passers-by who continued apparently neither seeing his gesture nor hearing his appeal. 'It's the sugar plum fairy,' grunted Herbie.

'Great, great!' said the pasty young Hatt when he saw us. He stepped back and viewed our robes with the attitude of a husband viewing a wife's new dress. 'Great,' he repeated with less certainty. 'Great.' He handed us each one of his tracts with a triumphant thrust of his hand.

'You're preaching to the converted,' I pointed out.

'Take them,' he pleaded. 'Here, take a couple more. They're free. There's no payment. I don't seem to be holding people's attention. I think it's the singing. Nobody can hear me.'

Obligingly we took the sheets and stuffed them into the pockets of our trousers beneath our robes.

'You sure look the part,' enthused the Reverend Hatt, leaning back from the waist to take us in again. 'You should really stir things along, carrying the Cross in addition. I think we're going to be off to a real good start.' Two more New Yorkers went by his elbow, like fish teasing a novice angler, but by the time the tracts were held out to them they had gone in the direction of the worldly towers of Wall Street.

At that moment the door of the 'Jesus Lives' trailer opened and disgorged the Reverend Properjohn, Ambrosia and Poor Clare holding her mouth-organ like a nervous pistol.

'Glory! Glory!' Properjohn bellowed when he saw us. He had the face of a joyful hawk. Ambrosia and Poor Clare were arrayed in long white silky robes. As the young girl descended the short run of steps, with her mother clattering, half-stumbling, behind her, Herbie and I both looked at her breasts moving freely beneath the gown.

'Glory!' called Properjohn again as though he needed some confirmation.

'Hallelujah!' responded Herbie off-handedly. 'She's not wearing anything to keep those boobs quiet,' he whispered to me.

Winston then emerged from the trailer, stopping halfway down the steps to consider us in our robes. He whistled: 'Real nice. Humm, humm. Real nice.' He came down and walked to us. 'That jerk Jaye tried to get me in disguise too,' he observed.

'But I told him to show me where it said in the contract that I had to dress up, and he couldn't do that. Gave out with some crap about impressing the ethnic minorities. How about that?'

'Good thinking,' agreed Herbie sourly. 'This goddam gown would show up whiter on you than me.'

Winston grinned at him. 'But I ain't got it,' he said. 'You have, brother.'

Properjohn, Poor Clare and Ambrosia were now hurrying in a tight group towards a wooden rostrum set up in front of the refreshment rooms, the silk robes of the two women blown behind them like wings in the waterside breeze. The singing stopped impressively and as Properjohn jigged skittishly up the steps of the platform so the assembled people fell to warming applause. Even at a distance it was easy to see how he loved it. His large, carved head went up and down and his arms waved like a marionette.

'How did they get all these people here?' I said to Winston.

'They get them, man, just like they got you and Herbie and me.' He rubbed his fingers against his thumb. 'Dollars.'

'They hired them?'

'Some they hired. They figured they'd need some good, strong voices out here on account of the wind. But mostly they just come from churches up-state where everything is kept cosy by the Helen J. Jaye Foundation for Christian Love. I'm telling you that confidentially as a friend and a participant, man. If anybody else wants to know, then they came of their own sweet motivation.'

Herbie laid his hand against the side of the 'Jesus Lives' vehicle. 'Home sweet home?' he suggested.

'For us all,' agreed Winston. 'The Properjohns are sharing "Jesus Loves" and we're using "Jesus Lives". I hope you guys can drive one of these rigs.'

'Nobody asked us,' said Herbie. 'But for the money, I'll do it. I drove a ten-tonner in one of my films.'

'Sure, *Truck-driver's Fun Girl*,' said Winston.

'For Chrissake,' hissed Herbie, looking sideways at the Reverend Hatt who was, however, twenty yards away trying to interest an old blind man in one of his tracts. Herbie glared at Winston. 'Okay,' he muttered. 'So you know. But maybe this circus wouldn't like a guy who went to see those dirty movies any more than a guy who was in them.'

Winston smiled and put up his hand. 'Easy,' he said. 'You just took the words right out of my mouth. Brother, I never missed one of your pictures.'

Oliver Jaye appeared at that moment, creeping swiftly around the edge of the vehicle like a successful spy. We fell back, almost colliding with each other in our anxiety. 'Okay, okay,' he said. 'This is no movie fan club. So let's get moving.' He shot a quick inspection glance at Herbie and I. It turned to a scowl when it reached our feet. His nasty face came unbelievingly up to meet ours, first Herbie then me. 'What gives with the boots?' he said.

'What gives?'

'You can't,' he snarled. 'You can't wear those boots. You'll make us a joke before we start. Get them off. Jesus and the Disciples had bare feet.'

'Not so,' interrupted Winston firmly. 'Not so, according to the gospel. St John, Chapter One, talks about the latchet of the shoes of Jesus. And New York City Ordinance 331, subsection b, says "Anyone walking in the streets of the city unshod can be accused of Vagrancy." Besides maybe they could injure their feet and not be able to walk another inch towards Las Vegas.'

Oliver Jaye stared at Winston but swallowed whatever he was going to say. 'Okay, then,' he muttered eventually. 'You win on the shoes issue – temporarily. But I'll see we get something more suitable than cowboy boots.' He lapsed into an unpleasant laugh. 'Or maybe we'll get a longer hem on those ball gowns.'

We stood, none of us speaking, for almost a minute, like a lull in a battle. Then Jaye said: 'Okay, you guys. Let's get this Cross operational. It's on the rack on the second motor home, which is where it's got to be stowed when not in use. Now let's move to it. The Cross is to be transported down to the assembly over there, and you just stand there holding it, Turpin. Okay? And you, Cato, you just stand beside it looking as though you're thinking good thoughts. If you know any of the prayers or hymns join in. If you don't – and I bet you don't –

just keep opening and shutting your mouths. Give a good impression. On the journey Properjohn will be teaching you a selection of hymns and prayers so that by the time you get to Vegas you'll have a look of deep sincerity about you. Right, let's move.'

The Cross was on a special grid on top of the 'Jesus Lives' motor home, fitted beneath a plastic sheeting cover. We took it out with more care than reverence. 'This balsa crap snaps like candy,' confided Herbie as we lowered it to ground level. 'We had a bed made of it for a joke scene in *The Organ Grinder's Night Off*, where it had to fall apart as I pushed this chick into the sack.'

'I think you ought to forget your film career for a bit,' I suggested quietly. 'I thought old Jaye had heard too much a couple of minutes ago.'

He nodded and with exaggerated care, as though we were handling some true religious relic, we brought the Cross down from the roof of the trailer. I took it in my hands for the first of many times. It was light, illogically light for such a tall and wide thing, and it immediately moved like a jib sail in the wind. Anxiously I steadied it and then looked down again to see Herbie regarding me with that unnerving sincerity which had come upon him that morning when I first tried on my robe.

'God,' he sighed. 'It's great, you know, man. It's real great. It looks *right*, if you get me. Right. If de Mille was walking the earth just now you'd be in his next picture.'

'Let's get on with it,' I said. 'I can feel my trouser leg coming down.'

'I'll fix it,' he said with a residue of the reverence still in his voice. 'You just hold the Cross, pal, and I'll roll it up.'

'You're getting kinky about this,' I said.

'No,' he said. 'But I can see how it's got possibilities. If a heathen like me can see the possibilities, just looking at you, and I *know* you're not J. C. but just Willy Turpin from England. If *I* can do that, think what somebody really stuck on it can do. Somebody who *believes*.'

I hoisted the Cross a few inches and, my face consciously moulded, I set out on the first steps of that lunatic journey.

*   *   *

We mouthed our way through the hymns and prayers, initiating a technique which we followed thereafter until we had become familiar with the words through their repetitive use or learned them from Properjohn during our journey west. I stood with the Cross to the side of the dais, like a stage spear carrier, Herbie at my side, standing with unemployed embarrassment not even having the static occupation of holding the Cross, but merely having to look religious. Our jaw movements were necessarily of a gum-chewing variety at the start, a simple mechanical opening and shutting, with longer openings at the end of the last lines of hymns and a grateful pronunciation of the 'Amen' – the one word we knew in context – at the conclusions. At least, I knew it and Herbie picked it up very quickly. Later, when we were able to recognize and go along with some of the other phrases, it must have appeared more convincing.

An edgy wind riddled us as we stood on the raised wooden platform, cutting through my robe and into the innermost crevices of my trousers and shirt, while Herbie had goose pimples on his neck and his chilly legs were held close together. After the first hymn and a prayer I could see he was occupying himself by running his expert eye along the virginal front line of a girls' choir which, sweetly gowned and squarely mortar-boarded, was trilling below him, their eyes at a level with his cold thighs. I could almost feel his shrug of sacrifice as he took his gaze from them and turned it on Properjohn who was flinging out his theatrically pitched notes to the fresh air of the Manhattan shore.

Properjohn was a natural rabble rouser. He could only have been a religious fanatic or a politician or a trade union leader. I watched him that first time, as I was to watch him on too many occasions later, pull the crowd up with his arms, almost physically it seemed; raising those long ugly branches of his, up and up, lifting their voices and indeed the people themselves. And his summoning voice, the ridiculous elk sound of it, baying, calling, exhorting them. He used his hands and his arms with his voice, the arms going up and down on their black hinges, seeming to control the pitch and the volume of his words. When I was a child, and I went to a genuine church,

I was given the job of pumping the organ by pushing a lever up and down, a sword-like thing plunged into the very gut of the contrivance. If ever I failed to use it with enough power or verve the organ would cough and wheeze like an ancient man. But if I pumped it extravagantly the whole ungainly instrument would rise and sing. It was that way with Properjohn's arms. There was power in them.

He had this paid congregation with him from the first moment. They were there to sing praises at a price and the very novelty of the man encouraged them.

Eventually we moved off from the Battery in loud procession, myself and the high-borne Cross to the front, Herbie beside me scraping his feet and making mournful Middle-Eastern noises which he thought fitting to the occasion. Properjohn strode behind us, his voice blaring past my ear like a sousaphone, the sound swinging perceptibly from side to side as his head went first one way then another to bellow greetings and blessings to the people of New York on the sidewalks and behind their imprisoning windows. Ambrosia and Poor Clare were on the flanks, the girl stringing her Sprott's auto-harp and Poor Clare running her harmonica through her lips, pressing and releasing the little side valves and periodically pausing to knock the spit from the cavities of the instrument with a deft blow on her large and protruding hip bone. It was the only thing she did gracefully. Ambrosia, pink faced in the chill day, looked like a well-fed angel, playing with sureness and serenity. Poor Clare's performance was jagged as the mouth-organ's path across her lips. At the long, corner notes, when she was almost at the edge of the fluted front, she would sometimes hold a note, drawing her whole face to one side as though trying to pull a stubborn molar.

In the procession from the Battery through Wall Street, along Mott Street, Chinatown, and from the Bowery to the arch in Washington Square, the choirs marched and sang. Behind them came the twin motor homes 'Jesus Lives' and 'Jesus Loves' driven by two temporary volunteers and with the sinister shotgun figure of Oliver J. Jaye riding alongside the first driver. The rear of the crusade was taken by the solitary inhibited figure of the Reverend Hatt, holding his sheaf of tracts like a pink country girl cradling a bundle of corn. Because of our relative positions in the succeeding processions across the country I was never able to witness this unhappy man, trying to give away his printed good news. Once, much later in Memphis, he tried throwing the sheets to the crowd but collected a litter summons. Not even his hopeful, hopeless, call of 'It's free! Nothing to pay!' would encourage bystanders to accept either his word or the Word of the Lord. He found it very frustrating, with an accumulating feeling that he was merely bringing up the back of the procession in case anyone at the front dropped something. If they had decided to have me travelling on a symbolic mule then the Reverend Hatt would have been given a practical bucket and shovel. It was not a happy experience for a young and sensitive minister. He confessed as much to me the night he attempted to kiss me in the mountains of Northern New Mexico.

This odd array of the spiritual, the temporal and the sheer incompetent, progressed below the peering windows, the streets and walls of Wall Street, through the coloured closeness of Chinatown and the morning sadness of the Bowery, in what the following day's report in *The New York Times* called 'the funniest farrago seen in this city for a long time'. I felt hurt and annoyed about that.

There were television cameras travelling with us, sitting like modern metal birds on the roofs of special vehicles, a presence which made Properjohn shout louder and appear to grow longer and blacker as we walked. Naturally my Cross and I got a good deal of coverage and I must say I looked pretty good. Herbie on the other hand kept covering his face like some frightened key witness in a scandal trial, in case any of his former movie fans should recognize and expose him.

In Chinatown, Properjohn, predictably, began to bellow phrases like 'Converting the Heathen' and 'Come to Jesus you Heathen People' which, fortunately, no one seemed to understand or at least take seriously. An exquisite Chinese teenage girl broke from the sidewalk and, placing a creamy face and a bosom wriggling with silk dragons before me, produced an autograph book and requested in a complete American voice my autograph. It was awkward holding the Cross and signing the book at the same time but no one had ever asked me before and I was not going to miss it. I stopped and signed, leaning the book on the wood of my burden to do so. Herbie smiled a frank and filthy smile directly into her wide pale face and whispered to me, 'Sign it with a cross, man.' I signed it 'Willy Turpin, Littlefold, England', which seemed to cause the girl some disappointment because she read the inscription as she walked away, glanced back with a wry face, and then tore out the page and ungraciously handed it to a minute Chinese child standing blandly on the sidewalk.

In the Bowery the drying drunks shuffled along with the parade for a while, apparently equating the sign of the Cross and the words of the preacher with a free handout. Only here did the Reverend Hatt find any willing recipients for his handbills and this enthusiasm quickly fell apart when the poor miseries realized that nothing more negotiable than words was being handed to them.

As we progressed up the lower limb of Manhattan Island we began to encounter thicker traffic, the high proportion of Catholic taxi drivers in New York being demonstrated by the obedient swerve to one side or the other when we approached. But one man shouted from his car: 'Get that goddam crucifix outa here!' The remark caused an escorting policeman to trace a quick and horrified cross on himself before going over to admonish the driver.

We were joined at our own pedestrian pace by a moaning police car which howled slowly, like something undergoing a terrible death, until we reached the Parisian arch and the comparative peace of Washington Square Park. The siren effectively stopped the bawling from Properjohn. Even he could not compete with that.

Our hired congregation gathered around in an obedient circle for further singing and additional supplications and blessings. Eventually we boarded the two motor homes, the Cross stowed on the rack of the one labelled 'Jesus Lives', and commenced our strange journey. Properjohn, Herbie and I were in the front vehicle, with the volunteer driver still at the wheel to manœuvre us out of the city difficulties.

All the fresh little girls in the front of the choirs waved

dutifully and beautifully as we prepared to move off. Then one of them blew a kiss to Herbie, which seemed to please him more than a five-hour orgy would have done in the old days. On the fringe of the crowd, moving about like a suspicious spectre, lurked Oliver J. Jaye, watching grimly before leaving us. Winston said: 'He'll be back.'

Our driver started the engine of 'Jesus Lives' and I heard the roar of 'Jesus Loves' just behind us. Properjohn stood up and I thought he was about to cast a blessing. But, instead, eyes alight, arm curving, he shouted: 'Waggons roll!'

Five

The road to Bethlehem is through the Lincoln Tunnel and out onto the New Jersey side of the river, through Phillipsonberg and Easton, through, at first, a countryside struggling to rid itself of the residue and rubble of the big city.

It was a slow battle. Houses, inserted between factories and scrapyards, loomed over by hoardings advertising everything wonderful, struggle to keep a single tree upright or to hold to themselves a patch of grey garden. Smoke stacks stand out on the landscape, there are flocks of seagulls come inland for the winter and the rubbish dumps. Waterways, cut through to the New Jersey skyline, strangled by debris, wept over by tarnished trees. Then, like a sniff of fresh New England air, we saw a horse running in a slum of a field and someone feeding chickens in his rusty backyard.

A couple of miles beyond the tunnel we dropped our pilot drivers. Herbie went back to drive the second motor caravan, and we got the Reverend Hatt in exchange. To my amazement he immediately sat behind the wheel and began to handle the vehicle with the languid aplomb of a professional bus driver.

'I used to work in a parish which had a community coach,' he explained blithely, pleased at being able to show a positive achievement. 'I used to drive my people almost everywhere.' Then, sadly, he added 'Once.' The wet road was whispering hurriedly under the tyres and 'Jesus Lives' was travelling at a steady seventy. It had a windscreen like a double shop window. Winston and I sat on two bucket seats on the right-hand side, while Properjohn, quiet for once and examining the landscape ahead like Columbus, sat behind the Reverend Hatt.

'My country!' the pink American clergyman suddenly exclaimed. He threw out both arms from the wheel in an impulsive and dangerous gesture. 'My country!' he repeated like an actor going back over an enjoyable line. 'Just take a look at it will you!' We looked out on the dreary industrial landscape, on the hills of rusted cars, the ragged fields of factory waste, the smoke creeping through disgruntled trees, solitary birds flying across hunched housetops as though seeking some place to rest. 'This is my America!' cried Hatt.

'My people settled this land,' he went on strenuously while we gazed out, all of us looking to find a green field or an unstunted tree which he could see but we could not. 'They came here from the Old World and they planted this land. Generations of Hatts have been born and grown up in New Jersey.'

'I was a singer once,' Properjohn interrupted. It was as though no one had been speaking, and he had felt obliged to say something. For once I felt grateful to him. 'A secular singer, you know. With a dance band in Wales.'

'They have good voices in Wales,' said Winston, reinforcing the resistance against the Reverend Hatt.

Properjohn was dreaming. 'Oh, yes, I sang in the band. Aberavon Raggamuffins. But then . . . then . . . I saw the Lord, you know. Right there in the dance hall one night . . .'

'He gets everywhere,' said Hatt sincerely. 'Hallelujah.'

'Hallelujah,' we all grunted.

Properjohn glared at him for his interpolation. 'And that was the end of the whirling lights and the patent leather pumps for me, boys. I saw Him and He called me. No more razzamataz. Finished me with secular singing for good.' He waited as though hesitating over a confidence. 'I've had information from the Lord ever since,' he added making it sound like a racehorse tip. 'Haven't I, Willy?'

I was astonished that he should have sought confirmation from me. But then he patted the pocket of his waistcoat confidingly and winked at me like a hooked-nosed owl. Then I remembered what he had said was written on a piece of paper in that pocket and I nodded dumbly.

'She's a good girl that Clare,' he went on reflectively and for no obvious reason. 'Poor Clare. Had her jaw removed, you know. Whisked out completely. It's exhibited in Cardiff Orthopaedic Hospital in a bottle in a glass case. They've got a sort of museum there, see, tidy little place, very nice, and Poor Clare's jawbone is in that. I suppose it's quite a thing really having your jawbone exhibited for people to witness. It makes her famous in a way, if you see what I mean . . .' He appeared to be soliloquizing, but suddenly, with a short guilty turn of his head and an expression of bovine guilt in his changing eyes, he looked at us. At that moment I realized how vain he was; that he was making excuses for himself, for his wife looking like she did without her jaw. 'Aye,' he reflected. 'I was a good-looking chap when we got married. She was quite pretty too, having got her jaw and everything. I was still a secular singer then. Going places they said.'

'Well, you're going places now,' I interrupted to stem the embarrassment that was choking me. 'Bethlehem, Pennsylvania.'

'Is it far?' he inquired innocently and without umbrage at my obvious interruption.

'There and back again,' I said.

Properjohn laughed enjoyably. 'You know that too?' he said. Then he shrugged: 'Ah, well you would, being a writer. Clever like that. How does it go?'

To my surprise and perhaps his, certainly to Winston's, we recited it together, like children:

'How far is it to Bethlehem?
Three score miles and ten.

Can I get there by candlelight?
There and back again.'

He exploded with an almost indecent bellow of mirth, rolling
one way and the other with the full enjoyment of it. Then
Winston tried to recite it, and Hattie, and suddenly we were
singing it to some pop song tune.

It was a strange moment, a point of realization, of discovery.
Released from New York, or back beyond that from our own
homes and former lives, we were like fresh shipmates embarking on a voyage into the unknown.

We would be journeying together, living, eating, sleeping in
these idiotic craft labelled 'Jesus Lives' and 'Jesus Loves'
until, perhaps, we reached our almost mythical destination, Las
Vegas. Fluctuating friendships and enmities would mix among
us. One day we would be happy and hopefully travelling, and
the next sullen with failure and boredom. We were to find
interest and even joy, love perhaps, and always surprise,
among our good companions, and in the next hour a flame of
anger, frustration, dislike and even disgust. It would be
strangers on an up-and-down emotional ride, tied together for
better or, frequently, for worse; nursing our private thoughts,
fears, and memories, each with our special selfishness, but, in
the adjoining moment feeling protective and comradely to our
companions, in an odd way building a defence around ourselves against the world we were supposed to save. There
were times when those of us who believed and those who did
not believe were closely one. It was the same journey for us all.

That singing of the Bethlehem rhyme, followed by more
laughter, and then an opening of the coffee flask which
Winston had brought along was the first sign. I had never
before drunk from the same cup as a black man.

And it was then, as we travelled down the road to Bethlehem,
through the neon villages, the motels and the gas stations, the
cars and the scars, that I allowed myself to think that somewhere in the approaching country, perhaps in the Christmas
City, as they called it, where we were now going, I might find
and claim my wife again. Somewhere along that line that
stretched to the distant west I would know the sensation of her

skin again, to smell her face, to know the love of her mouth. She might even be here.

'That's Bethlehem right ahead,' said Winston. 'I can see the goddam smog from the steelworks.'

Six

That night we dined on Bethlehem-burgers – the local hamburgers – and Coca-Cola at the Downtown Bethlehem Hotel. Our march into the city had been less than triumphal for it is a centre for a number of rich religions and the Helen J. Jaye Foundation for Christian Love had few adherents and beneficiaries. At Easter in the little city they play the Easter Hymn from the tower of the Moravian Church – on trombones – but on this day only the Sprott's autoharp and Poor Clare's howling harmonica heralded our entry in light Pennsylvania drizzle.

A damp, unwilling group of about twenty people and an infant reporter from the local College newspaper greeted us at the city limits, and me and my Cross to the fore, we went in the dying wet light of the October afternoon down sloping Broad Street with its abutting shops, the first of many identical American towns we were to enter in the coming days. People waiting for the Greyhound bus in the steamed-up shop window of the American Hotel watched us as we walked, their fingers rubbing loopholes for their eyes on the glass. A few other watchers came to shop doorways, and others stopped for a moment of curiosity on the sidewalks. Across the river valley the steelworks smoked as though demonstrating its indifference. Some kids called rude comments from a corner coffee shop on Raspberry Street and a damp dog did a cursory shit right in my path as I walked, stony faced, with my Cross. I think Jesus would have been upset that the place was called Bethlehem.

Winston, who had a briefcase full of plans and programmes, had told us that, according to the itinerary, we would park the motor homes in the courtyard of the Sun Inn ('Hospitality since 1758') where we would have dinner that night, a thought which cheered me along the drizzling street.

The inn, on Walnut Street, looked old and quiet. When, after parking the vehicles and joining the local adherents with a quick hymn and a rainy prayer, we went to the door we found that it was deserted and hollow with disuse.

'George Washington slept there,' one of the local people called back helpfully from the arch to the main street.

'Seems like he was the last one,' Winston observed quietly as he squinted through a crack in the door.

'Ain't been open for years,' returned the man. 'Some say knock it down, some say keep it up.' He apparently considered he had done enough to justify his church's faith in Helen J. Jaye and her Foundation, for he hurried off through the rain to his home. We were left grouped forlornly around the barren door.

'These Bethlehem inns,' sighed Winston, straightening up. 'Always been the same.'

'There might be a back door,' suggested Properjohn.

Winston invited him to look through the crack. 'If there is,' he said. 'Take a look at what's inside. I don't see no home comforts there. I guess somebody boobed. Or maybe it was its little joke to see us on our way.'

'Oliver J. Jaye,' I muttered. Winston, moving over to make room for Properjohn, nodded and said: 'It's great to know he's got a sense of the ridiculous.'

We suddenly felt very foolish and lonely there. Seven of us, out to save the world, standing, crouched together, in the wet gloom of a small town afternoon, locked out of a ruin, our clothes and faces wet, no one paying any attention to us, and our Cross parked against a damp wall like the banner of some vanquished rabble.

It was Ambrosia who moved. 'Well, we're not going to stand around here, all wet, like a load of ninnies, are we?' she

69

demanded. 'Better get ourselves sorted out in these lorries. See who's going to sleep where.'

I fancied I saw a little glow come to Herbie's eyes, set into his black, wet-haired face, like the last spark in a doused fire. But the girl did not even look in his direction, nor at anyone in particular. She turned and went towards the two motor homes parked in the courtyard, pushing her rainy hair back with a short-tempered thrust of her hand as she did so.

She was gone around the corner before the rest of us began to stir. As I was collecting my Cross I heard her call: 'There's a door open at the back here.' I put the Cross down again and followed the others. They were timidly grouped about the door but Ambrosia was already inside and calling to them to go in and see. Properjohn, reasserting his leadership, went first and we followed.

There was not much light left in the day and inside the abandoned hotel it was like a cave. Why we explored, what we expected to find there, I do not know. But we went around, bent in single file like the seven dwarfs in the witch's castle, through the reception hall, into the gaping dining room, and the dried-up bar, the cold kitchens and the comfortless lounge, some with dead furniture, all with squared windows looking in at us blankly.

'Take a while to get this place homely,' muttered Herbie. He blew an explosion of dust from the top of a table, his hairy cheeks ballooning and the dust shooting away like the drawing of the wind on an old map. Properjohn and Hatt were gazing about them with clerical sadness as though they had reached heaven and found it uninhabited. Poor Clare seemed frightened and kept bumping into Winston as they both looked around up into the gloom with curiously similar expanded eyes. I was cold.

But Ambrosia appeared to be enjoying it. Suddenly the dumb dumpling, that afternoon's dull-eyed player of a Sprott's autoharp, became a young girl exploring a large and echoing house with the excitement of a heroine in a Victorian children's story. It was she who led the way up the straining stairs, we others following, much slower behind her, and still not knowing why. If anyone had carried a candle our shadows would have gone in ghostly file along the old American walls and probably frightened us. As it was we were in the growing dark, except where the light from the street came through the naked windows and caught our creeping forms. We progressed in a curious crocodile in and out of the bedrooms until Ambrosia stopped stiff at one doorway and we clumsily closed up like a concertina behind her. She stood in the door, staring, saying nothing, her hands pushed out slightly as though she had seen something startling before her. I felt some softly retreating steps behind me and glanced to see Winston and Herbie backing with sedate cowardice towards the stairs.

'What a room,' Ambrosia breathed suddenly and joyfully. 'What a beautiful, fantastic, brilliant room!'

'You might have told us before, girl,' said Properjohn sharply, the tension falling from him with the rest of us. 'You ought to have said. Keeping us standing here like that. I thought you had witnessed something spiritual or indecent.'

We followed her into the room. It was large enough for a modest ballroom, with a splendid rank of windows down one wall. The floor was of oak, laid in long fine planks, and almost at the centre of the room was a great four-poster bed, slewed sideways like a carelessly parked car. Its canopy was missing and the four posts stood up bare. We stood looking at it, a timid little audience, as Ambrosia almost tiptoed towards it. None of us moved now. We just watched. She reached the side of the bed and touched it with her fingers as though no one was watching. Then, to my utter astonishment, she laid herself across it like some happy bride instead of a dumpy teenager in a woollen sweater and jeans.

Frozen with embarrassment we stood while she languorously turned herself on the old mattress, in a slow ballet, first one way, slowly, and then the other, caressing it as she did so. I heard Herbie make an odd sucking noise with his gums. It was Poor Clare who split the silence. 'Ambrosia!' she bellowed astonishingly, like a Monday morning washer-woman. 'Get yourself off of that thing. It might be damp.'

The moment was broken, the spell was gone. The girl sat up as though awakened from deep sleep and stared at the group of us in the gloom. Then she climbed angrily from the bed and came back to us, face down, silent, and we turned and left the ghostly place to return to the miniature modern comforts of the mobile homes.

The Properjohns were to live in 'Jesus Loves' and Winston, Herbie, Hatt and myself in 'Jesus Lives'. It was an easy arrangement although, as Herbie was to point out in rueful sexual frustration in Custer County, many nights later, that while living was permitted in 'Jesus Loves', loving was not allowed in 'Jesus Lives'.

Wearing civilian off-duty attire we went to the Bethlehem Hotel for our Bethlehem-burger supper and then returned through the moribund streets to the motor homes parked darkly in the courtyard of the inn. Everyone was subdued, tired and dispirited, and there was little talking done. With curious male modesty the four in our truck formed a square and turned outwards to undress. Winston and Herbie went almost immediately to sleep and Hattie, after saying a short but loud prayer while propped up, hands properly together before his nose, followed them. I lay awake in my bunk thinking about it all and then finally, inevitably, wondering how far away were Silvie and my children. That day, I thought, I must have decreased the separation by a hundred miles. Somewhere at that moment she was, in all probability, doing the splits in the lights of some cowtown nightspot. Then I thought again that she might be right there in Bethlehem.

In the lobby of the Bethlehem Hotel I had idly noticed that someone, with an eye to making good in this world whatever the consequences in the next, had opened a nightclub blasphemously called The Stable. I wondered now if it were possible that she could be there.

I dressed easily without even stirring the others and went out into the damp night. A pessimistic taxi was mooching like an aimless cat along the street and he took me to The Stable apparently by the long route since we crossed the Leighigh River three times before we arrived.

Two girls in dusty costumes, and a man in a purple tuxedo, greeted me with what seemed like enormous relief at the door. The place was not doing well. Even the candles, quietly having fits in deep alcoves around the walls, were sufficient to show that the only people there were the barman and a waitress, reading opposite sides of the same newspaper at the end of the bar, a man stumbling at the piano and a middle-aged couple, stiffly holding hands across the table at the edge of the small, vacant stage. They took no heed of my entry for their eyes were hard and intent upon each other, apparently engaged in one of those contests of strength where the object is to press your opponent's hand to the table.

A moment later, however, they relinquished the combat and the man rose and asked me to join them at the table. 'We might as well sit together,' he explained. 'It saves dirtying-up another table, if you get me. Keeps the overheads down.'

With some reluctance I accepted. But he ordered me a drink. 'I'm Harry Benner,' he said. 'I own this dump, for God's sake. And this is my wife. Rose, I think she's called.'

'Rose,' nodded the woman as though confirming it as much to him as to me. 'Rose.'

'Nice to see married people holding hands,' I observed.

'Oh, that,' he said. 'Don't count on that, mister. It's just a little act we put on when somebody comes in – to give the place a romantic atmosphere. We figure if we hold hands then other people will too. But when there's just one like you, well you can't hold hands with yourself without looking a kook, can you?'

'That's very true,' I agreed.

'You're English,' said the woman with that touching tone that American women keep for Englishmen in small towns. 'You're English.' It appeared she always said the same thing twice.

'Yes,' I admitted. I drank my first bourbon and gratefully let it sink to my deep inside.

'And we tried to fool you with the hand-holding crap,' sighed Mr Benner. 'Imagine that! Trying to fool an Englishman. Hitler couldn't do it, but we thought we could!'

'You fooled me,' I admitted flatly.

'You're being nice,' said Mrs Benner. 'You're being nice.'

'No, you really fooled me. Honest. I felt romantic as soon

as I got in here and saw you holding hands. It's very convincing.'

'You're being nice,' affirmed the man. 'It's a goddam shame you can't see the cabaret. We just sent her home.'

God, I thought foolishly. Right first time.

'What a shame,' I said. 'Is she any good?'

'Not great,' he shrugged. 'And it's no use her performing for us. We've seen it all. And once she's gone you can't call her back because she takes the bike and the tightrope and that fucking monkey of hers, and getting that back and setting the whole thing up is just too much.'

The monkey did not sound like Silvie unless one of the children had changed for the worse. 'You've not had an English girl in a show here have you?' I ventured. 'A dancer. Very beautiful, called Silvie.'

'Never,' he said firmly.

'Never,' she said. 'Never.'

'I thought you might, that's all,' I said. 'It was just a possibility.'

'No,' mused Mr Benner. 'We had a Scotchman once who was the best laugher at his own jokes that I ever heard. But he was Scotch and he wasn't called Silvie. Not on stage anyway.'

'I just thought it was a possibility,' I repeated.

'It's no town for a nightspot,' he said moodily. 'When you came in it meant that we are only fifty per cent down on last night. The fun goes out of it. All I get is a sweaty hand from Rose.'

'I suppose it's because it's Bethlehem,' I said. 'It's the image.'

'Founded Christmas Eve 1741,' he grunted, then asked: 'Have you seen the graveyard?' I said I had not. 'All the old tombstones are flat, all lying flat in rows because nobody wanted to be up before anybody else on Resurrection Day. And that's how folks still are, I guess. Everybody, all over town. Lying flat out, three feet between each one, just lying there and doing nothing. What chance has a classy place like this got?'

I bought them a drink for which they seemed grateful and I

left them. As I got to the door he called after me morosely:
'If you see the dame from the cabaret walking with her
monkey, don't touch the monkey. The bastard bites.'

I took a cautious, circuitous route back to the Sun Inn, along
Raspberry, down Main and around the corner on which the
inn stands forlornly, into Walnut and the archway to the courtyard. As I reached the arch I saw the door of the nearest motor
home – 'Jesus Loves' – slide open like the vertical eyelid of
someone slowly awakened from sleep. I had placed myself on
the dark side of the wall, away from the mixed shaft of street-
light and moonlight, and I stood still and hidden while
Ambrosia came carefully from the vehicle and with precision
closed the door behind her. She stood like a quiet night spirit
for a moment in the cold courtyard. I could only see her
indistinctly, little more than a shadow.

She turned lightly, almost a dance movement, and went
towards the unlocked door of the inn. My immediate thought
provoked a curse for Herbie and his silent seduction. Christ,
he had hardly the opportunity to say two words to that girl all
day. I was angry that he should think so little of the risks and
the dollars involved that he should break the compact on the
first night out and only a hundred miles west of New York City.

I hesitated, then followed the girl into the cobwebbed building, creeping from the outdoor dark into the dark indoors.
Once inside I realized the size of the moon that had come up
over Bethlehem and was shooting through the many naked
windows and striking the floors, the stairs and the walls in a
dozen places. Keeping to the dark canals of shadow I reached
the stairway. All I could think about was that huge, ill-parked,
bed upon which she had performed so strangely a few hours
earlier. Choosing each step of the stairway as though it could
be booby-trapped I went up. On the middle landing I stood
still because through the damp air of the place I heard a soft
laugh and the light rustle of her voice; a whispering, like conversational mice, from the big room where the bed was. If I
made for the door where we had all stood that late afternoon
then I would be exposed in a chute of moonlight from a high
window. There was a corridor breaking off at right-angles to

the main landing and I slithered along that, guessing that in its length there must be another door.

There was. It was closed, but one of its dried panels had split and parted for almost an inch. I was immersed in darkness there and I stood and looked into the stark moonlight of the room and at the girl. She was alone.

My surprise at this was only surmounted by my amazement at the charming little dance she was performing across the disused and dusty floor. I could see her excellently for the moonlight fell from the ridge of windows filling the entire room like a pool. The bed was like a beached boat with four bare masts only a few feet from my spyhole. Ambrosia was wearing a lumpy patchwork dressing gown and her dark hair was tied behind her neck in a long pigtail. She danced lightly, humming to herself, eyes closed and with a tubby smile.

Her dance lasted a minute more and then she curled a final turn in the full moonlight and curtseyed low and charmingly to an imaginary partner. Then she stood upright and expectant at the side of the bed only a few feet from me. Her expression was turned up, her eyes still closed, as if she were facing someone with happy anticipation. Her hands went to the clumsy bobble-buttons of the quilted dressing gown but she held them at an unnatural, awkward angle, as though they were meant to be someone else's hands. Deliberately she undid each of the buttons and with a broadening of her smile she let the lumpy garment fall open down her front. Her lips pursed and she whispered something. The hands moved to her again, going under the robe and touching her puppy-fat breasts beneath the Crimplene jacket of her Marks and Spencer's pyjamas.

She sat on the edge of the bed and it emitted a surprised and rusty squeak. The girl shifted sedately. Her face remained serene, minutely creasing at each easy upward caress of her fingers on her own body.

Her legs opened on the side of the bed and she eased herself back, so slowly that there was no hurt squeak from the old contraption. She arched up at the knees. The misshapen pyjama trousers hung like Oriental pantaloons. She began to stir her hands against her breasts more firmly now as though warming herself. Across her calm face the shadow of one of the bedposts, carved and curved, lay like a totem. Her backside began to raise itself from the bed and fall back, a small leverage at first, then her right hand emerged from within the jacket and carefully undid the uneven row of buttons up the front. She pulled the two edges of the jacket away, the first quietly so that it ran over the white hump and the smudgy nipple and slid down the further slope, the second with a touch of haste, tugging it aside to uncover the other one to the moonlight, its soft whorl lying almost touching distance from my own concealed fingers.

Her stomach, even flat out as she was, looked fatty and trembling. The elastic waistband of the pyjama trousers cut into it like tightly tied parcel string. Abruptly she stopped and lay still for a moment, lounging in the cool moonlight, her hands full of her own breasts. Then they eased themselves down her wobbly stomach and the points of her fingers nosed under the top band of the trousers. She pushed them down as deeply as they could go. Her hands and her wrists went burrowing beneath the brief material.

She pushed the ungainly trousers away from her loins. Her belly, the trunks of her legs, her whole private landscape, was displayed to me by the moon.

She remained still, briefly. I feared she would hear my heart beating against the door panel. Then sweetly, her pale, podgy body curved with temporary grace, she began to masturbate. Her fingers rubbed quietly and her buttocks rose and fell in short movements to meet them. My male excitement was at once engulfed by compassion and tenderness for her and sudden shame for myself and my eavesdropping. A protective love welled within me so that I wanted to break out of that hiding place and embrace her, hugging her loneliness to my loneliness. At that moment, while I was sick with excitement and emotion, a wandering woodlouse, roaming down the cracked door, clumsily fell onto my extended eyelash as I peered. It balanced there like a man on a trampoline, staggering on my stringy eyehairs until my annoyed blink sent it plummeting to whatever eternity awaits doomed woodlice.

She had moved until then, with her back as the spring, but abruptly she began to writhe to each side of the bed, left and right, rolling each way, and then I realized that she was using something else upon herself and not her fingers any longer. She was using it with both hands, pushing it and taking it away, thrashing about now with the sensation, up and down and side to side, her body glistening with sweat even in the coldness of that room.

She arrived at her climax with a small, snapped-off cry and a shudder. And at that moment I put my foot through a rotten floorboard.

Ambrosia heard that. She stiffened with fright and in a moment, scrambling guiltily, she pulled her clothes about her and tiptoed hurriedly but deftly across the floor. She reached the door and paused and I saw her go like a rounded ghost along the corridor ten feet from my spying place. I stood there for five minutes with my foot trapped in the floor, ragged edges caught around my ankle like a beartrap, before carefully withdrawing it and creeping down and out to my bunk in the motor home. The moon came through the square window in there shining on the wall like a cinema screen without a film show. I lay and thought about it, that tender and private thing, and then I slept and woke on another day in Bethlehem, with the sirens sounding across the Leighigh River at the steelworks, and it was time to start our journey again.

Seven

'Jews!' exclaimed Properjohn.

'Wrong,' said Winston. 'They're not Jews.'

It was a fine countryside. Windless fields quiet, idling towards winter, trees standing on elevated ground as though to get a better view of the landscape, their leather leaves split by the silver streaks of birches. The rain had travelled away and we were journeying under a blue, good-humoured sky with frail autumn light collected on rivers, streams and farm ponds. The farms themselves, spread with rural orderliness, barns prettily coloured with hex signs, each like a decorated ark, silo towers splendid as lighthouses, chestnut horses shining in perfect fields. Even the pigs looked clean.

'Lancaster County, Pennsylvania,' Winston had announced. Herbie was driving 'Jesus Lives', Winston and I were in the bucket seats and Properjohn behind the driver's hairy ear. Hattie was in 'Jesus Loves' with the ladies.

'Jews,' repeated Properjohn, looking out. 'Anybody can see they're Jews.'

'Amish,' corrected Winston patiently. 'Amish people. They're Dutch.'

'Dutch Jews,' insisted Properjohn triumphantly. 'A blind man can see they're Jews. Black hats and coats, long beards, long noses. Jews!'

Herbie, the Hebrew in him stirring, glanced around rudely from the wheel and observed: 'You got a black hat, a black coat and a long nose.' He was squinting violently sideways, trying to take in Winston and myself and to get a glimpse of Properjohn sitting behind him and slightly to his right.

'WHAT DO YOU MEAN?' howled Properjohn, as though struck by a hot spear.

'Well, man, you could be a Jew,' said Herbie, blinking at the bellow.

'A Jew? Me, a Jew!'

'He said you dress like one,' pointed out Winston in a conciliatory tone. Then apologetically but with determination, 'And then, of course, there's your nose.'

'My God,' cried Properjohn, his huge Semitic head abruptly collapsing into his hands. 'I've never been called a Jew before. Never. Never, never, never.' He slowly came up from his palms, as though he had realized something even more horrific. 'The Jews crucified Christ,' he whispered, adding unnecessarily, 'on the Cross.'

'The Pope forgave them,' pointed out Winston coolly. 'Couple of years ago.'

'Nice,' muttered Herbie. 'That's real nice.'

'The Pope?' croaked Properjohn unbelievingly. 'The Pope? What's it got to do with the bloody Pope? He's a heathen. I'd listen to a druid before I'd listen to a heathen like that.'

'Okay, okay,' said Winston, his hands making a calming motion. 'No need to get incensed. So all we're saying is that people who maybe *look* like Jews don't have to be Jews. And some that don't look like Jews, are Jews.'

Properjohn was staring from the window at the strange people gathered at a fruit and vegetable market. The sides of the road in the small town were blotched with the men's black hats and dotted with the white gauze bonnets of the women and girls. It was very animated, people bargaining and spitting dramatically on their hands, greeting friends and making jokes. It was like a happy funeral. 'They look like Jews,' Properjohn grunted. 'And those horse buggies they're riding in. They look like Jewish buggies.'

'They're Amish,' repeated Winston. 'Jews ride in Cadillacs. These are strict Christian farmers. They won't have anything modern. No cars, no television, no combine harvesters. They do it all like it was two hundred years ago.'

'And they look like Jews,' mumbled Properjohn.

'Okay, so they do. But they've been kidding that they're Christians, and everybody in America believes them. It took you to find out they were cheats.'

Properjohn seemed defeated and looked sulky at the sarcasm.

'They have strong family alliances,' said Winston. 'The home and the farm. And they don't have any churches. They pray at home.'

'Ah,' said Properjohn knowingly. 'In secret, you see. That's when they bring out the little skull caps and the candlesticks.'

'And they are rumoured to bundle,' continued Winston doggedly.

There was a three-point silence at that. I was first to ask. 'What's that?' I said. 'Bundle.'

'Bundling?' shrugged Winston. 'Alleged to be done all over the world by various sects. It's just young people, teenagers you know, getting bedded down together before marriage.'

We all waited for the predictable howl from Properjohn. But

no sound came from him. When he turned slowly towards Winston we saw that the howl was trapped on his face. 'What did you say?' he said hoarsely.

Winston smiled reassuringly. 'It's okay,' he said. 'It's merely the custom, so they say. They kinda get into bed together, but they've still got all their clothes on, if you get it?'

'Do *they* get it?' inquired Herbie beneath his breath.

'Heathen practices,' seethed Properjohn. 'The devil's work.'

'Now I come to think of it, I've heard it's done in Wales,' I said. Then, as his face began to expand, I added: 'In remote areas.'

'Never!' he shouted. 'Not never!' He exploded into an abominable shaking rage, spluttering to spitting out his words, shaking his fists and becoming an extraordinary aubergine hue about the cheeks and brow. He frightened me, he frightened Winston, and Herbie, looking fearfully over his shoulder, let 'Jesus Lives' take a corner too sharply and sent two Amish buggies careering onto the sidewalk, their horses crying out, their passengers astonished and stiff as an old photograph.

Properjohn was thrown sideways but this did not prevent him scrambling up like a rugby player from a scrum, flinging down the window and howling back at the aghast Amish men: 'Jews! Jews!'

'How's the Cross today, man?'

'It's a bit spongy,' I said. 'It must get damp on top of that roof. Look, I can just about dig my fingers into the wood.'

'Harrisonburg, Virginia,' said Winston, as we reached the top of a broad hill cut through by a dual road. 'The Shenandoah Valley.'

Herbie, who had asked about the Cross, looked suspiciously at him from my other side. We were walking in light, cold rain again, and wearing green waterproof plastic capes.

'You sure know a lot,' he observed.

Winston glanced at him with mutual suspicion. 'I learn something before breakfast every day,' he said.

'Sure, I do too. Like I'm a day older and it's cold. But you know *things*, man. Like where we are, and where we're going, and about those Amish characters and whole pieces of shit from the Bible. Where did you get it all?'

'You sound like you think I'm a spy,' said Winston defensively. 'That's the way they used to find out about spies in the war movies. How did they know about this and how about that.'

'That's where I got it,' agreed Herbie. 'But you sure know your crap, man.'

'Excuse me a minute,' I asked, shifting the Cross from one shoulder to another. It made my neck sore if I kept it on one side too long. Nobody had come out to meet us from Harrisonburg. Cars went by sending spray up onto the wet ends of our robes, but nobody stopped. 'It's difficult to keep up with you two when you argue,' I said. 'With this lump of wood in the way I can only see one of you at a time.'

'We'll make you a peephole,' said Herbie, but not to be taken away from his intention he made it an aside and continued after Winston. 'Well, how do you know, then? Tell me now.'

'I'm educated,' shrugged Winston, the one I could see. 'Some have gotten education, some have gotten other things. I've gotten education. I know the capital city of every State in the Union, I know the name and date of every President back to Grant, I know . . .'

'Not before Grant?' asked Herbie quickly.

'No,' admitted Winston. 'I had to quit the course. We were poor people, sir. But like I told you, I'm ambitious. I was named after Winston Churchill, police chief of the city of Indianapolis. I would have made a great white man, man. I voted for Nixon like Sammy Davis.'

'How come you know the Bible stuff then?'

'All us coloured folks know de Bible,' said Winston.

'Not like *you* know it, Mac. How about that stuff you was giving to Jaye back in New York. Quoting it like a script. Also like a script *you* wrote.'

I put the Cross on my other shoulder to see Herbie, but realized the argument was now back with Winston so I shifted it again. 'Sorry about this fidgeting,' I said.

It was Herbie began again. I moved the Cross once more so I could see him.

'The point I'm approaching,' he said meanly. 'How do we know that you ain't some spy planted here by the selfsame Oliver J. Jaye just to see that we don't break the contract?'

'Did I tell him, or anybody, about *The Truck Driver's Fun Girl*?' asked Winston potently. 'Boy, if I was his spy you would be back screwing those worn-out broads in front of a camera right now instead of walking along, making like St Peter in this nice, soft, Virginia rain.'

Herbie knew there was no answer to that. 'Okay, so you're no spy. I'm sorry I said that and I apologize.'

'I didn't tell him you're a Jew either.'

'No. No. Okay, man, you made your point.' Then, I could almost hear his eyes click. 'How did you know? Did I tell you? Did Willy tell you?'

'I didn't,' I protested swinging the Cross and almost hitting Winston.

'Keep that totem still, please,' said Winston patiently. Herbie continued, 'How did you know? I don't look Jewish.'

'Seems I've heard this argument before,' said Winston. He raised his voice a fraction. 'Sure you look Jewish, man. I can tell. It takes one member of a minority to tell another. But don't let it bug you. You just don't have to think about it. One millimetre under this skin I'm a white man. You know, in the summer I can take my watch off my wrist and see the shape where it's been. That's the sort of thing that gives a guy encouragement. Hope.'

'You're sneaking off,' warned Herbie. 'I want to know how you've gotten all this Bible stuff. Just put that plainly my way, if you don't mind.'

'Okay,' said Winston. 'Like I told you I was weaned on it. Every day I had that stuff slung at me and I was too little to duck. Where we lived was just stinking, and I guess they thought the good words would sweeten the air. School, too, they always gave it to us at school. "For in my Father's house are many mansions. If it were not so I would have told you." "The meek shall inherit the earth." "Blessed are the poor." Christ, man, that stuff could have been written just for our block.'

Herbie and I were impressed. All I could remember of

religion, apart from pumping the organ, was dropping my penny collection so I could look up the Sunday School teacher's skirt. Herbie said: 'You sure know it. I can't remember a goddam thing they taught me like that.'

'The Jews are richer than the blacks,' said Winston logically. 'With them it's a kind of a hobby. With us it was serious stuff. Feeding on the living bread, they used to call it, because we didn't get too much of the everyday eating stuff.'

'And you remember it all this time,' said Herbie. The argument had gone from his voice, drained quickly away. 'Just from your mammy's knee.'

Winston nodded. I was now his side of the Cross. 'I figured I'd forgot,' he said. 'But when I got assigned to this circus I got myself a Bible and read through the Jesus period, Matthew, Mark, Luke and John. It's easy reading and it all just came back to me. It's the same story four times over, like reading about the same ball game in four newspapers. Nothing to it.'

'Ah,' said Herbie sagely. 'That's just tough titty with the Jews. We have all the prophets and the flood and Adam and Eve and God, and guys begatting broads, and suchlike. There's fucking miles of it, man. It's no wonder we can never remember it.'

Before we had taken the route to Harrisonburg, Virginia, a strange thing had happened. We had approached Baltimore from Lancaster and as the buildings of that city appeared above the horizon like some overpopulated graveyard, we prepared ourselves for what we now called a Triumphal Entry. The Cross was unshipped, we attempted to smooth the creases from our robes (which turned out to be of tatty material) and readied ourselves for the last mile of road. Our replacement footwear seemed to have been overlooked and Herbie continued as St Peter in cowboy boots while my casuals, brown and British, nodded along stoically beneath the hem of my robe.

At Baltimore a considerable crowd of welcome was expected, for the Helen J. Jaye Foundation for Christian Love had half a dozen dependent churches there. I had quickly perfected a sort of holy shamble when I approached a town, head down, Dolcis shoes scraping the road, a look of religious dejection about me. Herbie, having been told that St Peter was not the Dancing Dan he somehow imagined, had subdued himself to a degree where his winks at women could have been a mere sadness of the eye, while Winston could at will adopt the expression of one who has sinned and knows forgiveness is uncertain. We were always immediately followed by words and music of the Properjohn family and the hapless Hatt following the two motor homes which were driven, on these town approaches, by volunteer drivers from the local churches.

This had been accomplished at several small towns on the route, in accordance with the schedule in Winston's possession, but Baltimore was to be the first of the big Triumphal Entries. At the other places the procession had been short and decorous, with a prayer meeting in some hall or open space, two or three hymns, a quick harangue from Properjohn, and then off westwards once again.

At Baltimore we had been promised five hundred voices and eighty collection boxes.

We were genuinely keyed up; looking forward to putting on a show, Herbie conscientiously wiping the mud from around the seams of his cowboy boots, the Reverend Hatt sorting his pamphlets and practising his salvation smile and Poor Clare spending half an hour cleaning the spit from the crevices of her harmonica.

A mile before the town we had waited for the volunteer drivers, but none appeared. Eventually we advanced cautiously, in our normal formation like a timid little army, with Winston and Hattie driving 'Jesus Loves' and 'Jesus Lives'. Around every bend, beyond every junction we expected to be greeted by an outbreak of white-robed song, but no choirs were there. Winston checked the schedule to make sure we had the time and the date right. He said we had. We stood in the town's suburbs confused and worried before an establishment which announced: 'The Crabs you eat today slept last nite in Chesapeake Bay'. Two blocks along the road were 'Continuous Topless Girls' poetically adjacent to 'Smithy's Surplus'.

We progressed along the street. It was very cold, with little fractions of snow beginning to spangle my beard. Eventually, almost in front of 'Continuous Topless Girls', we halted.

'Well,' said Properjohn woefully, 'I don't know what's gone wrong. There was supposed to be a lovely turn-out today. I was awake half the night working myself up.' He glanced at Winston. 'This is the place you say it is, I suppose?'

'It's Baltimore,' nodded Winston patiently. 'It looks just like it always did. Maybe we ought to go and sound the Liberty Bell.'

'Will that get the people out?' asked Properjohn. 'If it will then we must do it.'

'No,' said Winston hurriedly shaking his head. 'It's not that easily arranged.'

'What shall we do?' moaned Poor Clare, as though we were suddenly shipwrecked. She ran a practised eye along the teeth of her harmonica like someone inspecting the maw of a dead shark. 'I thought it was going to be so nice today.'

'Shut up, Clare,' snapped Properjohn. Then he said, 'We'll have a service,' and suddenly brightened with the notion. 'Yes, we'll have one. When in doubt have a service, I say. A hard pray will do us the world of good.'

'Just us?' I asked, looking around. Bits of snow were drifting among us and the street was almost empty, although I could see black faces from the windows of the slum across from 'Smithy's Surplus'. While we looked about us at the dismal prospect unexpected support came from Poor Clare. 'A service!' she exclaimed brightly. 'That's a grand idea, don't you think? These little streets remind me of Wales. I think we could have a good service here.'

We shuffled into a semi-circle and sang 'Praise To The Holiest In The Height', our faltering voices dropping dead within twenty yards. Ambrosia plucked stiffly at the autoharp, poor Clare blew her way from end to end and back again. I hung pathetically to the balsawood Cross. Black people began to come to the windows and doors of the houses, children, women and old folks mostly, regarding us with intense indifference. Their clothes, their skins, seemed to merge with the dinginess of the houses. Properjohn prayed theatrically and they stood blankly, the pearly pieces of snow settling upon their heads and faces.

We sang another hymn and when it was launched Properjohn leaned towards me and whispered: 'Where are all the white people, Willy?'

'They live somewhere else,' I suggested.

'I thought the darkies lived around the Mississippi,' he hissed.

'These came up to get a better standard of living, I expect,' I told him looking at the hopeless faces set in the squalor.

He nodded me back to the hymn because without us the tune was faltering. 'No use taking a collection, I suppose?' he whispered when the hymn was on its feet again.

I half-turned and my eye caught someone in the doorway behind us. It was one of the Continuous Topless Girls, a lard-coloured, large woman, with a shawl over her breasts and face like a paint palette. She was leaning against the doorjamb and singing with us, while mascara-coloured tears ran down her cheeks like a stream from a coaltip. As I glanced furtively the shawl fell away from a large, weary tit, leaving it momentarily exposed to the cold. She covered it again and continued weeping and singing.

'I don't think you'd get much in a collection,' I said belatedly, answering Properjohn. He had not seen her. 'If we gave *them* something, they might get interested.'

'No, we can't do that. It's all in the accounts. It's got to be banked. Let's go and leave it. I think we ought to find some white people. I get a bit frightened here. I told you before didn't I?'

I said he had. We stopped the hymn and self-consciously loaded the Cross and ourselves into the motor homes and drove away from that place in silence.

Properjohn seemed defeated. 'No,' he said decisively, emerging from his thoughts. 'I never was one of those who could have gone to Africa. I wouldn't know what to say to them.'

Winston said nothing but Herbie said philosophically: 'You can't get those people to repent because they've never had enough dough to do anything wrong. I guess sin is something you gotta be able to afford.'

We drove through the town and the snow and out the other side. Properjohn seemed to have forgotten about hunting for some white people. He sat hunched like a large and ugly rabbit behind Herbie who was driving. A mile out of town, on the road to Washington, Oliver J. Jaye was sitting in his limousine at the side of the road. In his sinister way he was not so much waiting for us as lying in ambush. He looked more gaunt than he had in New York, even I could see that although he never left the back seat of the car. A chauffeur like a Gothic water-chute sat in the front and on the rear of the vehicle was a badge incorporating a reverend cross and the word 'Clergy'. Proper-john and Winston, like army officers negotiating a truce, walked forward and spoke to Jaye from outside his window. The conversation was brief and as they returned to us the limousine went like a silent shot down the highway before us and vanished before we had driven a few hundred yards.

Properjohn sat in the seat behind Herbie again. 'We are not going to Washington,' he said. 'Mr Jaye says we mustn't. That party's been cancelled, he says. That's why there was nobody at the last place. That was cancelled too.'

Winston said: 'I can't figure it out. How could he want to skip Washington? He won't say. He says we now go to Harrisonburg, Virginia, instead. And Harrisonburg ain't no "Washington".'

'Maybe there's someone in Washington he don't like,' said Herbie.

'Or some guy who doesn't like him,' suggested Winston quietly.

We turned from our southern route and took the road again west towards Winchester. 'Willy,' whispered Properjohn after a while. 'What would you say are Continuous Topless Women?'

I said I didn't know, but I would inquire.

It had been Properjohn's idea for us to carry the Cross through the damp Virginia evening into the town of Harrisonburg. It would, he thought, provide a sort of trailer, for the following day's Triumphal Entry upon the small, sedate town.

It had been the sort of day that seemed glad it was over. The low afternoon clouds had prevented us viewing the mountains or the green, red and yellow of the Shenandoah Valley, although Winston and Herbie, in an odd and spontaneous American patriotic alliance, assured us with every wet mile that it was all around us and would be beautiful to see if we could only see it.

'Like heaven,' I observed half absently as we trudged alongside the dismal dual road that lifts itself and then descends in a steep bend, past the Christ Against Communism Church And Health Stores into the middle of the town.

'What is?' asked Herbie.

'I wish you two would make things easier for me,' I complained. 'Why is it that every time I say something the one I can't see has to answer. If the bloke the same side of the Cross as my head could do it I'd find life a bloody sight easier.'

'Okay, what is?' asked Winston.

'Well, it is,' I said. 'Like heaven. All beautiful and marvellous, but we can't see it. We just have to believe it's there. It's like your saying about the Shenandoah Valley which we can't see because of this drizzle.'

I sensed an embarrassed silence from both sides of the Cross. We shuffled on towards the bleary neon lights of the town in the valley.

'Hmm,' said Herbie eventually, like a diagnosing doctor. 'Maybe you would repeat that.'

'Oh, come on,' I said. 'You heard. I just said about not being able to see heaven, but knowing it's there, that's all.'

There was a further silence, then Herbie said: 'Carrying that thing is going to your head.'

'Certainly is,' confirmed Winston.

'A couple of days ago your idea of heaven would be hand-to-hand combat with Jane Fonda,' said Herbie. He sounded genuinely disturbed. 'Now what do we hear? Angel voices and tweety birds.'

I stopped angrily and swung around on him. I sensed Winston ducking under the top half of the Cross as it whistled above his head like a cutlass. 'Don't talk balls,' I protested. 'It was merely an observation. I do *think* about things, you know. I don't live my life like some do, depraved day after depraved day . . .'

The swines began to sing then, 'Jesus bids us shine with a

pure, clear, light' and I marched sulkily on ahead, with the childish hymn following me like a prolonged catcall. I swung around again and confronted the laughing black face and the delighted hairy white face. 'I know how Jesus felt,' I bawled back at them. 'With a couple of thieving sods like you each side of him.'

They dropped on each other's shoulders and howled vulgarly. I saw a gas station to my right and just by it a bus parked in the forecourt of a place which said 'Snackery' in red neon. I marched ill-temperedly towards it, hitching my robe up into the top of my trousers so that it was hidden by my green raincape. After some hesitation I put the Cross around the corner from the exterior door, hidden from sight, and went inside. The warmth of the plastic place engulfed me. Herbie, with his robe hitched up around his waist in the same fashion as mine, entered cautiously just as I got to the counter, and Winston, anxiety now replacing his smirk, followed.

'Listen, are you guys crazy?' he whispered. 'What are we *doing*? What are we risking?'

'We're getting some coffee,' I said brusquely. 'I'm cold and wet and cheesed off with carrying that lump of wood. We're just blaspheming, the lot of us. I hope you realize that.'

'You'll blaspheme some more if you screw up your bonus for a lousy cup of coffee,' murmured Winston. Nevertheless he accepted a cardboard container from my hand and we sat like conspirators in one windowed corner from where we could observe the road. There was a steamed-up girl behind the counter and a shadowy man flitting in the vapour at the back. The place advertised forty-seven different varieties of ice-cream and the girl after a few minutes of bored inaction ran a rapid finger down the displayed list and decided on Number 30, Caramel and Orange Bonfire. While she was concocting this, Herbie, as though to test whether his seduction art had diminished, said smoothly: 'Working your way down the runners, honey?'

'Certainly am,' she replied, without bothering to look at him. 'It's my thrill of the day. I been here thirty days and this is how far I am down the chart. When I get to the bottom, I quit.'

'I don't,' smiled Herbie horribly.

'You should, mister,' she said. 'Your slip's showing.'

Herbie made a grab down and we looked under the table and saw that his robe was hanging below his raincape. I gave a hasty tug at mine folded into my waistband. Three youths in motor cycle leathers sitting at the distant end began to take interest. They had been quiet, their heads close together, but now they looked along at us and laughed openly.

'Steady, boy,' muttered Winston catching Herbie's tightening arm. 'Is it worth it?'

'I'll kill the bums,' said Herbie but below his breath. 'They'll need a shoemaker to patch 'em up when I've finished.'

He remained seated, however, living proof of the sedative qualities of the prospect of money. There was an immediate diversion when an old, bulky car, a blue Buick, suddenly careered off the road and came like a charging rhino at the window behind which we were sitting. Gravel flew like bullets as its brakes pulled it up six inches from our transfixed faces. Six young men, all laughing boisterously, descended from the heavy vehicle and barged showily into the snackery. Two were tall, two were fat, one was lean and mean, with acne spread like red currants on his face; the sixth was small and bustling, trying to get to the counter first, and taking a sickeningly familiar lick at the girl's Caramel and Orange Bonfire, when he got there. The others all had a lick too as she held it out sensually and obediently to them. They shouted to the man in the fog at the rear and then began to horseplay around while they waited for six large and sickly ice-cream cones to be prepared.

We were watching them quietly and I noticed that the leathered youths at the far table were doing the same. The six remained standing while they sucked and swallowed the ice-cream, one of the fat ones leaning back against a chrome bar which bulged his backside out spectacularly in his elephantine jeans. Across the back of his denim jacket he had: 'Virginia State Champions 1970'.

Towards the end of their cornets they fell oddly silent and then, the last biscuit crunch finished, they filed out as quietly as they had been noisy on the way in. In a few moments the acne sufferer came around by our window, got into the car and drove it around the corner out of our sight. I got up and went to the door.

As I reached it the car belched and shot away. I knew it! Horrified I twisted into the snackery. 'Those bastards!' I howled at Herbie and Winston. 'They've nicked our Cross!'

The realization of the situation paralysed us. Herbie and Winston had rushed to the door of the snackery, as though they did not believe me or were somehow capable of stopping the awful happening. But once they got there they stood with me stiff and horrified.

Then there was a shout behind us and the three leather boys were rushing towards the door like a fire-engine crew, pulling their jackets around them as they came. My immediate thought was more trouble but the youth in the front said: 'Come on, you guys. Get with us.'

I had only been on a motor-cycle once before in my life, years ago, as the petrified passenger of a mad rent collector who used to circulate around my boyhood home, getting his kicks out of frightening young lads who were foolish enough to mount his pillion. Now I found myself, unbelievingly, climbing behind a meaty stranger with a skull and crossbones splayed across the back of his powerful jacket. He gave his machine a vicious kick and it seemed to leap up and hit me in the crotch. I hung on, my arms and legs stiff as wood, the rest of me like jelly. I sensed that Herbie and Winston were mounting the two other cycles flanking me but I could not look at them. I heard Herbie shout with a sort of joyous excitement and I guessed he was familiar with these things, probably as some nude Steve McQueen in one of his films. No sound came from Winston and, as my machine bolted forward, I caught a brief view of him cringing against the back of his rider in the same way as I was grovelling against mine.

At the moment we moved forward it was all I could do to prevent myself abandoning the machine by sliding over the side. But the same fear nailed me there while we slid on the soaking gravel of the open area in front of the snackery, turned like a speedboat into the main highway and flew down that with the spray and the frenzied air rushing by us. I did not know whether we were the first or last of the motor bikes. I could think of nothing, not even the stolen Cross, but to clutch on to preserve my precious life. My head bent down against the young man's shielding jacket like a young bird against its mother. My eyes were clenched, for to open them was to see the wet road skimming by a few inches below my knees. I thought my man must be going beyond a hundred miles an hour when, smoothly and extraordinarily, Herbie and his rider overtook us on a wide bend, Herbie whooping maniacally through the dark drizzle as they went by. I opened my eyes briefly for that sight and then again as Winston, a pathetically tiny bundle on his pillion, curved by on the opposite flank. We went swooping down a long incline and then decelerated with such a frightening pull-back that I found myself muttering the name of Silvie and mentioning my children like some sort of magic litany.

Then we began to climb, a rougher road by the feel of it, but at least it cut our speed. Trees were gathered close around, dropping showers of rainwater on us; then another suicidal turn, a quick burst on the main road again, and finally plunging through a screen of low trees and bushes, along a path with stones flying like bullets, and water cascading from the disturbed branches. My driver grunted. I did not hear it but I felt it. Then we stopped suddenly and I fell thankfully over the side onto some boggy grass.

Trembling everywhere I attempted to stand up, almost did so, fell down again, then pulled myself to my feet and began to run on a wobbly course after the others who had gone through the trees. A moment later I was in a clearing and in a fight. The Cross was hanging out of the window of the big car, already claimed by Herbie and Winston. Herbie was pushing Winston forward to fight the tall youth with acne who was swinging his long, bony arms like wheels. The motor cycle boys were fighting vividly with three thieves, obviously a single battle in a long-waged war. One of the fat youths was lifted bodily over the bonnet of the car.

There was a slippery rush from my right and I turned to see one of the youths coming at me with a stump of wood. I had a quick feeling of gratefulness that it was the smallest of the six.

I've never been much of a fighter but I lifted my foot and to my astonishment he ran right into it, catching it in his groin and collapsing with a surprised little wail. I went to him, picked him up and threw him down again. 'Right, mate,' I found myself saying excitedly but with enjoyable righteous power. 'Nick the Cross of Jesus, would you?' I looked around hoping the others had seen what I had done, but they were busy grappling. I picked up the log of wood but whatever my intentions were with the small youth they were quickly interrupted by the second of his fat friends appearing from around one side of the car and running straight at me like a pig. I swung the piece of wood in a fierce half-circle and caught him with superb if accidental timing on the very top of his flabby head. I heard myself let out a triumphant squawk, like a novice soldier who had shot his first enemy, as he fell down spectacularly almost at my feet and remained there, the 'Virginia State Champions 1970' legend heaving across his fat back.

When I looked up from my personal carnage, the little fellow having crawled away into the wet copse, I saw Winston still dodging like an exhibition bantam-weight around the tall youth. He was getting nowhere and I was about to stride forward to put my new-found fighting powers to further use when Herbie pushed Winston impatiently aside and then with a fist like a casual sandbag knocked the tall youth over in a cartwheel. There was no fighting left. I strode forward and pulled the Cross from the car, examining it for damage, putting my arms about it and carrying it like some rescued maiden away from the scene of conflict.

Blood was satisfied quickly and Herbie and Winston emerged from the trees with our well-satisfied allies. There were introductions and we thanked them and courageously allowed them to drive us at a sedate pace back into the town – six miles away now – with the Cross loaded on the left shoulders of good old Archie and myself. It must have looked fairly effective carried like that. Anyone who is planning any future Cross-carrying over long distances should really consider a motor-cycle cavalcade.

Eight

The sun shone benignly on Harrisonburg the next day and we marched around the town, around the square to Woolworth's and back, then left to the Post Office and Courthouse before about-turning and advancing through the main street past the cinema and the woolshop and the bookshop where china-faced young ladies, with gauze bonnets, came out to wave shyly. One of them gave Herbie a book called *Hang Loose with Jesus*.

There were willows in the gardens and brilliantly dying leaves set against white houses which had little toy towers at their corners. The people came into the street to watch and wave approvingly and for the first time I was really glad to be carrying the Cross. 'God bless you, Jesus,' an old lady called.

Outside the drug store were some wholesome young girls in lettered yellow sweaters and short socks. One of them advanced into the road and handed Winston a bottle of coke. He gave it to me and I opened the trapdoor at the foot of the Cross and put it in there for later. We had never had cause to use the walkie-walkie and, in any case, Properjohn refused to operate it. He was frightened of it like an old person might be afraid of the telephone, so we had disconnected it and left it in Herbie's bed locker.

The young girl's friends, stuffed with good things by the look of them, waved suggestive hot dogs in greeting, and some old men and women in unwieldy black hats nodded enjoyably from the benches in front of the grave city hall. The sky was unmarked, stretching away down the street to where the Blue Ridge Mountains waited lazily. Ambrosia was twanging her Sprott better than I had ever heard her, Poor Clare saw the black bonnets of the elderly women and, between puffs at her harmonica, cried with pathetic excitement, 'Look at the 'ats, John. Just like Wales. Oh, just like Wales.' Properjohn was showering blessings in every direction, 'Jesus Loves' and 'Jesus Lives' seemed as majestic as elephants in a circus procession, and Hattie disposed of a hundred of his tracts at one time to the owner of an old-fashioned fish shop who said he would distribute them around the town. It was that sort of day.

The meeting was good too. We held it in a small open park decorated by willows and birches, with the town graveyard just behind to add a neat religious touch. Hattie, who was something of an authority on graveyards, indeed collected them as a sort of hobby, viewed this after the service and reported that it was as good a place to be dead and buried as any he had seen in the whole of the Eastern States.

It was near the middle of the day and there must have been two hundred people praying and singing in the little park. I found myself enjoying it. I glanced at Herbie while everyone was in full song and his great hole of a mouth was opening and shutting with the enthusiasm of a walrus at feeding time. Winston smiled at me in comradely encouragement and Ambrosia winked with a large eye. It was like being a member of a suddenly successful football team.

Properjohn, naturally, had sung louder and more extravagantly than any of the people there. Now he stood forward to speak. Waiting for his words was like waiting for his discharge of the ceremonial gun. He stood before them in the sunshine, his black clothes taking on a vivid sleekness in the bright midday, his Brylcreemed grey hair like a silver helmet, his face gaunt but illuminated. Everyone was waiting for him.

'People!' he abruptly bellowed, as though he had been bottling it up for hours. 'Dear people of Harrisburg.'

'Harrisonburg,' Winston said to him quickly.

'Harrisonburg,' said Properjohn, 'Fine city in this beautiful autumn weather. We bring you love and greetings.'

Any displeasure at the geographical error was immediately erased. I could see children smiling at him and dogs sitting silently wagging their tails. 'All around us,' he called out again. 'All around, everywhere the world is in turmoil, and that is why I am glad to find you here today – at peace.'

He braced himself, breathing in so powerfully I thought he must explode. 'People ask,' he bellowed. 'People here on this miserable planet, have the enormous nerve to ask: Would

Jesus Christ be able to deal with the problems of the world as we see them today? They ask that! It astounds me! It must make our Lord laugh fit to die. We make a shambles all around us and then we have the infernal cheek to question whether Jesus would be up-to-date enough to know how to put things right. It's funny, that's what it is, people of Harrisburg . . . Harrisonburg . . . funny! Is He who made the mountains, and the sky, and every last sheep upon that mountain and under the sky, capable of solving our paltry problems? What a damned silly question!

'I'll tell you something, my people . . .' His voice flowed over them all, over us all, in the afternoon sun. Holding on to my Cross I found my head moving closer to him, not to miss a word. Herbie stood beside me in the same awkward attitude. I don't know how long the sermon lasted. It seemed very short, but in those few words the world became so easy and logical. The Reverend Hatt stood with a smile of rapt admiration, Poor Clare's mouth had dropped to where her jaw had once been, and Ambrosia was looking at her father as though she had seen him for the first time. We all could see it at once. Properjohn had power.

When he stopped it was abrupt but appropriate. The sensation remained like the light shining below a door that has just been quietly closed. Some children in the crowd began to clap, either children or timid adults. It was the immediate signal for a great explosion of applause, and even cheering, that sent the pigeons scooting from the eaves and gutters of that small Virginian town. My arms were looped around the Cross and my hands were applauding on the other side. Herbie glanced at me and began to clap. Winston stood with a professional smile, as though he had got something he wanted, or almost, and quietly tapped his hands against each other.

'I think we got ourselves a star,' said Herbie, as we walked back to the motor homes. The people were still milling around the park like a huge picnic crowd. Properjohn was among them, like a busy black spider among all the coloured clothes, giving away blessings as though they were surplus stock, signing autographs on the backs of the tracts provided on the relieved initiative of the Reverend Hatt.

'He's certainly got something,' I nodded. 'I was believing it all myself. And I *know* what he's really like.'

'Star quality,' mused Herbie. 'You either got it or you ain't. And he's got it. He could do a strip and make it interesting. It's a real shame he's wasted himself on this stuff.'

The unexpected euphoria of that bright day was with us into the evening when we were again on our journey, going through an apricot sunset on the way west through the valley of the Shenandoah. We came to a place where the road crowned a long slope of gentle grass, where beeches and birches stood by the river like people enjoying the last of the day's warm sun. The Blue Ridge Mountains seemed to be supporting the sky with one hand and the entire landscape was settled and quiet.

From 'Jesus Loves' travelling behind us came two short and two long toots of the horn, our stopping signal. We pulled to the side of the highway and Ambrosia, light as a child, ran forward to us and called up to her father: 'Can't we stop here, Dad? Look at it. It's brilliant.'

'Hardly brilliant,' said Properjohn looking out sagely like a captain examining an anchorage. 'But very tidy and quiet.'

'Can we go down by the water?' she pleaded. 'Can we stop down there and have a camp? I'll cook for everybody tonight.'

'The Lord help everybody!' exclaimed Properjohn, like a benign Victorian father. We all laughed and watched her eager face clamber at the window aperture.

'I will, I promise,' she said. 'I got some fish in Harrisonburg – all wrapped up in our leaflets too. We'll have fish and chips.'

'There's a sort of track turning off just ahead,' I pointed. 'I'll go and have a look, if you like, to see if we can get down there.'

'All right, lad, you go on,' said Properjohn affably. 'I wouldn't mind some fish and chips.'

'I'll come too,' said Ambrosia hurriedly. Her face coloured quickly and she climbed down from the side of the vehicle to the road again. 'It needs a woman to tell if it's all right for a camp.'

I glanced at Herbie and I saw his reaction. I hesitated, but

Properjohn surprisingly said: 'Yes, all right. Go on, both of you. Go ahead.' He waved his finger waggishly. 'But no playing "kiss in the ring" or anything like that when you're down there.' He crumpled with enormous laughter at the childish joke and thumped me on the shoulder gasping: 'Good boy. Good boy.'

Ambrosia was already running along the tufted grass verge of the road, her fat little arse bouncing in her jeans, her lovely black hair loosely dancing down her back. She looked back over her shoulder, slowed down, then stopped and waited.

'Are you allowed out of school?' she said tauntingly when I got there. 'Did the nice headmaster let you out?'

'Any of that and you'll get my hand across your backside,' I said.

'Promises, promises,' she sighed. I thought she was going to add something, but her eyes died for a moment and she began trotting again, off the road and down the stony track which curved considerably through the dropping meadow until it became a towpath alongside the riverbank.

'Mam keeps crying,' she said as we went down. 'She keeps saying everything reminds her of Wales.'

'Poor Clare,' I said.

'That's what everyone says about my mam,' she said taking my hand, casually as though by accident, and then releasing it again. ' "Poor Clare," they say, whatever she's doing. If she won the football pools they'd say "Poor Clare". They'd probably be right too because she'd never get her hands on the money.'

'Who would get it then?' I asked quickly.

She said, 'The survivor out of my dad and me.'

'Poor Clare,' I said.

'Poor Clare,' she nodded. 'Everywhere's like Wales. The trouble is when she's in the bleeding place she's crying like mad to get out of it. She says it rains coaldust where we live. How she can think *this* is like it, God only knows. All this lovely soft green.' She reached out to touch a hummock of thick moss; she lifted a piece and held it against her cheek as though it were expensive fabric.

'Wouldn't mind living here, myself,' she said. We were

reaching the level part of the valley now by the river. It was running more rapidly than the landscape suggested, running straight at one bank of trees and then whirling at an angle to make for another group on the opposite side.

'In America, you mean?' I said.

'Right here. On this very spot. Here.' She kicked a divot with her heel as though staking a claim. 'Not too far away from a town, and not all that far from New York really even though it's taken us ages, so I could go and have a rave-up every weekend and then come back here and be peaceful all through the week.'

'There are times,' I said, 'when you don't sound much like a clergyman's daughter.'

She sat down and seemed to be examining the river minutely, following a current from one side to the other and off around the following curve. 'That's my business,' she said dropping her tone to a whisper. 'There are times, mate, when you don't look like you ought to be hiking that Cross about. I've seen you looking at my breasts, you and that sly sod Herbie, having a quick ogle when you think nobody's noticing.'

'Don't flatter yourself,' I said without heat. 'If we're staring at you, girlie, it's probably because you're playing poor old Sprott off-key or you've got a bogie hanging from your nose.'

'You nasty bugger,' she said, her voice only a little sharper. 'I know what you're looking at and when you're looking at them. Why don't you stare at my mam, she's always out of tune and she quite often has a bogie coming down her nose. You don't look at her, do you?'

'I think we'd better go back up,' I said. 'I didn't come down for a fight.'

She seemed immediately deflated. 'Nor me,' she shrugged. 'Not with you.' I stood up but she remained on the grass, her face following me. 'Would you like to have a look?' she suggested calmly. 'At my whatsits? I'll show you if you want.' She said it like a child wanting to share a top it has previously held selfishly.

'No,' I answered, taking her hand and helping her to her feet. 'I don't think we ought to start that.'

Her fingers went to the wide neck of her blouse and she undid one button, opening it down until the beginning of her deep breast valley was exposed. The young pudding sides were swollen out and about an inch of the divide was showing.

'Are you sure you wouldn't like to see?' she asked genuinely. The gulf in our ages seemed a thousand years.

'No, Ambrosia,' I said. 'I'm sure. Thanks very much for the offer.'

She released the edges of the blouse and we began walking back up the slope in a matter-of-fact way as though the viewing offer had been for family photographs. When we were almost at the summit and we could see 'Jesus Lives' and 'Jesus Loves' on the road, she said: 'I think you would have enjoyed it. Seeing them.'

'I'm certain I would,' I replied. I almost said: 'I did.'

That evening, beside the river, a fire going between us, and after such a fine day, there was a new and settled contentment with our company. Ambrosia cooked the fish and chips on the range in 'Jesus Loves' and brought them to us under the growing stars. We sat and ate and drank a permitted glass of local cider each, with the fire fanning our faces and the Virginia night breeze tickling our backs. I could not recall such a mellowness, such a well-being, for years, certainly not since childhood. There was a special friendship, a comradeship, suddenly among us, even, God help me, a feeling of common cause. We talked and told stories from our lives, made up other stories from our heads, sang and recited, did conjuring tricks, danced, and had a splendid time.

Properjohn, in the firelight, looked like an amiable old Toby, Poor Clare's absent jaw was hardly noticeable and she danced a neat polka with Herbie, who certainly learned a lot of odd expertise in his films. Winston shone like coal and told droll stories of Madison Avenue, Indianapolis and somewhere called Reddish Knob, which he said was in our present locality. Herbie took a lot of childish chaffing, demands that he should shave off his beard so that we could see if there was a man underneath. Ambrosia, her face glistening from the fat of cooking, waited upon everyone, making little nudging jokes like a mediaeval serving wench, and I sang three rugby songs I knew, a sort of panic-stricken spontaneity enabling me to change the filthy words when I had all but collided with them.

The Reverend Hatt, who had been watching these diversions like a well-pleased scoutmaster, suddenly stood and did several female impressions, including Grace Kelly, Carmen Miranda, and Eartha Kitt, which drew general applause and an exchange of raised eyebrows between Herbie, Winston and myself. It was a time of good fellowship and the cleanest fun. Everyone enjoyed it. That evening by the river we had found peace. I think we would have done anything for each other.

Winston refused Herbie's offer of a quiet joint and said that he had taken to smoking Peter Stuyvesants.

Properjohn had smoked innumerable cigarettes while this ambiance was growing in the firelight. The stumps were broken and piled in front of him as he sat cross-legged upon the ground, still in his black garb, like some off-duty vulture. Then he rose stiffly from his patriarchial place, pushed the pile of cigarette ends to one side with his foot and, as though fulfilling a long-awaited moment, took his stand before the fire.

'Clare,' he ordered. 'Ambrosia. Get the instruments.'

Mother and daughter obediently rose and went to 'Jesus Loves' to fetch the Sprott's autoharp and the harmonica. They each played a tune, formally introduced by Properjohn in the manner of the chairman of an old-time music hall. When Poor Clare mislaid the notes in the middle phrase of the Londonderry Air, and attempted to recapture them with some frenzied bites up and down the instrument, he rallied her with a loud reminding hum and a conducting wave of his extraordinary arms. I shall always remember the look of appreciation and love she gave him over the little tin horizon of the mouth-organ when she was safely with the melody again.

Ambrosia, angelic Ambrosia in the rosy light, then played some old Welsh tunes, touching the little keyboard of the harp tenderly, her face beatific, slightly held up as though hoping to catch a glimpse of some night bird flying high above. She played the instrument very well when she wanted and the liquid notes floated out across the ruminating river and the hidden fields. From somewhere a farm dog began a melancholy howl, but this seemed to enhance the soft wildness of the harp's melody and the smile that grew on the girl's face as she played was remote and private as though she were alone in the night.

At the end she curtseyed with mock shyness at our applause. She had put on a long green skirt and a frilly blouse loose over her top. Watching her, distant from all of us, made me wonder how she could ever be the same young girl who had confronted and challenged me by that same riverbank that same evening.

Her father's clapping was enormous, his hands resounding like two pieces of wood hitting each other. He bowed to her and then took the centre of the floor and demanded musical accompaniment which his wife and daughter struck up with apparently well-practised ease. They played an opening to 'Moon River' without even being asked and Properjohn fell into it, crooning the honeyed song, eyes closed, nose quivering, hands splayed out, like the most tinny dance hall singer who ever stood in a pink spotlight. It was astonishing. He finished the song with an appropriately sad flourish, bowed to our broken applause, and then, like Sinatra making a signal to Nelson Riddle, he jerked his finger at Poor Clare and Ambrosia, and flew into an extraordinary stringed version of 'Get your Kicks on Route Sixty-Six'. He staggered about in front of the fire, sticky hair against his wild face, feet apart, hands spread and trembling, twisting and rocking at the waist, like some dark devil against the fire. When he had done we had to applaud loudly to cover our embarrassment. Winston called out gamely, but lamely: 'This is Route Eighty-One, swinger, not Sixty-Six', and with cheap spontaneity Properjohn did a sharp flashback to his former wiggle and sang, briefly: 'Get your *fun* on Route Eighty-One!'

We all pretended to be delighted at his quickness and that was a mistake because it encouraged him to go on. First he drank a glass of cider, which he had refused earlier, then he called: 'Spoons! Spoons!'

Poor Clare, like some conjuror's assistant, obediently produced a pair of tablespoons from somewhere about her person. Her husband greeted them like old friends, clacked them a few times up his arm and down his leg, very expertly, too, before dropping into a crouching stance before the fire in the manner of a Japanese waiting for a karate lunge. Both Ambrosia and Poor Clare gave him a chord and then he launched himself into a frenzied, gymnastic, clacking of the spoons, up and down his arms and legs, his knees, the soles of his shoes, even the front of his forehead. There was no doubt as to the virtuosity of the performance and Properjohn was intoxicated with it, his face seeping sweat, but lit with a bright gleam of almost manic delight. Across his shoulder blades went the singing spoons, down his thigh, delicately up his arm from wrist to elbow, and then to a crescendo across his chest until the finale, three resounding blows on each knee. There was astounded silence when he had finished and then the nearest six of us could come to thunderous applause. Properjohn pranced about, sweating and bowing, and spreading his hands, graciously pointing at Poor Clare and Ambrosia, his background accompanists, as though his triumph was at Carnegie Hall not a bank of the Shenandoah River.

It was the next thing that was so grotesque. I was pushing Winston forward with pleas to sing a piccaninny song or anything to get Properjohn off-stage, but Winston was reluctant and slow and in the hesitation the mad Welshman was performing again, this time doing a pathetic Jolson act with Ambrosia dragged in to be Sonny Boy and squirm on her father's knee. He crooned his way through the moony song, then, with terrible seriousness, began his own monologue about Ambrosia, his little girl, whom he loved well, named after the Food of Heaven, who was sweet and good and who honoured and loved her father and, to some extent, her mother also.

We sat, withered with embarrassment, the girl, her face set red like a hard apple, on his knee, while he mused: 'Remember when you were a little girl, Ambrosia, how I used to tell you stories in bed. Till midnight sometimes. All cosy. You in the middle of your mam and me. And how we used to walk and look at the coaltips and the pit ponies having a rest in the fields. And games we used to play, girl. Ah, yes, the games . . .'

It was at this point that I sensed something was going to happen. His face had become shiny with the power of the memories, the excitement of his prancing and dancing and the dynamics with the spoons was still on him. Now it seemed to heighten. Ambrosia switched on a sharp, concerned, expression. She tried to wriggle from her father's bent knee, but he caught her with his big hands, saying 'Come on, don't you remember? The games. Oh, the fun we used to have!'

'No!' she said in frightened protest. 'No. No, you don't. Not now.'

'Come on,' he encouraged madly. 'Remember this one. When you were little . . .'

In the next extraordinary moment he looped his arms around her waist, swung her out and whirled her about. Around and around. His spinning countenance was bright with the fun of it. Each time the girl came around to our view her face was fixed with terror. She knew what was coming next.

He caught her confidently under the arms and then with a complicated, but adroit movement, he turned her over and upside down. He hung her by the ankles, shouting with laughter, as a father might with a very small girl. Her long skirt tumbled down her legs engulfing her head, while her white legs right to the tight pink triangle of her pants were exposed for everybody to see. In that firelight, in that open country, it was like some gipsy scene, so wild and grotesque that we could only squat, stunned and gaping.

But Properjohn was laughing like a maniac. From beneath the skirt came the muffled cries of Ambrosia. Her round, white body wriggled like a captured cod. Poor Clare was standing, less transfixed than the rest of us, emitting little toy-engine toots that were half moan, half protest.

In that firelight we saw this huge man in black, laughing as though drunk, holding the ankles of two chubby legs, curved and white and trembling as the girl tried to wriggle. At that strange angle they appeared to sprout from a receptacle draped in green satin, and pelmeted with a frill of pink nylon. Then he began to revolve once more, slowly at first, but increasing his speed until the poor girl swung out and around in a whooshing circle. Her cries fluctuated as her orbit neared us and then went away again. Properjohn was going 'Wheeeeeeeeee' through tight teeth.

'Mind the fire!' I protested idiotically, still stuck to the ground.

He slowed, like a carousel when the ride is over, and eventually stopped with Ambrosia still hanging from his grasp. He must have been very strong. Then he dropped her gently to the ground where she lay in a sobbing heap, her pink backside jutting up like the saddled hump of a small camel, her head just poking out of the hem of her skirt. We all stood up together, slowly, as though in acknowledgement that the entertainment was over, while Properjohn stood beaming pleasure like someone who has performed something exceptionally clever. Suddenly he seemed to realize, from our lack of applause I suppose and from the increasing sobs of his daughter, that something was amiss. He knelt to her and tenderly took the skirt away from her face. Her complexion was bright red, I suppose with the combined effects of embarrassment and the blood rushing to her head. Tears had run amok over her cheeks, but were now gushing in a more orderly course down to her mouth.

'Ambrosia,' pleaded Properjohn. 'Oh, Ambrosia, love, what's wrong? Whatever's the matter?'

'You . . .' she began but did not finish it then. She never forgot that she was afraid of him.

'It was only fun,' soothed Properjohn. 'Only a game. Like we used to play.' His spreading hand went to her shoulder and this seemed to electrify her for she leaped from the ground, shouted and sobbed something for the benefit of all of us, which none of us deciphered, then bolted like some mad night spirit.

Properjohn, with the rest of us, watched her escape. He then turned a tragically hurt expression on us and began to say some words which refused to come out, but which would have been: 'What have I done?'

'She's heading for the river,' said Winston abruptly, starting to run in that direction.

'The river! The river!' shrieked Poor Clare.

'The river?' asked Properjohn as though the reference meant nothing. But he only said it to me and I was the last to run after Winston. Herbie was way out in front going like a tank, with Hattie squeaking on his tail, and Poor Clare running and pushing her arms out in all directions like some ambitious early flying machine trying to get off the ground. When I caught up with them they were all slowed along the dark riverbank cooing cautiously: 'Ambrosia, Ambrosia.'

I found her in a short bay they had already passed. She was lying flat in some shallow water, kicking her feet, and grinding her teeth.

'You'll never drown in that,' I said kneeling on the bank.

'I know,' she muttered. 'That's why I jumped in here, didn't I? I'm not bloody daft.'

She looked up. She was about four feet below me, pathetically lying among the water and the mud. 'Are you by yourself?'

'The others are along the bank,' I said.

'Oh that bastard,' she sighed. 'I really will kill him one day. Did my legs look terrible? When I was upside down?'

'No,' I said reasonably. 'I thought they looked quite good.'

'Not too fat?'

'No. I thought they were fine.'

'Thank God I changed my drawers,' she went on.

'They looked all right too,' I said. She was kicking her ankles gently. 'Isn't it cold down there?' I asked.

'Bloody cold,' she confirmed. 'But I want that swine to think I've drowned.'

'He'll simply enjoy doing a funeral oration,' I pointed out.

'He would too,' she agreed. Her head came around to one side and she looked directly up from the mud and the little currents. 'Listen, Willy,' she said. 'Will you do something? Come in and get wet and then we'll get out on the bank and you can kid that you've rescued me.'

'What for?' I said.

'If the old sod turns up and I'm lying stiff on the bank and you're giving me the kiss of life, he'll really think I've snuffed it. I'd love to give the bastard a scare like that.'

I did not consider the proposition very much. I simply said: 'All right.' As I slithered down the muddy bank I had a strange passing feeling of relief that I was not wearing my robe. It's very odd how you get attached to things.

It was not until the water had taken hold of my ankles that I realized fully what I was doing. It was icy. It gurgled down into my Dolcis casuals a moment before I fell forward on my knees and then it ran in a chilly rush up my legs.

'Get right in,' she urged lying almost alongside me. 'Go on.'

'Christ, it's cold!' I protested.

'Don't I know,' she shivered, reaching up and pulling me with surprising force so that I went flop on my belly in the stream. I repelled a howl and splashed vainly in six inches of water. 'Let's get out. Quick. Please,' I shuddered. Her answer was to grasp me around the neck and pull us together in a wet and brutal kiss, with her large soggy bosom flopping into me and her legs thrashing through the water like an octopus trying to get a hold. I pushed her away and gasped: 'They're coming back along the bank.'

Twice we slid back into the damned river while trying to reach the grass but at the third attempt I got there and tugged her up after me. We both lay flat out and shaking on the bank, but I could hear the others calling through the dark as they hurried, so I told her to turn onto her back and look as though she were drowned.

Shivering, I knelt across her and put my mouth to hers. She opened hers like a snorer but then stuck her tongue blatantly halfway down my throat. I pulled back. 'Pack it,' I threatened. 'Otherwise you're on your own. Here they come.'

'Sorry, Willy,' she whispered. She closed her eyes and went limp as rubber on the grass. They all arrived in a bunch, even Poor Clare, who must have reached a good pace to keep up with Herbie.

'She's dead!' howled Properjohn, dropping on his black knees on the opposite side of Ambrosia. 'I knew it, she's dead!' His face, his voice, his clasped hands went up to heaven and he began to pray loudly for the soul of the departed.

'Don't, John, don't,' pleaded Poor Clare. 'Give her a chance. She might not be gone yet.'

'She's not,' I confirmed bringing my wet mouth up from the girl's. 'I'm doing my best. I think I can save her.'

Herbie caught me by the shoulder and pulled me strongly away. 'Let me,' he said. 'You're not blowing up a balloon. Any more of that and she'll float away. Here.' His eyes were fixed on her and he hustled me aside and took my kneeling place at Ambrosia's hip. Then the rotten swine pressed his hands down on her crammed chest several times before fixing his hairy mouth to hers. Winston was fidgeting, circling, hinting that he wanted his turn, but Herbie's heavy treatment caused the victim to open her eyes quickly.

'There,' said Herbie leaning down for a final, entirely gratis, blow and puff. 'That's great. I guess she'll be okay now.'

Ambrosia gave him a hard stare through the dark, its intention obvious by the attitude of her head, but then collapsed and moaned: 'I wanted to die . . . to die . . . forever . . .'

'There's no temporary way,' murmured Winston, disappointed he had missed his turn. The Reverend Hatt, who had been muttering supplementary prayers a few yards away, saw Ambrosia sitting up and collapsed spectacularly to his knees with thanks for a quick reply. This was mere background, however, for the howling repentance of Properjohn's descent upon his risen daughter. His embrace, and the peripheral flappings of Poor Clare's thankful arms, engulfed the girl, piling her to the grass again with such force that Herbie had to pull them both away with cries of 'Give her air! Give her air!' The Properjohns obeyed and after that, with unstinted tears and words of thanks and rejoicing, Ambrosia's hideous parents carried her back to our encampment between them. We followed behind. A spiteful night wind was zipping through my wet trousers. I looked up and saw the girl hung between Properjohn and Poor Clare, head down. Like a prisoner.

'You didn't pull her out of that river,' said Herbie abruptly when we were in our beds in 'Jesus Lives' and the light had been out an hour. I propped myself up on an elbow and dipped a warning finger down to the Reverend Hatt's bunk below. There was enough light for Herbie to see the intention.

'Asleep,' said Herbie, but whispering anyway. 'Said his prayers and asleep.' He waited a moment and then repeated his charge: 'You didn't pull her out.'

'I did,' I said truthfully.

'Sure, sure. Okay, so you pulled her out. But how far was she in? Tell me that, hero.'

'How far? What d'you mean? She was out in the middle. Floating away. If I hadn't grabbed her she'd be out to sea by now.'

'Shit,' he said quietly. 'Plain shit. Listen man, the back of your shirt wasn't even damp.'

'It's quick drying.'

'And that broad was no more unconscious than I was. We had a kid in *Swimming Pool Sex* who *really* went under. The guy got so engrossed in what he was doing to her that he forgot she had her head under the water. It was nearly bye-bye baby. And when we got her out she looked different to our Ambrosia. And I'll tell you something else. No broad who is drowned sticks her tongue in your gob when you are supposed to be breathing life into her.'

'Did she do that?' came Winston's voice drowsily from the bunk below Herbie.

'Certainly did.'

'Jesus,' sighed Winston. 'Why is we black folks always last in line?'

'She just wanted to scare her father,' I shrugged in the dimness. 'And you can't blame her can you?'

I heard Herbie rustle his big head. 'No, man,' he agreed. 'You sure can't. When he did *that*, when he did *that* to her. Man, have you ever seen anything like it.'

'Never upside down,' said Winston.

'He's stark raving potty,' I said. 'Can you understand how a man who gave that performance in Harrisonburg this afternoon could do that sort of thing tonight? It floors me.'

'It's oddball,' agreed Herbie. 'I guess he just does whatever he thinks he will at that moment, whether it's preaching or indecently exposing his daughter.'

'Right,' agreed Winston's voice from below. 'This guy is the last of the windjammers, man. He goes whichever way the breeze comes along. And he uses whatever he's got to hand, whether it's his ever-loving kid or a sermon which Archbishop Todd preached to ten thousand folks in Dallas last month.'

We digested this in a space of silence. Then I said: 'It wasn't his then? The sermon?'

'Oh, don't get me wrong. The way he put it over was one

hundred per cent Properjohn. I doubt if Archbishop Todd would have recognized it. But it came from *Time Magazine* of October 14th. I know because I showed it to him. It was said to be one of the great sermons of the century. *Time* gave the whole of its Religion page to it.'

'And Properjohn nicked it,' I said.

'Nicked it, like you say, friend,' replied Winston. 'I showed it to the man because he told me he didn't know what to say to the people here. He was looking for help. I figured maybe he would pick up a few crumbs from it. Instead he took the whole loaf. That's some man we've got with us.'

'Don't any of those people in Harrisonburg read *Time Magazine*?' asked Herbie.

'They do,' said Winston. 'But I don't think they'd recognize it. He stirred it up real good. I didn't realize until he was some way through.'

'Nor me either,' came the Reverend Hatt's wide-awake voice from below me. 'And it was *Newsweek* not *Time*. October 18th, friend.'

Nine

There were times when, frankly, I thought I was the only sane person in the whole crusade. Ambrosia, after the night of adventures on the Shenandoah, descended into a sulky stillness from which she emerged only to occasionally grunt. Her mother continued to see Wales in everything, mountains, vales, chapels, towns, weeping with homesickness over them and playing flitting snatches of native melodies on her harmonica. The appearance of a neat white church – they were all neat and white and prettily steepled as though assembled from a universal kit – this one with the notice 'Cardiff Baptist

Chapel' set her off into a deluge of grief and Herbie, who was driving 'Jesus Loves' at the time, had to stop so that she could be emotionally reassembled. She continued her home-sickness with even greater remorseful gusto until even the ketchuped smell of a Hamburger Paradise was for her the aroma of her native fish and chips.

The Reverend Hatt's madness was at least quiet. He was collecting graveyards and crematoria as we journeyed, visiting them whenever a stop made it convenient, whistling blithely around the rural ovens, lisping little bits of sorry poetry and other epitaphs, private thoughts on public stone, committed there forever like a fixed grin. Some he copied into a notebook. He was patently delighted at Troutville to discover the scenic Radar Chapel and Mortuary there with a pile of wrecked cars close by as though they were an advertisement for the place.

Properjohn continued in his moods of volcanic insanity, his secular singing on the road, his phenomenal gaffes irrevocably damaging relations between Britain and a dozen decent communities in rural America. At Staunton, a sturdy little town folded about a river, he spoke outside the Stonewall Jackson Hotel and somehow confused Woodrow Wilson, who was born in the place, with Harold Wilson, much to the puzzlement of the people, most of whom had never heard of the latter. Asked about his attitude to the English Speaking Union on television at Lexington he shouted extravagantly that he was all in favour of trade unions as long as they kept their place. I had never known a man provoke so much noise and so many silences.

But, at about this time, Winston and Herbie went mad too. Anyone witnessing the unforgivable violence over an old rat-bag in a bar in Bristol, on the border of Virginia and Tennessee, could confirm that. That night they risked everything.

As for myself I was continuing modestly, the average Jesus, toting my Cross through each town with one of my four, now perfected, expressions, slightly varied according to which side of the balsawood my head was that day, and which side of the town sidewalk the majority of the inhabitants had gathered. If they were evenly distributed I used to walk a hundred yards with it on my right shoulder, sad expression turned left, and then a hundred yards again with it on the left, sad expression facing right. My Dolcis shoes, after the soaking in the Shenandoah River, were authentically careworn, and my robe was dusty and limp. I was looking the part more each day.

Indeed it was while I was practising a couple of new expressions, during a short night-walk near Ronoake that we suffered our road accident with the Cross. Ronoake, a key town for janitor and sanitary supplies, has hills standing around it like tents, and is noted for a big illuminated star on one of these hills. Properjohn, naturally, concluded it was in our honour and made much of it at the meeting and Press conference there, until it was quietly pointed out by a newspaperman that the star was a permanent feature illuminated when no one had been killed on the roads in the area and blacked out when they had. That night we nearly saved them a week's electricity costs.

We had gone forward on a night reconnaisance, so called by Properjohn although in this instance it was more of a rearguard action since we had already sung the hymns, said the prayers and counted the collection in the town. He thought, however, we might like 'a walk to stop you getting stiff' and, without asking further, we donned our robes, took up the Cross and started for the town. I was always glad of these excursions for it gave me the opportunity to take off my robe, leave the Cross with Herbie and Winston, and make a swift guilty visit to each of the nightspots of the place in my continuing quest for my wife. She was not in Ronoake, which did not surprise me, although a girl with a boa constrictor act at the Tip-Tap Club said she thought there had been an English dancer in a floorshow at Bristol about a year before. We returned, shuffling along the dark, mid-week-empty road, singing mildly 'She was Poor but She was Honest', while I was rehearsing a new expression of humility which I thought might be added to my repertoire.

The sum of these activities, though, was that we were not watching the road. Not until two ferocious headlight beams staggered around a sightless bend and fixed me and the Cross in their instant whiteness. The car itself seemed to emit a cry. It began to skid almost as soon as it had rounded the bend and came wildly towards our group as we cowered foolishly against our balsawood emblem in the middle of the road. Only twenty yards short of a spectacular and unusual carnage it screeched off the highway as though itself frightened by the sight of us. It jumped into a steep nose-dive down an embankment to our left, flinging bushes and small trees out of its way like some excavator. Fifty feet down it expired with a tin bang, a whimper and a long plaintive hiss.

'Hell,' said Herbie.

'Come on,' I said moving forward.

The guilt complexes in America are formidable. Instead of running as I was, towards the embankment, Herbie and Winston, entirely misreading my intention, set off like escapees in the opposite direction. Angrily I called them back and after some hesitation they returned at a shuffle. We stood staring down the long scarred decline like timid tourists on the rim of a volcano. I started down the slope, still stupidly carrying the Cross. When I realized this I had to scramble back, lay it down, and then go down again.

Stiff with bourbon and shock the marble-headed driver and his wife were motionless in their seats, staring out through the broken windscreen as though they expected at any moment to continue the downward journey. They knew we were at their window but neither would look at us. Finally, after some tentative knocking, Herbie, the bastard, went around to the front, poked his St Peter's head in at them through the holed screen, and making a sign of the cross said: 'Peace be with you.'

'They speak English,' the man muttered to his wife.

I went to Herbie's side and looked in at them. They were very frightened of me. The grey hair fringing the man's bald middle head was bristling. Eventually the woman, a wiry little thing with a nasty bruise on her forehead, bent forward to get a closer view of my face.

'He only had a coupla whiskies,' she began as though anxious to get the slate straight. 'Just a couple.'

'Are you all right?' I asked.

The man's eyes were distant, as though he were thinking of somewhere else. 'Just a little celebration,' he began. 'Generally I lead a good life, don't I, Martha?'

'You do, Henry,' Martha confirmed. 'A real good life.'

They wanted us to do nothing for them, nor to call anybody. They said they would prefer to remain there and rest. We mounted the embankment again, leaving them staring through their broken windscreen. We retrieved the Cross at the top and then set out again. But now Winston and Herbie carried the Cross, one each end. Like the piece of wood it was.

'Sister Anna,' I said to Herbie. 'You carry the banner.' I handed the Cross over to him in the dark behind the nightclub in Bristol.

'Remember I'm subscription-paid-up Jewish,' he pointed out.

'All right,' I said. 'You can be Sister Hannah. Hang onto it anyway. I want to get this maxi-dress off.'

'I ain't never been scared of going in a nightclub before,' whispered Winston. 'But, man, I'm scared now.'

Herbie said there were times when Winston looked like Rochester, a bad image for a coloured man. Winston nodded miserably. I could see his eyes wide and white in the dark too. 'Sometimes I feel like Rochester,' he admitted. 'I've sprayed around a few dollars in better places than this, but ain't never risked a thousand bucks plus, just poking my head in the door.'

I had taken off my robe, folded it, and put it in the cubbyhole in the Cross. I tried to smooth out the crumples and creases in my suit and shirt. Herbie said to Winston: 'Listen, we know one drink in here could cost us a lot of dough if anybody sees us and figures out who we are. But you voted with us on it. We either have a night on the town or we stay in and suffer the pangs of Christianity with poor old Hattie.'

'It will be safe,' I reassured them, wondering if it would be. 'We've only just got into town.'

I looked anxiously at the Cross pushed in among some wooden cases and general rubbish at the rear yard of the nightclub. Winston said: 'I guess that will be okay.'

'As long as it's not nicked again,' I said.

'Maybe we could take it in with us,' suggested Herbie impatiently. 'Or leave it by the sidewalk, like it was a car. We could only get a parking ticket.'

He moved off to where the lights from the front of the place were blinking into the road and we followed. But I was still concerned about the Cross. 'It's such an inconvenient thing,' I said to Winston.

'Sure,' he answered. 'I guess it always has been.'

It was one of those places that looks as if it were excavated not built. The room was like a jagged cave, with candles in crevices, peopled by shadows, and with a band hunched in one corner. The barman moved around like a rumour behind the long counter. We were glad of the dimness and we sat more comfortably and had our first drink in a week. Winston paid.

The stage, about the size of a window, glowed faintly from underneath. I tried to see Silvie slowly uncoiling her naked legs in a front windmill. It was easily big enough. She had done it one night at midnight for me, at home in our small bathroom. At a party once she had done a somersault in a wardrobe. She was very good in confined spaces. But America was very big.

'Where does Tennessee begin?' Herbie asked the barman.

'Right across the street,' said the barman. 'You can smell the sweet Virginia air on this side. On the other it's cottondust.'

'Did you ever have an English girl, a dancer, in the show here?' I asked immediately. 'Small, dark. Nice body.'

'For me, mister, they all got nice bodies,' said the man. 'You just have to get used to it, that's all.' He was trying to get some glasses from below and he put his head forward on the bar and rested there as though fatalistically awaiting the chop. 'English,' he muttered into his crooked elbows. 'English. Yeah. Sure, I think I remember one.' Then he was definite. 'Sure, there *was* one. Nice little boobs.'

I felt my face freeze. 'She was in the . . . naked . . .?' I said. I sensed Winston watching my expression and Herbie smiling with distant cockiness at me through the dusk of the place.

'Naked?' echoed the barman. 'Sure. Not only naked. NUDE.' He glanced at me and thought he had gone too far. 'Well, maybe just a feather or a bead here and there. Beads, yes. She had beads. But most of 'em was sweat.' He laughed coarsely. Then he said with some concern. 'She your sister or something?'

'I wouldn't mind if it was my sister,' I said.

'His wife,' said Herbie brutally. 'It's his wife.'

'My, my, my,' said the barman. 'You send your wife out doing that kind of nude work?'

'No,' I said defensively. 'I didn't send her. She went. She likes the work.' I waited. 'How did she seem? Was she all right?'

'All right,' he shrugged. 'As much as I remember she was great. But it was a bad week. Rained all the week and she didn't get much business. I used to get the guys from the kitchen to come out front and applaud. They liked to see it anyway and the place seemed so empty. It was just like when we had the Japanese comic. Will you listen to that? A Japanese comic. In Bristol. The guy who booked him shot himself.'

We all had another drink and then another. More people began to arrive in the place and the musicians became more interested and began to play together instead of wandering off in different lonely directions as they had been. A woman came and sat alone at the bar stool to my right, a few stools away. I only saw her from the edge of my eye, but Herbie turned his seat a fraction so he could observe her fully. But he had decided to bait me.

'Listen, man,' he said lazily, finishing his drink and putting it up for another. Before going in there we had agreed on two drinks each with Winston paying, to be reimbursed when we got some money. 'Listen. Why are you gazing all goo-goo-eyed at that stage? Picturing Silvie doing handstands?'

'More or less,' I said. 'Anything wrong in that?'

'Sure there's something wrong,' he answered. He could not have more than three without getting difficult. 'You should have done your worrying years ago, back in England. Look at you man, wallowing in it like a sow in shit. Loving it. Boo hoo, I lost my ever-loving wife. You should have thought about your ever-loving wife when you had her and you were screwing around with other guys' ever-loving wives.'

'Shut up, you objectionable bastard.' I said.

'Sure, shut up, you objectionable bastard,' echoed the woman sitting behind me. We all stopped to look at her. She was in a black dress with black hair and black blotches under her eyes. She was smoking and, for effect, she took a deep draw and dispatched the smoke in our direction. It drifted among us and Winston did a little sea-lion act trying to catch some of it in his mouth. Herbie forgot me and moved across to the woman.

'Oh, boy,' he said, standing above her. 'What some people will do just to get in on some company.' She did not look up at him.

'It's a better pitch than dropping my handkerchief,' she shrugged. 'You're the sort who would pick it up and send it to somebody for Christmas.'

'Okay, okay,' nodded Herbie, subdued and at once affable because she was a woman. The front of her dress was even lower than it was meant to be. It looked white and tired down there like cold cooking left in a pot but Herbie was leaning over so far his whiskers were almost brushing her. 'You win,' he smiled extravagantly. He turned to me generously. 'I'm sorry, Willy, old pal,' he said. 'I didn't mean a word of it.'

'Why don't you buy me a drink?' suggested the woman.

'Tell me your name for a drink,' coaxed Herbie. To watch that man operate on a female was sickening.

'Dearest,' she told him. 'I'm called Dearest around here.'

'Because you're the most expensive!' exploded Herbie. He rocked about with huge laughter. The woman remained absolutely straight. 'Right first time,' she said. 'Vodka on the rocks.'

'Oh,' said Herbie his hilarity quelled. He turned sheepishly to Winston. 'Can I buy her a drink?' he asked.

'Who's that?' asked Dearest. 'Your Poppa?'

'He has the money,' explained Herbie unhappily. 'It's what's called Black Power.'

Winston paid up patiently. Dearest composed a wan smile for him but was right away confronted with the widespread face and chest of Herbie, who sat on the next stool, three feet away, turned his back on us and his nauseating expression on her. I thought that sort of approach went out with acne and concealed contraceptives. Dearest unerringly fixed his period. She regarded him with a sort of disgusted amusement.

'Baby,' he muttered eventually, through the whiskers and

the whisky. All three of us closed our eyes and so did the barman. He said it again. 'Baby.'

'Yes, Baby,' replied Dearest dutifully.

'Why don't we get outa this place. Maybe you could take me across to the motel across the street.'

'There's a Federal Law,' she replied quietly. 'And it says you can't transport minors across a state boundary for an immoral purpose.'

The barman and Winston fell towards each other across the bar, howling with delight. I was a bit slower because I did not immediately appreciate what she was saying. But then I began to laugh too. Herbie flew around on his stool, knocking his glass backwards for effect. He roared with a mountainous fury and rushed first at me, hitting me with an off-target punch that caught my cheekbone and sent me spider-legged over the floor. I landed stupidly, sitting on the feet of a woman at a table across the room. The club seemed to be rocking fiercely but even through the distortion I could see and hear Herbie making for Winston.

Winston was swift and deft. Two blows went sweeping across his head, but then he made the mistake of losing his temper too and holding his ground. I got to my feet with confused apologies to the lady on whose feet I had been squatting in time to see Winston foolishly square up to the next onrush of the large and fearsome Herbie. I winced and I felt the people at the tables all around wince too. I sensed them ducking, which is more than Winston did. Herbie went straight at him. That night there might have been race riots in Bristol if Dearest had not thrown her quickly emptied glass and struck Herbie behind the ear just as he was about to deliver the killer blow on our coloured friend. As it was Winston half got it. The ham fist bounced off him, but with enough force to make him see wisdom and get over the bar in one leap and a hurried scramble. His black head came up. 'You hairy honkey!' he piped at Herbie. 'Honkey!'

Herbie stopped. 'Honkey?' he said, with surprisingly quiet anger. 'Honkey?'

Winston's small, neat head came up from behind the bar again like part of a carefully rehearsed puppet show. 'Honkey,' he repeated flatly but with a decided apprehension in the tone.

'Sure, sure,' breathed Herbie, standing feet planted apart on the other side of the bar. It was like a western.

'Sure,' he repeated as though he had forgotten his lines. 'Honkey.' He made a big sigh. 'So you niggers have got a word at last. You never did have one before, did you? White trash never sounded right, did it? It never had that ring. We had all the best words. Nigger, darkie, blackie, coon. They're all real easy, but you didn't have one easy word for us. But now you've got one. Honkey.'

I turned to a man at the table behind me. 'Is that bad?' I asked.

'Very bad, I'd say,' confirmed the man. His companions nodded gloomily.

I moved forward at the same moment as Herbie. At the back of my mind was the thought that if Herbie killed Winston in a nightclub brawl then none of us would get our bonus. Shakily, from the effect of the blow already landed and the possibility of more to come, I stumbled forward to try to stop Herbie's rush. I was a fraction too late to prevent him getting to the bar. He flew at it insanely, a bellow like a furnace issued from him, like fire blowing through his beard. Winston's cautious head emerged from his wooden trench in time to see the start of the onrush, and he withdrew it with a squeak. Herbie reached the bar and his body shook it, his top half going over the top, his arms and fists flailing ahead of him.

I reached him just then and fortunately so did the barman and the courageous Dearest, who grabbed at him bodily in a way he would have enjoyed in a different situation. I had him around his thick, bristly neck and the bartender, a heavy, round man, was kneeling on the bar with his own body trapping Herbie's to the wooden surface. Winston popped up and grabbed Herbie's hair, hauling down on it like a circus hand with a tent rope. He fought madly. I was rattling about as I tried to hold on. Dearest slid spectacularly down Herbie's left leg, taking part of his trousers with her, while the force of Herbie's fight made the prostrate barman bounce up and down like someone having vigorous and enjoyable sex.

Even then I doubt if we could have held the maddened

monster for long. Foul and fierce language was flying from his head, held half over the bar by Winston, who having committed himself that far could not let go. He held onto Herbie's shaggy hair while crouching on the floor behind the bar, only inches from the awesome face of a man in the full flight of uncontrollable fury.

It was left to an outsider, the lady on whose feet I had landed, to decide the contest. Seeing that four of us were getting nowhere in holding Herbie with our various methods, she strode smartly across the floor, selected a cheap liquor bottle and brought it down with an odd rubbery sound on Herbie's head. He was immediately quiet. The bottle did not even break. The lady replaced it in the rack, walked back to her table, and sat down again.

Herbie was so still that I thought for a moment she might have to start sorting out a defence to a murder charge. But he groaned encouragingly as we slid him like a conquered whale from the counter. With Dearest, the barman and myself supporting him, he lapsed to the floor. Blood was coming plentifully from the nasty knock of the bottle. Winston, shaking like a stick insect, emerged from the back of the bar, looking in extreme worry about him and mumbling: 'I'll never say honkey again. Never, never again.'

We laid out Herbie on the floor. He looked dreadful. Dearest went to borrow an ice pail from a table, and the barman stared down at the hairy, bloody, unconscious man.

'What is the guy, anyway?' asked the barman. 'A stunt man or something? Maybe he's a wrestler?'

'Actually,' I said with foolish absentmindedness, 'he's a sort of evangelist.'

It said a lot for Herbie's constitution that he was able to walk back to camp. It was a wobbly walk with my support, Winston humping the Cross and a dainty lace handkerchief donated by Dearest pressed to the lump on Herbie's head.

Conversation was limited on the road and I had some time to watch Winston's technique with the Cross and to grudgingly realize that the effect would have been startling if he were permitted to carry it every day. Apart from the inherent interest of his black face, he was a small man and the Cross was large; he carried the light balsawood with an ease that was really effective. Naturally I never mentioned this to anyone else.

The night's events were not concluded. We had parked the motor homes inside the broken-down stockade of a derelict drive-in cinema , an area as big as a football field with the listening posts still sticking up in rows like war graves and the gigantic screen holed in one or two places, standing at the front.

At that point the road was sunken and we mounted the final rise, with Herbie now breathing heavily as though sleepwalking, to find that Properjohn had gone mad again. With their headlights and spotlights full on, 'Jesus Loves' and 'Jesus Lives' were drawn up in the middle of the deserted drive-in area, their beams flung right onto the screen. Properjohn was in mid-fling on the platform his arms soaring, his sticky hair built up like a hat on his big head, and his body shadow flung gigantically across the screen. It was enormous and frightening, twenty feet high, fingers outstretched and seeming to reach for the corners of the sky. He was shouting his usual sermon, but for once the sound was diminished by the sight. His voice piped through the vivid light and the darkness beyond in which we stood transfixed. Timidly we moved forward. I took the Cross from Winston and gave him the weight of Herbie, which was less now because he too was standing and blinking at the extraordinary sight.

We walked forward, in automatic procession, as though long rehearsed in the ritual. It is amazing how these things can get hold of you. Once we were in front of the van lights the Cross was suddenly and dramatically shadowed on the same great screen. Properjohn, who had seen us, stopped and then, immediately realizing the spectacle, hammed it to its fullest extent. Ambrosia and Poor Clare, who were sitting with the Reverend Hatt, on camp chairs facing the screen and were not aware of our approach, let out frightened cries that augured badly for them on Judgement Day. They leapt up in panic and the equally panicked Hattie clutched onto them. They stood stupidly embracing each other in the middle of the deserted place, with the shadows of Properjohn and the Cross fixed above us all.

Properjohn's cackling laugh went through the atmosphere like streak lightning. We all stopped and looked sheepishly at each other. He came down from the stage shouting: 'Just a rehearsal. Just a little rehearsal.'

Ambrosia, her face drained, turned to me and whispered angrily: 'Never do that again. You frightened me out of my wits. For a minute I thought the old sod might be right after all.'

Ten

Our days had been warmed by the late-year sun, through a landscape that seemed to breathe deeply in its natural contentment. Trees losing their final leaves, as delicate as dandelion clocks in their autumn frailty; looking fulfilled and old and prepared for the temporary death of winter. We were framed by mountains too for most of these days; first the Blue Ridge Range, then the Smokies, striding along the landscape, near at one time, then withdrawing to their private distances; sharp at mid-morning, merging in turquoise with the sky at evening, a brief resting place for the rising moon.

The lives of the people we passed on our journey touched us also, for a moment. Amid the defensive islands of neon, Buzz's Heroburgers, Hawk's Wrecking Yard, Dr Pierce's Favorite Prescription, Bear's Grocery Stores, Tinker Mountain Antiques, the English Village Court Motel, Susie's Bakery (Positively no Loafing), amid all that in tubular lights, would be a slum of shacks and a fat Negro woman pulling up her stockings on her doorstep. Going by people's houses, perhaps when we were driving late, and seeing them in their evenings, sitting, rested perhaps or exhausted by their day, on verandah chairs, working among their garden flowers, walking their dogs in fields, eating a lamplit meal, or sitting in the deathly television glow. Sometimes when the houses were poor and near the road, and we had slowed in traffic, it was difficult not to feel the covetous guilt of a homeless eavesdropper.

One night when we were driving on to make up for a long lunch stop when the sun had been so benevolent that it was difficult to wake Properjohn from a deep, black-clothed sleep, we slowed at a crossing on the Norfolk and Western Railroad and from the front cabin of 'Jesus Lives' I looked into an orange-lit window and saw a young woman pulling a dress away from her body. She was standing in the light with her back to me, long black hair running over pale shoulders. I sat staring at her. When the dress was free of her body she flung it aside and stood naked-backed, allowing her fine hair to run through her hands like a rope. She must have enjoyed having that hair. I found I was a Peeping Tom once more, guiltily hoping she would turn around. Herbie saw her too from the driving seat of 'Jesus Loves' because I heard him brake suddenly as he followed us around the bend and he was irritable for the rest of the night.

Inside Tennessee, the weather changed. We awoke to a drizzling morning after the unfortunate fracas at the nightclub. Herbie did not apologize to anyone but we were satisfied enough to see him walk like a huge hunchback for several days, seeking to conceal the bottle-lump on the back of his head. My cheekbone was sore and bruised but this added effect to my new sorrowful expression which I used while at two Triumphal Entries into small towns on our route that day. If Winston was bruised, it did not show on him and the business was never mentioned again.

As we went on, the highway cutting through the tobacco fields and the small farms, poorer now, the clouds hung pot-bellied on the declining hills until they broke in a spectacular deluge that reminded Poor Clare of the last August Bank Holiday Monday before the war at Porthcawl. 'We all crowded in the shelters along the beach,' she recalled. 'Standing there with our sopping sandwiches and the rain running from our things and out into the street. But we had a bit of singing and this boy from Cardiff kissed me when we was jammed behind all the other people.'

'You didn't tell me about that,' said Properjohn with a nasty turn in his voice.

'You know we always went to Porthcawl on August Monday,' she said worriedly. 'We always did.'

'No,' he growled. 'This kissing business. You never told me that, Clare.'

'Oh, John,' she replied nervously. 'It was when I was eight years old, after all.'

'How old was he?' he said.

'About the same I suppose. Eight. I mean, he didn't mean any harm, John. I expect he only did it because it was raining and that.'

'Yes, I expect he did,' he said bitterly. 'I just think it's a great pity that we've been married all these years and you never thought to mention it before. And now you mention it in front of total strangers. I don't like to think we've got any secrets. Any skelingtons in our cupboard.' He said it like that too. Skelingtons.

He sulked for the rest of the morning until the sun came out and steamed the fields and Winston said that in these hills Davy Crockett was born. Properjohn began a little private mumble of the song. 'Good secular song, that,' he nodded at last. 'Lovely words.' He hummed it and sang a bit. 'I'd like to have one of those hats,' he said.

'Raccoon hats,' said Winston, grateful like the rest of us to have him out of his depression.

'Yes, yes,' agreed Properjohn. 'I like the thing that hangs down. I can never understand why they let it dangle at the back. If it's a wild front ear it should be at the front. Stands to reason.'

We hoped Winston would not say anything. He did not. Like the rest of us he was learning. Properjohn said: 'Born around here was he then, Davy Crockett?'

'Sure,' said Winston. 'Up in the mountain near Morristown.'

'There's a Morristown in Wales,' said Clare wistfully.

'Shut up,' said Properjohn sharply. 'We're talking about Davy Crockett.' He hummed a morsel of the tune again and then began to sing loudly: 'King of the Wild Front Ear'. We all joined in and sang it with him. There was nothing you could tell the man.

Now, along the road as we travelled, there were signs which said: 'Finger Lickin' Country Ahead', there were bridges over the watery wanderings of Cherokee Lake and the Tennessee River, there were shanties among the weeds and automobile dumps, short hills leapt along the horizon, and the Confederate flag flew outside Jolly Joe's Firework Company. We were in the South.

Properjohn, who was as pleased to see such towns and sign-posts as Salem, Damascus, Carthage, Lebanon, and Palestine, as Poor Clare was to see Cardiff and Newport, became very moved when we came upon huge painted banners, desecrating the country, and beseeching: 'See the Holy City at Ruby Falls.'

Winston muttered: 'That must be a real high mountain,' but Properjohn was pleased and said: 'I think we are coming to a very religious part of America.'

In most places we had a Triumphal Entry and service, a sermon and a collection before moving on. And it was at one of these that we became aware of the sly shadow of Oliver Jaye. Herbie spotted him in Sneedville and both Winston and I saw him in another town leaning against a shop saying 'Pistol Sales', his white face like some bleak overseer among the Negroes trudging through the chilly autumn leaves. He made no contact with us, but he was there and we knew he was watching.

'Maybe he thinks we'll steal the collection,' said Herbie on the night in Knoxville.

'Peanuts,' said Winston. 'He's not concerned with dimes. The money for this business comes from the big people, the rich folks – and there's plenty of 'em – who think the Helen J. Jaye Foundation for Christian Love has got the ticket concession for heaven. And I guess they think Oliver is the box office manager, because he takes the cheques. No, man, he's just making sure we're still on the road and we ain't gone over to the Baptist Union or nothing. This is a little showpiece, man, just to demonstrate that things are moving. We're showing the flag, showing that Cross. The churches who get dollars from the Foundation fall in behind and sing, every town we get to. And those that give the dough can see it's doing a *great* job. All those people, marching for Helen J. Jaye and Jesus J. Christ. It's in the newspapers and it's on television. It keeps the money rolling in.'

'I wish we could see it rolling our way,' grumbled Herbie. He glanced at me. He had a nasty criminal quirk.

'Why did we skip Washington?' I said to Winston.

'I tell you why we skipped Washington,' he answered. 'At least why I *think* we skipped Washington. Because there's a Congressional Committee on phoney religions, and their finances, sitting there right now, and if we had gone into Washington, or Baltimore, or any neighbouring place, toting that Cross and singing loud, they would have been out of the committee room and right on our trail, making note of every cent and every hallelujah. I guess Oliver J. Jaye wouldn't want that.'

I could see suspicion accumulating in the area above Herbie's whiskers once more. 'Boy, do you know a lot,' he said yet again. 'I just don't know how you know so much.'

'I just know things,' replied Winston. 'I'm bright – for a black man.'

We travelled on through Finger Lickin' Country, through the tobacco and into the cotton, from the hills into the flat lands with rivers engulfing woods and the trees standing hopelessly like men caught up to the knees in a quicksand. Each town had its shacks sitting on dust or mud, depending on the day's weather, and its separate clean suburbs of oleanders, lawns, barbecue spits, basketball nets, and miniature models of Negro jockeys grinning in front gardens. Each place spelled out its name proudly at its entrance road, with sometimes a list of churches as a sort of certificate of righteousness. And then the road would have to push its way through the inevitable gulch of used car lots, gas stations, tyre depots, wrecking yards, greasing, oiling, braking and breaking depots, so that each town seemed to have one sure industry, revolving around the short life and sudden death of the motor car.

In some places oily men crawled from beneath jacked-up vehicles like soldiers emerging from shell holes and bunkers, to watch our Triumphal Entry, the Cross and me, followed by our immediate entourage, then local clergy, bands, and gowned choirs. I thought that perhaps, in some way, the crusade was doing some good. I was doing my best with my sad faces and the way I carried the Cross, while Herbie loved acting up, and the response of Properjohn never fell below his own loud standards. Hattie was sure we were succeeding, lighting lamps, or at least candles, wherever we went as he said, and I thought that perhaps the sight of the Cross gave one or two people a jolt. I don't say that it made any man about to mount his neighbour's wife, stop, consider and then zip-up and walk away to his own wife, but at least it made him think.

I said so to Ambrosia. We did the shopping together sometimes, Properjohn delegating me to carry the load because he patently did not trust Herbie with his daughter, nor, for his own reasons, would he allow Winston to go with her although at times Hattie did. Poor Clare, he announced, must not be allowed to go into shops because she would only fritter her time away buying lipsticks and cheap magazines.

On this day it had been arranged that 'Jesus Loves' and 'Jesus Lives' would continue west to the outskirts of the next town and we would catch them up on the local bus. I enjoyed going shopping because it was a breath of freedom from the religious life we more or less had to observe, and I was able to leave my robe and my Cross behind because they would be awkward in supermarkets. Ambrosia was plump and sweet on these outings, as happy to be away for a while as I was, and pretending, I knew, that we were a young married couple shopping for the weekend. In one town she even attempted to imitate an American accent and to make me an accomplice in this. She liked playing games.

It was when we were together in the three-dollar rooming house that I told her I thought the crusade might be doing some good. I was sitting in a rough chair by the wash-basin and she was sitting on the bed. A few shreds of rainy afternoon sun came through the grubby curtains at the window. The town was Knoxville and, I remember, across the street was a sign saying 'Clapp Sales. Beauty Aids.'

'You what!' she exclaimed, sliding forward on the bed in my direction. 'You what?'

'Well,' I said, embarrassed at her reaction. 'It just seems to me that even if something is make-believe, all right – phoney, like this is, it *might* just do some good for one or two people. I mean, it *might* have the same effect as the *real* thing. After all they don't know it's *not* the real thing. Maybe there's somebody who wants a jolt to make them change for the better . . .' I trailed off because of the way she was looking at me.

'Jesus Christ,' she breathed unbelievingly, and then added sharply, 'and I don't mean *you*, Willy Turpin. You sound just like my old man, arch bloody hypocrite that he is.'

'You're not very charitable to him.'

'Why should I be?'

'Well, I know he's crackpot and suchlike, but he *is* your father . . .'

'Honour thy father and thy mother in the days of thy youth that thy days may be long in the land which the Lord thy God giveth thee,' she sneered. 'Love Daddy and Mum or you die.'

'I don't think he's that bad,' I said lamely. I wondered what we were doing in that grimy room. It was her idea.

'You haven't had the time to grow to hate him like I have,' she said. 'I've had seventeen years.'

'Listen,' I said, leaning forward so the ratty old chair creaked. The movement brought me abruptly close to her and I could smell her clean, quiet smell. 'Listen,' I repeated. I stopped again, suddenly choked by her nearness. Her face was half-grinning with the realization of what she was doing to me, straight into mine, her breasts were like a sweet parcel just below my nose.

'I'm listening,' she said more softly.

'Yes, well listen,' I warned irritably. 'I've seen you looking at him when he's up there preaching. Just like the rest of us. And you don't look like you hate him then. If you do you've got a bloody funny way of showing it.'

I had not been swearing very much during the crusade, and

yet I knew I had said bloody now to bring myself down to the level of that bed on which she was sitting so beautifully. Her skirt had gone up above her smooth, chubby knees. And it was a rainy afternoon in a room in Knoxville, with three hours to wait for the bus.

She was watching me closely but she pursued the conversation. 'I'm fascinated by the bastard,' she said flatly. 'I can't believe that there could be anyone like him, and that he could be *mine*. Sometimes I feel like a kid watching her father burgle a house.' She screwed up her shoulders and we said nothing for a minute or more. Then she said: 'It's cold. I always thought it would be warm in places like Tennessee. It's very chilly in here, isn't it? If you don't mind I think I'll get under the covers.'

In the manner of a child scrambling late into bed she went on all fours to where the doubtfully pink bedspread bulged with the pillows, pulled it aside and, having treated me to a prime view of the tops of her legs, her pants and her backside, turned and pushed herself between the sheets. Then she tugged the cover over her head and lay there lumpy as a corpse. I sat and watched her for a minute or more, saying nothing. It was very curious sitting there, like that. The sun had gone from the pallid window and I could hear it was raining again. Somebody had to say something.

'Do you really know what we're doing here?' I said quietly.

'I thought you'd never ask,' she said, muffled below the cover.

'Well *do* you?' I persisted. 'Sitting here on a wet afternoon in a crummy room in Knoxville, Tennessee, or wherever it is. It's almost beyond the limits of human imagination.'

She pulled the covers sharply away from her face. It was red, like it was when her father held her upside down. It must have been difficult to breathe in that bed. 'We're sitting here,' she replied with heavy sulkiness. 'Because it *is* a wet afternoon in rotten old Knoxville, Tennessee. And because the sodding bus doesn't go on to the next lousy town until five o'clock. I wasn't going to stand at the bus stop for three hours.'

I remained in the chair and she lay taut in the bed. It was like a doctor having an argument with a patient.

'We could have walked around the stores,' I said. 'Or gone to a museum.'

'I find it very difficult to spend three hours in Woolworth's,' she said tartly. 'And I can't stand museums. I've lived in a museum all my life.'

'They have cinemas here too,' I pointed out primly.

'My father doesn't like me going to the pictures with strange men,' she said.

'But you can come to a room with one!' I exploded. 'That's all right, isn't it?'

'This,' she huffed, 'is not a place of entertainment. And you can say that again. He doesn't like me going to places of entertainment with men. He's spelled that out. But he never mentioned rooms.' She was staring miserably at the ceiling. Then she said: 'I don't know why you're so worried anyway. I paid the three dollars. You didn't have to come in.'

'You said it was a place of shelter,' I argued shittily.

'It *is* a place of shelter,' she said. 'You're not getting wet are you? No wetter than you are already.'

I blazed with sudden, paltry fury, and went across the room and around the bed, so that I stood over her. 'Listen,' I almost spat. 'You *know* what would happen if we were found here together. Do you think anyone would believe we came in out of the rain? I thought we were going to sit in the lounge and watch television. I didn't want to come here.'

She stared at me. 'You,' she said, dragging the word out. 'You must be the biggest snot in the world. A snot, that's what you are, Turpin. A priggish, hypocritical snot!' I saw her eyes fill with tears. 'You really *believe* you're Jesus, I think, hanging onto that Cross, with a face like a fucking bloodhound.' She was trembling with the anger and her sadness now. 'And all the time you're just worried about your sodding bonus. That's all you're really concerned with.' She must have been lying exactly flat on her back because her tears began to run evenly both sides of her face.

'Don't cry,' I said. 'Stop crying, will you.'

'All right,' she promised. 'If you stop being a snot.'

'All right,' I nodded.

We were silent for a while, just remaining there. Then she

said: 'You didn't really think we were coming in this place to watch television, did you?' It was almost a plea. I had believed nothing of the sort. As she had brought me into that three-dollar place, I knew where we were going, right enough. I knew. But I just suspended everything and let it happen, in the knowledge that whatever occurred it was not my fault. She was right about me. I was a snot. Silvie would have understood.

'I'm sorry,' I said dully. 'I didn't mean that at all. I seem to need an excuse for everything.'

'Me too,' she sniffed. 'The trouble is I'm a bit slow in thinking them up. I can't even think of a good excuse for us being here now. Not even the rain. Is it still raining, Willy?'

I got up and went to the window. I felt like James Cagney or Bogart, holed up in a cheap room, watching for the gang coming to get him. 'Still coming down,' I said, staring out at Clapp's Beauty Aids. 'There's nobody in the street.'

'They're all in three-dollar rooms,' she giggled. Her voice was still wet from her crying.

'Somehow it never occurs to you that it rains abroad just like it does at home,' I said still looking down. 'It's as wet and cold out there as March in Manchester. Tennessee always sounds warm and rivery and full of the smell of flowers.'

'That's nice,' she said. I could hear her fidgeting and I thought she might be wriggling out of her clothes. 'You say some very unusual things sometimes. Are you any good as a writer?'

'If I was I wouldn't be doing a long-distance haulage job with that Cross,' I said. '*I* think I can write, but I'm in the minority. And the jobs I get, like writing brochures for pesticides and wickerwork furniture, don't really lend themselves to a lot of poetic stuff. The wickerwork isn't so bad, but pesticides give you no room at all.'

She had stopped fidgeting and I turned and went over to the bed and sat on her side of it. My leg went against hers with the blankets between. Her pretty, round face was fixed on mine, her eyes smudged with her tears. I knew that she was naked now beneath the covers and I had to do something. I reached out with one friendly finger and touched her chin.

A quick, brief, memory came to me about the night I

watched her in the inn at Bethlehem. Now her fingers emerged from beneath the bedclothes like raiding parties on the flanks of a hidden army. They came up each side of her and curled around the top rim of the bedclothes. Then quietly and unfussily, as though she were making the bed, she turned the covers down in a broad fold and showed her pale staring breasts. I recognized them immediately. And I was glad to see them again.

'Hello,' I said. 'What have we here?'

'Snot,' she smiled. 'You know very well what they are.'

I could almost hear that Cross clattering down the concrete stairs to hell, and my bag of dollars falling after it. I put the flat of my tongue against one nipple, holding it there as though lost in thought while licking a postage stamp. I heard her head go back and a brief gasp come from her. I leaned across her, taking her other breast in both my hands and squeezing it until it bulged. Then I laid my tongue against that too.

When I rose I saw that her head was flung back hard against the wooden bedhead and her eyes were clenched. 'Do that again, Willy,' she muttered. 'Please, for Christ's sake. I want to get used to it.'

I let her wait for a moment while I got out of my clothes. I had almost forgotten what an erection looked like. She opened her eyes and saw what I was about. When I was stripped she put out both podgy hands and caught me by the tool and coaxed me back towards her.

'I've wanted this,' she said, squinting down at it. 'I've wanted it like mad.'

'I've wanted you to have it,' I said. I lolled over her again and lapped at her blind nipples.

'I'm fat,' she whispered as if she had suddenly found out.

'Puppy fat,' I reassured her, lying my cheek against her breasts as though they were pillows. 'You're young and pretty and podgy.'

'Do you like that?'

'Yes. I think I'm going to.'

'Are you a dirty old man.'

'Well, I hope to be some day. I'm only twenty-five at the moment.'

'That's right, I forgot. I suppose I have a fantasy about older men.'

I was going to blame her father, but for once I kept my mouth shut. Now I kissed her on the lips, a fresh, sweet-smelling experience, her fine hair touching my forehead and my eyes and nose as I leaned in to her. I drew back and regarded her. The face was very tight and pale, the eyes glittering and fixed on me. Her shoulders were white and puffy and her arms the same. Lying as she was, flat on her back, her breasts sat up firmly, slightly spreading at the bottom, but evenly. She saw how I was examining them. 'Are they all right?' she asked anxiously, as though it were a medical problem.

'They look all right to me,' I replied.

'My father took me to a sea captain's house once, in Cardiff,' she said chattily. 'And this man had a pair of ship's decanters on his sideboard. They're very broad and round at the bottom – so they don't tip over in a storm – and they taper up to the stopper. More or less like my tits. And my old man kept looking at them in a really funny way, until, in the end, he couldn't stand it any longer and he asked this captain to put one of them on another table. Just to separate them. I was thirteen then and even then I could see what he meant.'

'Well, let's keep this pair together,' I said, kissing them again.

'Why don't you come into bed?' she suggested encouragingly. 'I promise not to charge you half the rent. It's warm now. Well, this side is. Look, I'll move over to the cold bit and you can have this side. I wouldn't like you to get a chill now that I've got you.'

The suggestion of conquest, of permanence, inherent in the remark occurred to me uncomfortably. I had forgotten there were another thousand miles to travel. But she was holding back the bedclothes for me to climb in and the white body was lying sheathed there. I went in beside her. She was like a warm lozenge. We embraced softly at first and then in earnest, almost crushing each other, my thin bones against her comfortable podginess. Her hands went to my thing.

'I bet you don't know what that is,' I said.

'I could make a wild guess,' she said.

She felt enjoyable. Velvet warm from the bed, smooth skinned, with wobbly parts that trembled and moved as my hands moved over her. Her stomach was like a quivering pudding but her backside was compact and her legs felt firm. Her pussy hair was as curled and splendid in texture as the hair on her head. Her bosom stood like a rounded rampart between her face and her belly. From the moment I had crawled in with her she had not let go of my root. Both hands were holding it like a cook grasping the handle of a particularly hot and important saucepan. And she was not gentle either. She was squeezing it like fury and the more my explorations excited her the tighter she squeezed.

'Do you think you could relax a trifle on my cock?' I eventually inquired. 'You're not trying to get the last drop of toothpaste out of a tube, you know.'

She glanced at me anxiously, then laughed and let go. 'I just wanted to make sure it didn't escape,' she said. She cuddled closer in an almost wifely fashion. 'I think we can have a lot of fun, Willy, don't you?'

'Let's try,' I said ambiguously. I eased her legs apart and began. It was very simple. We slid together easily, bringing a sweet gasp from her and a sharp memory suddenly returned for me. Sex is like taste, for me; I can never remember precisely what it's like until the next time.

Once we were joined we did not move, but lay there engulfed in each other, her flesh holding me, accommodating me, sticking to me, everywhere. It was curiously as though, having got this far we did not know the next stage. I made a cautious move, feeling her belly's rubbery rubbing against me, pushing me away, and then retreating as I went in again.

'Don't,' she whispered. 'Steady on for a minute, love. It's been a year and a week for me and I want to get used to it being there. The bus doesn't go for more than two hours.'

'We'll get on the bus,' I said. 'What do you mean a year and a week?'

'I bet you thought I'd never done it,' she said. 'Go on, you did, didn't you? You thought I was trying to unload my virginity on you?'

'No, no,' I lied. 'Not like that. I thought you were, though.'

'When I had it,' she said reflectively, 'my virginity, I couldn't wait to get shot of it. I didn't just want to lose the bloody thing – I wanted to trample on it.'

'I must admit, I thought you were,' I said.

'I'm a second time around virgin,' she said. 'I was, then I wasn't, then I was again, and now I'm not again, thank God. I've had it and I've not had it. Having it is better.'

'Do you want it now?' I inquired. 'I don't think I can lie still like this for long.' I am inclined to get on with things.

'Yes, now,' she decided. 'You can do it to me now, love. I'm ready.'

Some women are thin screws, some are loose screws, some tight, some expansive. I've known women who needed a whole bedroom to perform, bed, floor, wall, dressing-table, stool, washbasin, and window sill. Others have been neat and compact, economical in every movement. There was a girl at BBC Television once who would have fucked comprehensively on a matchbox. But Ambrosia was the first I had ever known to do it in absentia. From the moment I began to move she simply was not there. Her body was doing all the things, indeed half a dozen at the same time, but emotionally she had gone, departed. I leaned up on my hands and wrists and looked down at her. Her eyes were screwed up, like they were that solitary night of hers in Bethlehem, and her face was shut. Her body was moving rapidly, with mine, and those big breasts, dodging from side to side now seemed to be following me around. Then I realized that she had taken herself back to that room in Bethlehem, and a hundred lone rooms before that, and was doing it herself. I was merely a substitute for masturbation! She had, as they say in America, a lot of things going for her. But I wasn't one of them.

Her climax was volcanic while I came only as a sort of courtesy. We lay quietly, sweating, after that and I retreated down her body and the bed until I was curled up in the vicinity of her accommodating stomach. I felt her wake and she looked at me over the top of her breasts with an expression that said, for sure, 'Are you still here.'

'Lovely,' she whispered. 'Really lovely, Willy. I feel so satisfied.'

'You may be more than satisfied,' I said from my place against her belly. 'You may be pregnant.'

'Ah,' she said, still softly. 'Having a little worry down there are we? That's betting after the race, Willy.' Her hand came down to my head and touched me as if in thanks for my modest assistance. 'Don't think about it,' she said. 'The first thing I did when I knew I was coming on this trip was to get myself on the pill. I had to go miles by bus to Cardiff to get them too. Everybody in our valley knows who takes the pill. We've got a mouthy chemist. They used to be pointed out in the street.'

'That's what I call foresight,' I said. I moved up the bed towards the pillows. Our bodies were still sweating and we slithered together like a couple of lizards. I lay beside her on the pillow and her puffy arm came around my neck in a companionable half-lock.

'I meant to have it,' she said. 'I was determined. I wanted to pull more over here than the strings of Sprott's autoharp, I can tell you.'

'You're amazing,' I said, meaning it. 'You look so angelic.'

She laughed out loud. 'That's a good one coming from you, of all people,' she said.

I saw what she meant. 'I suppose you're right. None of us is what we're acting out, are we? Not one.'

'Winston is,' she said. 'Unless he turns out to be a secret Chinese. He just knows it's a job. We're all selling something we don't believe in.'

I remembered Oliver Jaye had said that. 'That's what I was trying to say before,' I answered. 'The thing is we might be selling it as good as, or better than, some people who truly mean it. Perhaps it's no good real Christians trying to sell Christianity because they're too close to it. Maybe it *needs* people like us.'

'I think that's why my father is so good at it,' she agreed. 'He's a hypocrite, but a *true* hypocrite, if you see what I mean. He really *means* all the things he says, but he doesn't believe them.'

'Never stops acting, does he,' I said.

'Never. And, God, he's so vain. Do you know, Willy, he burst into tears a few days ago when he saw a picture of an American archbishop or somebody in one of those magazines. And do you know why? I'll tell you why, because this archbishop looked so young it made him feel old.'

'It's supposed to be policemen who make you feel like that,' I said. 'But he got his own back, didn't he? Pinching the archbishop's sermon.'

'That's right,' she said unsurprised that I knew. 'It was while he was cribbing bits out from the magazine that he saw the picture.' She paused as though debating something. She decided. 'I'll tell you another thing,' she said. 'But not a word to anybody. If you tell then I'll tell my dad you raped me. Is that agreed?'

'You've found my weak spot,' I said. 'Tell me.'

'His name's not really Properjohn,' she whispered. 'He just called himself that when he started in Christianity. He thought it sounded right.'

I was surprised, but only said: 'He thought it would look good in lights?'

'That's it. When he was a singer with the band at Aberavon he was called Johnny Jerome. I've seen some of the old pictures and bits from the local papers. But his real surname is just John, a good old ordinary Welsh name. His Christian name is John too. John John. His dad didn't have a lot of imagination, although he always swore that he just repeated the surname for the registrar because he thought he was deaf. And the man put it down twice.'

'The origin of surnames. Theology,' I mused lying close to her. 'The things people talk about after sex.'

That appeared to remind her of something. Her other hand slid down to the joint of her legs and she began to move her fingers. 'I wish this was a better room,' she said wistfully. 'A room like that one in the old inn at Bethlehem. Remember that? With the big old bed in the middle?'

I said I remembered it.

'That was nice,' she said, as though re-relishing a steak and kidney pudding she had once eaten. 'I loved that place. I have a sort of fantasy where I meet a lover in a room like that, all cobwebs and dust and moonlight, and we dance and then he puts me on the bed and screws me something wicked.'

Her fingers were working more quickly now. I lay unemployed for a moment then I put my own hand there and took her hand away. 'Let me help you out with that,' I said.

Her warm, wet fingers guided mine to the place and I carried on where she had left off. I had never done that before. It was quietly exciting and selfishly unselfish, giving a nice feeling of sacrifice. I really enjoyed doing it and watching the brightening expression on her young face. 'Quicker, quicker now,' she asked me at the end, and I did. The effect was amazing. We had a second-hand washing machine once that used to leap up and down on its base when it was spin-drying and this is how Ambrosia went. She lay there panting her life away when it was done while I lay and smiled at her. She recovered sufficiently to kiss me.

'I'm sorry I said you were a snot,' she murmured. 'You really are a good sport.'

Despite the fact that the bus only ran at wide intervals we were the sole passengers when it left Knoxville. We went to the seat at the back. Eventually two nuns and a garage mechanic with a monkey wrench, who appeared to be travelling together, sat in the front and we set off.

'I had a baby once,' said Ambrosia conversationally as we were going from the soaked city to the rain-sodden country. I suppose my expression said enough as I turned to her.

'Boy or girl?' I said.

'It never got that far,' she muttered. 'It wasn't a baby, really, it was an abortion.'

'That's why you went to Bristol?' I said.

'You're good at remembering things,' she said. 'I suppose that's why you're a writer. Bristol, that's right. My mam came with me and we got shot of it.'

'Your mother? God, I'm amazed.'

'Spent all her savings on it,' she said.

'She must love you.'

'No. But she loves my father. She didn't want him to know.'

'And he doesn't?'

'Of course not. He'd cut my throat. Especially as it was one of the visiting lay preachers. Good name for that one, too. Lay preacher. I was fifteen and I was in bed with streaming flu, head, runny nose, temperature. The full house. And this man, he's in his thirties, was staying with us while he was preaching in the various chapels around about. And one morning when dad and mam were out he came in with a bowl of creamed rice pudding. "Ambrosia for Ambrosia," he says all kiddishly. It was that Ambrosia stuff they advertise on the telly. He insists on spooning it to me and before I knew what was going on he was spooning something else to me too.'

'Christ,' I said aghast. 'What a thing to do.'

'That's what he said,' she replied. 'But we'd done it anyway and I enjoyed it like mad. For a kick-off it cleared up my flu. And I kept following him around to get some more. Every time he spoke at one of the chapels in the district, or even some way away, I'd be there in the front pew waiting for him to finish with God and start on me. Brynglas, Pontyllewellyn, Dinas, Mountain Oak, all over the place. We even had it once in a disused pigsty behind the minister's house at Cwm-Corner. I think that was the day I actually got it. The old man was pleased as hell I was going to all these meetings and services. He really thought I had got the message. Then I realized that I *had* got it and I told my mam.'

The bus passed 'Jesus Lives' and 'Jesus Loves' parked in a muddy clearing at the side of the road. We got out at the next stop and began to walk back through the drizzle. 'We'll do it again, won't we?' she said with sudden anxiety. I nodded and she grinned, 'You might as well be crucified for a sheep as a lamb.'

Eleven

'Say, what was with you in Knoxville yesterday? What was going on there?'

'Shopping,' I said.

Thin slices of fog drifted about us as we walked towards Nashville with the Cross. We went past a hoarding which said: 'Visit the Lost Sea'.

'I know – you went to visit the Lost Sea,' persisted Herbie. He could be an annoying bastard at times.

'I told you we went shopping.' I had to call over to him because I was around the wrong side of the Cross, as usual, with my head next to the stoically tramping Winston, his small wet head poking like some bleak tortoise from his plastic raincape. Winston took on a very miserable appearance when he was wet and he did not talk much.

'Shopping,' I repeated to Herbie when I had got the Cross on the other shoulder. I swear it was getting heavier. I don't know whether it just felt like that as the miles of our journey went on or whether the rain of those few days had been soaking into the balsawood again.

'Six hours for ten dollars worth of groceries,' mused Herbie. He wasn't looking at me, but face forward into the mist and drizzle like an explorer expecting, at any moment, the vision of a new land.

'Could I help it if there's only a bus twice a day?' I said. 'We just had to kill time.'

'You didn't visit the Lost Sea, then?'

'No, we didn't visit the Lost bloody Sea!'

'Steady, Jesus,' he warned sideways, blowing a little channel in his beard as he did so. He nodded ahead and I saw a man and a woman standing at the gate of a small wooden house staring at our approach. 'Stea-dy,' said Herbie again. 'Fix that look of humility, man. We don't want folks seeing the Lord saying wicked words to St Peter, do we now?'

I dropped my face professionally and Herbie treated them to a brief blessing, like a motorist's hand signal, as we tramped by.

'Where y'headin'?' asked the man.

'Nashville,' called Winston dolefully from my other side. He always handled situations which he regarded as within his function of giving information.

'They won't know you there,' said the woman enigmatically.

We trudged on. I hoped the interruption would have stemmed Herbie's curiosity, but I knew it would not. 'Six hours for ten bucks worth of groceries,' he whistled. 'That's choosy shopping.'

'Listen, you prize berk,' I said. 'If you want to know, we went to the pictures, to the movies, but it has to be kept quiet because Properjohn won't let her go into a cinema with a man.'

'What did you see?' he asked briskly like a detective. 'What movie?'

'Oh, come on,' I breathed angrily. 'What's it matter? What are you getting at?'

'Slow down, pal,' he said, flapping his hand quietly at me. 'I wanted to know about the movies in Knoxville. Is that so bad?'

'*Curse of the Mummies*,' I blurted.

'Wow,' he grinned. 'That picture sure gets around. It must follow you. Remember you told me you saw it in Bonapart's in New York. In the waiting room.'

'I knew I'd seen it somewhere before,' I muttered. Christ, how I hated him sometimes.

The arrival behind us of 'Jesus Loves' and 'Jesus Lives' stopped any further embarrassment. The volunteer drivers had picked them up a mile or so back and now they stopped and we were joined by the Properjohns and the Reverend Hatt for the Triumphal Entry into Nashville.

'A big welcome awaits us!' Properjohn bawled in our direction. I allowed myself one look at Ambrosia but she did not return it. She was plucking short snatches on the autoharp and Poor Clare was banging the spit from her harmonica on the front off-side wheel of 'Jesus Lives'.

Someone had to answer Properjohn. 'What about the rain?' I called. 'That's not going to help.'

'It's been arranged!' he called excitedly. 'Mass prayers yesterday and again this morning for a change in the weather. The sun will be out when we get there.'

It was too. Open mouthed we saw the prophecy fulfilled before our eyes, the clouds obediently peeling away, the mist retreating to holes and crevices in the Cumberland River valley, and a steamy sun bright over the land and the approaching city.

He was right about the welcome too. The river bridge was crowded with gowned choristers and spectators. There was a uniformed band with a sousaphone semaphoring in the vivid sunshine. People hung from the windows of the Post Office, the Courthouse, and the headquarters of the Baptist Sunday School Union. On the river a tugboat captain gave his hooter a toot as I bore the Cross over the bridge and into the town. It was midday and the lunchtime people were crammed on the sidewalks, under the trees. We had rid ourselves of our plastic raincapes outside the town and in my travel-weary robe and my broken-down Dolcis casuals I honestly looked the nearest thing to the real Jesus you are ever likely to come across in this world. It was the best Triumphal Entry we had experienced, and the biggest.

Herbie was enjoying himself too, measuring up the young girl choristers as though it were a slave market. Hattie was handing out his pamphlets like a sower scattering grain. I saw several people wearing hats they had made from them for the sun was extraordinarily strong for the time of the year. We halted on the riverbank after crossing the bridge and there seemed to be hundreds gathered around. There were television cameras on platforms, and Winston was skimming busily around talking to newspapermen. Then, through the crowd, like a rat emerging from a nice cake, came Oliver J. Jaye.

This was a smiling, expansive, Oliver J. Jaye, his tombstone face wreathed with happiness. Happiness must have been a difficult accomplishment for such a man and I could, that day, imagine him actually composing his face somewhere on the fringe of the crowd, pushing a bit up here and a bit there, making it up into something approaching a glad thing, before coming through the crowd and the choristers. His arms were flapping as though he were learning to fly and Properjohn's big bladed arms began to flap too as the two sombre frauds advanced on each other like the reunion of long-parted twin crows.

'Praise! Praise! Praise!' shouted Properjohn.

'Glory! Glory! Glory!' bellowed Oliver.

'My ass, my ass, my ass,' Herbie breathed next to me.

But for all the people around, the people who did not know, who had just come out of curiosity or Christianity or the fact that their neighbourhood church was due for its subsidy, it was a joyous moment. On some emotional impulse Poor Clare began to play 'God Save The Queen' with great gusto, was joined immediately by Ambrosia's harp, and was then drowned by the Nashville band's 'Anchors Aweigh'.

Properjohn and Oliver lashed themselves about each other in an embrace that would have left most of the great screen lovers to shame. It was a scene overflowing with emotion, from the crowd and from our own party and followers. The Reverend Hatt, a pile of his pamphlets like a prayer mat under his knees, was crouched to one side, hands together, despatching words to Heaven like a telegraphist. When the crowd surged forward towards the two leaders it thoughtlessly engulfed him, treading over him in its cheerful blindness. In Ambrosia's eyes I saw the bright splintering of tears as she watched the emotive scene. There was no doubt. She was crying. The whole family were *real* hypocrites.

There was a furious swopping of Praises and Glories going on between Properjohn and Oliver, who had now stepped back from each other but continued to shout alternately like rowdy bidders at a cattle auction. Winston was laughing and shaking hands with a man wearing earphones. The Reverend Hatt was crawling awkwardly from between the uncaring legs of the girl choristers and Herbie was watching covetously. Poor Clare was pretending to play 'Anchors Aweigh' with the band, but her hopeless lips were nibbling an inch from the harmonica holes. Ambrosia was bent with happy emotion over her harp. I stood holding the Cross in the way a man might hold a signpost when he felt lost.

'People!' howled Oliver J. Jaye above all the noise. 'Dear People.' The band and the tumult stopped at once.

There was no doubt he had presence. 'Dear People of Nashville, Tennessee.' A huge cheer burst from them and sent river birds flying panic stricken downstream. It was as though, after years of doubt, someone had, at last, fixed the town's geographical location. 'Dear People of Nashville,' he repeated. 'Tennessee.' He was standing on tiptoe, a big man stretching up to shout across their heads. His difficulty brought forward a quick and astonishing demonstration of regard and agility. Five young coloured men ran forward, all in white slacks and white vests with the name of some church on them, and, kneeling before him, formed a human platform upon which he could stand. He had the sense of public relations to take his shoes off first, but he stood on their backs and balanced there to a further storm of cheering that caused the river birds, who had been over-confidently drifting back towards the bridge, to turn about and hare downstream again.

'People,' called Oliver again, wobbling on the young men's backs. 'I don't know how long I can stand up here . . .' Great laughter came at this, including some from the young men forming the platform, the latter quickly silenced by the unsteadying effect it was having on the man on their backs.

Judging by his anxiously dropped glances, it was the sensation of shifting beneath his feet that prompted Oliver to get on with what he had to say. 'People of Nashville,' he said for the third time. 'Tennessee. I bring you greetings in the name of Our Lord, from the Helen J. Jaye Foundation for Christian Love.'

'Our greetings back, sir,' called a man from the congregation, someone obviously the Helen J. Jaye Foundation had well pleased or well paid. The words were crowned by further spontaneous cheering. I glanced at the river birds, but they were warily circling the distant bank.

Oliver Jaye glanced uncertainly down at his human platform and shifted like a skater worried about the ice. 'Today,' he continued, 'we come to your fair city carrying the Cross of Jesus and we hope this demonstration will impress you with its simplicity . . .'

'And cheapness,' Winston muttered by my ear.

'This little charade . . .'

'Good word,' whispered Winston.

'. . . parade, is brought to you by our friends in Christ from across the mighty ocean deep – The Reverend John C. Properjohn, his wife and his daughter, from Wales.' His waved hands encompassed the Properjohn family, although the gestures were curtailed in the cause of keeping his balance. 'An Englishman, William Turpin, who carries the Cross with prayer and humility . . .' I bowed briefly, having been caught by surprise by the introduction, although afterwards I thought I might have done something a bit more impressive.

'And . . . three of our fellow Americans.' He nodded at the Reverend Hatt, whose blush was visible even in the mid-day sunlight, at Herbie, who treated them to his holy nod. Then he carefully pointed out Winston who merely acknowledged the introduction with a wave like a small, modest, boxer.

Oliver Jaye then launched into a lurid version of our journey, the crowds and the conquests; a Path of Light, he called it, sweeping across America, bringing love and illumination to millions. He seemed to have become accustomed to his circus rider position by now, shifting his weight as the boys in the platform shifted, and the length and trend of his sermon was only briefly interrupted when one of the crouching boys below his feet was caught with a fit of gasps and had to be removed. This was done neatly. Officials helped the youth to back out on his hands and knees and a new volunteer was quickly inserted like a brick in a wall without Oliver Jaye having to get down at all.

When Oliver had completed his harangue Properjohn was invited to take his place, but extraordinarily declined, a decision which brought a look of gratification from the platform boys and a nasty scowl from Oliver. Properjohn contented himself with standing on tiptoe and announcing that the big service would be there on the riverbank that night at six o'clock. There were some hymns sung after this and a thorough collection before the people dispersed and we retreated to the enclosure of 'Jesus Loves'.

We sat around uncomfortably on beds and stools, Ambrosia perched on her bunk up somewhere near the roof, while Oliver Jaye sat down heavily, his smile wiped away by his normal thick grimace. We sat silently for a while as though we were waiting for someone to deal the cards.

'Properjohn,' grunted Jaye eventually. 'Why did you decline to address those people? For God's sake what's the matter with you?'

'I've got a hole in my sock,' said Properjohn plaintively.

Herbie, Winston, Ambrosia and I each looked at the next one in a rough circle, as though trying to pass around the severe temptation to laugh.

'A hole in your sock?' growled Oliver disbelievingly. 'A HOLE IN YOUR SOCK!' Foul anger was crammed in his face now. Poor Clare's bevelled lower lip began to tremble and I thought she was going to explode with weeping. Hattie looked as though he was trying to think up quick private prayers.

'Yes,' nodded Properjohn nervously. 'That's right, Mr Jaye. A hole. You see, if I was going to stand on those darkies' backs like you did I would have had to take my boots off, wouldn't I? And I couldn't do that because I knew that my big toe is sticking through my sock and everyone would have witnessed it.'

Poor Clare did begin to cry now, tears seaming her funnelled face. And as she cried she sobbed: 'My fault, Mr Jaye, my fault.'

'Stop her,' Jaye ordered Properjohn, as though it was a matter of turning a knob. 'Stop her.'

'Stop it, woman,' snarled Properjohn at his wife. Clare tried; she shuddered like a truck braking hard. She appeared to have succeeded, and raised her red, ruined face to look at us all again, with those terrible lost eyes and the awful missing jawbone. But the effect of our stares was only to start her off into a great jelly of tears again, uncontrollable, gushing out, with her guilty words: 'My fault . . . my fault . . .' fighting to get out like drowning men in a torrent.

'QUIT!' Oliver Jaye abruptly rounded on her and bellowed fully in her face: 'QUIT THE SQUAWKING!'

There was a swift, angry movement from overhead and there was Ambrosia in her bunk, her expression scarlet, poised as though about to drop her considerable weight on his upturned face. 'Don't you speak to my mother like that, you two-bit vulture,' she threatened. I liked the 'two bit' part. It's strange in America how quickly one picks up their idioms. Oliver's mouth fell open. His gaunt finger pointed towards her in the manner of one who has spotted a devil in the rafters.

'I mean it,' she spat at him. 'If you bully that man there, or these here, I don't care. I know what sort of men they are.' She took us all in with one contemptuous swivel. 'But if you shout at my mother again I'll come down there and pull your great big nose until it's twice as long as it is now, and that's saying something, mate.'

There was a vacuum of amazed silence. Then: 'Mate!' howled Oliver Jaye. 'Mate!' The term apparently shocked him more than the interruption or the threat contained in it. 'Mate!'

'Don't call Mr Jaye, mate,' said Properjohn feebly at the girl.

'Not mate, not mate,' sobbed Poor Clare into her red hands. 'My fault, my fault. I'll darn it. I will . . . I promise.'

Ambrosia was hanging out of her bunk in the attitude of a sloth from a tree. 'Listen,' she told him. 'You need us more than we need you, mister. You just watch your step or when we do one of those sickening television shows again I might take it into my head to throw up over the piano. Do you get that? And let's see how *that* would look in the papers.'

Amazingly Oliver did get it. She was threatening, talking a language he understood, I suppose. He rose hurriedly: 'I'm getting out of here,' he announced. 'I don't feel safe.' He went to the door and we thought he was about to close it on the crusade. But he said: 'That meeting tonight had better be a wow,' and then went out. So we were still in business.

'We can't do this every afternoon.'

'It's only when we do the shopping.'

'But it will cost you a fortune. Even at three dollars a room. I haven't got any money at all. Herbie and I borrow from Winston.'

'That's all right. I cheat with the shopping money. Who is going to know?'

'This is a terrible room,' I said. 'Worse than Knoxville.'

'It's not meant to be the Ideal Home Exhibition,' she said. 'Close your eyes and just see what's in the bed.'

'I know what's in the bed.'

'Love, can you find it?'

'I'm searching.'

'I know. Is that right?'

'You should know.'

She giggled. 'It feels nice there. Just leave it like that. Just touching.'

'I don't know whether I can keep it like this – only with the snout in.'

'Try. See how long we can stand it.'

'Games, now.'

'Let's have a talk. I'd like to talk with it just resting there, peeping in.'

'All right. What would you like to talk about?'

'You start,' she suggested. 'Better make it something of sort of general interest, not sex or it might start us off. I think we can stay here a long time like this.'

'Well, this is of general interest. Herbie twigged that we were up to something in Knoxville.'

'Oh God, he would.' She was disturbed. 'Dirty old smutty Herbie. What did you tell him?'

'I said we went to the cinema.'

'Oh no, that's almost as bad as saying we went to bed, you fool. If my dad finds out I went to the pictures with you . . .'

'Listen, I had to tell him something. He won't say anything. He's my pal, and anyway I've got too much on him.'

'Like what?'

'I'm not telling you.'

'All right. Keep it. What film did we see then? I ought to know.'

'*Curse of the Mummies.*'

'That's appropriate.'

'Sorry, it was the first thing that came into my head.'

'Do you want to start now?' she said.

'Try and leave it there a bit longer. You must admit it's new.'

'It's nearly all new to me, Willy. I don't know much about it, yet. Remember that. Just one lonely lay preacher in the Welsh hills. He knew one position only and so did I. Fortunately the same one.'

'It's what they call the Missionary Sandwich,' I said.

'That's why he knew it, I expect. Very effective it was. Very.'

'It must be terrible having a father you can't go to when you're in trouble.'

'Don't be so bloody pious. Millions of fathers don't even know their daughters have monthlies. My old man would think I was talking about *Home Notes* or *Woman's World*.'

'Yes, I suppose he would. Can I put it in now?'

'Wait a bit, can't you?'

'I remember feeling like this when I was the last in the queue outside a cinema when I was a kid, and wondering if I was ever going to get in.'

'You'll get in, don't worry, even if you have to stand.' I don't think she meant it as a joke because she didn't laugh, but said: 'What were we talking about?'

'Your father.'

'Yes. He ought to have had a dog not a daughter. At one time he was doing all the little girl stuff with me, you know, my lovely little daughter and all that. This was in the days when he used to dangle me upside down for fun.'

'Those days haven't gone yet,' I pointed out.

'They have. The next time, I kill him. No, he was doing this lovesy-wovesy thing and he said, "Ambrosia, if ever you are in trouble, my darling, anywhere in the world, and whatever the trouble is, you just pick up the phone".'

'That's reasonable,' I said. 'What any father might say.'

'Yes, but he told me to phone the bloody police.'

I laughed and she did too. 'What could you do with him?' she said. 'He's just mad.'

'I thought you had gone mad today,' I said. 'Having a go at Jaye like that.'

'I wondered when you'd bring that up. What did you expect me to do when he was shouting at my mother? That poor cow has enough to put up with anyway, without him. And all you lily-faced buggers sitting there, not saying a word.'

'You didn't give anybody a chance.'

'Rats. You wouldn't have said anything. You're too worried about your bonus. You're good for nothing – well just one thing and you'd better start getting on with that.'

'If you put it like that I won't bother.'

'Oh, don't say that, Willy. I was only joking. And I've paid for the room after all. Come on, darling, don't disappoint me now. I look forward to it.'

Afterwards while we lay and let our sweat cool, she asked: 'Are you still looking for your wife?'

'Yes,' I said.

'I hope you never find her,' she said.

Twelve

Our Grand Evening Rally at Nashville attracted seven people, three of whom went home when the rain became too heavy. The rain began in the late afternoon, no fragile drizzle this time but an uncompromising deluge that had the Cumberland River gurgling like a glutton below the bridge. We stood pathetically in our green plastic raincapes, while the congregation, four of them covered by a single tarpaulin sheet, chewed at a few damp hymns. The sheet quickly swelled with a great belly of water over the heads of the three men and a woman who held it. It hung between them like an imminent pregnancy.

Oliver Jaye had returned and sat in his chauffeured car, his face framed in the window like a disagreeable portrait. After a few minutes he left, the jerk which carried the car away a testimony of his ill-tempered instruction to the driver. We were left praying while God bucketed water down upon us. No one had the heart to take a collection.

'We've got to do something,' muttered Properjohn from the crinkled recesses of his green rainhood. It was as though he spoke from the centre of a wet cabbage. 'We can't just give in. Not like that. Come on, boys, let's have a march.'

So, to cheer him up, we had a march, down the inevitable Broadway that streamed with water on its steep descent. Two pessimistic people stood by the door of the Broadway Barn which advertised 'The Biggest Square Dance In The World' presumably doomed, if no others turned up, to become the smallest square dance in the world. A man regarded us from beneath a cowboy hat from the entrance of an establishment exhibiting a Cadillac and a notice 'See The Car That Hank Williams Died In', while a waxworks invited us to view life-sized figures, fully dressed in their own clothes. Souvenir and music shops, each blaring a different country and western record into the rainy street, were lit gaudily in the galloping dusk, and a photographer's place suggested 'Blow Yourself Up To Poster Size'.

But then, quite suddenly, there were people, hurrying through the rain or lined in cars, waiting for a turn into a side street. Our procession became spectators, trying to fix where the cavalcade was heading.

'It's a church!' cried Properjohn, the power of his exclamations sending a cascade of rain from his garments. 'What a cheek – it's a church!'

'It's a dry church,' I pointed out.

'It's a Saturday,' said Ambrosia.

'It's a synagogue,' suggested Herbie.

'It's the Opry,' said Winston.

'Opry?' said Properjohn. 'Opera?'

'Opera, Opry,' said Winston.

'In a church,' breathed Properjohn.

We advanced along the street, collecting scant attention from the people hurrying through the rain. They seemed to be all white. 'Country and western music,' sniffed Winston, strangely caustic. 'Truck driver stuff.'

'The Grand Ole Opry,' smiled Herbie with a quaint smile of patriotic discovery. 'Nashville.'

'Tennessee,' muttered Ambrosia.

'In a church,' muttered Properjohn.

It was a church. Or it had been. The familiar big chapel, red brick and pointed windows. Properjohn advanced on it like a priest come upon a desecrated temple. 'Union Gospel Tabernacle 1891,' he read aloud.

'Grand Ole Opry House,' I read beneath.

'National Life Accident and Insurance Company,' read Ambrosia beneath that.

'Sacrilege,' whispered Properjohn. 'Sacrilege.'

'Cool it,' Winston told him cautiously. 'Just cool it. They get a couple of thousand people in here twice every Friday and again on Saturday. We got seven. Right? Right. So maybe we'll go in. If we can't get the crowd to us, we'll go to the crowd.'

Winston paid for everybody. The attendant in the foyer was a man surprised at nothing. 'Please, sir,' he said to me politely. 'Maybe you'll put that Cross in the cloakroom.'

'That was very generous of you,' I said to Winston. 'Considering you say it's truck driver music.'

'Twelve dollars well invested,' he smiled. He looked around. 'Just look at all these white folks. He never did have an audience like this, man.'

'You're going to push him up there?' I said, nodding towards the great bare stage.

'He won't need no pushing, baby. You know that,' said Winston.

'He could be lynched,' I said. 'Maybe they'll turn nasty. They didn't come here to hear him.' We were standing at the rear of the place. The wooden chapel seats swing around in a wide semi-circle. There was a balcony above our heads and bleak lights overhead. Every seat was taken.

'He could be lynched,' agreed Winston with a shrug. 'Whatever happens, man, the publicity could be great. This show goes out on the air.'

I glanced at him with an odd new respect. 'He might get torn to shreds,' I pointed out.

'He knows what he's doing' said Winston. 'He knows more about more things than maybe you give him credit for. He knows about getting attention.' He paused and then said: 'Some way.'

The first thing that happened when the show began was that a big coloured placard saying: 'Odom Sausage – US Borax' was lowered and in front of this three performers sang plaintive songs about lost love, lost hearts, and lost fortunes, the double nasal tone of the country voices and the guitars bringing instant happiness to all around. I liked it and I liked the next act, sponsored, according to the backdrop, by Beechnut Chewing Tobacco, which featured the Crook Brothers and the Stoney Mountain Cloggers.

Winston muttered again: 'Truck driver music.'

It was a four-hour show, act succeeding act as their commercial board was lowered behind them, the audience getting warmer and louder in their applause as the evening went on. Winston remained scornful: 'These people would clap if you went up there and blew two consecutive farts, man,' he said.

At one point a breezy master of ceremonies strode across the boards in buckskin boots and announced cheerfully that the Grand Ole Gospel Time, with the Reverend Jimmy R. Snow and Special Guests, would take place at eleven o'clock. I said to Winston: 'He'll have more special guests than he thinks, eh?'

Winston shook his head. 'Our Boy won't wait for that,' he forecast. 'He don't want to share it with nobody. Not even Jesus.'

He was right. Stephen's Work Clothes had lowered their advertisement and the crowd was anticipating the big star of the night, Hank Snow accompanied by The Fruit Jar Drinkers, when Our Boy stood up and marched down the chapel aisle with the faithful Clare and Ambrosia hurrying behind him. There was a blind, surging confidence about Properjohn. Halfway to the stage he began to shout his: 'Glory! Glory! Glory!' and to fling his arms in all directions. He was at home in chapel.

'We'd better go with him,' I said to Winston. But he restrained me and Herbie who was sitting on his other side. Hattie was beyond that, white faced, as though about to make a sacrifice. 'Maybe we'd better stay,' Winston cautioned. 'We don't want no unnecessary bloodshed.'

'Ambrosia,' I said anxiously. 'We shouldn't have let her go.' I caught Herbie's eye. 'And Clare,' I added.

But debate was now academic for Properjohn had reached

the stage and was hauling Ambrosia and Clare up, one with each hand. 'Praise! Praise! Praise!' he bawled. The two thousand were immediately still. Somewhere behind I saw the glint of a guitar. Mr Hank Snow and the Fruit Jar Drinkers were obviously waiting to get on.

But the great silence held. I thought: 'My God, he's done it again.'

Properjohn was silent also. But suddenly he seemed to make up his mind about something. 'Sacrilege!' he bellowed at them. 'Sacrilege!'

There was an eerie, disconcerting murmur around the pews. I heard a little whimper come from Hattie. I had fixed the nearest exit. Herbie said he was just going out to the toilet, but we held him back.

'Christ threw the money-lenders from the temple!' howled Properjohn with instantly-summoned fury. 'And I'm going to throw you out of here! Using the tabernacle of The Lord for this . . . this . . . TRUCK DRIVER MUSIC!'

His fury was marvellous to see. He reached up and caught the canvas hoarding for Stephen's Work Clothes with his great hands, tore it down with a spectacular rip, and then threw it at the audience.

Jesus, that did it. People seemed to come from everywhere. From the sides of the stage, from the audience. Uproar broke out. Above us the gallery was on its feet and throwing things. I had a brief glimpse of Properjohn's black arms lashing out and I heard Poor Clare's wail among the commotion. The four of us got up. I started down the side aisle towards the stage and Herbie was with me with Hattie trembling just behind. Winston turned to go out of the back exit, but Herbie grabbed him. 'Quit it,' pleaded Winston. 'I only work here. I'm a black boy and this is Nashville, man.'

We got him, though, and dragged him with us. Everybody in the place seemed to be out of his seat. Hundreds were crammed around the stage, shouting and waving their fists at Properjohn, who was struggling in the arms of half a dozen men. I could not see either Ambrosia or Poor Clare, but in the middle of the mayhem I briefly and curiously heard a pitiful note from the harmonica, like the last trump of a stricken bugler.

'This way,' called Herbie. We followed him through a side exit and then with a sharp elbow bend to the left we found ourselves with a comparatively unobstructed way to the stage. We brushed by performers in cowboy suits and sequins standing in the wings watching the uproarious scene. Properjohn was still fighting. He had floored two younger men and another was holding his face while squatting on the stage boards as though trying to fit two halves back together. Poor Clare was free, but pursued, screaming around like some ugly mermaid chased by fishermen. Ambrosia was behind a barricade extolling Shoney's Big Boy Restaurants, fighting off three men with her swinging autoharp.

In the middle of this extraordinary scene was a man wearing earphones and shouting 'Stop it! Stop it! We're on the air! We're on the air!' He saw us as we reached Properjohn and, guessing right, charged at us angrily. 'Get this madman out of here,' he demanded. 'Get him off. We're on the air.' We pulled at Properjohn and he came away from the morass of men quite easily, as if they were only too glad to let him go. But he immediately rushed at them again, snatched a guitar, and smashed it savagely over someone's head.

We pulled him away again, collected Ambrosia and Poor Clare on our way to the wings, and made for the exit. The cowboys at the sides split rapidly at our approach. But the audience had not finished with us. We went along a corridor and were abruptly faced with a whole wolf-pack of them, women, children as well. We turned and went the other way where, very oddly, stood the attendant I had previously seen in the foyer, his arms full of our green raincapes and robes, and with the Cross ready to hand to me. I took it at the run. 'Across the yard,' advised the man calmly. 'Through Tootsie's Orchid Lounge.'

It was a short run, across a wet enclosed area and under a low door. Some of the crowd were still after us, and a terrible thing happened as we went through the door. I hit the Cross against the transom and it snapped off, clean in half. I actually caught the top piece, including the cross-member as it fell, and with what I now know was an awful cry of despair I stumbled after the others.

We ran through Tootsie's Orchid Lounge like a train, bundling innocent drinkers aside. A lady behind the bar blew strongly on a police whistle as we went by.

Then we were in the rain, in the street. The crowd no longer after us. Faces crowded the doorway of Tootsie's but none of them came any further. To my astonishment I saw that Properjohn was laughing crazily, and dancing about with excitement. 'We did it!' he exclaimed. 'By heaven, we did it!'

'I'll tell you what we've done too,' I said. 'We've buggered up the Cross.' I held the two pieces so I could show them. Everyone stopped and looked helplessly. 'I bashed it against the top of a door,' I said.

'Oh Lord, oh dear Lord,' said Properjohn. 'What a terrible thing.'

Nobody even blamed me. We ran first, then slowed and trudged along Broadway, past the Cadillac that Hank Williams Died In, past the World's Largest Square Dance, back to our homes, our refuges in the two vehicles with 'Jesus Loves' and 'Jesus Lives' adorning their sides. We stood around in the now diminished rain when we got there, looking at the two pieces of the Cross, and talking in whispers. Clare and Hattie, who had collected the first black eye of his life in the battle, were openly weeping. Winston prudently said we ought to drive out of town that night in case anyone came looking for us, and this we did, going on about ten miles before stopping.

We all stood around Properjohn, who held the bits of the Cross like a bereaved parent. Eventually, patting us on the shoulders, he sent us all off to bed.

'Tomorrow,' he said. 'We'll try and mend it with a bit of paste. I expect we'll be able to make it stick.' He looked back along the road in the direction of Nashville and growled: 'Sacrilege.'

We arrived late next day in Memphis, its streets and leafy gardens tilting down to the broad, brown, evening smile of the Mississippi. 'It worked,' said Winston. 'See man, I told you, it worked.'

It appeared he was right; that half the city had come out to the streets and parks and sloping gardens to see Properjohn, the man who had caused the riot in Nashville. The Tennessee newspapers howled over it that morning, angrily in Nashville and with rival laughter in Memphis, and we had been waylaid five times in our journey across the State by television crews wanting us to describe, yet again, the mayhem at the Grand Ole Opry. The nearer we got to Memphis the more they laughed and patted Properjohn's back.

Now there were people, white and coloured, thronged everywhere along our route, and our following choirs were the largest and loudest we had known. I felt very excited and proud. A coloured man in a bright blue suit called to me: 'Say, man, I don' know whether you's Jesus, but you sure got a pretty step!'

I held my Cross more carefully than usual for it had been repaired with twenty tubes of model aero-cement purchased from a surprised but pleased hobby shop owner at Jackson. Herbie, who was very useful some unusual ways, stuck it together and fixed some supporting bands at the fracture. It was fortunately a good drying day while we journeyed across Tennessee, sun and a flat-running wind, and by the time we took the Cross from the roof of 'Jesus Lives' outside Memphis it appeared as firm as it had ever been.

'You know what the Bible says,' said Winston, as we marched. 'It says in the Psalms that Promotion don't come from the north nor the south, nor the west, man. You know where Promotion comes from? From a good public relations man like me.'

Our trailing choirs were singing 'This is My Story' and behind my shoulder I could hear the voice of Properjohn spouting his usual 'Glory! Glory! Glory!' punctuated with the odd 'Praise! Praise! Praise!' but once he caught me by the shoulder and shouted exultantly: 'The people, Willy, the people. All for us.'

As usual it was not quite like that. I had sensed an odd attitude of ambiguity about the crowds from the moment we were in the city. Some spectators were obviously surprised to see us, shouting and clapping at us in a sort of supplementary way, as though they were waiting for something else. As we went in procession along the river and then up by the Confederation Park into the middle streets, many people on the grass and the walls seemed to be looking in the other direction. Then we heard the band.

'Music,' I heard Properjohn exclaim. 'They've brought a band.'

They had, but it was not for us. We rounded a bend, with our choirs rallying against the growing rivalry of the drums and the sounding brass, when we found ourselves advancing towards a huge phalanx of United States Marines, blaring and blowing as they, in turn, advanced on us.

'Oh, God, no,' I heard Winston protest. 'Not the marines.'

'Carry on!' ordered Properjohn from the second rank. 'Don't falter, lads.'

The crowd could not believe its luck. It rushed with joy and expectancy along the sidewalks to get a better view. Television cameras on two platforms at each side of the road were whirled and turned like guns, their crews crouching and aiming for the junction where the point of impact between us and the marines must come.

Being at the van of our procession I had my eye fixed on the bulky chest of the marine drum major looming larger with each stride. I wondered if the Cross would stand up to the collision. Herbie's steps were slowing and Winston, eyes bulging ahead, was down to a shuffle. The spectators urged us on. The noise of the band, of course, swallowed our singing, but the choirs gamely tried to keep together, and I could hear the disjointed squeaks of Poor Clare's harmonica and Ambrosia's autoharp, as they did their despairing best.

It was a policeman who arrived from a sidestreet riding a quaint three-wheeled vehicle like a small milk float, who saved us. Chugging fearlessly to the cross-roads ahead he dismounted and standing stiffly at its centre waved us into the left-hand street and the marines' band down the hill to the right. There was no more than a yard between their flank and ours as we passed. I felt the wind of them going by.

'Right in the goddam middle of America,' swore Winston. 'In the middle. A million miles from the goddam sea. And who do we meet? – the marines.'

We were sitting feeding the ducks in the pond in the lobby of the Sheraton Peabody Hotel. Herbie and I were wearing our robes and the Cross was leaning against the round ornamental duck pond. The others were sitting around waiting for television cameras to be set up and reporters to arrive. Properjohn was to give a press conference.

'The President's Own,' read Herbie from a poster across by the reception desk. 'The world-famous marine symphonic band – on its once-a-year visit to Memphis.'

'The President's Own,' echoed Winston dolefully. 'Why don't he keep 'em then? Once a year – and this has to be the goddam day.'

I said to Winston: 'I don't see it. In Nashville you were all for causing a riot, just for the cheap publicity. And that worked. We're not doing too badly on this.' I nodded around at the television cameras being fussed and the lights arranged.

He winced. 'Look, it's one thing to screw up the Grand Ole Opry,' he said. 'And, brother, it's another to screw up the US Marines. Who cares about the Opry? But all good, decent, clean-living, clean-fighting, middle Americans love our Marines. And them's the very folks who give us the bucks. Got it?'

'Got it,' I nodded. 'You'd better warn him then.'

'I already did,' he said glancing towards Properjohn. 'I just hoped he listened.'

Ten minutes later Properjohn was standing in front of the State's television cameras and shouting in his grotesque film-land voice. 'I gave them hell in Nashville and I'm going to give them hell here. In Nashville last night we were reviled and attacked. Now here, in Memphis, they turn the military on us! The Marines! And let me tell you, this town ain't big enough for both of us.'

Winston's head sank slowly into his hands. I could see the sweat of the lights on his black forehead. 'Cast your bread on the waters and you get wet bread,' he sighed.

'It's reported that you claim to have the date of the End of the World in your pocket,' said a man in front.

'It's not reported,' cried Properjohn. 'It's true! And when the appointed hour comes I will reveal it.'

'You're not going to tell that to the Marines?'

'Never. Let them perish in hell.'

I hardly heard him say that. From where I was standing with the Cross I could see a poster at the reception desk, next to the one about the Marine Band. At the top it said 'Memphis Bo-Peep Club' and directly underneath 'Sexy Silvie. French Dances.'

Thirteen

'Sure she was here,' said the girl. 'Couple of weeks ago.'

'Where is she now? Any idea?'

'You a friend?'

'Not exactly. I'm her husband.'

'That's different, I guess.' She smiled professionally at me. She was a redhead with a good, big figure. She had a dress high up around her neck and tied there as though it was meant to throttle her. I could never remember seeing a girl in a night-club wearing a dress as high as that before.

'She went back to Vegas,' she said unsurely. 'Or maybe to Los Angeles. She said they wanted her to do a month at The Losers in LA.'

'That's a club, The Losers?'

'Good class sex show,' she said. 'No picking up dimes with your you-know-what. Nothing like that. Just good-class sex acts.'

'Did she have the children with her?'

She looked at me surprised through the gloom. 'I didn't know she had kids,' she said. Then she shrugged. 'Well, I guess that's not the sort of thing everybody talks about in this business. Some do, some don't. She didn't say.'

'It *is* her?' I said, moving my hand towards the photograph in my pocket again.

'Sure,' she said. I had already shown it to her but I took it out once more and she nodded at it. 'Just like she is now. They liked her here. She was in the show last Fall and they asked her to come back. They flew her in from Vegas, just for the week, and they don't do that too often.'

'Did she mention me?'

'Your name's not Lionel is it?'

'No, not Lionel.'

'Then she didn't. She mentioned a Lionel, or maybe it was a Leonard, I don't know. But she didn't make a meal out of men. Some of the guys here wanted to lay her, naturally, because she's a looker and she's foreign, but I don't think any of them made it. She didn't seem interested. At first I thought maybe she was butch.'

'Oh, no,' I argued. 'She's not that. I can tell you.'

'Can you?'

'Well, yes, of course I can.'

She smiled. 'Well, I guess you're the one to know.'

'I've got to find her,' I said. 'Haven't you got any idea?'

She looked thoughtful. 'You know, she did give me a card of some kind. I think it was an agent in Vegas. She said he might be able to get me something so I could go legit again.'

'Oh, I see.'

She grinned frankly. 'I'm not one hundred per cent legit now,' she said. 'But I said I'd like to go back. I used to sing.' She sighed. 'The high notes bothered me.'

'Have you got that card, do you think?'

'It must be somewhere. Probably in my apartment.' She looked around. 'This place is dead tonight and the boss is away, anyway. Come on over and have a look-see. It's just two blocks.'

I very nearly told her I did not have any money. The drink I had bought her was by courtesy of Winston. But I did not say it, and we walked down the street together, me a fraction of a pace behind ready to bolt.

'You ashamed to be with me?' she asked.

'No, it's not that,' I said. 'I've got some good reasons for not wanting to be seen.'

'Sounds like something out of *The Godfather*,' she said.

'It's a bit like that,' I admitted. 'Not quite as bad, but something like.'

'Only I could pick up a fugitive,' she sighed.

Then I told her I did not have any money. She laughed wryly. 'Don't you worry, honey, you ain't going to have anything worth paying for tonight. We're just going to get that card. Okay?'

'Okay,' I said. 'I felt it was only fair to mention it, that's all.'

'Mighty thoughtful of you. Some guys want it for nothing and they expect green stamps. Here it is.'

Two minutes later I was experiencing that guilty thrill of being enclosed within strange walls with a woman who is a stranger. It was a small apartment but homely, or it felt like it after the confines of 'Jesus Lives'.

'Very comfortable,' I said from the armchair. She was getting me a drink in the kitchen.

'I'm a frustrated housewife,' she called. 'Not in the normal way, like a housewife who's frustrated. I'm frustrated in wanting to be a housewife.' She came through with the drinks. Her mouth was as loose as the dress was tight. It was very tight on her thighs when she moved.

'Gosh,' she said, as though it were her nastiest word. 'I subscribe to the Book-of-the-month Club, and I belong to the Consumers Association, and I get recipes from *Ladies' Home Journal*. I joined the parent-teacher association until somebody squealed on me. I make my own clothes and I go with a basket on wheels to the supermarket. I do everything like that. Everything. Gosh, I even like washing up. And every time I just end up bringing strange guys in here to screw me at fifty bucks a throw.'

'That's frustrating,' I agreed, not knowing how else to answer.

'It's sad,' she corrected. She drank her whisky and poured another one swiftly. I drank mine too and handed the glass to her. She filled it and said: 'I want to show you something.'

'What?'

'Something. Look, there isn't any card. Silvie didn't give me one. But I've been wanting to show some man this and you

163

came from heaven. Because I can show you and you can tell Silvie when you see her.'

'There's no card?'

'No, I was just kidding. Just to get you over here. Will you let me show you?'

'What is it?' I was very disappointed about the card.

'You will then?'

'All right.'

'And you won't get mad? And you won't touch me?'

'No. Nothing. What is it, anyway?'

'It's better in the bedroom,' she said. Her face was set and serious. 'Come on, I'll show you in there.'

Nervously I got up and followed her. An erection had crept up on me. I manœuvred it down my leg. The bedroom was all black with a white bed and a pink lamp by the bed. There was a smoky mirror along the length of one wall. She told me to sit down and I sat on a little stool at the side of the bed. She stood on the other side, next to the mirror. She smiled as though to reassure both of us.

Her hands went to the back of her neck, behind the oddly prim collar, and she pulled the zip of the dress down to its full extent, down to the out-curve of her spine. She was standing sideways so I saw nothing in the mirror then. Her hands flicked at her brassière hook and she let the straps part.

Then slowly she turned her back on me. It was a long, fine back, or it had been before somebody had been at her with a whip. Right down its length were vivid horizontal wounds, almost carefully placed six inches apart. I felt sick and full of that sense of shameful excitement again.

'God,' I whispered.

'No,' she said. 'A guy called Homer Bean.'

Then she pulled the dress down over her thighs and deftly pulled her pants away with it, half-revolving with the action until she was sideways on. Her breasts were large and lazy in profile. She turned her back to me again. Her buttocks were striped in the same way, geometrically, and the backs of her legs to the knees. There, right behind the knees it stopped. In the mirror I could see she was weeping.

'I just thought I would like another *man* to see it,' she said

164

quietly through the tears. 'I thought I would get some kind of revenge out of that.'

'Homer Bean,' I muttered, as if I knew him and recognized his work. I couldn't think of anything else to say. I couldn't believe what I was seeing. She turned away from the mirror and I could see that she had been beaten at the front too, on the tops of her legs, reaching almost to the apex of her pubic hair, three distinct half-cuts across her right hip, reaching towards her stomach, and a livid red stripe touching her breast.

'Homer did it,' she said again.

'What for?' I mean, I knew what for, but I couldn't believe how anyone got into a situation where they were allowed to do that sort of thing.

'A thousand dollars,' she said.

'He paid you a thousand dollars?'

'I certainly didn't pay him, you jerk.'

'Sorry,' I mumbled. 'I just can't believe it, that's all. I've never seen such a cruel thing.'

'You love it, don't you?' she said, leaning towards me across the bed. 'You like to see it.'

'No,' I stumbled. 'No. I don't like that sort of thing, really.'

'Most men do.' She turned slowly on the far side of the bed displaying all the lashes again. I could not take my eyes away. 'That's ten days ago,' she said. 'When Silvie was here.'

'Silvie?' I said startled. 'Silvie wasn't . . .?'

'Relax, Silvie wasn't. But she knew about this proposition.'

'From Homer?'

'Sure. He asked her if she would do it.'

'I'll kill that bastarding swine.'

'It was two thousand bucks in her case. She's younger. But she decided she didn't need the dough that much. She couldn't dance looking like this could she?'

Tears had rushed to my eyes. 'Oh, for Christ's sake, shut up!' I bawled at her. 'She wouldn't do that sort of filth.'

She laughed like a taunt. 'She thought about it,' she said easily. 'After all it's all over in ten minutes, and two hundred bucks a minute is good bread for anybody, baby. We sat here in this apartment and talked it over, Silvie and me, for hours.'

'Here? In here?' I sniffed and wiped my eyes. It was the first time that it had occurred to me that Silvie had actually been in there. I looked around and then into the other room, wondering in which chair she had sat.

'Hour after hour we discussed it,' she said. 'This guy made it clear that he wanted to whip one of us, or both, and he was willing to pay. I didn't find out until later that he had offered her twice as much as me. She didn't tell me. You can be friends in this business and still not talk about money.'

'What business?' I asked thickly. 'She's a dancer. She's not a whore.'

'Sure, sure, she's a dancer,' she said consolingly. 'But two grand would have been two grand even to Pavlova.' She took a pace forward and sat on the side of the bed, on the satin coverlet, elegantly, for she had a splendidly shaped body, her hair rolling red down her scarred back, her eyes full in the half-light. I thought she was going to lean across to me for a moment and I was making up my mind what to do for the best, but suddenly she became businesslike again. 'I said I would,' she sighed. 'For a thousand bucks. It took ten minutes.'

'Yes, you mentioned that,' I said.

She stood up and turned towards the mirror. Her fingers ran along the line of one of the weals on her torso, tenderly, and then across the angriest cut on her backside. I might as well admit that I was near boiling point then. Anyone would be. Any man. 'He came up at seven in the evening and he was out in the street again by twenty after, and that included the time he took to get me tied up.'

'Tied up? Oh, bloody hell . . .'

'It was,' she said tightly. 'Like you say, pal, bloody hell. He tied my hands and feet and put me on the bed. He wanted to tie my hair to the bed rail but I said it would be another hundred bucks for that, so he didn't do it. Funny how some people like to economize over the small things. But I let him gag me because he said that was important for him and anyway I thought if I squealed it might disturb the Rabbi in the next apartment. It was a Friday. And I squealed. Christ, did I squeal. I tried to keep quiet so that he wouldn't get the satisfaction of hearing me holler – Homer that is, not the Rabbi –

but I couldn't hold it. I had my teeth biting into that gag and I still couldn't. Christ, it hurt.'

She stopped then as though waiting for me to digest it.

'Why are you telling me this?' I asked. I dropped my gaze, but quickly put it on her again. 'Me?'

She sat wearily on her dressing-table stool and momentarily dropped her face in her hands. But she lifted her head again in a moment. 'If I don't tell somebody I'll go mad,' she confessed. 'I thought it would be better for me if I told somebody, and especially a man. And you can tell Silvie that I did it. Because she left that day.'

I didn't know what to say or do. I had a horrible, sick temptation to go to her and to touch the places myself. I really wanted to do that. But she went on in her low voice. 'He was pretty deliberate about it, that Homer. I was trussed like a Thanksgiving Turkey, and he stood just where you are now and kind of eyed me for a while, like the villains do in the melodramas. I was lying down there, all clenched up, waiting for the first one, but it didn't come so I turned my head around and sort of screwed my eyes up to him, and that's when he did it. Right across my ass. Jesus, I thought I was going to fly out of the window. Then he picked another place and did it again. And again and again. So careful and deliberate. He did it for five minutes in here and then got me in the other room and made me sit in the chair while he did it to the front of my legs.

'He tried to carry me in there but the cunt dropped me. He's only a little guy. In the end I had to hobble in there. It was curious because he didn't take his clothes off or anything. He just kept his street clothes on. And the whip was only a little thing, not like they have in the porny books. When he was finished he was all kind of dreamy and he went out and forgot to untie me, the fool, and I couldn't call after him because of the gag. Christ, I could have been here for weeks like that. But when he got down the block he remembered and he came back and undid the knots and apologized for forgetting. Then he went home to screw Mrs Bean, I suppose.'

'My God,' I breathed. 'I can hardly believe it.'

'I can,' she said. She began to weep again.

'Listen,' I said. I got up and went around the bed towards

her. She let out the most gruesome scream. 'Get out! Don't you touch me!' she cried. 'Go on, fuck off.'

I went. I hardly knew where I was going. Half-running I went until I was alongside the cool night-time Mississippi. A riverboat, lit like a stage, was going downstream, and I could see the lights of the cars moving over the bridge between Tennessee and Arkansas. The embankment runs steeply to the moorings there and some small boats were restless in the wash of the craft that had just gone by. A woman came idly along the bank. She appeared to be admiring the invisible shore of the next state. Then she said to me, as though continuing a conversation which we had been having: 'Well, do you want to try something really new. Twenty-five dollars.'

'All night?' I asked, not knowing why.

'All fucking week, honey,' she answered, and walked on.

I ran all the way back to the safety and sanity of my friends and comrades in 'Jesus Lives' and 'Jesus Loves'. Sometimes I felt that the world was too big for me.

Along the bank of the Mississippi, on the Memphis side, running down from Riverside Drive, there were tightly fixed cobblestones, falling to where the thick water muscled its way among jetties and boats. The morning was serene, the sky creamy, the city humming. Two girdered bridges, one on each side of us as we stood, reached out to Arkansas across the elbow of the river. Warner's jetty was below us with some tugs and other craft, a puffer named 'Mildred' and a tough tug called 'Mallard', resting their foreheads against its flank. A decorated paddler, 'The Memphis Showboat', was moored to another jetty, all colours and curly bits but tired and empty like a can-can dancer after a rough night.

'You should feel at home right here, Willy,' said Winston. 'These cobbles came from England as ballast in the old cotton ships and then they used them to build the riverbank. Slaves and donkeys used to carry the cotton down from the old warehouses up there.'

'Wow, there goes that mouth again,' muttered Herbie. We sat down on the cobbles in the mild sun and watched the coiling chocolate river. He eyed Winston. 'I never did hear any guy who knows as much as you,' he said. 'You *sure* you ain't a spy?'

It was the hundredth time he had said it. They were constantly digging at each other, friendly but still digging. In the confines of the mobile home it got on my nerves. Hattie had taken to praying loudly for unity among all peoples, colours and creeds whenever the argument began.

They liked to needle each other, bluntly sometimes, but at others with craft and slyness. 'You,' said Winston, crouching on the cobbles, unconsciously primitive, 'you have got the worse complaint of racial prejudice I have ever seen.'

'Crap,' answered Herbie, amiably. 'I've got no colour prejudice about you, baby. To me you're just another nigger.'

'And you, baby,' said Winston, just as amiably. 'You're just another ten-cent Brooklyn yid.'

'Why don't you two pack it up,' I said.

'The Limey wants us to pack it up,' said Herbie, trying to imitate my accent. 'Let's not take any notice of him, old chap,' mimicked Winston.

'You're like a couple of bleeding kids,' I grumbled, 'And anyway you shouldn't be arguing in your robe, Herbie.'

But they did not want to argue with me. They faced each other again.

'Okay,' said Herbie. 'So you know everything. But you don't fool me, baby. Maybe you got Sixth Avenue shoes on but, man, you got Jackson, Mississippi, feet in those fucking shoes.'

Still sitting, I had shuffled a few feet down the sloped embankment, just to divide myself from them. Their exchanges continued in the curious ritualistic manner they had formulated, each taking a turn to throw a vile insult at the other and then remaining silent while it came back. But there was no shouting and no violence. After the affray in Bristol they had arranged to conflict like this, sitting calmly, trading jeers, like cool tennis players. The insults, usually the same insults, would be lobbed to and fro with calm bitterness. Winston's remarks were the cleverest, and there were more of them for it took Herbie longer thought. Sometimes Winston would say something that would have Herbie grinding his teeth into his pillow half the night. But Winston had the disadvantage of being black which somewhat restored the balance because, as

Herbie pointed out, whatever insults you can think up appertaining to the Jews, the Jews are still white.

I sat in front of them, then, dully half-listening to their verbal tirade, sorting through, now, my doubts about Silvie. How could she even be *interested* in a proposition like that? Christ, she *must* have given the spendthrift Homer Bean some reason for supposing he could make her the same sort of offer he made to the redhead. I realized that I had never asked the woman's name. What with one thing and another I had forgotten.

I was ashamed of the very thought that Silvie, my wife, the mother of little Kathy and James, should be part of a world where men called Homer Bean could pay large sums of money for doing such things. I was angry with her for going, for leaving England, for leaving me; whatever things I did, and I was at fault at times, I was not denying that, she was at least safe and sound and not exposed to such terrible possibilities. So embarrassed was I by the knowledge that she was even on the fringe of a life where such things happened, that I had told neither Winston nor Herbie what had happened the previous night. As far as they were concerned I had gone out on my usual nocturnal patrol of the nightspots and returned, once more, empty handed. Sitting there by the Mississippi, the squalid enormity of the thing engulfed me again. She, my wife, whom I loved and I was seeking, had even *considered* being whipped by a pervert with two thousand dollars to spare (God, I was getting less than that for carrying the Cross). That this could even enter the thoughts and discussion of a girl who had lived in Buckinghamshire.

'The meek,' said Winston abruptly and loudly, two yards behind me. 'Shall inherit the earth.'

'Blessed are the meek,' responded Herbie.

'Blessed are they who hunger and thirst after righteousness,' intoned Winston.

'Blessed are they,' echoed Herbie.

Carefully I turned. Standing behind them was the gaunt and awesome figure of Oliver Jaye.

'In my Father's house are many mansions,' Winston flogged on.

'Okay, you guys, I heard you.'

They turned with well-managed surprise.

'Oh, my goodness,' said Winston. 'It's Mr Jaye, Herbie.'

'Oh, Mr Jaye,' bubbled Herbie. 'You scared us.'

Jaye lowered himself slowly, like a large and awkward bird trying to get its backside straight on its nest. 'Quit,' he muttered threateningly. 'Quit.' He glanced at me.

'Morning, Mr Jaye,' I said. 'Nice bit of river.'

'Listen,' he said nastily. 'What's going on?'

'We're having a rally right here this afternoon,' Winston informed him, 'and we just came down to see that the place was er . . . you know, *spiritually* right.'

'This, I mean,' said Jaye, brushing the words aside. 'And this.'

He produced two newspapers, that day's *Memphis Commercial Appeal* and the previous day's Nashville *Tennessean*. He hung them out in front of him as though trying to dry them.

'Jesus Freak Wrecks Opry' he read from the Nashville paper. Then, from the other: 'God will smash Marines, says Pastor.'

'Well,' shrugged Winston. 'You know the newspapers, Mr Jaye. They don't get everything quite right. They like to blow things up a little.'

Oliver was frying beneath the tight calm of his face.

'That madman,' he trembled. 'That crazy kook. Christianity may never return to Nashville after this, and as for saying that God will smash the Marine Corps.' Suddenly he gave one of his shouts 'GOD IS NOT A COMMIE!' He paused and breathed heavily, then said: 'Properjohn is bringing the whole project into disrepute! I could very easily dispose of him . . .'

A chill settled in my throat when he said that. But Winston, to my astonishment, smiled encouragingly and patted Oliver's arm. 'If you didn't need him,' he pointed out.

'I don't need any of you,' snarled Oliver. But he was not sure of himself. He grumbled: 'I thought you guys were going to keep a close watch on him.'

'How can you keep a watch on a loon like that?' asked Winston. He was at ease. 'Anyway, what have we got? We got ourselves on the front pages, Mr Oliver. Bad news is good news. It you want to stir up Las Vegas you've got to be right there, on the front, and on the TV screen. You're not going to stir them up by singing hymns and praying loud, mister. They won't even look up from the crap tables. It's okay, don't worry about it.'

Oliver seemed suddenly to find the slow progress of a barge going upstream of consuming interest. Eventually he rose, his long legs jacking like a heavily loaded spring. 'Make sure it's good today,' he said. 'We've got a lot of supporters who contribute their dollars in these parts. And don't tangle with the Marines. Okay?'

'Okay,' said Winston and we nodded. Then Winston said: 'Mr Jaye, would it be a possibility for you to advance me a little cash for disbursements. I keep having to buy these guys candy.' He said it with a small, dubious laugh but to my astonishment Oliver Jaye reached in his wallet, took out a hundred-dollar note, put it back, took out a fifty-dollar note, and handed it without a word to Winston. Then, still silently, he gave Winston a white form to sign. Then he went, striding ill-temperedly over the cobbles to where his car was standing on the highway.

'What about that!' exclaimed Herbie after we had watched him go.

'Fantastic,' I said. 'I can't believe it.'

'Something,' said Winston thoughtfully. 'Has happened. I don't know what it is, but I sure would like to.'

It was not our choice, of course, but one result of our brush with the Marines in Memphis was that our crusade became the rallying point for all the wild Jesus freaks, drop-outs, way-outs, peace campaigners and that general sort of individual. They arrived at our riverside rally in hundreds, like some Mongolian rabble, shouting and waving their fists, and carrying on about freedom, peace, love and all that type of nonsense. It was very frightening in its way, upsetting our established prayers and hymns, and making everybody feel uncomfortable. There seemed to be nothing genuine about them at all.

All the usual local choristers and people from the subsidized churches were also there, of course, and I think they were more embarrassed by the behaviour of the mob than we were. Some of the Jesus freaks attempted to adopt a sort of Christ-look, with the hair and the beard and the robes, but, quite truthfully, they were pretty poor imitations. One of them actually asked me if he could hold the Cross for a while 'just to get the feel of it'. Cheeky bastard.

Nor would they join in the prayers and the singing in a proper manner. Instead they were shouting slogans and falling down on the ground and ridiculous exhibitionist stuff like that. How they fancied themselves as actors; and the girls too, crying and wailing, and bleating on for some reason about Mary Magdalene. One of them, pregnant as hell, was galloping about saying she was bearing the Second Messiah. All she got was a quick shove from me.

It upset Properjohn too, of course, because he was accustomed to people *listening*. When he was giving his sermon these people kept interrupting him, arguing with him, and at one point apparently even prepared to rush the platform. Properjohn could not credit it. He jumped down in a fury and ran at the vanguard of the mob with such ferocity that they backed away in a hurry, pushing back the people behind them, and eventually causing a small Negro boy to be pushed into the Mississippi. There was a terrible commotion about this, people panicking and arguing and blaming each other (and Properjohn shouting: 'Pray for him! Pray for him!') but nobody thinking of getting the poor little devil out. Eventually he was hooked out by one of the Jesus mob who had a sort of shepherd's crook – one of the various phoney props, including several makeshift crosses, they carried.

The whole meeting looked like falling apart, if not becoming an actual battle, when the Marines arrived again. They came down Union Street and across Front Street, heading for Confederation Park. Their blaring brass, suddenly doubled as they turned the corner from the buildings of the town, stopped all the shouting and misbehaviour in our meeting. A shout was raised 'Sing! Everybody sing!' and in a moment the hundreds were bawling 'This is My Story', with guts and gusto that would have staggered Billy Graham, with Properjohn, as rabid as any of them, conducting with fierce panache

173

from the rostrum. But unfaltering the Marines strode along Riverside Drive, towards us, playing 'St Louis Blues March'.

I was feeling uneasy about the whole business. To crusade for Christ is one thing. To fight the US Armed Forces is another. But now Properjohn was urging everybody into the road. Encouraged by the Jesus freaks and others, he was preparing to march around the park to meet the marines coming in the opposite direction. I was rushed forward with the Cross and reluctantly at the head of the strange army of choristers, solid citizens, and raggle-taggle drop-outs, we marched up one flank of the park while the marine band marched up the other. At the top they would turn right and we would turn left. No Memphis policeman could avert the confrontation this time. In the distance, I could hear police sirens but I knew they would be too late, and I felt very apprehensive.

Properjohn, carried along by his own idiot enthusiasm and with Poor Clare, Ambrosia and even Hattie, close behind him in euphoric support, led the charge. I noticed that Herbie and Winston were moving gradually, separately, to the sides of our procession, making ready to run as usual, but I was forced forward with the Cross by the pressure and enthusiasm of the crowd behind me.

We turned the bend at the top of Confederation Park about ten seconds before they did. We advanced on each other, the Marines playing, eyes steady, stride full, caps like axes, while our disgraceful mob sang and shouted and waved things in the air. Almost at the centre of the street at the top of the park we met. A single steely order and the marines halted both their march and their marching. We pulled up raggedly a yard from them. Both formations were stretched right across the road on either side. There was no way past.

' 'ello,' said Properjohn meekly to the drum major, a man as big as a carthorse, standing directly before me.

'Hello,' answered the drum major surprisingly. 'Drum Major John Drew, United States Marines, sir.'

'The Reverend John Properjohn,' said our leader pedantically. 'Representing God and Jesus.'

'The old firm,' smiled the drum major. 'Southern Baptist, myself, Reverend. Anything you would like us to play?'

"Onward Christian Soldiers"?' asked Properjohn.

'No trouble at all, sir.'

At this moment the rabble element in our procession, who had been as silent as everyone else, realized they were being sold out. They began shouting protests and obscenities (so much for their Christianity!) but they were too late. The band did a springy about-turn, struck up with 'Onward Christian Soldiers' and the decent people on our side strode forward joyfully singing. We left the riff-raff jeering and shouting at the side of the park, but doing nothing more. Properjohn and I were rushed to the front of the band with the rest of our group, and we marched along the Mississippi, Cross high, hundreds of solid citizens singing behind us. I was very proud. I think Jesus Christ himself would have been proud.

Fourteen

We crossed one of the high bridges and drove our motor homes on through Arkansas, confused and elated by the adventures that had happened. But all the riotous things, the bands and the noise were left behind us as we entered the new state, as though the Mississippi had closed behind us like a great door, and we were restored to that strange, conclaved half-family that we had been before. We sang songs and talked among ourselves of our past lives as we drove and during our stops for food. It was as if we had all, to our relief, survived something and were back together again. Winston told us airily how he had talked to the US Marines public relations officer and arranged that miraculous about-face by their band, and the boisterous peace between us that followed. 'I told the man it would look better in the newspapers, and it sure did,' he said, with his subdued boastfulness. Properjohn refused to believe him and said it was an act of God.

Now we were in a landscape of flooded woods, cotton, rivers, shacks, and slogans. The country was so flat you could see another vehicle moving like a beetle miles away, the elevators of the Riceland Rice Company stood up like a lonesome cathedral, and the sky was the pale blue of the Fall season with groups of clouds like small forests gathered on the far horizon towards Oklahoma. The land seemed as clear as the sky. It stretched on and on and only here did we strangers realize in full the size of the country. 'It never seems to stop,' sighed Ambrosia, as I lay with her one afternoon, for a quick hour, at Brinkley motel. 'There's yards of it. On and on and on it goes.' She meant America. The motel was near a level crossing of the Santa Fé Railroad and two trains rolled by, right beneath our window, in the still afternoon. When we stood and dressed and looked out of the window before picking up our baskets of groceries to go, we could see right along the length of the straight flat railway line until it became a point in the distance. It was like looking down a man's throat.

The shanties, the shacks, each clutching its motor car, were strewn along the highway. Some of the cars were bigger than the houses. Wong's Food Market at Clarendon stood rightfully among the rice fields, as did more of his Chinese brothers settled there in Arkansas; at Palestine, where Properjohn insisted we stopped to imbibe what he imagined would be the religious atmosphere, there stood a shed labelled Ron's Dance Studio, where the dancing must have been really tight. Coloured people stood in the streets talking deeply as if something sad and momentous had happened on a day when nothing had, children played among the squalor of weed-filled cars, and old people lay tired on their broken verandahs. The rivers ran chocolate through community rubbish, and the stores announced 'We accept US Government Food Tokens'. In a village a man advertised 'Minnows, worms and crickets for sale' and in a town a notice like one from the slave days simply said 'For Sale, Fred Usher'.

There were richer parts, in Forrest City and at Main and Maple Street, Brinkley, and in Stuttgart, there were the standard American lawns and cleanly spread trees, shading the standard porch and barbecue. Here the dogs remained indoors. In the poor places they played in the rivers and the rubble with the little children.

There was water lying everywhere in the state. It was as though a great deluge had preceded us. It ran regulated in the rice fields and wild among the woods where trees stood about helplessly in the floods like people searching for something lost beneath the surface. Some of that water must have been there a long time for it had turned the trunks white, and trees lay on their backs like big corpses.

Cotton waggons stood like cages in the streets of small towns and the rice elevators grew tall and naked on the flat land. Ranks of black motor tyres stood chained prudently together in the streets of gritty towns like the Negroes of old had been chained. We drove and rested and drove on again through one hundred miles after another. It had not looked very far on the map.

I did not look for Silvie at all in this state. Somehow I could not see her performing at Ron's Dance Studio. She was beyond this long plain and the cities and the hills beyond that. Now, at least, I was sure that the trail led straight to Las Vegas. One night I dreamed that I saw her covered with Homer Bean's lashes and heard her shouting at me: 'It's your fault! It's all your fault!'

'You don't love me by any chance, do you Willy?' Ambrosia had asked that afternoon in Brinkley, the only place we had intercourse in Arkansas.

'No, I can't say I do, love,' I said.

'I don't love you either. In fact I hate you, you bearded pig.'

'Why do you say that?'

'Because you tell me so bloody blatantly that you don't love me. You might just humm and haa a bit.'

'Sorry. I thought you wanted to know straight.'

'No woman, no man either, I suppose, wants to know straight. I might say I do but I don't really. Can I ask you again?'

'You could try.'

'All right. Do you love me?'

'Yes. I adore you.'

'You soon change your bloody mind. I'm not sure I like a man who changes his mind that quickly.'

I went close to her in the motel bed. I was paying half for this one because it was a motel and not a rooming house. It was part of the money from Oliver Jaye. She felt warm and sulky, stretched there ignoring my penis lying against her leg like a rampant caterpillar. I moved it jerkily up her thigh.

'Every time we come to somewhere like this,' she suddenly giggled. 'You spoil it by bringing that thing along.' Then she looped her pale, fatty young arms about me and we kissed for longer and with more relish than most real lovers ever would.

It was about this time that Properjohn discovered the map. Until then he had let Winston or Herbie do the navigating, having no idea where he was in America, and not caring beyond the odd grumble that everywhere seemed a long way. But when he saw Palestine, Arkansas, marked on the route map and within minutes it appeared out of the real horizon he was excited and impressed.

After that he kept putting his finger on random places in the state and insisting that we drive there. Winston or Herbie argued him out of it sometimes, but not all the time, and we would drive for two hours or more off the route to find ourselves in some backwater creek surrounded by silent rural children and suspicious adults. Then we would have to turn and find the main highway again. But experiences like this did nothing to deter Properjohn and one day he spanned three inches on the map and suggested that as we were so near we might as well go to Canada for a few hours. Dissuaded with difficulty, he continued to sit behind the driver in 'Jesus Lives', selecting names from the map like a child picking out interesting sweets from a bag. In a few days we arrived perplexed in three Salems, two Babylons and a place whose name I forget but where the church notice board had the invitation 'Try Jesus'.

General bouts of childishness, as distinct from his bouts of adult idiocy, had shown themselves in Properjohn far back in the journey. There had been a strange two hours at Natural

Bridge, a rock arch in Virginia, where he and Poor Clare had screamed with astounding delight as they were being whisked through the scenic wonders of that place in little gay cars slung on a cable. Poor Clare thought it was like Porthcawl and talked of nothing else for two days. Properjohn, like a hideous truant schoolboy, had whooped through the air, hanging perilously over the side of the container, ice cream in one fist, hat in the other, taunting us for not joining him. Eventually Ambrosia paid for Herbie and me to take a trip, and, soberly embarrassed, we followed his whooping through the treetops and scenic rocks.

Spouting as he did at every corner and every opportunity about sin and degradation he nevertheless seemed blind to the true evils of the land through which we travelled. At Humnoke, Arkansas, in the midst of a crouching settlement of shacks with mud around the doors and despair seeming to hang from the very trees, he was delighted with an illuminated sign which proclaimed: 'Jesus is Coming Soon'. It was as though the poor people could hardly wait. But Properjohn cried: 'Look! Look at that! These people really know the secret of life.'

There were further manifestations of his childishness. He rode on a mule at a country fair outside Little Rock and walked around the Museum of Cowboy Fame in Oklahoma City with a cloud of candy-floss exploding from his huge hand. In Fort Smith he choked on a toffee apple and had to be pounded on the back by the gallows in the old stockade, and his quietest two hours of the entire journey from New York to Vegas was while he was engrossed in the comic paper antics of Bat Girl as the scenic beauties of middle America slipped by unadmired outside the window. At England, Arkansas, he strode into the inevitable Bank of England and loudly demanded that the Union Jack be raised from their roof forthwith, while we explained in a group to the security guard that Properjohn need not be shot dead. Outside England he spied the Brahmans P. J. Ranch and like some excited boy exclaimed: 'Oh, my first ranch! My first ranch!'

And yet he was afraid of children as of nothing else. When they approached him at rallies or Triumphal Entries into towns he would back away from them as though frightened they would do him some hurt. On the road by the school at Scott, the next town after England, there were children piling from a yellow bus outside Scott School ('Home of the Boll Weevils') and Properjohn crouched with an embarrassment approaching fear when they crowded round our stopped vehicle to ask us who we were and where we were going.

The same afternoon in Little Rock, he found an establishment called The Guardian Church Goods on Seventh Avenue, where they sold robes and cassocks, ornate crosses, 'heavenly gifts' and 'imported Christmas cribs'. Taking Hattie he entered the shop and with Winston and I on uneasy patrol outside he spent an hour dressing himself and Hattie in the most sumptuous and elaborate of church vestments, robes and crooks and funny bonnets, parading around like some poncing primate, preening himself in front of the long ecclesiastical mirrors and egging on Hattie to try more fanciful robes and garments with each change. I have never seen anything like it. Winston and I walked up and down the street praying that Properjohn would be quitting the shop every time we approached it. But he was still in there, among the gold and the purple, enjoying himself immensely and childishly. Eventually he and Hattie emerged having bought a ten-cent scripture card between them and leaving the proprietor dazed amid scattered and glorious church clothing. Properjohn laughed and danced all the way back to the vans, seeking and getting reassurances from Hattie on how good he looked in that thing and how regal in that thing. There was no doubt about it, this man was a clerical cretin.

We went across the square hinge of Texas that hangs onto the door of Oklahoma, on through Amarillo and then as far as somewhere in New Mexico, where Properjohn had one of his navigational brainstorms and set us off through the mountain passes north of Route Sixty-Six.

It had been benign autumn weather, through the midwestern states, with daylong sun lying dry along the flatlands, and touching red on the curious chimneys of the desert mountains. But as our two motor homes left the main highway and began to climb the curling road through rocks and upland cedars we could see mats of snow in the hollows and a smatter-ing on the wider mountain flanks. When we stopped for the night it was set bitterly cold. It was pointless being angry, asking, or wondering, what was in Properjohn's mind. He had commandeered the main road map and was keeping it to him-self like some secret document. But he had become very excited and conspiratorial, creeping about with a look like Guy Fawkes in his changing eyes.

At about nine o'clock, after we had eaten Ambrosia's evening fry-up, the four of us in 'Jesus Lives' sat down to play cards. Within two minutes a terrible trembling scream filled the mountains and we ran out into the cold darkness to find Poor Clare folded up in terror on our doorstep. 'It chased me,' she bleated. 'Oh, it chased me. I'm sorry, I'm sorry.'

'Don't be sorry,' said Herbie, firmly taking hold of her arm and hauling her into our van. 'What chased you?'

Properjohn and Ambrosia arrived at our door, Properjohn angry as he always was when Poor Clare did anything like this. 'What's the matter, woman?' he demanded. 'Stop shivering.'

'She was chased,' said Winston.

'First time in her life,' muttered Properjohn.

'Why were you out there?' I asked.

'I went out to the toilet, Willy,' she trembled. 'Ours is broken and I didn't want to disturb you lads. I thought I would go quietly at the back of our van, away from the wind . . . and then this thing chased me . . . ooooooooohhhh.'

She collapsed again. Properjohn was still irritated. 'Fancy doing that outdoors on a night like this,' he said angrily.

'It's your fault,' Ambrosia said. 'Bringing us up into this damned wilderness. If we'd kept to the road she could have gone to the toilet in a motel or something. There's nothing up here.'

'That's what you think,' said her father quite madly. 'That's what you think.' His eyes were theatrically bright. There were times when I thought he could have been locked away without conscience.

'Let's go and look-see,' said Herbie, still attending to Poor Clare. He made for the door and, in the nature of her life, Poor

Clare, who had been resting against his legs as she sat on our floor, fell heavily backwards. We eased her up again with apologies. 'Be careful, please, please,' she wailed, as we went into the night. Herbie with the torch was in front, followed by myself and then the reluctant Winston. 'I'm only going with you in case you don't come back,' he muttered.

Around the corner nuzzling against the side of 'Jesus Loves' was a large bush of trembling tumbleweed. Poor Clare's yard of toilet paper was pathetically shivering against the van wheel. We set the tumbleweed free, as though it were some animal, and watched the wind roll it off through the darkness. We went back and told the others and we all laughed about it except Poor Clare who had another sniffle and said she was sorry she was such a fool. We all went to bed but an hour later Ambrosia was banging at our door to say that Properjohn had disappeared. And so had the Cross.

Herbie and Winston, with the two women, took 'Jesus Loves' down the narrow valley road to search, while Hattie and I drove on up into the mountains. We had no idea where we were going because Properjohn had kept the only large-scale map carefully with him all day and it seemed he had it with him now.

Hattie moaned and mumbled like some vexed old spinster, but nevertheless drove the bulky motor home around murderous bends and curves with the skill of a rally driver. It began to snow heavily, the big flakes rushing at us through the cliffs and gorges. Then, quite shortly, there were dim lights ahead.

'It's a town of some sort. He could be here,' said Hattie. 'He can't have gone far unless he got a ride. What's this place, I wonder?'

We knew almost before he had asked the question. Outside the town was a name-board. Our headlights caught it through the snow and we slowed and stopped. It said: 'Las Vegas'.

Hattie did not start again immediately. We just sat there dumbly. Then I said: 'It looks as if he's found the wrong Las Vegas.'

'This sure isn't the right one,' said Hattie.

'Do you think he's mad, sometimes?'

'He's mighty peculiar.'

'Oh, for God's sake . . .' I began, looking at the growing blizzard.

'For His sake,' muttered Hattie.

'Sorry, Hattie, but you'd think, wouldn't you? You'd think he would realize.'

'I don't think the man knows where he is,' allowed Hattie regretfully. 'Not at any time. He knows he's in America and that's all. He's got no idea of place or distance.'

'Let's go down to the town or whatever it is,' I sighed. We started forward. 'He's been having fun and games with the map recently,' I said. 'He must have seen this place just off the route and thought this was Las Vegas, the fool. He thought he'd grab the glory himself, so he nicked the Cross and carried it in. Crafty old devil.'

The town was hollow and cold, hardly a light in any of the wooden houses, and trees rattling like bones in the street. We drove in the tentative way of an armoured car on curfew patrol up Lincoln Street. The Vegas Barber Shop was near the junction with Main Street and next to it Gullermo's Wig and Beauty Salon, with its neon sign lighting the bitter white and empty street. Phil's Shoes, Joe G. Maloof's saloon on Douglas Street, the Greyhound Bus Station, the Marine recruiting centre and the deer hide collection box; all were dumb with a wandering snowy wind poking around their doors and shutters. It was late and desolate.

'Even Properjohn must have known this is not Las Vegas, not the real one,' I said to Hattie, who was peering over the wheel along the gloomy street. 'The man's potty, I tell you.'

'He's at the end of the next block,' said Hattie. 'I can see the Cross standing against the mortuary wall.'

It was easy to see the mortuary for it had the brightest neon advertisement in the town, a yellow and white design of almost oriental curves, and the words, 'Johnsen Mortuary' ablaze in the middle. Somehow it seemed right.

Properjohn was hunched outside the establishment's door. Snow had drifted against him. He was squatting low and the Cross was standing just as wearily under the neon sign. He hardly seemed to notice us pulling up.

'It's the wrong place, the wrong place,' he moaned as we got out and walked towards him. 'There's nobody here.'

'You should have told us you were coming,' I said sharply. I lifted him to his feet with difficulty for his overcoat was stiff with cold. There was snow rimmed along the side edge of his clerical collar and his hat was white with it.

'I'm so cold,' he complained. 'So very cold, Willy. And it's the wrong place. There's no sin. There's nothing.'

'This is Las Vegas, New Mexico,' said Hattie patiently, as we helped the old fool towards the motor home. Snow fell from him in pounds. 'We aim to get to Las Vegas, Nevada.'

I lifted the Cross and put it on the roof rack, quickly fastening it with one strap. 'Why didn't somebody say,' Properjohn complained, his teeth chattering. He sat hunched behind Hattie at the wheel as we started off through the bleak white channel of the street again.

'Why didn't *you* say,' I argued. 'If you had told somebody you were going off like that we could have put you right.'

'It seemed all right on the map,' he moaned. 'I'm not used to maps, Willy. It's easy to make a mistake when you're not used to things. I could have frozen to death there.'

'You were conveniently near the mortuary,' I said sourly. 'They wouldn't have had to travel far to get you.'

'Don't say such things!' he howled. 'My time is not yet. You forget the work I have to do and the secrets I have in my possession.'

'Secrets?'

'Yes, secrets. The date of the End of the World and that manner of thing, Willy. I can't die with that sort of information on my person.'

The big snow seemed to have been waiting in ambush. As we left the last hushed house of Las Vegas it swooped from the mountains and engulfed us. It flew against the windscreen with such strength and size that the wipers could not keep pace with it. I stopped talking to Properjohn and glanced at Hattie.

'Can you see where you're going?' I said.

'It doesn't matter,' he said hurriedly, as though glad to get a confession off his chest. 'I've got to tell you I'm lost, Willy.

It's the wrong road. This road is climbing. If we were trying to get back to the others we ought to be dropping down.'

'We're lost, we're lost,' moaned Properjohn to himself. He was making little blowing forays at his hands. He looked up. 'Did you secure the Cross on top of the van, Willy?' he asked.

'Don't worry, I did,' I said. In fact I had only fastened it with one of the three straps. I hoped we still had it with us, but I wasn't going to look. Poor 'Jesus Lives' was straining through the blizzard now, like a pilgrim up to his knees while going to a high mountain. Eventually Hattie stopped it.

'I don't think we are going to progress much further,' he said, turning his pink worried face to me. 'I don't think she's going to climb much more in this snow, and in any case we're going in the wrong direction. We'll either have to stay up here until tomorrow . . .'

'Or turn around and go back down,' I said.

'Yes, or do that.'

'Well, we'll have to turn round,' I said. 'We can't just stay up here in this stuff all night. We'll be completely snowed under.'

'It will be difficult to turn it around,' he answered piteously, all his confidence behind the wheel now evaporated. 'Real difficult.'

'If we stay up here,' I said. 'Heaven knows what will happen. We stand a good chance of being swept over the side of one of these mountains anyway. I think we ought to go back while we've got the chance.'

'Lost, lost,' groaned Properjohn. He was beginning to sound like his own wife.

'Let's turn it around,' I said decisively. 'I'll get out and guide you. I'll see if the road is wide enough first.' I pulled my coat about me. As I was about to get out I could not resist turning fiercely on Properjohn and saying: 'This is all your fault.'

'Oh, Willy,' he pleaded. 'Don't be long out there.'

'I won't, don't worry about that,' I promised sourly. I opened the door and jumped out into the slicing snow. It was black and white mingling up there on that mountain; black night riven with a million fragments of snow, flying through it on a howling wind. First I climbed on the bonnet of 'Jesus

Lives' and scraped away as much of the hungry snow as possible. Armfuls came away with each sweep, but it piled up again almost as quickly as I got it away. We would have to be quick.

Hattie was staring through the windscreen at me and the cadaver-faced Properjohn then appeared at his side. They looked liked men encased in a glacier for a thousand years. I gave the windscreen one further clearance with my arm and then dropped to the road. I paced it out as far as I could to see how wide it was. A wall of mountain rock reared up on the left-hand side and another wall fell away with hideous anonymity on the other. There was not much room for the turn. But there was enough.

Hattie had the headlights full on as he went gingerly into the initial manœuvre of getting the nose facing the other way. The two men of God crouched together trembling against the windscreen. I stood in the road and guided his inching forward until the front wheels of the vehicle were as near the edge of the right-hand drop as I dare allow them. Then I motioned him back and he edged away from the abyss and pushed the rear of the truck back to the rising rocks on the other side. I let him get to within six inches before signalling him to stop. There was no doubt about Hattie, he could drive. Properjohn was sitting stiff beside him. It had not occurred to us to tell him to get out. Forward again, a slithering inch at a time through the snow. At least it was driving against the side of the vehicle now. Right to the edge, then back against the rocks again. There was a crunch and a sound of glass as the rear window was forced through by some projecting stone. The Cross swivelled on top. That rattled Hattie because on the next forward movement he tried to turn the whole thing around, to get it all over in one movement, and with a terrible slip and a fatalistic lurch 'Jesus Lives', Properjohn and Hattie, all went skidding over into the emptiness. I shouted out the most terrible cry, but I heard their desperate screams from over that. The Cross somehow flew from the roof of the vehicle as it toppled and was flung in the snow ten yards from me. With a strange blind impulse I rushed to it and picked it up. I clutched it, praying to God like mad that they had not gone forever. It worked.

186

From the swirling black-and-whiteness down there I heard their voices calling to me. I went to the very edge and almost collided with them as they came scrambling over the top. I threw my arms about both and we danced together in joyous relief in the snow.

'It's only a little drop,' said Properjohn off-handedly, as though he had arranged it himself. 'We only went down a few feet.'

'Let's pray in thanks for our deliverance,' said Hattie simply. He dropped on his knees in the snow and Properjohn fell beside him. Reluctantly I went down with them, hands together, eyes shut against the snowflakes, mumbling now to a God to whom a few minutes before I had been bellowing for help. It's funny how the Almighty grows and diminishes depending on the circumstances.

'We'd better not pray too long or we'll freeze,' said Properjohn practically. 'Then all the Lord's good works would come to nothing.'

'Gee, I'm sorry,' said Hattie, taking the responsibility for everything. 'I guess I panicked when I heard the Cross sliding from the roof. I didn't realize what it was.'

'Yes, it's all your fault,' said Properjohn typically.

'Listen,' I said to him forcefully. 'If it's anybody's fault, it's yours. Coming out by yourself on a night like this.'

'Yes, yes, Willy,' he said immediately contrite. 'I was very silly.'

'Let's get going,' I said. 'We'll get snowed up otherwise.'

I went cautiously to the edge of the descent and sniffed more than looked over. But only a few feet below I could see one headlight and one red rearlight of the motor home. 'You left your lights on,' I said to Hattie. He smiled through the snow and touched my hand.

Properjohn had reached the Cross and was prising it up from the drifts. 'We'd better take it with us,' he said dubiously. 'I wouldn't like anybody to walk off with it.'

I took the familiar weight of the Cross from him and we began trudging down the mountain road. The snow was thick around our feet, reaching up to our knees in some places and still it tumbled from the bottomless sky. Wheezing noises began to issue from Properjohn and I didn't like the sound of them. Twice he fell in the snow and we had to haul him out. It was obvious we were not going to get down the mountain with him that night.

Our prayers, however, seemed to have left us in good credit because only a few paces after Properjohn's second fall we came abreast of a large notice at the roadside and we pushed away its coat of snow to find it said: 'Hunters' refuge hut one hundred yards'.

'Thank God for that,' I said, helping Properjohn forward.

'Thank God, indeed,' echoed Hattie.

We staggered down the incline and almost passed it in the darkness. Then we saw it square among a crop of trees and thankfully reached it, pushed open the door, and groped our way into its salvation.

I let Properjohn down fairly heavily to the floor where he lay for a while muttering the odd 'Glory, glory, praise, praise' between laboured breaths. From his pocket we prised a box of matches and struck one. There was a kerosene lamp on the table and we lit it, standing thankfully and letting its safe glow grow around us. We were like three snowmen, covered with the stuff. Hattie's face was crusted white with his pink cold nose poking through. Properjohn looked up from the floor and suggested we should have a second session of prayers for deliverance once we had our circulations running again.

'There's a stove,' I said, nodding to Hattie who had the matches. 'Let's hope the thing's working.'

It was too. The kerosene lit easily and the hut began to warm quickly. There was a cupboard marked 'Food' where we found some tins of soup which we heated and ate gratefully. Finally we were able to loosen our coats and sit quietly on the long bench exhausted by it all.

'Las Vegas,' grunted Properjohn eventually. 'Tin pot place. Doubt if there's any sin to be saved there. Wouldn't waste my time and energy on them.'

'She's a good girl, really, you know. Ambrosia.'

He said it through the near-dark for we had turned out the lamp and kept the kerosene stove going; he said it as though

188

continuing some running conversation although we had not been talking about her. He was lying on the hut floor, piled with blankets. The place smelled of the soup we had cooked and eaten. Hattie was prone on the other side of me, also on the floor, on his back, eyes closed, hands clasped in moribund manner across his chest.

'Ambrosia?' I said, through the firelight. I made it sound as though I was trying to think who she was. My guilt I suppose.

'Yes, a good girl,' he confirmed from a crevice in the blankets. 'Still a child, of course, Willy. Only seventeen yet.'

'Plenty of time,' I said.

'For what?' he asked, his nose emerging from the mound with a touch of suspicion.

'Well, for living, seeing things, going places,' I replied uneasily.

'Oh, not Ambrosia. She's a home-girl, you know, underneath it all. Oh, she tries to pretend that she's up to date, and mod, whatever that may be, but she likes her home in Wales, she does. Peace and quiet. Even when she went to Bristol that time to see her sick friend and to view the Clifton Suspension Bridge, she didn't really want to go.'

'No?'

'No, not likely. And she insisted that Clare went with her. She wanted to have her mam with her, see. Cried when she left home. Aye, cried. Never been away before, see. Couldn't get used to the idea. And she was only gone for a few days.' He paused. 'Funny place to go, Bristol,' he said. 'If it's your first trip away from home, if you see what I mean. Most people would like to go to London, but I'm glad she didn't go there. I can't see my Ambrosia in London, somehow. It's too smutty. It just wouldn't suit her.'

'If her sick friend was in Bristol, and the Clifton Suspension Bridge, that's where she had to go, wasn't it,' I said, I hoped logically. 'It would have been no good looking anywhere else for either of them.'

He laughed, an elderly, sleepy laugh. 'No, no,' he agreed. The blankets nodded vigorously. 'There's that about it.' He waited for a few minutes more and I thought he had gone to sleep. 'Did you ever find your wife, Willy? The one you said you were going to look for when I was talking to you on the aeroplane?'

I swallowed in the dark. First Ambrosia, now my wife. 'No,' I said. 'I've not actually come across her yet. Not a sign of her.'

The blankets sighed. 'Ah, there's so many people here,' he said. 'It's a sizeable place, America. All these people and mountains and towns and fields and rivers. You know, you may not believe this, but there are times, Willy, when I just don't know where I am.'

I could not resist a snort. 'Like tonight,' I told him. 'Getting the wrong Las Vegas.'

'Oh, that. Well, anybody could make a mistake like that. I mean, how was I to know there was two. Did you know?'

'No,' I agreed truthfully. 'But Las Vegas is in the desert. It's not stuck up in the mountains like this. And I don't think they get much snow there.'

'I don't care about whether the place is hot or cold,' he said defensively, from the little crack which he had opened up more or less permanently in the fold of the blankets. 'That doesn't concern me, Willy. I was just surprised when I couldn't find any gambling clubs or lights or shows, or any of that kind of thing. Now, that's when I began to suspect that there was something gone wrong. I put my head in that bar they had there and asked them where the night-life was. They all seemed to think it was a great big joke. One of them shouted "it's her off-week this week" or something of that nature, which I couldn't really make any sense of. Does that make sense to you?'

'No, I don't understand that,' I lied. 'Perhaps you didn't hear it right.'

'No, perhaps I didn't.' He left hardly a pause. Then he went back to Ambrosia. 'She'll make somebody a fine wife one day, Willy,' he said. 'In fifteen or twenty years' time.'

'She'll be getting on then,' I said. 'She's seventeen now.'

'But young, Willy, very young. Do you know she's still like a little girl in some ways. I think of her as a little girl.'

'I know,' I said.

'Ah, don't take any notice of that silly tantrum by the river that night. She loves me swinging her around by the legs. She really loves it. But she just put on that bit of temper to show off to you lads, that's all. She's still a child. Do you know she still carries the leg of the china doll she had when she was a tot; still carries it around in her handbag.'

'That's a funny thing to keep,' I said.

'Yes, it is. I looked in her handbag once. Looking for some change, I was, and it was lying there, handy.' His pointed face came completely out from the blankets. 'Not that you must ever tell her that,' he warned. 'About me going in her hand- bag. I don't want her to know that. I couldn't find any change anyway. Only this doll's leg. Goodnight, Willy. Thank you for coming to find me.'

'That's all right,' I said quietly, through the gloom. 'Good- night.'

'I understand that,' said Hattie suddenly. I had thought he was asleep. 'Keeping a doll's leg. Inanimate things concern me, you know. I like to keep things because I worry about what might happen to them if I let them go. People can always come back to you.'

'Sometimes,' I said.

'But things, that's different. When I was a kid we used to have a beach house we used to go every summer. At Biddeford, Maine. In September we would lock it up for another year, storing everything away. And in the winter I would lie awake wondering how the chairs were getting on, or maybe if the clock could be lonely. Worrying about them up there, locked up on the coast. Does that make any sense to you, Willy?'

'It doesn't to me,' grunted Properjohn ill-naturedly from his pile. 'Go to sleep.'

'I can see it,' I said to Hattie.

'I wondered what they did all the winter, there in the beach house. If the time seemed to go slow. I suppose it's like that when we're dead.'

'Rubbish. Go to sleep,' growled Properjohn again.

'Goodnight,' said Hattie sadly.

'Goodnight Hattie,' I said.

I lay there for half an hour, weary but unable to go to sleep, thinking about it all. The strange things about it. That doll's leg. The big bed in Bethlehem. Poor Ambrosia. Then I drifted to sleep and woke with a sharp start to find Hattie leaning close to me and his hand on my leg.

'Hattie,' I whispered in alarm, thinking he might be doing it in his sleep. 'Hattie, what's going on?'

He was awake all right. 'God moves in a mysterious way, Willy,' he said pleadingly.

I stared at him in the dimness. 'That's not the hand of God, mate. Take it away,' I said.

He did. But he did not retreat. Sorrowfully he said: 'Willy, I thought we were going to die tonight. When the truck went over the edge.'

'I thought there was a fair chance of it,' I said guardedly.

'I've never done anything I really want to do, Willy. Never in my life. I realized that at the moment when we were plunging over that precipice.'

'So you're going to start now,' I said. I was whispering in the dark so as not to wake Properjohn.

'Your voice is low,' he said. 'I like you very much, Willy. Do you like me?'

'Of course, of course. I just don't like your hand on my leg, that's all.'

'I thought . . . I thought being English you would understand,' he moaned. 'You have a liberal outlook. We don't seem to have it here in America.'

'Even with a liberal outlook we only like what we like, so don't do it again.'

'I'm angry with myself, Willy. I think I'll go out in the snow.'

'Captain Oates did that and never came back,' I said. 'Mind, not for the same reason. Why don't you just settle down and go to sleep. You've had an exciting day and it's upset you.'

'Sure, sure,' he muttered like an incantation. Then without wait or warning he leaned over and kissed me on the cheek. I nearly went through the roof of the hut. My howl woke Properjohn and he called out to find what had happened.

'A rat,' said Hattie promptly.

'Yes, a rat,' I said firmly, staring at Hattie through the dark.

'Goodnight,' mumbled Properjohn.

'Goodnight,' we both returned.

We waited. Then I said to Hattie, 'Do that again and I'll kill you. Okay?'

'Okay, Willy,' he sniffed. 'I just promised myself I'd try it just once. I won't again. I admire you, Willy, tremendously.'

I did not trust him. There was not much room on the floor of the hut and none of us could go outside. Along the wall was the Cross, so I crept to it, picked it up, and placed it between the Reverend Hatt and myself so that we were like a maid and a knight of old sleeping each side of a sword.

Fifteen

It took two days before 'Jesus Lives' was retrieved from the ten-foot gorge in the mountains. The garage man from Las Vegas said it was the only ten-foot gorge in the entire range. None of the others stopped before two hundred feet. We returned gingerly through the declining snow to Santa Fé and then on to the main highway at Albuquerque with Properjohn in subdued mood. The first thing he did when we re-started towards the west on Route Sixty-Six was to hand the road map disdainfully to Herbie. 'I haven't got time to do it,' he said. 'I am writing a special hymn for Las Vegas.'

He brightened in the Navajo Indian country where the landscape was all turbulent red sandstone piled against the sky, adobe huts and Spanish churches, and big signs saying: 'Over thirty major credit cards accepted at Indian City.' He went down into the fastnesses of his deep black coat to find hidden money for a pair of steer horns and a genuine squaw blanket, bought with childish zest from an Indian wearing pince-nez in an imitation tent outside The Refrigerated Navajo Motel.

'That,' remarked Winston, as we helped to get the steer horns into the cramped space of the motor home, 'was the original refrigerated Navajo. Did anyone ever see a happy Indian?'

'No Indian's ever had anything to be happy about,' grunted Herbie. 'Their life's real miserable and always has been real miserable and always will be real miserable until they're finally wiped out. These guys haven't developed the face muscles to smile.'

'Why don't they?' I asked.

'Because nobody's ever told them anything funny,' he said, looking with his usual racial challenge at Winston. 'Or nice. They've never had any good news.'

Winston sniffed. 'The Negro ain't had a lot to laugh about,' he said. Then in his Uncle Tom voice, 'But we's famous for our smiles.' He flashed a manufactured grin.

'The black man always liked to show off his teeth,' put in Herbie, philosophically nodding at Winston, as though he were a lecturer and Winston a specimen. 'Even when he didn't have another thing he had his big white teeth.'

'The black man's jewellery,' said Winston cynically.

Herbie said: 'Well, the Navajo ain't even got good teeth.'

Properjohn had seen a sign for Laguna and was happily singing to himself about the Lily of such a place while arranging the crop of curly hair between the steer horns like a hairdresser. The argument between the Jew and the Negro meant nothing to him. Just short of a place called Grants there was an Indian sitting in a broken armchair in the middle of his muddy yard, looking at his slum shack, his dejected motor car, and the great beautiful rising of the clean sky and muscular mountains behind them. To Properjohn it would have been just a man sitting in a chair in the open air. In Grants itself, a sublime example of man's indifference to nature's finery, a town backed by great dumb mountains and choked with trash heaps, smashed cars, shanties, supermarkets, and all man's rubble, a front and an *aff*rontery. Here we stopped and Properjohn devoured a Stuckey's Pecan Walnut Fruit Divinity because it sounded religious.

There were many Indians in the street there, men with incredibly bowed legs and bowed mouths. Herbie continued his appraisement of the Negro and the Indian until Winston fell silent and finally asked quietly: 'How come white man know so much about redskin?'

'I just know,' answered Herbie, waving the question away.

'And I know how you know,' said Winston craftily. 'Because, man, I remember seeing you in a movie *Night-time Wumpum*. Boy, that was really something to do with the lot of the Indian.'

We were hurrying for Las Vegas now. The delay in the mountains of New Mexico had put us behind schedule but, in any event, there were no Triumphal Entries planned for the desert and snow country of Northern Arizona. Some sort of arrival ceremony with an edited rally had been on the list for Flagstaff, but we were a day late there and a blizzard was blowing. Properjohn professed surprise that 'the faithful didn't bother to wait' but he said no more and we descended from that high plateau down to the sunny level of the winter desert. The Indian signs continued, 'Navajo Jewellery, Papoose shawls. We take pawn' and 'Visit the Chief's Cave and the Tomahawk Nightclub'. It was sad to see a whole people reduced to making an exhibition of themselves.

All through the burnished country of petrified forest, painted desert and stormy sunsets Properjohn had dismissed the awesome landscapes as 'cheap tourist rubbish' and fell into howls of derisive laughter at a notice which proclaimed 'Two Guns, Arizona – Site of the World Fair in 1999.'

Eventually, at Kingman, an airy and open place where Properjohn played for half an hour on the footplate of the Santa Fé railway locomotive bedded in commemorative concrete, we turned away from Route Sixty-Six, released it to continue on its way to the Pacific sea. We went up into the mountains again towards Nevada, crossed the bow of the Hoover Dam, and at evening arrived in the lofted peaks overlooking the flat desert and the shining city of Las Vegas.

We knew it was coming even while we still climbed the bent road on the far side of the hills, for its million lights projected up to that height like a broad and majestic searchlight, lighting the undersides of the low wintertime clouds.

'I guess this is what it's like approaching heaven,' said Herbie, then glancing at Properjohn. 'For some folks.'

'Hell,' said Properjohn predictably. But his hunched face was pushed forward in anticipation and those eyes were alive with a light of their own.

We reached the apex of the road and there it was – a city flung far out like an explosion, fiery with lights and neons, its long streets, and The Strip streaming outwards like a tail from a disintegrating star. That was the first sight. But then we turned the two vehicles off the road onto a wide, flat area that was to figure so much in our misfortunes in that place. We got out and in every face of ours there was some form of happiness. The city was not an explosion; that had been the first dazzling sight. It was a great brilliant lake of light, and peaceful, so peaceful, winking and blazing away with a strangely quiet rapture in the dark of the desert. Light intersected with light, light curled and circled, splashed and rose and fell in many colours; light travelled through light as cars moved through the streets far below us. The Strip stretched out like a bright handle from the city, and beyond that, in the night sky, at our eye level, were the red insect lights of aeroplanes coming in to the distant airport.

'It's lovely, it's so lovely,' breathed Ambrosia. She had her hand violently around my elbow as we all stood and looked out. I glanced quickly at her father and she released my arm. But the sight still held her eyes and she said again, but quietly because of him: 'It's the loveliest thing I have ever seen.'

'Sin!' Properjohn shouted at last. 'Sin, sin, sin.'

'That's a whole lot of sin,' agreed Herbie, whispering on my other side. 'I pray for it. I pray I'm going to get some of it.'

'It's like Newport Docks!' exclaimed the incredible Clare. 'All the lights on the ships. Just like the docks.'

'The enemy!' howled Properjohn in everybody's ear. 'Behold the enemy!'

'Newport Docks,' insisted Poor Clare to herself. 'Just like.'

'Toy town,' said Winston, with a wry laugh.

'Las Vegas,' said the Reverend Hatt as though pinning it down.

'Silvie,' I thought. She was down there, somewhere, under

one of those signalling lights, performing French dances, or whatever they called them here. Or something. And down there she lived too and the children went to school. It was strange because it did not look like anywhere people really lived.

We stood observing it for another five minutes, the dazzling sameness of its billiance, the only changes the unchanging blinking of the eternal sky signs and the endless belt of the traffic. Nobody spoke until Properjohn called, not to us, but to the city: 'Death and destruction will visit you, and very soon too. I have the date in my pocket. Don't repent – it's too late!'

At that moment I thought I'd put my money on Las Vegas.

We went down the descending road to the city, out of the turreted desert mountains and down to the asphalt and lights. A mile outside we unshipped the Cross and set off on our final Triumphal Entry.

Flaming torches greeted us, and choirs and bands with young drum majorettes dressed in little cassocks that were hemmed on a level with the bottom of their small, crowded backsides and with heaving ribboned bows over their American girl chests. It was powerful and exciting. I, naturally, entered into the spirit of the night completely, carrying my Cross with my finely formed expression of suffering until Winston suggested that I relax because if there was one thing they did not like to see in Las Vegas it was somebody miserable.

The city was like a tempest of light, jumping and waving all around from every street and every roof and window. In the downtown district people crowded from the gambling arcades to see us and to join in the hymns before going back to their own heaven with the fruit machines. Some people in evening dress got on top of 'Jesus Lives', the front of the two motor homes, and sang louder than any. There was no sense of enmity among these sinners, who looked strangely like ordinary American people, and indeed they welcomed us in a manner which suggested that they anticipated us joining them rather than them joining us.

Downtown Las Vegas was like a funfair, bright but enclosed, intimate in its streets, and noisy with pintables and souvenir shops, but with everyone glad to see our new diversion and giving us a marvellous reception which was very sporting, as Herbie was quick to point out, as a good proportion of them were Jewish. They applauded as though we had won a fancy dress parade. They cheered the Cross as much as any of the Christian gamblers, and, as far as I could see, were just as liberal when the collecting boxes were toted about. Winston said that people are apt to live in a strange, generous cloud when they are in Las Vegas. 'This is the place,' he said. 'Where they say people arrive in a twenty-thousand-dollar Cadillac and leave in a seventy-thousand-dollar bus.'

We marched through the tight town streets, like some roistering circus band, but then we turned and headed for The Strip and we left the intimacy of the town and marched down the broad neon arm that stretches out into the desert. Here the great gaming buildings, The Dunes, Circus-Circus, Caesar's Palace, and the others winked at us knowingly like rich and randy ladies. The extraordinary illuminations splashed and jumped and curved about us on each bank of the broad avenue, a perpetual firework display. There were no people on the sidewalks now, only faces from slowed cars and a chill breeze blew down the gully of the highway, pushing against our clothes and bodies, our faces, and buffeting the Cross in my arms. We could have been walking through a wasteland.

'Sun-Up, Vegas,' said the man expansively. 'Is a great little show. We transmit at seven every morning and we aim to just catch our audience before they hit the pillow.'

He waited for the laugh, as he doubtless did every morning from his guests, and Winston nudged Herbie and I into projecting two early smiles. 'We aim,' he said. 'To bring a little uplift to people who need it. A little song, maybe a sensitive poem or so, a recipe here and there, a little surface religion. So that the couple who have lost a few thousand at the crap tables all night don't think that the end of the world is coming.'

'It is,' said Properjohn firmly. He was sitting hunched at the end of the row in front of the producer.

'What's that?' queried the man.

'Coming,' confirmed Properjohn. 'The End of the World.'

'Ah, yes,' beamed the man uncertainly. 'I think you have some information on that. Well, let's wait for the show.' He blinked at Properjohn. 'That's if it's not going to be too late?' he simpered.

'You'll have time for the programme,' replied Properjohn solemnly. 'Anyway, we want to sing our new hymn.'

'Great, great,' breathed the man uneasily. 'I sure wouldn't like to be wasting anybody's time.'

'Especially when it's running out,' said Properjohn. Winston turned a small dark glare on him and Ambrosia nudged him discouragingly. The man gave a tenuous laugh and built it into a large grin when another man in a red suit appeared from behind the screens and lights of the studio. 'Barney Gallatio,' he announced, as though he were making the revelation to millions. 'The star of our show.'

Mr Gallatio looked as though he had gone to bed at five, risen at six, and had spent an hour on his make-up. He was a tall, slim young man with a battery-operated smile, and the batteries were low that morning. To my astonishment Ambrosia made a little squeaking noise and rose from our row, to be the first to be introduced. Mr Gallatio took her hand sickeningly in both of his and his smile made her blush. Then, back in order, he was introduced along the line by Winston because the producer had already forgotten our names.

'During the programme,' said Mr Gallatio, 'I would like the Reverend Properjohn to occupy that chair directly across from my chair and I would like the rest of you to form in a semi-circle behind us, with the man with the Cross in the middle.' A voice came across the studio floor and he broke off and walked over to the man who had called. When he had turned his back we all glared like a family at Ambrosia who was watching every step of the star's tired legs.

He returned. 'No – we've taken a rain check on that and I guess the guy with the Cross had better place himself to one side, to the right maybe, because otherwise the Cross is going to get in the way of the name of one of our sponsors, Testament Ground Coffee. Is that okay, Cross-man?'

I nodded sourly. Testament Coffee was in heraldic letters

over the dais at the end of the studio, flanked by Trinity Autos, and Miracle Furnishers.

'We'll have a great little half-hour, this morning,' exclaimed Mr Gallatio, as though trying to rouse himself. 'Bringing comfort and hope to many people in Las Vegas.'

'Don't count on that, buddy,' said Properjohn in his Edward G. Robinson voice. Winston nudged him and smiled at the producer who had arrived to usher us to the dais before the cameras. Nobody seemed to be awake. One of the cameramen was actually hanging onto his instrument, eyes closed, like a weary cowboy holding the neck of his horse.

We were arranged woodenly, as for a group photograph, behind the two chairs, and the programme began almost before we had time to compose our expressions. 'Do you believe in miracles?' Mr Gallatio inquired of one camera. 'I do, friends. I firmly believe in miracles. Miracles, 496, East Flamingo Road, in downtown Las Vegas, is the furniture store *you* can believe in too. Later in this show we will be demonstrating some of their fine, fine products. We will also see some of the great, great cars *you* can buy today from Trinity Autos, Tropicana Boulevard, and sample some of that *heavenly* Testament Coffee. But, right now, I want you to meet our guests for today. They are members of a group who have been travelling across our country bringing the Word of Christ to many people who need it in these troublesome times. Their leader is the Reverend John Properjohn, Minister of the Church of the Living God, Wales, England.'

'Livid God,' corrected Properjohn testily.

'Livid God?' queried Mr Gallatio. 'Oh, gee, sure, I get it, now. I thought it was a typing error. Oh yes, folks, I see, Livid God. And what more appropriate in these troublesome times.'

'And Wales is Wales, not England.'

'How right you are. Okay. Let's get this address right. The Church of the Livid God, Wales, Wales.'

'Llanbergowonyth, Wales,' Properjohn pursued him.

'Sure, right on the dot,' said the man wildly. 'Okay, then. And this is your group.'

I don't think he intended individual introductions but Properjohn half turned and pedantically pointed each one out.

'That one's Clare, my wife. She's had an operation on her jaw, you know. And then Ambrosia, my daughter, a young girl of seventeen – keep your hands off, big boy.' He delivered this towards Mr Gallatio in his pre-war film track voice again and crumpled with idiotic laughter. He wiped his eyes and recovered sufficiently to introduce Herbie, whom he called Harold but quickly amended, and then me, 'the one who looks like Jesus' and finally 'the black bloke is Winston, named after our great war leader'.

'Mr Properjohn,' Mr Gallatio broke in firmly. 'Has been delivering the Message of God on his long journey. More about that in a moment. But first a message from our sponsor.'

A vacuum settled on his face as soon as the commercial had taken over the screen. Then he seemed to remember we were there and he turned, first to Properjohn and then to the rest of us, and with that dim, aching smile said: 'Well, folks, it's going real good.'

The real good ended there, however, because from that point Properjohn took over the programme. He sang, he recited, he told mindless jokes, praised God, did a stiff clerical dance, and splattered the Testament Coffee all over Mr Gallatio.

'Mr Properjohn, Reverend,' Mr Gallatio had purred. 'I want the opinion of an honest-to-God man on the quality of Testament Coffee, an honest-to-God product. We would like your . . . ah . . . testament . . . about this heavenly beverage.'

Knowing Properjohn as we did we stood cold like people ranged before a firing squad, except for Winston who was standing next to me with a settled contentment on his small, smooth face. Properjohn took the proffered cup and with his wrecked smile held it up as a sort of toast to the viewers. Mr Gallatio nodded in a pleased fashion and then Properjohn took a deep drink. It would be too much to say he spewed it back, but he certainly splattered it back, half-rising and spraying a shower of the heavenly liquid all over Mr Gallatio's red suit.

The man let loose a wild cry that quickly dried into a stupid stony grin since he was still on the screen. 'Oh my, oh my, oh my,' he cooed horribly, wiping impotently at the spots. 'What a sad accident we have here, ladies and gentlemen. Went down the wrong way, I guess. And what a waste of Testament Coffee, a great product. Are you okay, Reverend?'

Properjohn said nothing but sat back as though in some state of shock, regarding the coffee cup, now set on the low table, as though he had narrowly survived an assassination attempt. Gallatio was professional enough to get away from the incident as quickly as possible. The producer was sitting in a corner with his head in his hands. 'Well,' said Gallatio. 'Let's get back to your great crusade, your great crusade.'

'We want to sing our song,' said Properjohn truculently.

'Your song? You have a song?'

'We've got a song, all right,' boasted Properjohn. He did not wait for the invitation, but stood and conducted us in the hymn he had composed on the road:

'Jesus is coming,
Everyone watch out!
Hear the trumpets trumping,
Hear the angels shout.

'Jesus is coming,
Hear the song – and how!
Sinners start shaking,
You'll be sorry now.'

It went on for several more hideous verses to a tune filched from the *English Hymnal*. Despite its sentiments it might have proved a reasonable salvage ending to the disastrous show had not Properjohn spotted that the armchair standing vacant almost beside him, a commercial prop for the Miracle Furniture Company, was bulging with hurried and haphazard stuffing at the back. As we sang and in front of the horrified but helpless Gallatio he proceeded to pluck great lumps of synthetic horsehair and foam rubber from the piece and to throw them airily about the studio. The stuff came out in handfuls as we sang to the climax of our hymn. The silence that came after was broken by the sobbing voice of the producer far back in the studio calling weakly 'Cut it, cut it.' He and Mr Gallatio were in tears, half-exasperation, half-sorrow, while Properjohn stood and looked around with an amazed face as though wondering what had gone wrong.

'That guy don't need no public relations man,' said Winston confidently. 'He wants a keeper.'

'I thought the whole idea was to *save* Las Vegas,' I said. 'He's telling everybody it's doomed.'

'I guess he wants to save it first,' said Winston. 'Like spiritually – and then whap! Down comes the big fist of God.'

In two days Properjohn had shattered the decent, middle-aged peace of Las Vegas. People who were accustomed only to the religious low drone of the croupiers' voices, the innocent rattle of the dice and the remembered voices of The Ink Spots in cabaret, who contentedly ate hamburgers with iced red wine, who clutched each other convincingly in their second-honeymoon beds while the myriad colours of the frenzied advertisement lights flew in through their hotel windows and across their especially summoned passion. For beneath all its illuminated blatancy it was revealed as a sedate and timid place, a place of pilgrimage for people who had always promised each other they would go there. Until Properjohn arrived I doubt if Las Vegas was ever aware of sin.

He had caused a riot in Circus-Circus, the great, striped, imitation tent where on the high trapeze tumblers flew unheeded above gamblers. He went to the balcony and threw great storms of Hattie's leaflets over the people below and, commandeering the circus band leader's microphone, howled his message of doom to acrobats and fruit machine players alike.

His entry into Caesar's Palace, clutching the Cross, which I had gladly handed to him when, like a coward I had halted on the entry steps, was joyfully recorded by television, radio and the newspapers, tired with the dullness of their celebrity-ridden lives. He stormed into the great betting concourse, scattering lever pullers, knocking over mountains of chips, grabbing cards from intense hands, and throwing people bodily aside, all the while bellowing: 'Glory! Glory! Glory! Praise! Praise! Praise!' From the main door we watched the stormy progress of the wooden Cross, heard his battlecry, and the screams of the mothers and fathers from Dayton, Ohio, caught at their innocent pleasures. Right at my ear a television reporter, alerted naturally by the ecstatic Winston, was shouting into his microphone: 'Until now "action" in Vegas meant a poker hand. But now . . . Wow! This crazy guy is turning the place upside down.'

The crazy guy was on the far side of the immense gambling floor, only the top of the tossing Cross was visible above the thousand heads, but the cries and protests as he went through like some black avenging angel were all we needed to hear. Then we saw him again, this time mounting the prow of Cleopatra's barge, a life-sized vessel moored in an indoor pond to one side of Caesar's Palace. He was still waving the Cross, but now he was pursued by large men in tuxedos, and he staggered on enormous bow legs and with that mad, illuminated expression, up the ornate figurehead of the boat like an elderly Errol Flynn fighting against some pirate horde.

'Sinners!' he bellowed across the concourse. 'You're all doomed. All bloody doomed!' Whereupon the men in pursuit made a rush at him and he tumbled spectacularly with the Cross, and with one of the pursuers, into the ornamental pond. 'I think,' said Herbie prudently. 'Maybe we ought to wait outside until they deliver him. I don't like the attention we're attracting around here.'

Winston glanced at him and shrugged: 'Same old St Peter.'

We went out and waited until Properjohn, soaked and gloriously defiant, and still, I was relieved to see, clutching the Cross, was placed outside the main door by Joe Louis, the large former heavyweight champion of the world. 'I ain't never seen a fighter like that,' he said, as he put Properjohn down the steps. 'And I don't want no return bout either.'

'Reverend,' said Winston. 'This poor guy, Willy, has just got to have twenty-four hours' rest and recuperation. I guess it's been too much for him.'

I sagged convincingly against his arm and quietly rolled my eyes. 'He was found lying on the ground,' he continued. 'He can't take any more.'

'My poor boy,' exclaimed Properjohn, violently fixing my

face in a rough chute formed by his big hands. 'This is terrible. All been too much for you. All too much. Some of us are spiritually tougher than others.'

'The Cross is heavy after all these miles,' murmured Winston.

'That too,' agreed Properjohn. 'It always was an awkward thing, and he's never looked very strong to me. A bit sickly, I've often thought. But we need him for the big night to-morrow. Nobody carries the Cross like he does. Get him into his bed.'

'Well,' suggested Winston quickly. 'I think he needs to get away from this location for a short period. It's pretty noisy all the time with sightseers poking around and people wanting autographs and all that kind of activity. I know a priest here, a good guy, who runs a little place for people like this. He'll see he's okay in a day or so.'

'Make it a day,' said Properjohn, businesslike again. 'And who's paying?'

'There's no charge,' hurried Winston. 'It's a charitable thing.'

Properjohn grasped my eyelid. It was amazing how heavy he could be even with the smallest parts of the body; with his usual violent energy he lifted it and dropped it again. 'Very nasty,' he said to my private annoyance. 'Don't like the look of him at all. But make sure he's back tomorrow. It's a pity we have to do without him for this afternoon's attack on the Hilton Hotel.'

Not the most trusting of men, Properjohn insisted, under the guise of concern, in accompanying me to the Serendipity Center for Rest and Recovery, where he became predictably disdainful of the small Chinese pastor in charge, but left me lying on a bed with a quick theatrical blessing and a warning not to leave the building.

'He's turning this town upside down,' said Father Sunley, the Chinese pastor, when Properjohn had gone. 'What's he going to do next?'

'Attack the Hilton Hotel,' I said almost indifferently. 'This afternoon.'

'He sure gets the attention,' he acknowledged. 'Every time I turn on TV he's there. Most of us here are content to go quietly about our ministry, hoping to save a little maybe, enough to open a wedding chapel, or at least get the wedding concession from one of the motels.'

His face was expressive in a muted Chinese way, although his voice was completely American. 'I try in my modest way to help people who find Las Vegas a little too much for their emotions and, of course, their pockets. We try to give them a . . . a *soupçon* of peace. This, after all, is the city where people arrive in a twenty-thousand-dollar Cadillac . . .'

'And leave in a seventy-thousand-dollar bus,' I finished.

'You heard.'

'I did, but it won't happen to me. I haven't got the price of a single pull of a fruit machine handle.'

'Then you're rich, Mr Turpin. You *can't* lose. In these cubicles are people who are paying good money just to be brought back gently into the sunlight. After a week without seeing the day, just walking from the gambling floor to their hotel room in the same building, they come here to sleep and we gradually lift the blinds in the room so that they are introduced to God's sun again.'

'They pay?' I said.

'They pay some time. When we take them in they probably don't have the money, only a credit rating, but they pay eventually. They may need us again.'

'Winston said it was a charity,' I said.

'For Winston, and for you it is. He was a good friend in New York.'

'Good. Thank you.'

He said: 'This Properjohn, he's a Nonconformist, right?'

'Yes, I'd certainly say that. He conforms to nothing.'

'I remember the Reverend Jaye coming here,' he smiled.

'Ah, you knew Jaye. He died here, didn't he?'

'He came several times, but I was here when he died.'

'That's why we're here, you know, that's why the Foundation launched this thing. It's a sort of revenge because he died trying to save Las Vegas.'

'Yes,' mused the Chinest priest. 'He was excellent with

sinners. He was with one, Lulu Broadbent from the Fantastique Club, when he actually died.'

'No! My God, and they said he died of a broken heart!'

'More of a jolted heart,' he said blandly.

I laughed sourly. 'And they said he had been taken home by Jesus. Those were the actual words.'

'He was taken home by Lulu Broadbent,' said Father Sunley.

'Who'd credit it. It makes you wonder what *is* genuine.'

'Life's genuine,' he said. 'You couldn't fake that.' He paused then added: 'You won't be needing a cubicle, according to Winston.'

'No, thanks. I just want to slip out and give this town a going over. I'm looking for my wife.'

'Sure, Winston told me. You calculate she's here.'

'Yes, I'm pretty certain. She's a dancer.'

'There's a whole lot of dancers and a whole lot of places to look. Could you use twenty-five dollars from the poor box?'

'Could I? I really could. That's very kind of you.'

He went away and came back with the money. 'When you're heavy with the stuff maybe you'd like to send thirty dollars back or send it to Winston to forward. We have to make a little profit.'

'Of course, what else. I'm very grateful.'

'Okay,' he smiled in a final sort of way. 'I hope you find your wife, mister. And I hope she finds you.'

'That's important,' I nodded. 'Can I ask you how you get a name like Father Sunley.'

'I adopted it,' he smiled sadly. 'I have a Chinese name, of course, but people don't trust Sun Lee like Sunley and if he's a pastor as well they think they're going to end up in a horror movie. Sunley is much more reassuring.'

I had taken a list of cabaret booking agents from the yellow pages of the telephone directory, but walking from the Serendipity Rest Home to the bus stop I went by a school with children in the playground and the realization that my children could possibly be among them stopped me. They were small kids, about the right age group, and they were screaming and skipping about the yard as children do everywhere.

There was a little girl standing alone surveying the others and I had a sudden illogical thought that it could be Kathy. I stopped and bent down by the railings to get a better view of her. With a sad and hopeless realization I had to face the fact that it was two years and I did not know how she would look. The child half-turned and I saw her profile. God, she was like Silvie. I could *not* forget Silvie. She was wearing a pale blue dress.

Could it be? I must have been mad. I crouched at the chicken-wire fence and pushed my face as close to it as I could. My nose poked through one of the holes and my mouth came conveniently level with the next hole down. 'Kathy,' I called. 'Is that you, Kathy? Hi . . . little girl'.

She turned. I swore it was. The miniature pretty face, the hair, that very expression. Her mother all over. 'Little girl,' I called again. She came confidently to the fence. She stood there, two feet away, saying nothing, just staring at me, the crouching man. 'Kathy,' I said. 'Are you Kathy? I'm your father.'

The child took a firm pace forward and reached out with her dainty fingers. She caught hold of my nose with one hand and my emotionally protruding lips with the other and she twisted them viciously, my nose one way and my lips the other. Then she turned and ran off screaming hideously: 'Teacher! Teacher! There's a trippy man! There's a trippy man!'

A trippy man, I thought, my eyes full of water from the sharpness of her twists. A trippy man! Christ, that must be me! I glanced up to see her weeping against a formidable flowered overall at the distant end of the yard and pointing in my direction.

God, I had to get out! The fear straightened me up. I wiped my eyes and began running down the street, a quick right turn and then another and there was the bus. I had not intended to go to Lake Mead that day, but I went anyway. Anywhere would do.

*　　*　　*

That night I went to every club in the downtown area, like some private eye, producing a photograph of Silvie and showing it to the barman or the doorman. None of the booking agents I had seen had ever heard of her and there were only shrugs and shaken heads in the clubs. She was not very big time.

At midnight I shuffled into somewhere called 'Feathers' and in the doorway gloom displayed the photograph to yet another man in a greasy peaked cap. This one did not shake his head. He said: 'Are you a cop?'

'No. I'm just looking for her, that's all. I'm her husband.'

I suppose there's a touch of the theatrical even in nightclub doormen. This one pulled away a draped curtain and nodded into the dark hole of the club. Beyond the silhouetted heads, in a white spotlight on the stage a naked girl was having simulated sex with what appeared to be an equally naked man.

'That's her,' said the doorman. 'I see her every night so I notice her face as well.'

Stunned I stood there. That arrow of a body, the easily swung limbs, the fine tilt of the head, the hair caught at the neck, the shadows around the breasts. Silvie! Transfixed I caught hold of the door curtain and stood there.

'If you're looking for a divorce, mister,' muttered the doorman. 'I guess what they're doing is as good as the real thing. And there's witnesses.'

'Thanks,' I grunted absently. I moved forward, hesitating at first but then with short hurried steps because there was one seat at a table in the front. It was next to the stage and the other seat was occupied by one of the house girls.

'You want to buy me a drink?' she inquired, leaning across, a strong face, mounted on strong breasts.

'No,' I said briefly.

'You can't sit there without a drink, buster.'

I was staring at my slowly gyrating wife, white, smooth, lovely in the spotlight, only a few feet away and above me.

'Have what you want,' I muttered sideways at the woman. 'Get me anything.'

'Champagne?' she said.

'No. Beer.'

'Beer? And he said anything.'

At that moment the male partner in the sexual dance, a fellow like a dago of some sort, who, I was relieved to see, was wearing a sort of codpiece over his thing, picked Silvie up and cartwheeled her across the small stage until, at the final revolution, she came easily down upon the palms of her hands and with her lovely, sweet, sweating face, right opposite mine. She smiled in an unsurprised way. The waiter bringing the drinks passed right between us. My head went around his hip so I could see her again.

'Hello, Willy,' she whispered, in her strange upside down position. 'Still buying drinks for girls?'

Sixteen

'Well, Willy,' she said calmly. 'What are you doing here?'

'I came to find you,' I said uncomfortably. She was sitting in her dressing room, or undressing room I suppose in her case. She had cleared three other naked girls out of the door before she let me in. They walked out without a stitch between them, nipples quivering right under my nose, but Silvie, my wife, familiar as I was with every piece and part of her, was sitting in a robe. 'You don't just turn up in Las Vegas by accident and find your missing wife,' I went on because she did not say anything. 'I came looking for you, Silvie.'

'You took a long time about it.'

'I had to *find* you, didn't I? Well now I'm here.'

'Did we ought to shake hands or are we still on a kissing basis?' she asked.

'A kissing basis, I hope. Can I?'

'Sure, it's freebees.'

The word with its associations of Bonapart's jolted me. 'Americanisms don't sound right coming from you,' I said.

'I've been here a long time,' she answered. 'Were you serious about kissing me? Or have I been building up my hopes for nothing as usual?'

I stepped to her and we kissed, hesitantly as though unsure what went where, without passion but with a touch of familiarity, a taste of recognition.

'Sit down,' she invited. 'Be careful of the razor. Marie's been shaving.'

'Shaving? Oh, yes, I understand. I suppose they have to.'

'*We* have to,' she corrected. 'I'm a big girl now, Willy.'

'What about the little girl?' I asked deliberately. 'And the little boy.'

'Ah, you remember our children.'

'Of course I bloody-well remember them!' I shouted, then dropped my voice. 'I didn't come all this way to hear snide remarks from you.'

'Well *I* did come all this way,' she said tartly. 'I should have made with the snide remarks back in England, not wait until I got here. What have you come for anyway? Did you run out of crumpet back home?'

There was that strong impulse to hit her. But I caught the painful look in those drained blue eyes, more appeal than anger, and I stopped and collapsed inside and sat down resignedly on the razor.

I shot up at once and saw the relief and mischief in her face. 'I told you,' she giggled. 'You never listen to my warnings. It's just as well you didn't have your Jesus outfit on.'

'You know about that?' I put the razor next to some foam shaving cream on the dressing table.

'Know about it? Everybody in Vegas knows about it. It's in the papers and on TV all the time. That crazy man, what's his name? Rightangle?'

'Properjohn,' I said. 'He's crazy all right.'

'He was arrested at the Hilton this afternoon, wasn't he?' she grinned.

'Arrested! God, no! I didn't know. I wasn't there.'

'That's what it said on the news tonight. Wrecked a Jewish wedding and injured some Japanese tourists, so they said. Honestly Willy, when I first saw you in that robe thing carrying that Cross and with that awful face. Christ, you looked like a drunk hanging onto a lamp-post! I said to Angelo . . .'

'Who's that?'

'Angelo? Oh, he's just a chap I know here.' She looked up and went on '. . . I thought I would pass out just laughing.' But she was crying now, not much, but crying, the tears smudging over the smile.

'Sorry,' she sniffed. 'This is not as easy as you think. Not for me anyway. Look, why don't you clear off for a couple of hours and come back and pick me up later. I've got another show to do. The children are all right. The desert suits Kathy's hay fever. I'll tell you all about them later. And about everything.'

'All right,' I said, getting up. 'I could watch the show, I suppose.'

'No, don't do that. I know it sounds stupid, but I'd rather you didn't. Come back at two. Don't lose your money at the tables, though, will you?'

I smiled: 'Why, do you want some housekeeping?'

There was an all-night souvenir shop in the same street where they sold coloured T-shirts and had your choice of name and things like 'Stolen from Las Vegas Prison' printed across them while you waited. I bought two for the children and asked them to print 'A Present from Swinging London' on them. They did it but said it was the first time they had ever had an order like that.

Then I bought a newspaper and went into a subdued bar, bought a drink and sat in a corner. Two old men were playing cards for matchsticks at the next table. Las Vegas is a strange place.

The headline said: 'Jail then Bail for Jesus Prophet'. The second deck said: 'Battle at Vegas Hilton' and the rest of the tabloid page was taken up with a riotous picture of Properjohn, clutching the Cross, being manhandled from the lobby of the Hilton Hotel by a dozen policemen. His expression was wild and his mouth open in an extravagant bellow. I could almost hear the shout from the page. To one side, next to a wedge of astonished and entranced spectators, were Herbie and Winston, their hands raised in abject surrender and being held in custody by an official-looking girl in a cowboy hat.

Turning the page I was confronted with my own picture in my robe and with the Cross and the caption: 'Cross Carrier Vanishes. Police ask: Is he in Heaven?' I found my teeth gritting at the official blasphemy, but there was no doubt the picture looked quite impressive. It had been taken during the torchlight entry into Las Vegas and I certainly looked anything but a drunk hanging onto a lamp-post. One of the best things about the Cross, of course, was that it was light but it looked heavy, so I could carry it high, giving the illusion of strength. It was not a bad likeness at all.

The paper was full of it. 'Jewish and Japanese Protests' howled page three. 'Bride in tears as wedding becomes battle-ground.'

Eyewitnesses quoted said that Properjohn, carrying the Cross, had gone thundering through the ground floor gaming hall of the Hilton Hotel and had then collided in one of the corridors with an expensive Jewish wedding wailing in the opposite direction.

Properjohn had gathered around him an echelon of supporters and hangers-on, in addition to the usual people from our crusade. The Jewish bridegroom had come along the corridor held by the arms in the customary procession, with a hundred male friends and relatives all chanting and incanting behind, him and collided head on with the rampaging Christian. The confusion degenerated into a battle which was added to when a party of weary Japanese tourists, just off a plane from Tokyo, crowded into the hotel foyer and found themselves at the centre of the mayhem. Page four had a full picture of the extraordinary scene during the fight, with the Cross slewed sideways over the confused heads. In one corner of the photograph was Ambrosia, hair hanging, dragging away her mother across the floor, Poor Clare's face distressed, her hand still waving her harmonica. Properjohn, said the report, had been bailed and would appear on television to make an important statement that evening. Whatever he had said was now several hours old.

I had three drinks and made each of them last half an hour.

As far as possible I kept my face hidden from everybody there but as I went out the barman said: 'Say, I get a feeling I've seen you somewhere.'

'Ich bin Berliner,' I grunted and went out into the night.

'We can take the bus along The Strip,' she said, nodding along the road. 'It runs all night and it's only fifteen cents.'

'Las Vegas can be cheap,' I said. We were walking separately along the sidewalk among the ever-leaping lights. It was cool and there was a moon but it was a poor competitor for the unflagging neon. It cruised high up, a remote loser, a sickly face in the sky.

'It can be cheap, okay,' Silvie said. 'If you've been here long enough. Most of the expensive things you can do without.'

'I'm sorry,' I said. 'But I couldn't send you any money because I didn't know where to send it did I? All I got were those daft postcards you sent. What did you expect me to do, save it up and bring it out in a big bag?'

Unexpectedly she put her arm in mine. We were standing at the bus stop with, unaccountably at that early morning hour, a small lad in boy scout uniform. We were so engrossed in our own delicate conversation, carefully building it, that neither of us thought it strange.

'I'm not complaining,' she sighed. 'Honest, Willy. *I* left and *I* took the kids, after all. God, I'm tired, you know. You'd be surprised how tired that job makes you. Simulated sex three times nightly is just as exhausting as the real thing.' Having said that she turned and stared at the boy scout who blinked back. 'Are you okay?' she asked him.

'I'm fine,' he said. 'Just fine.'

'Oh, good,' she said uncertainly. 'I just wondered that's all.'

'Just fine,' he repeated.

'How long did it take for you to notice we had gone?' she asked. She was smiling ruefully.

'Oh, I noticed,' I hedged. 'I asked for it, love. You can't tell me anything I haven't told myself, drunk or sober, a thousand times these last two years. I should have looked after you better. I know now.'

'Yes, you should have. And the children.'

'I know.'

The bus came along, a modest bug of light through the canyon of exploding signs. There were two dozen people or more on it, late workers in the city, some in evening dress, some with groceries. Several said hello to Silvie and nodded at me.

'You know people,' I said, as we sat at the back.

'A lot of these people live on Tropicana,' she said. 'They have mobile homes, you know caravans, like me. It's only after you pay your rent that you can live cheaply here.'

'You live in a caravan?'

'Like a pedlar man,' she said. 'The kids love it. It's big and it's dry. Better than some crummy apartment. How did you manage? In the house, I mean.'

'Not very well,' I admitted. 'I tried to dust around a bit but the place got worse. You'd probably find the same washing up as you left . . . if you ever went back.'

'Straight back to the sink, eh? Waiting for the lad to come home. No chance of that, I'm afraid, Willy boy. None at all.'

'Are you very friendly with this Angelo?' I said.

'Pretty friendly, I'd say. Did you leave the key with the Patons next door?'

'What made you ask that?'

'Well, if ever I went out they were always asking if they could have the key. I think they thought we had dirty books all over the place, or something. They couldn't wait to get in.'

'I left the key with them,' I nodded. 'They said they were afraid of flood and fire.' I did not say anything about the letters I had forged. 'They've got the cat too.'

'Levicticus,' she sighed.

'Now Tussy,' I corrected. 'He went to live in there more or less as soon as you'd gone. He didn't fancy his chances with me.'

'Don't blame him,' she said.

'You're very bitter still, aren't you?' I said.

'No, not now. I've sort of buried it and built over the top. It's still there, but it's way down in the muddy foundations. I'm glad I did it. Honestly. I like it here. The kids like it. The funny thing about Vegas is it's a great place to bring up children. Schools, recreation facilities, open country, Lake Mead.'

'And it's good for Kathy's hay fever,' I put in.

'I told you. All that stuff back there, all the gambling and the lights. All that's just industry. It's like the factory area to us. It's just a place to work. People actually live here as well.'

We left the bus and people called their suburban 'Goodnight'. We walked along the broad avenue, far away from the big lights now, but with the red beacons of the airport just ahead against the black sky. She had not taken my arm since leaving the bus and we walked apart and, after all this time, having apparently nothing to say to each other. She kicked her toes along the paving like an idling child. Then she laughed briefly. 'I nearly had a fit when I realized it was you hanging onto that Cross,' she said.

'I was carrying it, not hanging onto it,' I said defensively. 'If you look in the paper tonight you can see I'm carrying it. Everybody thinks I look like Jesus.'

'I can't see it,' she said. 'But there, I probably think about you in a different context, if you get what I mean.'

'I do,' I muttered. 'But most people think that there's a striking resemblance. A lot of people have asked me for my autograph.'

She laughed genuinely, putting her slim hand to her mouth and looking at me over the fence of her nails. 'Oh my God, Willy,' she said. 'You'll never change, will you. How did you manage to get fixed up with a job like that in the first place?'

'I was picked,' I said huffily. 'If you want to know. I was on my way here anyway – I was coming especially to look for you – and I was on the plane when that nutter Properjohn spotted me and insisted that I was going to join the crusade. I'm due to pick up well over a thousand dollars in a couple of days.'

'That much?' she said impressed. 'That's not bad, is it? I mean you wouldn't get that for being Santa at Christmas, and it's basically the same thing.'

'It isn't,' I protested. 'It's not the same at all.'

She did not reply, but continued walking a few feet to my left still regarding me with hardly stifled amusement.

'Herbie's with me,' I said.

'Herbie! Oh no! Herbie! What's he, the Virgin Mary?' She did a little dance of genuine delight. 'I can't believe it, I just can't!' she cried.

'He's grown a lot of hair all over him,' I said. 'You probably wouldn't recognize him.'

'I saw him!' she exclaimed. 'Good God, that was Herbie! I saw him on the TV news at the Hilton thing. He was with a coloured chap and they had their hands above their heads, surrendering.' She was laughing again helplessly. 'Oh Herbie,' she exclaimed. 'And . . . for God's sake . . . they had a meter maid arresting them! The girl in the ten gallon hat.'

That sent her off into another huge laughing fit. I walked with my face ahead. 'He's St Peter,' I said. 'If you've ever heard of anything so ridiculous.'

I began to laugh then because I could see the funny side of that. It had never occurred to me that it was so hilarious before. Herbie Cato as St Peter! We had a good laugh together at the thought, Silvie, and I, even putting our hands on each other's shoulders while we were laughing.

'And you!' she exploded again. 'You . . . Jesus, for Christ's sake!'

'All right, all right,' I said wearily. 'So it's provided you with a good laugh.' I nearly said: 'You do exhibitions for a living too.' But, for once, I avoided it. 'I'm risking a thousand dollars plus coming to look for you,' I said. 'If I'd been spotted in that club tonight that would have been that.'

'Risking it!' she said aghast. 'Have you sneaked out or something?'

'I'm supposed to be suffering from exhaustion. I'm supposed to be in a sort of rest home for twenty-four hours.'

'All that money,' she repeated. 'You shouldn't have come out.'

'I wanted to see you,' I said honestly. 'I really did. All the way along the route I've been dodging off and going to night-clubs and suchlike to see if I could find you or if anybody knew you.'

'Oh,' she said quietly. 'You *have* been looking for me, then. Straight up.'

'I have,' I said. I felt her hand return to my arm again.

'Oh, dear, Willy,' she said sadly. 'You shouldn't have come, you know. You should have stayed away and enjoyed yourself.'

We went into the trailer park, Silvie stepping with her casual grace around the muddy puddles, dull and yellow with the indifferent reflection of a single high floodlamp over the caravans. The only sounds were our gritty footsteps in the mud.

'We've had a lot of rain,' she whispered, as though it were a secret. 'Just this week. And it hardly ever rains here.'

'Perhaps it's to make us feel at home,' I replied. She said nothing to the plural inference, that we were together again; us and home. But as she unlocked the trailer door she said: 'This is home for me now, Willy.'

She turned on the light as she stepped in and flipped off her shoes. 'Take yours off, will you?' she asked. 'These things are like tin boxes when it comes to noise. I don't want to wake the children.'

'Who keeps an eye on them?' I asked, pulling off my shoes and leaving them on the mat.

'Now you wonder,' she said without malice. 'There's a woman across the park who has a key and comes and looks in during the late movie commercials. If she gets bored with the film she goes to bed, but I have to risk that. I have to earn a living.'

'Do you think they would know me?' I asked. She was filling a kettle at the sink, putting the back of her hand under the stream of water to prevent it sounding when it fell in. I watched the profile, the runaway dancer turned into a housewife in a moment, waiting for the kettle to fill. I watched her as I had watched her, at times, at home.

'They know your photograph. I've shown them that regularly, just in case you might turn up one day,' she said without looking at me. 'It was the one you had taken the day you tried to play tennis.'

'At the Hammonds?' I remembered. 'I thought I played pretty well considering I don't play regularly. I beat Geoffrey Hammond.'

'He's got half an eye and arthritic hands,' she said. 'You stick to carrying Crosses.'

I wasn't going to argue. 'Can I have a peep in at the kids?' I asked. 'Just to see them?'

She looked doubtful. Then she seemed to decide firmly and said: 'Listen, not tonight. You can wait a bit longer. If they woke up and saw you . . . Well, you are a stranger, Willy, more or less.' She gave one of her sad giggles. 'I suppose you could get into a pair of shorts and take a tennis racket in with you. That might remind them.'

'You're really enjoying this, aren't you?' I said patiently. 'Taking the piss out of me. You sound like you've been saving it up.'

She looked sorry. 'I shouldn't do it, Willy, I know. There's nothing to be gained by it now. I suppose it's the hurt woman in me.' She had made the tea and she brought two cups to the metallic table. 'Still one sugar,' she asked, her hand over the basin.

'Two, please,' I said formally. 'I increased the dose when you cleared out.'

'Thought you'd better start building yourself up, eh?' she smiled. 'For all the energetic nights and days ahead.'

'There you go again,' I sighed. 'It was nothing of the kind. In fact it was a sort of compensation, I suppose. For not having you. And I didn't start tearing around like a randy racehorse, either. If you really want to know I shut myself in like a bleeding hermit and tried to settle down to some writing. I did the novel I was always going to write.'

'You did?' she said surprised. 'You really wrote it?'

'Yes. One hundred thousand words, not counting commas and full-stops and such like. *The Long Dawn*, it was called. It went out to a different publisher every week and every week it came back. The old postman and I started to have a sort of running joke about it. "Here's your Tuesday parcel" sort of thing.'

'Poor Willy.' Her genuine fingers touched my hands. 'You never were appreciated, Willy. Not by anybody. Not for long. How did you raise the money for the trip?'

'The usual brochures, weed-killers, sanitary fittings, all the classic stuff. I thought if I got across here then Herbie could put me up in New York and I could get a job and start working my way across country. I knew you'd be heading in this direction. You always said you would.'

'*We* always said,' she corrected. 'Well, you've found me. Maybe you ought to give up writing and become a detective. You might be really good at that, you know.'

'Stop it, Silvie,' I said. 'I'm doing all right, although I've got to admit carrying a Cross does have its limitations.'

'Ah, yes,' she said, remembering something. 'There's a late, late newscast. Do you want to see it? See what your nutty pal's been doing.'

'Yes, I would, please,' I said. She turned the set on. 'I'll keep the sound low,' she said. 'I don't want the kids coming in.'

'They might think I was Angelo,' I said spitefully.

'He never comes here,' she said carefully. 'Not at night. I wouldn't want that. Not with the children . . .'

I did not pursue it then. The jagged picture on the set solidified itself. 'I never thought we'd spend our reunion night watching television,' I said.

'It passes the time,' she replied. 'I usually have something to eat now. Would you like something? It's chilli and stuff out of tins.'

'Now you're feeding me,' I said. There was the final kissing clutch of an old film on the television.

'You're my husband, still,' she said simply. 'If you're hungry I'll feed you.'

I thought it was an invitation. I stood up and went to her. She looked up and confronted me calmly. 'Just kiss me properly, will you,' I asked. I put my arms about her and felt the familiarity flood into me, every small ripple of her slim body, the breasts pressing through her blouse, the bone at her hip, the small insistent stomach. I kissed her and she allowed it and then lay her head back and did it to me. We did it three times. My hands ran down to the curve of her buttocks. She pulled away.

'Let me get on with the food,' she said. 'You're confusing me. Let's get back to where we were a couple of minutes ago. You watch television and I'll get the tins opened. Okay?'

'Okay,' I agreed, moving away from her. I sat in front of the set, my inside churning exultantly and my throat dry with the excitement. There was a commercial on the screen. I stared at it, seeing nothing.

'It's the news next,' she said. She tried to say it conversationally, but I could hear the tremble in her voice.

'Do you want any help?' I asked her. 'Opening tins or anything?'

'You never did, so there's no point in starting now,' she replied. Then she said: 'Willy, you mustn't think you can come here like this, just sort of drop out of the sky, and everything will be all right, you know. I didn't run all this way to let you catch me. Do you understand what I'm saying?'

'Yes, I understand, I think.'

'You had your chances . . . no, that's unfair, *we* had our chances in England, and it was no good then. Just because we're here in Vegas doesn't mean it's going to be any different. So get that fixed in your mind, please, whatever you do. In this town, when you've staked your bet and lost they don't give you your dough back because you look sorry.'

'All right,' I said, my inside going cold after the stimulus. 'I understand. I said I did.'

The news began. Immediately the screen was filled with fighting people, a great mound of them battling on the steps of the Hilton Hotel, with Properjohn, Herbie, Winston, and the others all being led off in custody, and the Cross being carried behind by an embarrassed policeman who held it under one arm like a long parcel.

'This,' said the newscaster, 'was the scene at the Hilton Hotel this afternoon, the latest battleground in the rip-roaring crusade conducted by the Reverend John Properjohn, self-styled minister of the Church of the Livid God, England, who has taken Vegas by storm.'

I felt Silvie move familiarly behind me, standing, a fork in her hand, at my elbow to watch the picture. 'Tonight,' said the announcer, 'the Reverend Properjohn was bailed from the city gaol and he appeared on this network to warn Las Vegas about its impending doom. . . .'

'Oh, my God,' I muttered. 'The silly bugger's done it . . .'

'Done what?' she asked. I was very conscious of her hand on the back of the chair.

Watch,' I said. 'Here it comes.'

The screen was filled with that great cracked face, the eyes burning, the hair spiky with Brylcreem, the mouth opening and shutting on its protruding hinges. The voice seemed even more voluminous on television. 'Now,' he bellowed. 'Now – the time has come to warn everybody, every single soul, in this wicked, wicked city that the End is coming. And very quick it's coming too. So get that.' The final three words were in his pseudo-film accent.

He advanced challengingly right up to the camera and his face went out of focus. Then he retreated, drawn back by a disembodied hand on his shoulder. 'Enjoy yourselves tonight,' he continued. 'For here . . .' He began fumbling in his waist-coat pocket and produced a slip of paper. He held it up un-opened, then undid it dramatically. 'Here,' he repeated. 'Is a personal message from . . . guess who? From God! Delivered to me a year ago and with this prophecy – that tomorrow night, at midnight, this city will come to a very sticky end. A great hole will open in the earth and swallow it, lights and all. And you will all die!'

'That's going to cut business in the club,' muttered Silvie.

I put my head in my hands. 'I knew he wouldn't be able to resist it,' I said. 'Fancy actually fixing a time for it. I hope for his sake that he's right.'

I turned to Silvie staring at me. 'Christ,' she said. 'Fancy saying that. You're as batty as the rest of them.'

'How could you get mixed up with something so ridiculous, so phoney as that?' she said. We were sitting eating now, as we used to once, one each side of the kitchen table. 'And by the sound of you, you really believe it. All that rubbish.'

'It sort of grows on you,' I admitted, embarrassed. 'I hardly know what I'm saying myself sometimes. He's got that sort of power. I think he's stark raving potty . . . but he's got something. You see him standing before a crowd of people and you'll understand. If he says the world is going to end at mid-night tomorrow, there are going to be a lot of disappointed people around if nothing happens.'

'If?' she said. 'You said "if" as though you thought it *could* happen. You don't believe it surely. God, how can you sit there and talk such tripe? How could you get involved with such a nonsense?'

'Listen, Silvie,' I said. 'There are people, thousands of them, who firmly believe that Jesus is circling the earth in a space ship. They're not mad, they're normal people. Well, except for that. There's others who believe that the secrets of life are locked up in a tin box in Bedford, in England. It's what they *believe* in, Silvie. People hang on to things they *want* to believe in. Sometimes it's all they've got.'

She was going to say something else, but she paused first and looked at me. Then she said: 'So you're saying that telling people that the last trump is about to blow is going to spread joy and happiness.'

'It will spread some satisfaction,' I said bluntly. 'And when it doesn't happen there'll be a whole lot of disappointment too. Even if these things seem phoney they *do* things for people. They might give somebody a jolt to start again . . .' I ended lamely '. . . if they need to start again.'

'Until tomorrow at midnight,' she said.

'Listen, it's a sort of shock treatment if you like. Even when it's all over, and everybody knows it was a lie then it still might have done some good for *somebody*. Don't you understand that? It might put somebody on an even keel.'

'Oh sure, and scare the living daylights out of thousands more.' She looked at me suspiciously, as she had done, in the end, in the old days, and said: 'Don't tell me that you're doing it for that reason, Willy Turpin.'

'I'm doing it for the money,' I shrugged.

'But you're trying to justify the means,' she smiled. 'Same old priggy Willy. You'll be telling me soon that you went around screwing all those birds in London for medicinal reasons.' She laughed because she had thought of a joke. 'A sort of mercy emission,' she said.

I was going to raise my voice, but she held up her hand and nodded warningly towards the children's bedroom at the end. 'All right,' I said heavily. 'I didn't come all this way to fight over religion or women or anything else. I came to find you.' I looked up at her. 'Have you missed me at all?'

'No, not all that much,' she shrugged. 'I've been too busy. At least I had to think for myself here and not hang around until you made the next move, if you ever got around to making it. I've been lonely, bloody lonely, but the kids have got me over that. It's strange when you think about it, but life for the three of us has been a lot less uncertain here than it was in England. Can you understand that?'

She walked away towards the kitchen part of the caravan. 'It was a long ride getting here,' she said. 'Christ, there's no end to this country.'

'I've heard that said too,' I answered.

She wanted to tell me something. 'I came by Greyhound bus a lot of the way,' she said. 'Sometimes it seemed like we were going around the world. I was tired and unhappy and the children got fretful. I was pretty low then. One night the children were in the seat in front and a young guy got on the bus, a sort of student-type, I suppose, only a kid. He sat next to me and went to sleep on my shoulder. He was right up close to me and his hand was touching me you-know-where. And I let it stay there because I was glad of the feeling. I know he woke up after a while, but when he realized what he was doing and that I didn't mind, he just sort of snuggled down again and put his fingers deeper down between my legs. We stayed like that all night and in the morning he got out at some cotton town and that was that. We didn't say a single thing to each other. That's how lonely I was.'

It began to rain, heavy bullet drops that rattled on the metal roof. We were regarding each other across the table. 'Remember the old Goodnight and Loving Trail?' I said. 'I do,' she said wryly. 'It's supposed to end in Colorado not Nevada.' 'When we used to dream about coming to America,' I said, 'we never thought we'd ever end up eating tinned stuff in a caravan while the rain pelted down,' I added ruefully. 'And in Las Vegas, as well.'

She smiled regretfully, too, but said nothing. We sat each side of the plastic table like strangers do in snack bars, or sometimes like married people do when they have nothing else to say.

'Do you want some more tea?' she asked.

'No, thanks. That was fine.'

'Did you come here thinking we were going to end up in bed together tonight?'

'No,' I said truthfully. 'I couldn't see anything like that happening.'

She got up and took the plates to the sink. 'If you want to, I will,' she said quietly.

I thought I had misheard her because of the rain. 'You will?' I said.

'Yes, Willy. That's what I said. I can't even think why, myself, except that I'm your wife still and I still feel like your wife, no matter what has happened. It would not make any difference to anything else. I've opted for the alternative anyway. Going to bed with you won't make me change my mind about that.'

'Thanks,' I said. 'What you're saying is that I can borrow you for the night?'

'Yes. And I can borrow you.'

Clumsily I stood up and took the dishes from her hands. 'Steady,' she smiled. 'Let's wash them first. I never feel like it in the morning.'

'All right,' I answered, smiling at her. 'I'll wipe. It will make us feel domesticated again.'

'You never wiped a dish in your life,' she laughed softly. 'Not when I was with you.'

'Stop arguing, woman,' I said. 'Or I won't screw you.'

'Oh yes, you will,' she said. 'That's one thing for sure.'

The rain soon stopped. Its rattle on the roof died and soon there was only a regular drip-drip like a pendulum sound coming from outside. Silvie took a key from a hook by the door and motioned me to follow her out into the drying night. 'We can't go to bed in there,' she said. 'In case the kids wake.'

'Tell them we're married,' I said, following her across the wet compound. 'They'll understand.'

'We'll go to the annex,' she said. She took my hand and we walked stealthily across the gravel and mud. The trailers lay like coffins, all arranged under a bored moon. Over the square roofs coloured messages of The Strip lit the silent distance.

She led me to a caravan fifty yards away and quietly unlocked the door. 'I keep the key for a couple who only come at weekends,' she said. 'They're always hoping to make enough at the tables to buy a house here.'

I followed her in, excited by the prospect of her, dull with sadness that she had said it held no future. The place was a tin box; there was a deserted chill about it. 'It's not very welcoming, I'm afraid,' she said. 'But it's all we have.'

Going in there with her was curiously like following a whore into a business bedroom. There was furniture, a couple of lamps and some pictures, but they were disembodied; it was as though they were in a storeroom.

After the warmth of her own inhabited place we stood awkwardly, again like a harlot and a customer, the low sides of the stiff bed touching the backs of our legs. She felt it as I did.

'There's no wine or music,' she apologized. 'After all I didn't expect you, Willy. Do you still want to?'

'Of course I do,' I said. I half-turned and put my fingers gently on her waist, dropping my head tiredly against her neck. 'But like you say, it's not like you expect.'

'Nothing is,' she whispered. 'Nothing. Do you want to clear out?'

'Christ, Silvie, love, I want you. I've been searching for you.'

'Let's get into bed with our clothes on,' she suddenly suggested. 'It will be warmer like that and it will give us something to do before we do the other.'

I laughed at her serious expression. 'That's a good idea,' I said. 'It doesn't seem so . . . so . . .'

'Cold-blooded,' she finished for me. 'I thought that too. Take your shoes off, though. I can explain most things, but not mud in the bed.'

'I didn't intend leaving them on,' I said. 'But we keep everything else on, don't we?'

'Everything. It's a shame you didn't come in your robe.'

'I could hardly come in my working gear, could I? Come on, you get in first. You know I like to drive on the right.'

'I seem to remember.' She gave me a straight look and for a moment I thought she was weighing up whether or not to do it after all. But then she opened the bed covers and dropped lightly into the cold fold. Her skirt slipped up her legs as she did it and she moved over and lay there, watching me, her exposed slim legs stretched out. Her eyes closed then, briefly, as if she were very sad, but then she looked at me again and smiled. I lay beside her.

We remained apart for a moment and then turned inwards and clutched at each other as though we had been lost and had been found again. I had forgotten how small her face was. My hands held it and my face pressed against it. I felt her tears on my cheek. 'Don't cry,' I said.

'No, I mustn't, must I,' she sniffed. 'There's nothing to cry about, is there? Nothing much, anyway. Why don't you take your pants . . . trousers off?'

'You do it,' I said against her face. 'See if you can remember.'

'I hear the zip has replaced the fly-button,' she giggled sadly.

'You can't stop progress,' I said.

Her fingers alighted on me, fumbling for the ear of the zip. She remained very close to me, burrowing into me as if she were afraid of something outside. She unzipped me firmly and slid both her hands into the aperture, cool, sweet fingers that touched my rearing flesh.

'You haven't got any smaller,' she mumbled, her face jammed hard against my neck.

'You're still small, small and beautiful,' I said. 'You're as marvellous as the first time, and all the other times.'

My hands were caressing the plains of her legs, stroking them from the cups behind her knees to the tight mounds of her backside. Her skirt was lifted to her waist now, below the bedclothes. I turned my thumbs in the top-band of her tights and easily pulled them down over her buttocks and thighs. She had me naked up to the waist too and was exquisitely running my member through her delicate hands.

'Are you any warmer now, Willy?' she asked.

'Warming up,' I said breathlessly. 'It was a good idea to get into bed right away.'

'A blanket covers a multitude of sins,' she said. 'Your thing *is* rather noble, you know.' She poked her head inquisitively beneath the bed-covers. 'God,' she exclaimed. 'It is too. It's standing up like Nelson, looking at me with his one eye.'

'Very historic,' I said. 'Mind you I always did think that, for a cock, he is rather aristocratic.'

'Are you having a good time?' she asked sincerely, her head over the horizon of the bed again. 'Really?'

'Lovely,' I told her. 'Just like home.'

'Stop it,' she pleaded. 'Let's be satisfied with this bit.'

I had drawn her tights down below the junction of her legs and body. Even the tops of her legs felt slim. She had no dancer's muscles. Scooping my hand over the stretched band of the tights and under the tunnel of her body I laid the fingers and the palm against the soft roof, feeling the throbbing of her entire inside transmitted through that sweet fissure. It was familiar and yet strange. It had been my delight in the past, but it had travelled a long way since then.

'Take my dress off, darling,' she asked. 'It's all up like a ruff around my neck.'

I undid it and took it from her. Her shoulders were white, almost incandescent in the dim caravan light. I ran my mouth along the crest of her shoulders. 'Don't you sunbathe?' I said. 'I thought you would here.'

'It's not allowed,' she said, unbuttoning my shirt now. 'My contract says I've got to look white all over. The dirty old men like that because it's virginal, I suppose. They don't like to see nude showgirls with brown bodies and stripes where their bikinis have been. I imagine it's psychology – you mustn't suggest that you've got any life outside showing off your prat, if you'll excuse the expression. If you've got marks it shows that you've been sunbathing off-duty. See?'

I said I did. I nearly said something about the girl with the whip marks then, but I left it and undid her bra instead.

Silvie had many good parts, but her breasts were best of all. Now, exposed, they seemed to blink with surprise like small animals disturbed from sleep. They always brought out the hungry man in me and to see them again was to see a lost delicacy. But I kissed her mouth just to show I was not greedy. My God, I thought, how I am going to enjoy her.

228

'Wake up,' I said, kissing one nipple. Then: 'Rise and shine,' kissing the other.

'They get lazy,' she murmured. 'When they're not working. I have to give them a brisk slap sometimes before I go on-stage. Some of the girls do it to each other, but I haven't got that far yet.'

'I hope not,' I said.

'Oh, there's nothing like that to it, really. They horse around a bit, naturally, and some of them are really true butch, but you have to tone up a bit before going on and there's no room for cartwheels in the dressing room.'

'I've seen you do cartwheels in a wardrobe,' I said.

'I did too. You remember some strange things, Willy. Do I still look nice?'

'Magnificent,' I said. 'Small and magnificent, if you can have the two together.'

'You feel very good too. You never put on any weight, do you?'

'Stop the chat,' I said. 'We can talk later. I'm going to rub my hands all over you.'

'I'll look forward to that,' she promised. 'I'll do it to you afterwards.'

She lay stretched out, eyes on me at first, but letting her fine lids drop after I began. We had often done this at home, in our cottage some dull winter's night before we had become apart. Now I used my hands and my mouth and the front of my teeth on her breasts, massaging and sucking, and eventually running my tongue in a long snail-trail down her slim trunk until it was in the sweet, lemon-tasting, hump of hair, and then, pushing her legs firmly apart, burying my tongue and my face in her private valley.

'One of us is going to suffocate,' I heard her say in the distance.

I tried to reply while I was still tunnelling deep down there, but the mumbled mouth movements made her shout with hilarity. I emerged hot-faced. 'You're not supposed to laugh,' I said.

'And you're not supposed to talk,' she giggled. 'Not with your mouth full.'

'There are times when you're just a common bird,' I said. 'Turn over.'

She slithered over. Sometimes I used to think her back was better than her front, although I could never really make up my mind.

I laid my head like a dog, sideways across her shoulder blades, enjoying the sensation of the superb skin against my face. How careless I had been to allow her to go. Her backbone was white and curved beautifully, like the seam in a long piece of celery. I put my cheek to her cheeks. 'I think your arse has got a bit bigger,' I said.

'Oh, no!' Her jerk threw my head sideways. 'Oh, don't say that, Willy.' She saw my face in the dim light and saw that I was grinning. 'Oh, you are a rotten swine,' she said, but with relief. 'You know how I worry like mad about that.'

'Your arse is like it always was,' I said, kissing her mouth and eyes. 'Like a little tulip.'

'What colour?'

'A white one. White as ice-cream.'

'That's good. Willy, I want you so much. I want you inside me. Can we put anything else off for a bit and do it now. I'll do my rubbing bit on you afterwards. Do you mind?'

I turned her with one hand and felt her knees draw up either side of my waist. I was crouching in front of her, our eyes fixed with bright animal excitement on each other's eyes. Her little, lovely hands went out underneath me, caught my stem and tugged me to her. We were both slippery with anticipation. I eased myself an inch at a time until her gentle legs had closed about me like a trap. Then our parts touched with a soft shock. I swear we were not joined by more than a quarter of an inch. Her mouth opened and her face creased, becoming strangely old in the half-light. I watched her closely, then pushed myself into her and watched her sweet face clear. We were man and wife again. Briefly.

Seventeen

The following day, which was a Saturday, we took Kathy and James to the park and played at being parents. Silvie said: 'It's no use pretending that I bring them here very often because I don't. They usually play under the caravans and on the waste lot at the back. It's all new for me too.'

Both children had regarded me seriously in the morning, as though their worst fears had been confirmed. We all had breakfast together and I saw how close she was to them and they to her. Kathy was five now, a golden little girl, and James eight, with an air of manliness that I suppose came from growing up without a father. They were reserved at first, and on their best behaviour after their mother had explained who I was, but at the breakfast table James had emitted the tiniest of farts and it sent them into curls of laughter. That eased them and they began to ask me questions in their piping American voices. How was the Queen? Was England as big as Vegas? Why didn't we play baseball? Why hadn't we helped in Vietnam? The final question came from James, who had apparently been asked it as an Englishman on many occasions and had not known how to answer. I told him that it was because we didn't believe in war and he gave me a grateful look and said: 'Well, I'm sure glad I've got that one cleared up.'

They jumped with happiness when they saw the park with its swings and boating pool and carousel, but all the time I was playing with them, and Silvie, and she with me, I knew that time was running out. I would have to be back with Properjohn at midday.

Silvie had slept in my naked arms all night, but in the morning, when we had returned to her own caravan and seen the children she had, I could see and sense, detached herself from me. We had, as we had said in the night, only borrowed each other. And now I was borrowing the children for a brief space.

'What are you going to do?' I called to her from the other side of a little neck in the boating lake. She was crouching with Kathy on the opposite bank, about twenty yards away. We had looked up at the same moment and seen each other.

'Do what?' she called. 'What do you mean?'

I left James winding up a motor boat and walked around to her. Kathy passed me on the rim of the pond on her way to see what James was doing. I crouched by Silvie and the children were crouching on the other side.

'*Do*,' I insisted. 'With your life and the children's?'

'Live with them, I suppose,' she said.

'Here?'

'Here,' she said firmly. 'I told you, Willy.'

'With Angelo?'

'Maybe. Maybe not.'

'That's nice to know.'

'I'm filing for divorce,' she said, speaking to my reflection in the water. 'I've already sent the papers to you. They must have arrived after you left England.'

'Divorce?' I could not believe her. 'Divorce?' I repeated. 'From me?'

'You're the only one I'm married to,' she said simply.

'Why? What's a divorce for? Not after last night, surely.'

'That doesn't count. I don't remember it,' she said. 'And as for why. Well you've got a fucking cheek even asking why. Let's call it breakdown of the marriage. That's good enough these days, isn't it?'

'But . . . but I thought we might be all right. Especially after last night,' I said slowly. 'Fancy sending divorce papers to England. I bet the Patons had a good read of those.'

'Trust you to worry about whether the Patons read them,' she said angrily. 'Sod the Patons. And you too, Willy. I told you the marriage has broken down and a dozen nights like last night won't make it start up again. It would be just the same. And I wouldn't have the guts to run away again . . .'

Her voice died and I saw a large tear plop and make a target in the pond. 'Don't you see?' she cried, but stifling it back so the children would not hear. 'Don't you understand, you thickhead? I've got a bit of peace now. I haven't got lots of other things, but I've got some peace, and after the way you screwed me up in England that counts for a lot.'

'So you'll divorce me and marry dear Angelo even though you don't love him.'

'I might and I might not,' she answered. 'And I didn't say I don't love him either. There's a long way between a person's heart and their sexual organ, you know. Sometimes one doesn't know what the other one's doing. Do you get me?'

'I get you well,' I said. I was swelling with anger now, gritting my teeth to keep it back. I straightened up from beside her and walked away a few yards. Then I turned and stalked back. She was still watching her own crying face in the pond. 'But let me tell *you* a few bloody truths,' I started. We both looked up and saw that the children had heard and were staring from the other rim of the water.

'Kathy, James,' called Silvie, 'go and get some cotton candy.' She turned to me. 'Have you got a quarter?' she asked.

'No,' I said. I had some five-dollar bills which Mr Sunley had given to me, but no change.

'I forgot,' she said. 'You don't get paid until you hand your Cross in do you?' She was fingering in her handbag and she threw a silver coin towards the children who were walking doubtfully around the pool towards us. 'The cotton candy man is over there by the entrance,' she called. 'Don't be long.'

They went off together, still doubtfully, looking back over their shoulders at us. 'There's no need to be shitty about the Cross,' I said. 'If *you* haven't got an exhibitionist's job, nobody has. What happens when they get tired of you there, in that club?'

'When my face doesn't fit, you mean,' she said.

'I wasn't thinking of your face,' I answered nastily. She turned and started to walk away. I caught her by the shoulder and she did not resist. 'No, go on,' I challenged. 'I want to know. How will you keep the kids then? Go to another club, and then another?'

'I'll get work,' she said. She turned and her face was untidy with her crying. 'There's always work here.' She looked at me squarely. 'Maybe I could go on the sidewalks. That's very well paid in this locality, you know. It's even legal in Las Vegas county.'

This was it. 'Two thousand dollars, I hear, for some kinky bastard to whip you.'

What shook me was that she was completely nonplussed. I could see the reference meant nothing to her. 'That sounds like a good deal, if you like that sort of thing,' she said carefully. 'But why bring it up now? What's the significance?'

There was a children's helter-skelter and we stopped and she sat on the bottom step. 'I was told you had been offered that,' I said lamely. 'For . . . you know . . . doing that.'

She was grinning. 'Wow,' she said. 'Sit down, Willy Turpin. This I have got to hear.'

She moved up. It was a wide wooden step at the bottom and there was room for both of us. Embarrassed I said: 'The girl in Memphis. A redhead. I don't know her name. She told me.'

A fragile, grey-faced boy with a huge cap balanced like a burden on his thin head approached and stood by us. We stared at him until we realized he wanted to get to the steps to the helter-skelter. We shuffled aside and he gravely went between us without a word.

Silvie leaned closer. It was the closest we had been since we got out of bed. 'In Memphis?' she said.

'Yes,' I mumbled. 'She had been whipped by this man called Homer Bean and he had paid her a thousand dollars for doing it. . . . She said he had offered you *two* thousand. And that you had considered it.'

I knew I had fallen down a hole. She was suddenly laughing uncontrollably into her hands, lifting her face and looking at me and then collapsing with laughter again.

'I know, I know.' It was the small, grey boy returned. 'I know it looks funny,' he said patiently. 'But my mom says I've got to wear it because I have an allergy in my head. Okay?'

'Okay,' replied the bursting Silvie. She moved aside and he mounted the steps again wearily as though the cap was as heavy as it was large. Silvie was almost weeping with laughter.

'Are you laughing at him or me?' I demanded.

'Well both,' she gurgled. 'Christ, I've got the stitch. Oh, Willy, if only you knew.'

234

'Well *let* me know,' I grumbled. 'Tell me, for God's sake.'

The boy had taken his slide and was walking disgruntled across the park, kicking his cap ahead of him. 'Put it on,' Silvie called. 'You'll get a cold in your head.' He picked it up without looking back and placed it on his head like an archbishop replacing a mitre. Then he ran away.

'Now tell me,' I said. 'If you can stop pissing yourself for five minutes.'

'It was Sadie,' she said, touching me apologetically with her fingertips. 'Sadie the sadist.'

'Odd sort of sadist,' I said. 'She's at the wrong end of the whip.'

'That's just it,' Silvie said. 'There *is* no whip, you fool. Those lash marks – that's just cosmetics. She gets her kicks like that, don't you see? She picks up some guy in the club and takes him to her place and kids on she's got to show him this terrible thing that some other guy has done to her. And what happened, Willy? You go there and sit drooling while she strips off and shows you all the lash marks . . .'

'Well, no . . .'

'Well, yes. Oh, come on, baby, that's how the play is. The guy sits there dripping and she fawns around, showing him this lash mark and that bit, and telling him all the awful tale. And she won't let the guy touch her. Right?'

'More or less,' I said, miserably.

She was laughing again now, softly. 'Oh, Willy, I can see you sitting there with big tears in your eyes and a big hard in your pants. I bet she really enjoyed you.'

'Oh, Christ,' I muttered. 'And it's all just make-up?'

'Of course. That's why she takes you into the bedroom where the lights are right. And she won't let you get to her side of the bed, will she?'

'No. No, you're quite right.'

'She does it all the time,' nodded Silvie. 'Sometimes the other girls used to stand in that hamburger place right opposite her apartment and watch the guys come out. Some of them could hardly walk!'

'She's got a real sense of fun,' I said miserably. I stood up.

'Well,' I stretched. 'I'd better be getting back to work. The end of the world is tonight, remember.'

'You're going,' she said, suddenly sad.

'I've got to. I'll see the kids on my way across the park. Do you want me to phone you or anything?'

'There's no phone,' she said hurriedly. 'Not in the mobile home, only at the caretaker's place and I'm not often in.'

'What about the club?'

'The girls aren't allowed to take calls.'

The hurt and the unhappiness, the failure, then and again now, were weighing down on me, like the little boy's huge cap had weighed on him. 'Could I call in and see you then? I could be around for a few days. I'd like to see the kids,' I said.

She did not answer that. Instead she said: 'Goodbye, Willy. It will never work. Not for both of us it couldn't.' She bent forward and kissed me on the beard. I got up and walked away. The children were returning and I stopped and kissed them through their clouds of pink candy-floss. Then I cleared out.

Eighteen

On the side of a mountain above Las Vegas that night there were ten thousand people waiting for midnight and the earthquake that would signal the end.

There had been the most magnificent magenta sunset over the Nevada plain, the entire sky lurid with colour for an evening hour and the perpetual lights of the gambling town reduced for once to flickers.

'A sign! A sign!' Properjohn had shouted at a roadside rally as we were making our way towards the mountain highway to the plateau where we were to wait. His arms swept the sky from the roof of 'Jesus Lives' where he stood like some champion charioteer. People looked and wondered at the turbulence of the sky and I heard Poor Clare snivel close by: 'I *do* hope he's right. I hope he's not got the date mixed up.'

I trudged my last couple of miles with the Cross, along The Strip and into the downtown streets. There were thousands out to watch us, some of them apprehensive and angry, but quiet mostly, while others quite jovially called 'Good Luck, Jesus,' 'See you Up There!' and such things.

Herbie walking beside me appeared subdued. 'Maybe he's right,' he muttered. 'Maybe it could happen.'

'Shit,' I said. 'If you feel like that why don't you clear out.'

'What, quit now and lose my bonus?'

'Save your skin, lose your cash,' I said. 'Or save your cash, lose your skin. Take your choice.'

'I just don't like the feel about things today,' he said. 'Half the crazy people in Vegas are waiting for it to happen. I don't like the feel of the ground under these feet, man.'

Winston came towards us through the crowd. Hundreds were following our procession now, trudging under that boiling evening sky. 'Ready for the end, boys?' he said.

'Christ, don't you start,' I almost snarled. 'It's bad enough with this doleful bugger. He really believes it.'

'No,' protested Herbie. 'I didn't say that. I said I just felt uneasy about things.'

'Sure sign of a good campaign,' said Winston. 'Like in politics. When the people on the *inside* really believe the crap they tell others, then you've sold it good, man.'

'You're not worried, then?' I said casually towards Winston.

'Two things worry me,' he said seriously. 'First – what is this mob going to do when the earthquake don't happen. They ain't going home to bed quietly like good folks. They came for the End of the World and they're going to want the End of the World.'

'That crossed my mind,' I said, relieved that Winston did not think it would happen.

'Our boy is going to need some hard talking to explain that away,' nodded Winston.

The time had come to ship the Cross on the top of 'Jesus

Lives' for the drive out of town. As we handed it up to Hattie, who appeared astride of the luggage grid his face a strange hue in the sunset, I looked behind and saw, for the first time, the extent of the procession which had formed to follow us. There were thousands, a great tail of people, singing hymns, crying, bravely shouting religious slogans, carrying banners bearing large letters, presumably big enough for God to identify them in an emergency, and all shuffling up the hard road from the city to the mountains.

'Dear God,' I whispered to Winston. 'How are we going to handle this lot? If they get wild he'll be lynched – and so will we.'

'Try and make a noise like an earthquake,' he said. 'And keep an escape route open to the rear.'

I nodded and gave the Cross a final push up to Hattie. He smiled at me gratefully, a large magenta smile.

'What was the other thing?' Herbie asked Winston. 'You said you had two worries?'

'Sure,' murmured Winston. 'There's no sign of Oliver J. Jaye. I don't like it when he's here but when he's not here it bugs me. I called my office this morning and they said everything is okay as far as they know. But the fact remains he's not here, man, and he ought to be here.'

'Could be he don't like disasters,' said Herbie enigmatically.

The road to the mountain looked like some great exodus. They were in cars and buses now, for the journey up the rocky road, but there were still walking groups from outlying places on the way, or people who perhaps aimed to reach the plateau by midnight.

'All these people,' I said to Winston again. We always thought that Winston might just have the answer to everything. 'Kids and everything.' I looked back over the dusk trail, cars and buses, edging up the highway through the rocks. With Herbie we were sitting on the rack with the Cross on top of 'Jesus Lives'. 'What do they think they're going to see?'

'Entertainment,' said Winston simply. 'That's what the people want. They sure ain't going to see the Hoover Dam or Boulder City, I can tell you that, pal. I guess you could say there's a kind of sameness about what Las Vegas has to offer. Our boy makes a change from Milton Berle, that's all.'

Properjohn with Poor Clare, Ambrosia and Hattie were astride the 'Jesus Loves' vehicle behind, leading some vivid singing by gowned choirs standing like white cattle in three trucks which immediately followed. They sang all the evangelical stand-bys, including all those with a hint of Doomsday in the words, and of course our own Las Vegas theme 'Jesus is Coming – Everyone Watch Out!' Torches were lit in the new dark, swaying, shining red even against the retreating brilliance of the city on the desert plain. It was a stirring sight; people, travelling, singing, manufacturing even as they progressed a sort of generated passion. Locomotion, commotion and emotion, Winston said.

'When do we get our dough?' asked Herbie.

'You're contract's up tomorrow,' answered Winston. 'So is mine.'

'That *will* be the end,' I said, suddenly realizing that we would all be split again, separate people. No more Properjohn, howling like a Welsh wind, no more Poor Clare of the absent jaw and helpless eyes, no more ineffectualities from Hattie, nor afternoon nipple from sweet Ambrosia. Winston would go and eventually Herbie too. I would miss them all. And no Silvie either. I would go empty handed back to that cold cottage in England. And alone.

'According to what we're selling, it's the end tonight,' Herbie pointed out. 'But I still want to know about when I get the dough. What sort of a job is this when you only get paid if the whole thing fails?'

Now we were reaching the place where we had first stopped and seen Las Vegas spread before us like a scattering of hot coals.

'Whee!' exclaimed Herbie as the mobile home stretched itself up the final inclined bend. 'More victims.'

I could not believe it. There were thousands already there, awaiting us, a massive crucible of people, their flaming torches like some burning off of the gases of their emotion. They were singing their own songs when we lumbered up and these intermixed with the approaching anthems of our own procession clashed truculently in the high mountain air. Musical confusion continued along with the physical confusion, the singers surrounding 'Jesus Loves' and 'Jesus Lives' with frightening vocality. Amid all the jumbled tunes of praise, which even God would have been at difficulty in sorting out, Poor Clare, poor tone-deaf Clare, was gallantly blowing her own path on her harmonica. And, as always it was she, among the thousands, who was the victim of Properjohn's admonishment. With the great hysterical religious cacophony washing all about us, Properjohn shouted at her: 'Clare, stop making that unholy row.'

Ambrosia was looking frightened perched high above the excited mob, with more and more arriving at every moment as our procession fed onto the rock plateau. But her face went constantly to her father, astride the roof of his vehicle like a mad mahout on an elephant. People milled about, pushing and pulling, and ever singing. Somehow the choirs, recognizable at least in their robes, were channelled to the front and our two motor homes were edged that way also. From the front looking out on the thousands, the torches, the children, the family pets, all with their faces and their voices turned on us, was to see human turbulence at its most frightening. This massive pot of generated emotion, this wallowing of people and their minds, was a terrible thing. Above us the stars drifted and far below the lights of the city lay with equal serenity.

'Christ,' breathed Herbie over it all. He turned anxiously to me. 'And I don't mean you,' he added hurriedly. We hoisted the Cross high above the multitude and stood beside it trembling while they shouted their acclaim.

Winston said certainly: 'Sixty-five per cent of those who came to laugh, now believe. There's nothing that debases people like religion, man and there's no push-over like a crowd.'

'And when there's no earthquake, no End of the World?' I asked.

'Boy, these people are going to feel cheated,' he replied. 'And they're going to be real sore. All of them.'

A big white light had been set up and shone blatantly on

Properjohn singing and preaching from the top of 'Jesus Lives', his voice carried over all the people and bouncing off the Nevada rocks by an eerie loudspeaker. By half past eleven he had them all singing together, an emotive swaying sound filling the night to overflowing, while below Las Vegas blinked without concern and the red lights of aeroplanes made courses in the distant sky. The crowd were now with him, sinew, soul and song. There was a sort of doomed joy about them; their anthems were anthems with every note and meaning stressed, their prayers were so profound they choked over the words, their tears were real. They clutched their children and their dogs; husbands and wives held each other. Perfect strangers located each other's arms and sang as though their lives had been magically fulfilled in the last moments before disaster. For a people who were doomed they had taken on a new lease of life.

We stood arrayed around him, standing on the roofs of our motor homes, me holding the Cross which cast a great shadow on the rising face of the rock behind me. The white light was dazzling and it hurt our eyes. Ambrosia's autoharp sounded with sure sweetness next to my ear, Poor Clare was puffing like a breathless dragon into her harmonica, Herbie was singing with his mouth open so wide among his whiskers that the spotlights shone down his throat, while Hattie, in his maroon suit, his clerical collar like a bandaged wound around his adam's apple, conducted the singing with his arms only a foot or so less extravagantly than Properjohn himself. Winston's face was mesmerized with the power of the moment, the triumph of human feeling and fellowship under the pressure of good public relations.

I could feel my legs trembling beneath my worn-out robe. My feet were sweating into my Dolcis casuals. My eyes were hot as though the smoke of the torches were stinging their rims. It would be useless to deny that it merely moved me to see all these thousands singing, praying and waiting for the earth to crack under them. The sensation was extraordinary. It filled me so I had to breathe out to prevent myself exploding; it struck me in the guts like a sword that remained unwithdrawn; my fingernails bit into the soft wood of the Cross and I looked above me and saw that awesome cross-beam spreading out like great squared arms. I was part of something, for once, and a big part of something. There was I standing above this turbulent yet resigned throng holding the great and ultimate symbol of God's love for humanity for all the people to witness before we perished. And, by Christ, we were all enjoying it.

Properjohn, a black phantom against the stark lights, had been sweeping them in song and crouching them in prayer as the whim took him. We sang all the hymns we knew and some we did not know. Poor Clare, next to her husband's ear, had wandered harmonically off so far from one tune that the insensitive man had given her a sharp push which would have knocked her from the top of the van if Hattie had not grabbed her as she tumbled.

There were young people in the front of the crowd playing on guitars and singing the songs of hereafter as if they could hardly wait to get there. There were men and women who looked as though they had left their chips on the roulette tables, and others who had left their flowers in their gardens or cakes in the oven. Their faces were full of emotion and magic, uplifted, shining, the creases, the weariness falling away with each rising moment. They were engulfed with the immense sobbing happiness of the profound experience. As Winston had said, it was a change from Milton Berle.

At ten minutes to midnight Properjohn, his face dripping, his hair erect with Brylcreem like a man who has died of fright, hushed them all with a horizontal swimming motion of his hands. 'Dear people!' he howled across their heads. 'Dear, doomed people. The hour is almost come. The time when God shall snuff out this world like the worthless candle it is. The rocks will move, the rivers will steam, fire and brimstone will be upon us. Let us weep for ourselves, people, because now the day when we shall go naked before our God, to explain our sins and our misdeeds, is nigh. Tremble in your hearts in these final minutes. We were born with sin and we have added to it with every day. Now we must all die and give account . . .'

He spoke for five minutes, strong doom-laden stuff, the Welshness in his voice tumbling around the silence. Repentance, wickedness, the Forgiveness of God, fire and brimstone and the lovely fields of Everlasting Life. He had the people nailed down from the first sentence. Not just them; us also. His outsize power held us, it was as if no one was even breathing. The cool night had grown hot around us. Mouths were dry, eyes wet. A man in the front, a sweaty man in an excellent suit, began to take papers from his pockets and to tear them slowly and resolutely into fragments. The spellbinder was at work among us. We were all prisoners.

'Let Us Pray!' bawled Properjohn and the ten thousand dropped to their knees as though a mighty and invisible sword had whistled an inch above their heads. 'Almighty Father,' he howled into the microphone as though God had gone deaf. 'We beseech thee, in this our final five minutes . . .'

I saw Herbie check his watch and lick his lips. Ambrosia was clutching Sprott's autoharp with an expression that suggested it might be useful in the immediate future. I discovered I was clinging to the Cross with much the same subconscious motive. I glanced at Hattie, shaking as though with fever, and saw a trickle of blood start down Poor Clare's lip caused by her teeth clenching too fiercely into the hard-bitten harmonica. Winston, on his knees like the rest of us, was shuffling towards the rear of the motor home roof, prepared for the quick getaway from the wrath to come, from whatever source.

Properjohn ceased praying. His supplication had been rambling but potent, but now he seemed to have run out of requests and confessions. We had said the Apostles' Creed three times. The silence was taut and immense, a skin-bursting silence, hot, awful, and with ten thousand heads bent as if for some merciless blow. Above, the stars regarded us with slightly raised eyebrows, and a mocking wind sauntered uncaringly through the hills. The city blinked myopically. 'Two minutes to go!' called Properjohn. A shudder jolted across the plateau. A solitary couple with a child crept away from the fringe but no one else moved. 'Parents, embrace your children!' he shouted blatantly. 'Children – embrace your parents!' I felt sick. Herbie turned with a face like a frightened cow. Everywhere men and women, children and dogs were being kissed and embraced. 'Husbands, wives,' continued Properjohn. 'If you have secrets, tell them now.'

There must have been a lot of guilty stories unlocked at that moment because there was a babble of talking but it was silenced to stone when Properjohn shouted, 'One minute to midnight. Let us pray.'

I noticed more people making for the road, but still only a trickle. Then I realized that Ambrosia was beside me and her fat little hand slotted into mine. 'He'd better be right, Willy,' she said. 'If he's not it's the finish of him.'

'If he is,' I pointed out. 'It's the finish of everybody.'

I cannot believe now, at this sober distance, that I truly believed anything terminal was about to happen. My own grasp on reality would not let me accept that. But in those lingering moments before midnight I experienced, with the others, the power of superstition in the guise of God; unquenchable fear, stifling apprehension, a stiff panic, and the hideous dwindling of time. There were thousands who had come blithely to be entertained by this spectacle who felt the same powerlessness. They crouched and prayed knee by knee with the handful of crackpot believers and those whose genuine religion instructed them to be prepared for the end at any time, because no one was permitted to know the hour or the day. They had come to laugh and to enjoy themselves, to see a madman on a high hill. And now this. This hot emotive moment when, they were persuaded, it all seemed more than probable. They must have felt that they had walked into a trap.

I found myself staring directly at the astonishing Properjohn, Our Boy, the Man with the Power, standing in funeral garments and sweat, vast arms held out like a hovering black gull. At that moment he believed more than anyone. He *knew* it was coming. Held in his own spell, he was a great shadow waiting for the world to crack beneath his feet. Clare was at his side, staring at him too, like a weight lifter's anxious trainer. A whimper trickled from Ambrosia at my side. Her face was deathly shiny in the bleak light, her breasts heaving with the stress.

'Shit,' whispered Herbie in my ear. Then quickly, in fright: 'I mean hell . . . Well, I mean Lord help us . . .'

'Twenty seconds!' cried Properjohn. 'Make your peace

with The Almighty God.' Then the bastard began to count. 'One, two, three, four . . .' I shall never forget those moments. The tightening of the screw about those people, the curling of my own stomach, the cold sweat, the remote disdain of the stars, the peaceful lights of Las Vegas, the thousands crouched on the plateau, victims awaiting mass execution. 'Sixteen, seventeen, eighteen, nineteeeeeeen, TWENTY.'

Nothing happened.

I felt myself collapse inside. Then I looked up at the people. Questioning heads were being raised. Three women in the front fainted. Properjohn was standing motionless, his arms hung out as though to dry. I commenced a tentative shuffle towards the rear of the van roof. A similar secret movement was coming from Herbie. He glanced at me nervously and muttered: 'God's watch is slow.' Winston had already dropped to the ground from the roof. Ambrosia was still standing, waiting, eyes closed, but with a strange expression deflating her face.

People were staggering to their feet now, pulling their wives and children up from the ground. The fainters were being recovered. I saw a movement from Properjohn, as though he too had just opened his eyes. Hattie was shaking his watch.

'Cheat!' a man's voice called from the crowd. 'Lousy cheat!' Then a dozen shouts. 'Fake!' 'You scared my children!' 'Get down, you bastard!' And then everybody was getting to their feet, stumbling up, angry and disappointed and hugely relieved. There was a movement from the front towards Properjohn on the brow of the van and I saw him reflex away. The disjointed complaints from the people were swelling to a great and angry shout. The move forward thickened. People were around the base of our van too, their violent faces turned up to us their mouths open in shouts, their fists sticking out like spears.

'Stop! Stop!' I heard Properjohn howl. And then from the desert plain below rumbled a profound explosion. It rolled loudly and then, as the people stopped and stood in renewed fear, the sky in the distance turned red. At that instant I *really* believed it. I have to admit that. I was frightened and so were the people, dumb now, stumbling back, looking over the heads about them to the dull red clouds that were growing from the lower rocks. The lights of Las Vegas had gone. The night trembled with more explosions. I heard Properjohn cry and Ambrosia fell on her knees so heavily that she yelled out with the pain of her kneecaps hitting the metal roof of 'Jesus Lives'.

Next there was a firm grip on my elbow. It was Winston: 'Let's grab Our Boy,' he whispered. 'And get the hell out of here.'

I knew then that it wasn't the end of the world. Pulling Ambrosia to her feet I stifled her protests and pushed her in the direction of Herbie who was already dropping over the rim of the roof. Winston and I jumped easily across the space from our roof to the top of 'Jesus Loves' and got the baffled Hattie and the hysterical Clare down the side and onto the ground. Now there was only Properjohn, still standing, ecstatically believing it. Eyes closed, mouth open, arms out. The people were still cowed, hiding their heads in their arms and their children's faces beneath their coats. But the red smoke was clearing and behind it I could see that Las Vegas on earth and the stars of heaven were still intact.

'Come on, we're leaving,' I said loudly in Properjohn's ear. I caught him by one arm. He was steely, as though held by a trance. Winston tried to drag him backwards. But with a terrible despairing cry he abruptly swung his great fists around, like weights on the end of those huge arms, and with one complete circle hit both of us, first Winston then me, sending us staggering and then sliding over the edge of the roof of the mobile home. I slid over feet first but Winston, when I reached him, was lying stunned, having fallen on his head. He was resting on his side, like a slumbering piccaninny, but had fortunately descended on some tarpaulins and not on the bare rock. I caught him under the arms and lifted him across my shoulder. He recovered as we reached the back of the plateau area, well behind the vans and the crowd who were now shouting again. He insisted that I put him down.

'I've got a car and a driver waiting on the highway,' he said. 'This is where we quit.'

'What about Properjohn?' I said.

'You want to go back?' he stopped and asked. He plainly was not. We looked behind us. Properjohn was no longer on the roof of the van. The crowd were violently mad now, double-crossed, twice, and bawling for vengeance.

'They'll tear him to shreds,' I said, staring at Winston.

Then we heard it. 'Praise! Praise! Praise! Glory! Glory!' and saw Properjohn running like a black dog fifty yards away, coat tails flying, arms working, boots racing. He did not see us, or if he did he just left us. He went scooting out through the back way, wriggling around the rocks, and quickly vanishing.

'That's my boy,' nodded Winston. 'That's my immortal boy.'

'Come on, for Christ's sake,' I said, setting off after Properjohn. 'They'll get us.'

Behind us people were beginning to surge through the gaps between the two mobile homes. Fortunately, at that moment, somebody pulled out the plug of the floodlights and the plateau went black and left all the people struggling. We ran.

Outside on the road were Herbie, Ambrosia and Poor Clare. They shouted and ran with us, Winston leading the way to a black Chevrolet blocking the road between all the cars parked on the verges. The driver had the engine running. We fell on top of each other inside and we bounced around as he started off speedily down the descending road.

'Did he get away?' asked Winston when we were sorted out. He and Clare were in the front and Herbie and I with Ambrosia in the back. We had lost Hattie.

'Sure he got away,' said Herbie laconically. 'He got away on a motor-bike which was conveniently parked outside for a quick start.'

'He used to have a motor-bike,' reminisced Poor Clare. 'In the good old days.'

'Well, he's got another one now,' said Herbie. 'He would have left us to fry.'

We were speeding towards Las Vegas, still between parked cars, but with no people about. 'Thanks for the lift, Winston,' I said gratefully. 'It's a good job you thought of it.'

247

'Sure, sure,' nodded Winston. 'I have to think of these things.'

'Like the explosions and all these red clouds,' nodded Herbie.

'Jolly Jack's Firework Company,' agreed Winston. 'Las Vegas branch. I took the precaution of having those guys waiting just down the mountainside in case the real thing didn't come along.'

Ambrosia was pressed against me. I looked at her and saw she was crying. 'It was terrible,' she wept. 'Wasn't it terrible? All those people, all those poor frightened people. And the children. And then he goes and runs away on a motor-bike.'

'You can't *run* away on a motor-bike,' pointed out Winston kindly to stop her crying.

'He did,' grunted Herbie. 'You should have seen that guy's legs going either side of the thing as he started off down the hill.'

'Have you got your harp, Ambrosia?' asked Poor Clare seriously.

'No, I haven't got my sodding harp!' Ambrosia shouted at her.

'Ambrosia!' Poor Clare remonstrated. 'Your language! You wouldn't think your father was a clergyman.'

Only silence could greet a remark like that. Then Poor Clare said: 'It was all very unfortunate, though, wasn't it? He'll take it very hard, I'm afraid.' She paused, then brightening a fraction said: 'But at least they didn't laugh at him.'

We spent half an hour looking for Properjohn and then, at the downtown end of The Strip, we were flagged down by a police car. The cop walked back and looked in at us, then called back to the patrol car: 'Okay, Barney, this is them.'

'What's the charge?' asked Winston.

'We ain't finished making the list yet,' said the policeman. 'But right now you're wanted real urgent at Circus-Circus because that nutty guy of yours is up on the trapeze there. He's singing.'

Properjohn, who according to the police had drunk four beers and half a bottle of vodka and not paid, danced briefly with the frilly chorus at one of the smaller clubs, and had hit a doorman, was indeed high on the trapeze platform at Circus-Circus, a thousand faces once more turned up to him. He was singing 'Moon River' over a hand microphone and was accompanied by the band on the balcony.

As we went into the enormous imitation tent with the police an agitated under-manager approached and grabbed my arm.

'Get that loon out of here,' he ordered. We looked up and saw Properjohn on the little crow's nest platform high above.

'Is he in danger?' asked Winston soberly.

'He is when he comes down,' swore the man. 'From me.'

'It was real nice of you to get the band to back him,' said Winston calmly.

'To humour him,' grunted the man. 'He's drunk, that guy, and he says he'll jump if we don't let him sing.'

'There's a big safety net,' pointed out Herbie.

The man sneered. 'He's so screwy he could miss that,' he said. 'I don't want him landing on the fruit machines or the customers, okay? Just get him down.'

Properjohn was coming to the last notes of the song. He stood, higher than he would ever stand, above the upturned faces, arms held out, as he crooned it to its last sentimental word. I looked around at Poor Clare and saw the tears coursing down her ugly face.

Then Properjohn jumped. A truly magnificent leap from a hundred and fifty feet, flying spreadeagled through the air and bouncing spectacularly into the embrace of the wide safety net.

'That man,' said Winston slowly. 'Is an exhibitionist.'

'What can I give you first?' asked Winston. 'The bad news or the real bad news?'

We were sitting around a table by the side of the Holiday Inn swimming pool. We had stayed at the hotel for the rest of the night. Properjohn had not been bailed and Ambrosia and Clare had gone down to see him.

'Here it comes,' muttered Herbie, glancing at me. 'There's no dough.'

'No, no,' said Winston, holding up his hand. 'There *is* dough. It's just that nobody knows where the dough is right now.'

'Is that the *real* bad news, or just the bad news?' asked the Reverend Hatt. He had wandered the city all night without his clerical collar and had just found us after going to the police. He would not talk of what had happened to him.

'Mrs Helen J. Jaye is dead,' said Winston simply. 'I called my office today and they've got the whole story after a load of trouble. So she's dead. She died just after we started out from New York, just after that session at the Hilton. Personally I didn't think she looked too good then.'

'The dough?' asked Herbie impatiently. 'Tell us about the dough.'

'Oliver J. Jaye and two young broads who worked at the headquarters of the Helen J. Jaye Foundation for Christian Love have vanished, taking everything with them, including the light fittings. That's why he never got to coming to Vegas.'

'Why has he gone off with *two* ladies?' asked Hattie stupidly.

'The bags were too heavy,' said Winston patiently. 'The Senate Committee on Religions and Their Finances has been treading two steps behind our pal Oliver for some time and so, when the old lady died, he decided it was a good time to get out with as much as he could, including all the funds. Maybe they'll catch him in time.'

'They won't,' groaned Herbie. He put his hairy head in his hands. 'All that for nothing. For nothing!'

'We've got the two motor homes,' I said brightly. 'They must be worth a few thousand.'

'A few thousand peanuts,' said Winston. 'The people on the mountain last night kinda took them apart as souvenirs. All that was left was your Cross, Willy. They didn't touch that.'

'They wouldn't,' I said. 'They'd be too scared.'

'The cops brought it to the hotel this morning,' said Winston. 'The manager didn't like it in the lobby, so it's in the yard.'

'No dough,' muttered Herbie to himself. 'I even did better in pictures.'

*　　*　　*

'This is what you call a Welsh tan,' said Ambrosia, pointing at her pale belly quietly bulging from her bikini.

'Lovely,' I said.

'Do you feel awful about it?' she whispered like an anxious schoolgirl. I was lying beside her on the edge of the pool. Winston had borrowed enough from the Chinese Reverend Sunley's poor box to pay our bill. That afternoon we were all going back east by Greyhound bus.

'Well, I can't say I'm *not* disappointed,' I said. 'After all I only did it for the money.'

'But you liked some of it, didn't you, Willy?'

I touched her wrist. 'You know I did,' I said softly. 'Quite a lot of it.'

'You found her, didn't you.'

'My wife. Yes, I went to see her.'

'Any good?'

'Not particularly.'

'I'm sorry, Willy. That is, I'm sorry for you. We still don't love each other do we?' She shook her head as she asked.

I might have said something irresponsible and binding then, but the hotel loudspeaker called over the pool: 'Mr Turpin, telephone for Mr Willy Turpin.'

Ambrosia looked at me with abrupt concern. It was as though we both knew it would be Silvie. It was. I took it on the phone at the far side of the pool. I looked across at her, Ambrosia, dear tubby, pretty Ambrosia, stretched out white, her breasts full and young in the mild sun, her eyes closed beneath her splendid hair. 'How did you know where I am?' I asked Silvie.

'Angelo,' she said. 'He's a cop. All the cops know where you are after last night. That was quite a show.'

'It certainly was,' I agreed. 'Why are you ringing?'

She paused. Then she said: 'I thought you might like to come over and see the children again. They quite liked you.'

I was almost choking. 'I quite liked them,' I said.

'Will you come, Willy?'

'Yes, of course I'll come. Do *you* want to see me too.'

'If you want to see me. After everything.'

'Yes, all right. We're supposed to be clearing out this afternoon on the Greyhound.'

'Don't go,' she said quickly. 'You could stay around, couldn't you?'

'I suppose I could. But I'm broke. There was no money. You'll have to keep me, that's all.'

'I always did,' she said.

'What time shall I come?'

'About four. I don't work Sundays.'

'I'll see you,' I said.

'Okay,' she said. 'I'll see you then.'

I walked slowly back and lay down again beside Ambrosia. She did not open her eyes and I thought she had fallen asleep. But she said quietly: 'Come home, Willy Turpin. All is forgiven.'

'Something approaching that,' I said. Her face looked soft and white.

'It will never work,' she said. 'It never does.'

'Perhaps it won't,' I said.

She said nothing more and I closed my eyes too. But in a moment a shadow closed out the sun and I looked up to see Properjohn standing with Poor Clare simpering at his side.

'Willy,' he said, in his deepest voice. 'Willy, I have some great and extraordinary news.'

'What's that?'

'There was a mistake, a miscalculation. I've informed the policemen. You see, it's *next* Saturday night – the End of the World. Everybody will be . . .'

He never finished because Ambrosia began to laugh and then there came a spasm of shouts and a splash from the pool. We looked around. A boy was in the water and two others were about to throw our balsawood Cross in after him.

'Stop!' bellowed Properjohn. 'Stop. That is the Cross of Jesus!'

'We're Jewish!' shouted one of the kids and they threw it into the pool and dived after it.

I sat up and watched them. 'It's time somebody found something to do with that bloody thing,' I said.

Leslie Thomas
Dangerous Davies, The Last Detective £2.50

When Dangerous gets a murder case, it's a twenty-five-year-old sex crime. His witnesses range from a veteran of the Zulu wars to a mad policeman who thinks he's Peter the Great . . . and the mightily endowed Ena Lind, catsuit-wearer and crème-de-menthe drinker.

Exhibit A is the pair of pale green knickers that the victim wasn't wearing.

'Cheerfully vulgar . . . sharply observed' THE TIMES

Orange Wednesday £2.50

The interior-sprung mattress took the excitement out of sex for Prudence. Prudence took the excitement out of Lieutenant Brunel Hopkins. Then she told him of Orange Wednesday.

Tropic of Ruislip £2.50

'A romp among the adulteries, daydreams and nasty woodsheds of an executive housing estate . . . there are Peeping Toms, clandestine couplings, miscegenation on the wrong side of the tracks, the spilling of gin and home truths on the G-plan furniture, and the steady susurrus of doffed knickers' GUARDIAN

Tom Sharpe
Ancestral Vices £2.50

Left-wing academics, right-wing capitalists, true blue country gentry, workers, peasants, police and lawyers – all take custard pies full in the face in this boisterous knockabout farce' LISTENER

'Another bawdy and brutal romp of the kind he does so well' NEW STATESMAN

'Takes us at a gallop through the whole repertoire of British jokes' AUBERON WAUGH EVENING STANDARD

Porterhouse Blue £2.50

To Porterhouse College, Cambridge, famous for rowing, low academic standards and a proud cuisine, comes a new Master, an ex-grammar school boy, demanding Firsts, women students, a self-service canteen and a slot-machine for contraceptives, to challenge the established order – with catastrophic results

'That rarest and most joyous of products – a highly intelligent funny book' SUNDAY TIMES

Riotous Assembly £2.50

A crime of passion committed with a multi-barrelled elephant gun . . A drunken bishop attacked by a pack of Alsatians in a swimming pool . . . Transvestite variations in a distinguished lady's rubber-furnished bedroom . . . Famous battles re-enacted by five hundred schizophrenic Zulus and an equal number of (equally mad) whites . . .

Fiction

☐	**The Chains of Fate**	Pamela Belle	£2.95p
☐	**Options**	Freda Bright	£1.50p
☐	**The Thirty-nine Steps**	John Buchan	£1.50p
☐	**Secret of Blackoaks**	Ashley Carter	£1.50p
☐	**Lovers and Gamblers**	Jackie Collins	£2.50p
☐	**My Cousin Rachel**	Daphne du Maurier	£2.50p
☐	**Flashman and the Redskins**	George Macdonald Fraser	£1.95p
☐	**The Moneychangers**	Arthur Hailey	£2.95p
☐	**Secrets**	Unity Hall	£2.50p
☐	**The Eagle Has Landed**	Jack Higgins	£1.95p
☐	**Sins of the Fathers**	Susan Howatch	£3.50p
☐	**Smiley's People**	John le Carré	£2.50p
☐	**To Kill a Mockingbird**	Harper Lee	£1.95p
☐	**Ghosts**	Ed McBain	£1.75p
☐	**The Silent People**	Walter Macken	£2.50p
☐	**Gone with the Wind**	Margaret Mitchell	£3.95p
☐	**Wilt**	Tom Sharpe	£1.95p
☐	**Rage of Angels**	Sidney Sheldon	£2.50p
☐	**The Unborn**	David Shobin	£1.50p
☐	**A Town Like Alice**	Nevile Shute	£2.50p
☐	**Gorky Park**	Martin Cruz Smith	£2.50p
☐	**A Falcon Flies**	Wilbur Smith	£2.50p
☐	**The Grapes of Wrath**	John Steinbeck	£2.50p
☐	**The Deep Well at Noon**	Jessica Stirling	£2.95p
☐	**The Ironmaster**	Jean Stubbs	£1.75p
☐	**The Music Makers**	E. V. Thompson	£2.50p

Non-fiction

☐	**The First Christian**	Karen Armstrong	£2.50p
☐	**Pregnancy**	Gordon Bourne	£3.95p
☐	**The Law is an Ass**	Gyles Brandreth	£1.75p
☐	**The 35mm Photographer's Handbook**	Julian Calder and John Garrett	£6.50p
☐	**London at its Best**	Hunter Davies	£2.90p
☐	**Back from the Brink**	Michael Edwardes	£2.95p

☐	**Travellers' Britain**	} Arthur Eperon	£2.95p
☐	**Travellers' Italy**		£2.95p
☐	**The Complete Calorie Counter**	Eileen Fowler	90p
☐	**The Diary of Anne Frank**	Anne Frank	£1.75p
☐	**And the Walls Came Tumbling Down**	Jack Fishman	£1.95p
☐	**Linda Goodman's Sun Signs**	Linda Goodman	£2.95p
☐	**The Last Place on Earth**	Roland Huntford	£3.95p
☐	**Victoria RI**	Elizabeth Longford	£4.95p
☐	**Book of Worries**	Robert Morley	£1.50p
☐	**Airport International**	Brian Moynahan	£1.95p
☐	**Pan Book of Card Games**	Hubert Phillips	£1.95p
☐	**Keep Taking the Tabloids**	Fritz Spiegl	£1.75p
☐	**An Unfinished History of the World**	Hugh Thomas	£3.95p
☐	**The Baby and Child Book**	Penny and Andrew Stanway	£4.95p
☐	**The Third Wave**	Alvin Toffler	£2.95p
☐	**Pauper's Paris**	Miles Turner	£2.50p
☐	**The Psychic Detectives**	Colin Wilson	£2.50p

All these books are available at your local bookshop or newsagent, or can be ordered direct from the publisher. Indicate the number of copies required and fill in the form below

12

....

Name_____

(Block letters please)

Address_____

_____

Send to CS Department, Pan Books Ltd, PO Box 40, Basingstoke, Hants
Please enclose remittance to the value of the cover price plus:
35p for the first book plus 15p per copy for each additional book ordered
to a maximum charge of £1.25 to cover postage and packing
Applicable only in the UK

While every effort is made to keep prices low, it is sometimes necessary to increase prices at short notice. Pan Books reserve the right to show on covers and charge new retail prices which may differ from those advertised in the text or elsewhere